THE BENEVOLENT WORLD BANKER

M.K. Nielsen

MKN Publishing LLC

ACKNOWLEDGEMENTS

Several people have made important contributions along the way to shape this book. Jill French agreed to scan the very first version of the manuscript. She made some strategic observations that influenced the thorough re-write that followed.

Most importantly, I have benefited immensely from the guidance provided by two experienced, professional editors: Maria Lewytzkyj-Milligan, and K.J. Wetherholt. They have taken turns to follow this book through editorial assessments, copy edit rounds, proof reading, and formatting. My editors have encouraged and badgered me into writing in a more active style, with much more emotion, dialog, and sensory impressions. Dreaded "information dumps" have been splintered into lively exchanges. It has made this book quite different from anything I have ever published before, which was all non-fiction.

Another source of support has come from the Alliance of Independent Authors (ALLi) which produces an impressive amount of useful information for self-publishing authors.

Finally, my sincere thanks go to my wonderful, supportive wife who has graciously tolerated the many hours I have spent writing this book.

April 2023

M.K. Nielsen

Dear Reader,

For a more immersive experience, please look up and play the songs that are referenced in this book. Take a moment to reflect on how the characters felt at that particular time. If you enjoy wine, I invite you to look for the labels mentioned—or something similar—and savor those moments with the protagonist and others.

M.K. Nielsen

CHAPTER 1

Will They Come to Rescue Me?

The guards locked the solid metal door to his cell carefully every time they left. Only a thin, bamboo mat covered a strip of the dirt floor. The opening toward the hallway was high, close to the ceiling, and too small to crawl through. There was no window, nor was there anything he could use as a tool or a weapon.

Food, if he could call the porridge-like substance that, was delivered once a day at unpredictable times in a dirty, worn plastic bowl. A piece of bread lessened his cravings. He'd take a bite after brushing dirt off the bowl's lip to swallow the sludge. He resisted drinking water from the used plastic cup the first day for fear of disease. But when the heat built up in the small space, he gave in on the second day to dampen his raging thirst.

A banged-up metal bucket served as his toilet. One guard came in to empty it while another watched him, clasping his gun. Whenever they entered, they made hand signs to force him down on the ground.

"I want to speak to the village chief!" David yelled.

He could not understand the words…only the anger in the guard's outburst.

His belongings had been seized—his shoulder bag with a satellite telephone, passport, wallet, office ID, everything. Even his shoes had been confiscated to discourage any attempt at running away. There was nothing to bribe the guards with. He had never felt so naked.

David rubbed his wrists where the rope burns were still visible. His skin glistened as sweat dripped off his face to the dirt floor in the afternoon heat. He quit swatting the flies away. They were too many and too persistent. His stomach tightened as his desperate attempts to simply live through each passing moment crept through his head. His head fell forward, heavy.

But maybe it wasn't hopeless? They had captured him for a reason. David had read about a spate of kidnappings in the general region he had visited. Although unusual, foreign aid workers were among the victims occasionally. As far as he knew, they had all been released—probably after some ransom had been paid. Nobody talked openly about that, of course. Local people with means to pay up had been kidnapped. He had not heard of Islamist militant activity in this area of the country, so there was less of a risk that he would be used as a human prop to further propaganda. But he could have passed an international border in the hours he had been transported, blindfolded, on the back of some truck.

He lifted his head, looking around the cell, his brow furrowed as he struggled to wet his parched lips. What had happened to his interpreter and driver from the Ministry of Agriculture? Two armed guards were supposed to guarantee his security—what about them?

The kidnappers will ask for a ransom. If they are stupid enough, they will be tracked down and someone will come for me. If they are clever and can keep me hidden, let's hope someone is willing to pay, he thought. During his three years with the World Bank, he had heard of colleagues being robbed and beaten. But kidnapped? No, he had never heard of that.

CHAPTER 2

David's First Mission: Kangaland

United Airlines flight UA989 left the gate at Washington Dulles International Airport thirty minutes late. It was David's first trip—"mission" as the jargon went—on behalf of the World Bank, only two weeks after he had first entered the doors on 1818 H Street NW in Washington, D.C. to start his new job. The introductory sessions at HQ had been informative but unexciting. Now he felt that his real work was beginning.

David was happy to share the flight with Muhammed Hassan—known among friends as "Bob"—a friendly colleague from the legal department with lots of stories to tell and a breadth of experience. He closed the massive briefing file he had to read since he could not pass up an opportunity to hear some of Bob's insights.

Bob leaned over toward him. "So, why did you want to work for the Bank?" he asked with an ambiguous smile. He spoke softly with a slight Arabic accent.

David knew from the Bank's internal website that Bob had his roots in Lebanon and that he also spoke Arabic and French. The smell from Bob's suit indicated that Bob chain-smoked, but David did his best to ignore it.

Is he trying to put me on the spot? David thought. It was a very direct question, but, of course, it was not difficult to answer.

"Isn't it what anyone wants in a job? I want to contribute to something meaningful," he started. "Single-handedly, I cannot make the world better, but I can join forces with an organization that aims to alleviate poverty. What could be more important? The Bank has a lot of resources to get things done."

"So, are you convinced it's doing a good job combating poverty?" Bob continued—still smiling.

David felt unsure about Bob's angle. "I'll suspend judgment for the time being, but I'm very keen to find out." *Let's turn the tables now.* "You've been with the Bank for many years, so you've seen a lot of change, right?"

"Have I seen a lot of changes?" Bob seemed to ponder that, thumbing through a stack of papers before he flagged an air hostess, who smiled in his direction. He asked for a ginger ale. "The Bank is much less arrogant these days. We try to listen more to the client country."

"But there are still lots of conditions attached to loans and grants."

"Well … of course, but when structural adjustment lending started in the early 1980s, it was a cookie-cutter recipe. And we still believe that some things are fundamental for development. Without security, rule of law, breathing room for the private sector, and fiscal discipline, the economy will stagnate. But the package is more tailor-made these days. Targeted pro-poor policies have also become more common."

"What do you have in mind?"

"They could be things like conditional cash transfers. Say, you get your kids to attend school and have them vaccinated properly and you get a bonus," Bob explained.

9

An air hostess brought a trolley with pre-dinner drinks. David picked a red wine from Chile and was given a mixture of warm nuts in a small bowl. A heavy-set gentleman in a three-piece suit seated across the aisle was already on his second miniature bottle of whiskey.

"When I started twenty years ago," Bob said, peering up at David while sipping on his ginger ale and pursing his lips— "almost nobody talked openly about corruption. It was known as the 'C-word' even! You had to tip-toe carefully around that in reports. Some of our clients are not exactly model governments. There's a dilemma here." Bob rubbed his nose.

"And some companies in rich countries contribute to the problem. I've looked at the reports from Transparency International. Corruption is not confined to poor countries," David interjected.

Bob smiled. "Imagine if we demanded that the recipient government must be totally clean—as some of our critics do—we would be left with Norway as our client! We would lose the opportunity to assist a lot of poor people." He slapped his right armrest for emphasis and looked firmly at David with a broad smile. "Now we talk about corruption and actively work against it."

"So, what was driving that change?" David asked.

Bob grinned and looked quickly around him as if to check if anybody else listened. "Change in the Bank comes from the top, never from the bottom. We got a new president who got rid of the Orwellian acrobatics to avoid the issue. It was like we had our own Ministry of Truth back then."

Bob paused for a moment and shifted in his seat. It looked like he was trying to remember his early days in the Bank.

"Reports about poor governance had been brushed under the carpet," he continued. "The Bank's board directors from poor countries that felt targeted raised a stink. The donor countries' board directors were supportive in private but careful not to rock the boat in public. So, honest assessments were fed into the system at low-levels and gradually photo-brushed into anodyne statements that didn't offend the bigwigs. But now, it even happens that we close down a project if the corruption is too egregious."

Bob asked for another ginger ale with ice. The first course arrived, and they ate in silence. David's salad was delightfully fresh. He had turned down the offer of Russian caviar for a starter, as it seemed environmentally suspect and too extravagant. Bob put on a movie in Arabic.

David leaned back in the comfortable seat. He had not entered the Bank without reservations. It was a controversial institution admired by some but despised by others. He saw an opportunity to work with a noble purpose—to alleviate poverty. That had been a fundamental goal in his life plan for many years. He was also flattered to become part of what many regarded as an elite professional institution. With a PhD in Economics under his belt, he felt prepared academically. But was the Bank sincere in its attempts to increasingly present itself as "green" and more concerned about inequity? The recruiting manager had told him that he would be part of changing the Bank's culture in that direction.

Torben Nielsen, a PhD student at his Alma Mater in Copenhagen who was six years into his dissertation about Marxist economics, had lambasted him for taking the job.

11

"David, you're a sellout! That Bank and the IMF are just an extended arm of U.S. imperialism. It's their capitalism that has underdeveloped poor countries. You should read Walter Rodney's book *How Europe Underdeveloped Africa*. That would be an antidote to the brainwashing that they'll put you through."

David had read it already but found it shallow and one-sided in its virulent criticism of colonialism as the root of all evil. Yes, colonialism was oppressive, but the poor policies implemented by corrupt, national elites also deserved scrutiny.

Bob quickly lost interest in his movie and leaned over to David again. "Did you bring a family with you to the U.S.?"

"No, I'm single."

"Well, this could be a great place to start a family. The Bank is full of smart, attractive women, and many of them are single. So, look around," Bob added with a chuckle.

David blushed—as he was prone to—and he felt awkward about it. Bob had put his finger on the other main element in his personal life plan. First, a meaningful job, but once he got well into it, he would look for a life partner—someone to start a family with. A family better than the one he came from. A wife who shared his basic values but was also sufficiently different from him to be exciting. Not another economist! He often found women of color attractive, and the Bank certainly had its share. More importantly, there was plenty of color in D.C.!

"I need to focus on getting into the job first," David remarked. "But I would love to have a family. As the only child, I often felt a bit alone..." he started, but he felt he was getting too personal.

"I have a great track record of setting people up," Bob joked, as he put his headphones on again.

David found some smooth jazz on the airplane's selection of playlists, dozed off, and missed the main course but caught up later when he woke up. Again, a delightful dish of grilled rockfish and great service with a smile. The white wine was irresistible—the famous Cloudy Bay Sauvignon Blanc from the Marlborough District in New Zealand—and after the second glass, he gave up on his briefing book.

I could get used to this, he thought, but felt a pang of guilt.

Bob had turned off the movie again, so David turned to him. "Don't you find it incongruous to fly in the lap of luxury to one of the world's poorest countries?"

"Guilty about flying in first class?" Bob chuckled. "The Bank only pays for business, but the airline offers the free upgrade when there's capacity. You'll feel less guilty when you realize what the Bank is asking of you. You'll arrive pretty jet-lagged and stiff after two long flights and a change of seven time zones. No matter the hour of arrival, you'll be asked to 'hit the ground running,' as it goes."

An air hostess offered water, but Bob waived her off.

Agitated, Bob banged his hand against the right armrest to emphasize each point. "There will be an endless series of long-winded meetings with government officials, your own team, other donor representatives who are critical or even hostile toward the Bank. There'll be non-governmental organizations that want you to battle for their cause versus government, and field visits on dangerous, bumpy roads to meet the beneficiaries of your project."

Bob sipped his ginger ale and turned up the volume of his tirade. "You'll spend an enormous amount of time waiting for officials who are late or never show up. If they do, they'll fight over control of project resources and refuse to collaborate among themselves. Your schedule will constantly change. You'll sit in poorly air-conditioned meeting rooms where many are smoking."

David hated smoke and was getting uncomfortable already, but Bob was not finished.

"Meanwhile, Head Office will hound you with an avalanche of emails and demand immediate responses. You'll get sick because of the food by the second day and live on Imodium and Coke for the rest of the mission. You'll prepare your written inputs to the mission's final report carefully every night, but by the time you arrive home exhausted from the mission, a high-level meeting of managers has decided that the project no longer fits in this year's budget and will be postponed indefinitely ..." He took a big sip of ginger ale and peered at David with a mischievous smile. "Feeling less guilty about going first now?" Bob sank into his seat as if drained by his own outburst.

"I suppose so," David said. He felt rather anxious about the picture that Bob had painted so vividly. Was it really going to be that bad? Needing a distraction, he found Kenny G's album *Silhouette* in the airplane's playlist and unsuccessfully tried to get some sleep.

***

There was a change of planes in Frankfurt the next morning local time, so David had a chance to read through the extensive briefing package that he had received at HQ. Kangaland was a dictatorship. The country had a bitter history of an independence struggle against its colonizer but later also a war with a neighbor. The ethnic composition was varied, with a plethora of local languages, and Christians and Muslims dominated in distinct parts of the country. The independence struggle and recent war had fostered a culture of militarism. Corruption was not tolerated, and punishments for missteps—including vocal critique of the government— were severe.

They arrived in the late afternoon at the capital. The airport was small, and everyone disembarked via an old-style staircase that was pushed up to the plane by a tractor. The airport terminal had been damaged during the war, but repairs had started. The heat had mostly subsided in the late afternoon, and there was a pleasant crisp, dry breeze as he walked over the tarmac. It was a bit eerie to pass closely by several guards with automatic weapons.

At the first checkpoint before entering the arrival hall, all passengers had to show their passports before they received an immigration form, a customs declaration, a foreign currency form, and an electronic equipment form. Uniformed personnel checked the extensive forms thoroughly. A man in a worn-out, grey uniform counted David's foreign currency. He also had to show his laptop before the checkpoint officer duly recorded its serial number in a large ledger.

David and Bob were joined by two colleagues from the Bank who had arrived on the same plane, and together, they were met by two officials from the Ministry of Development who shook their hands, starting with their delegation leader, Wolfgang Fischer.

A small, air-conditioned bus took them to their hotel. Not many hotels in the country offered a standard that the Bank considered reasonable. David opened the creaky door into his very stale room. It had a narrow bed and a small table next to it. He placed his briefcase on the one chair. There was no desk, so he would have to find another place to work on his laptop. The wardrobe had only two wire hangers. He felt jet lag catching up with him and closed his eyes for a brief rest.

He woke up with a jolt only fifteen minutes later and went to the bathroom. A sign on the bathroom door cautioned that water would be on only between the hours of 7–8 in the morning and 6–7 at night. A sink and a bathtub mostly took up the entire room. The cover to the toilet was missing, and to flush, one had to reach into the water and manually lift the flapper. It was very basic, but David reminded himself that most of the country's population faced far greater challenges.

That evening, the Bank delegation gathered for an informal team meeting over dinner. Fischer was rather rotund, in his fifties, with graying hair, and a quick laughter. The fourth delegation member was a woman in her thirties—Melissa. As an architect, she was to lead the design of a large number of new schools and clinics that the project aimed to construct. The briefing material was extensive so there was little to add except some logistics for the days ahead. *I can work with these guys,* David thought as he left the meeting.

***

The next morning, Fischer introduced the World Bank delegation to a ten-person-strong Kangaland counterpart delegation. They were all men in their twenties to forties, thin, short, and dressed very plainly. The mood was official, but smiles were exchanged, and there was some small talk about the flight. David kept quiet but took the time to observe and attempt to settle his nerves.

The planned Community Development Project, or CDP, was broad in nature. The national government desired to confront several urgent issues at the same time: road building, water and sanitation systems, elementary schools, community clinics, soil and water conservation in erosion-prone areas, and so on.

The Minister of Development himself was scheduled to speak at 9 a.m. He was known to be powerful, temperamental, and critical of the Bank, but he needed the project funds to produce quick results. Otherwise, he would not last long as a minister.

At 9:30 a.m., an embarrassed official announced that the minister had been called to an urgent meeting in the presidential palace. Fischer suggested that they might start with the second speaker, but this would violate protocol. Everyone waited. Almost everyone from the local delegation was puffing away on a local, hand-rolled cigarette. The air became thick with smoke. David felt queasy, but it was unthinkable to step out.

At 10:45 a.m., the minister arrived with an entourage of three armed men. He took the floor with the self-confidence of a man who was used to being the star of the meeting. Rather than apologizing for his late arrival, he took the mission to task. He spoke through a translator.

"My country has asked for your assistance for several months. We cannot afford to waste any more time. Our nation is proud to build its independence." He elaborated on the years of heroic struggle for freedom and deplored the lack of international support. "Gentlemen, you are here to work for us," he concluded with a hint of a smile. Having set a rather stern tone, the minister departed hastily without taking questions.

A series of short presentations followed. The more junior the staff, the better English they spoke. Mission members had little time to weigh in, but the mission leader was allowed a summary speech at the end. He expressed the Bank's enthusiasm for getting the first CDP in Kangaland going. Fischer set the expectations right by talking about several formal steps that had to be completed before the funds could be disbursed. At the end of this mission, an *aide-memoire* would be agreed—a bit of French that was apparently part of the Bank jargon. There would be several more missions with subject-matter specialists from the Bank to cover all areas of activities that the CDP would be involved in. Gradually, the project documentation would be elaborated in detail, reviewed by management, and finally the legal documents would be signed in Washington, D.C. by the Ambassador of Kangaland to the U.S. "It might take us six to twelve months," he predicted.

The senior counterpart officer banged the table. "We're ready to move *now!*" he blurted out.

David met one-on-one with his project counterpart, a young agricultural engineer. The room was small, gloomily dark, and smelled of tobacco smoke. Jemal was in his twenties, a fit man dressed in worn jeans and a T-shirt with government slogans in the local language. He did not beat around the bush.

"Why are you here?" Jemal must have known about the long negotiations before the mission was allowed into the country and the discussions about the future project that emanated from local requests. But it was a signal to say: "I don't trust you."

David kept his cool. "I'm here at your government's request to prepare a community development project. You guys will implement it. I'm not here to dictate what you should do. But we will bring in money and people with years of experience in the kind of activities that you are planning. We will offer you opportunities to go to other African countries for capacity building."

Jemal sneered. "Capacity building! We have capacity! What to learn from other countries? We know our land. Those Africans, we are not like them! You think all Africans are the same?"

David was stunned at first, but he had heard about this attitude before. He shifted gears and let Jemal sketch out what he saw as the project's potential. Jemal explained how villages should be invited to submit project ideas to the Regional Administration. They would then prioritize a select few and forward those proposals to the Ministry of Development. This would ensure fair and equitable distribution of resources.

David wondered about that but could not openly express his doubts. The South of the country harbored some groups that were ethnically distinct and were not that supportive of the government. Open opposition was impossible, but it was known that central government officials were not well regarded there. To diffuse the situation, David tried another track.

"Jemal, how come your English is so good?"

His eyes lit up. "I study English very little. But I listen radio and read English books. Crime."

Jemal had finished twelve years of schooling with the last three much focused on agriculture. He had a wife and a two-year-old son. The government provided subsidized housing for its civil servants, which pleased him greatly. Jemal's pride of his country and its great future was evident.

The meeting ended much better than it started. They agreed to meet in the morning the next day. Still, David had an uneasy feeling as they parted. The Bank was not greeted with open arms.

***

Two weeks of lengthy meetings at various involved ministries and several field visits to project sites followed. The depth of poverty was striking. Everyone he met wore clothes that looked frayed and patched, and there was not a single overweight person to see. Some kids ran around in just a dirty T-shirt and looked stunted. The shelves in stores— mostly Mom-and-Pop-type— did have the basics of cooking oil, rice, flour, milk, onions, beans, bananas, and some canned goods, but there were certainly no luxuries. Cars were visibly run-down except for a few shiny Mercedes Benzes with government plates.

In spite of the poverty, no one begged, and people walked upright and met his gaze. There was also a can-do attitude among his counterparts. They were proud of their country and saw themselves as builders of a prosperous country—a role model for Africa. They argued for more resources to the project, wanting more cars and a bigger allowance for the first year's batch of projects.

The Bank team met daily and drafted an aide-memoire that sketched out the parameters of the future project with areas of activities, assignment of responsibilities, budget, and time plan. They tried to scale down the client country's bold ambitions to a more realistic plan, given experience in other countries. They could not resolve everything, as it was the first of a series of Bank visits needed to get the project going.

Bob and David met for a quick lunch to prepare for the final meeting between the Bank delegation and their counterparts. They sat outside at a restaurant they had come to appreciate. It served only one main course but a good one with local flavor. They laughed at how Bob's prediction had come true. David did get sick on day two, but after five days on Imodium and Coke, he had battled back to a cautious diet of well-cooked food. When their generous plates were put before them, David remarked tongue-in-cheek that Bob as a good Muslim should not eat. It was the holy month of Ramadan, and the sun was still up!

Bob smiled gently. "David, you have not read the Holy Koran, I guess. It provides an exception for travelers."

"You are making that up," said David, laughing.

"Oh no," said Bob. "Look it up, it's in 2:183. I know that one by heart because it's been quite useful. *Bon appétit!*"

Bob was the kind of mentor that David recognized he needed, and as the first Muslim who he had ever worked with, he was keen to better understand that part of his identity as well. Bob was a "pragmatic Muslim," as he called it, and married to a Christian woman. He prayed daily but not five times, he did not drink alcohol, went to a mosque about once every month, never ate pork, and gave generously to Muslim charities. In particular, he supported several orphanages in the Middle East. Without being prompted, he was unequivocal in his denouncement of terrorism in the name of Islam. He seemed keen to make that clear without any prompting by David.

"I have so much to learn from you, Bob," David emphasized. "We come from very different backgrounds, and that makes it all the more exciting."

***

The final meeting between the mission and the counterparts took place late in the afternoon in the Ministry's rather dismal headquarters in the center of the capital. The meeting room was poorly lit and lacked air conditioning. Several participants were chain smokers. It was the usual perusal of the draft aide-memoire that summarized the mission's findings and proposals—subject to management approval. Several senior officials from the Ministry of Development attended. Once again, the mission was lectured about the proud independence that guided the country's future development, its rapid progress under the new regime, the defeat of colonialism and foreign interference.

Then a line-by-line scrutiny of the draft aide-memoire followed. It was obvious that the text had been read from a defensive posture. Was the Bank trying to attach conditions to the project that would diminish the country's sovereignty? Surely, there was no need for "independent auditing by an entity approved by the Bank" when the government already had its internal system in place. Why did paragraph 37, line 4 say that the government "should" undertake certain actions before the next mission, when "could" was more appropriate?

The slow going exasperated David, but when the detailed discussion dragged on more than two hours, Bob wrote: "Don't worry, it's not always like this" on a piece of paper that he slipped over. Finally, there was agreement after some softening of wording and introducing "constructive ambiguity," as Bob called it. This would allow both parties to emerge with a sense of satisfaction and postponed disagreements to a later date.

When the meeting finally closed, there was at least a sense that a common understanding of the project had emerged. There was still tension on details, but the overall game plan had been agreed. Firm handshakes were exchanged, and surprisingly, Jemal made a point of thanking David for his contributions. David promised to bring a bundle of English crime novels next time.

***

The other mission members all had other stops to make in Africa, so David split from the group to return to Washington. The departure from Kangaland was messy, as the regular flight back via London had been canceled "for operational reasons"—whatever that meant. With a four-hour delay, he was rebooked on flights taking him first to West Africa and then to London.

Finally, he was able to board the smaller plane to West Africa with a seat in economy class. After another six-hour layover in a poorly air-conditioned, humid transit hall, another airplane took him to London. Economy again—no guilt there. As he settled down in a tight seat, an overweight White lady with a flushed face took the seat next to him.

"Hello, pet," she greeted him cheerfully. He could have been insulted, but David was a fan of the crime series *Vera* on TV. Vera, the impressive anti-hero of a police officer in northern England, was frumpy in appearance but sharp as a knife intellectually. Vera also addressed people as "pet" now and then.

"Hello, I'm David," he said as he helped her search for her seat belt. She required some help in her condition—the smell of alcohol on her breath was unavoidable.

She looked around in bewilderment. "When do they start with the drinks here?"

David hoped the answer would be "never" but kept quiet.

"I'll show you a picture of my boyfriend," she offered without any prompting. She held up her phone, and with some effort, found the right pictures. The boyfriend was a handsome Black man in his twenties about 6′3″ and of athletic build. "We met on the beach. He's so sweet, and you know he doesn't mind at all that I'm a bit older."

David put on his headphones and pretended to sleep. But he could not help noticing the large group of middle-aged White women with excessive suntans who filled the cabin with cheerful banter. A successful vacation in West Africa, no doubt.

David thought about the image of White people that these ladies brought to Africa. Male White sex tourism was more common but worked the same way in exploiting economic differences. Of course, the most severe exploitation was slavery and the extractive colonialism that had defined Africa for centuries. In Denmark, his Whiteness had never been something to reflect on, but here, it immediately labeled him as part of a group of people whose behavior was often seen as offensive to local customs and historically repulsive. It was an uncomfortable thought but something to keep in mind in his future work.

***

After a brief stopover in London, David caught a plane to Washington, D.C. He pulled up his laptop and started typing the compulsory back-to-office report. He reflected on the mission and felt discouraged and deflated. He had thought that the Bank mission would be warmly welcomed, as they potentially could bring significant resources to the country. But they had been met with arrogance and even suspicion. This country wanted the money but not the expertise or the oversight—that much was clear.

Is this representative of how clients feel about the Bank? he wondered. The pejorative image of the Bank forcing its ideas on clients had been turned on its head by this mission. *These guys in Kangaland are not being pushed around*, he thought.

Back at the Bank the next week, he met Bob over coffee to get his views. "The sentiment will change," Bob argued. "We'll build personal relationships over time with our counterparts. Once they realize that you respect them, and that you can bring lots of money and expertise, you know, they'll come around," he predicted. He also pointed out that their administration was not corrupt and very efficient in terms of implementation. "They will get the roads, schools, and clinics built," he stated with conviction.

At home that night, David was still actively processing the impressions from Kangaland. Bob's assessment felt reassuring—he was speaking from experience. He should not be judging the Bank's work based on a single mission, of course. A crisp, cool Chablis provided a pleasant diversion. He sat down in his reading chair and slowly sipped the firmly dry Chardonnay, making sure to enjoy every drop of it. His mind kept composing emails to be sent the next day—it was hard to close that down. In his small collection of CDs, he found one by Norah Jones and let himself drift into sleep with smooth jazz in his ears.

CHAPTER 3

Julia and the Benevolent World Banker

One Friday morning at the end of David's first month at the World Bank, the regular crowd approaching HQ was mixed with demonstrators. They carried signs and gathered in a small park on Pennsylvania Avenue close to the Bank's main building on H Street NW. A speaker with a megaphone stood on a park bench usually occupied by homeless people dressed in multiple layers of clothing and with overloaded shopping carts by their side. Various environmental groups were protesting the Bank's policies and projects and their allegedly negative environmental impacts.

"Close down the Bank, close down the IMF," the speaker demanded. Signs read: "Save the rainforests," "No loans to coal," and "Free Muhammed Hankari."

Next to David was a young woman dressed in a smart pantsuit—a paralegal taking a break from a law office? David asked her about Hankari.

She smiled and shook her head. "He is a rapper charged with drug possession. I don't see any connection to the Bank. These demonstrations attract all sorts of people. I am with the ICA," she said. Her ICA badge was clipped onto her belt, fully visible, and read: "Julia Chavez."

Seeing David's puzzled expression, she added, "It stands for International Conservation Action. It's a small non-governmental advocacy group mainly. But we also have some field projects in Costa Rica. We want to show that a well-managed environment can also bring economic benefits to poor people."

"I agree," David said. There were so many of these non-governmental organizations (NGOs), he'd learned. Sometimes, it was hard to tell the difference, but each proponent he had come across could fiercely defend their own distinct colors. Some were pure advocacy organizations, but others had projects in developing countries. Some had a cooperative relationship with the Bank. Others thrived on critiquing the Bank's every move.

"I'm David," he said and extended a hand.

"Julia. And you work for the Bank. Your badge gives you away," she added.

"Well, yes," he admitted, suddenly embarrassed by the situation as if he were guilty of the environmental crimes that the speaker enlisted.

The noise level kept going up. Police halted the traffic around them. More police officers kept pouring in—some with full riot gear and others on horseback. There were now several competing megaphones chanting slogans. "Forgive all debts to rich countries," demanded one, "All power to the people," demanded another. From one corner of the park, a police officer started shouting orders in a megaphone, but David could hear only bits and pieces of the message: "... ordered to disperse immediately ..." "unlawful assembly," which caused great commotion. He looked for a way out, but the mass of people was so compact, and the ring of police so tight, there was nowhere to go.

"Let's try to get out of here!" he shouted to Julia. He resisted an urge to take her hand to lead the way, but, of course, that would have been totally inappropriate. As they edged their way toward the periphery of the crowd, some demonstrators were being arrested. Not one demonstrator had acted with violence, but they had not had a chance to disperse since the order was given. Still, riot police forced demonstrators to sit down and cuffed them efficiently with zip ties.

David felt extremely uncomfortable. An arrest would be a blot on his record, he would perhaps be denied a renewal of his US G-IV visa, maybe they would even recall it, and that would be the end of his career in the U.S. As he came face to face with the line of police officers, he pulled out his badge and yelled, "I am on my way to work at the Bank" and held it close to a policeman's face.

The officer looked at it and yelled, "Get the fuck out of here, you idiot!" and grabbed his arm, pushing him through the line of black uniforms.

"She's with me," he yelled to the officer, but nobody cared, and the line closed behind him.

He could not even see Julia in the commotion. He felt like a coward, but he needed to save his own skin, so he hurried away from the police line. He had to walk a few blocks but was able to approach the Bank at a backdoor that was free from demonstrators. As he sank into his chair in the office, he decided that he would track down Julia Chavez right away.

He made a call to ICA later that day. The operator asked who was calling and from where. He hesitated to say, so he simply added, "It's a personal matter." His pulse went up as the operator said she would connect him. The call went to voicemail. He managed to convey his concern for her situation and asked her to call his direct number when she got the message.

***

Two days later, she called back. Still angry at the brusque treatment she had suffered at the hands of the police, Julia was eager to put it behind her. She'd been arrested and

29

bundled into a police bus, kept waiting for hours at a police station in a crowded room, then processed by hostile officers. One officer groped her while he fingerprinted her and leaned close to her face. "You're a pretty girl and shouldn't waste your time on communist demonstrations," he offered as unsolicited advice.

"Where do they get this from? I've never been a communist!"

"I understand that you're upset. Don't take it personally. It's just something some people here throw at somebody they don't like," David responded. "Would you be free to meet me this coming Saturday so that we could talk about all this?"

Julia hesitated.

"Oh ... OK, I didn't mean like a date," David quickly added. "But we're colleagues in the development business, right? And I'd like to learn more about the work you're doing." It was true but not the whole truth.

"I'd like that. Saturday would be good for me." Julia didn't hesitate this time and gave him her personal email.

***

They met alone the first time near the Vietnam Veterans Memorial on the Mall. It was a lovely Saturday morning with a comfortable temperature and no rain in sight. He brought coffee for them both—skim milk in her latte, black drip coffee for himself. No sugar—he had written it all down when they last spoke. He wanted the meeting to be perfect, though a vague sense of nervousness about being alone with her for the first time flustered him. Was it a date? He was unsure, as they had agreed simply to meet and talk about what had happened at the demonstration and its aftermath. She had also said she had lots of questions about the Bank.

Perhaps she was all about business? Why would she be interested in him unless solely as a Bank employee?

David waited at the agreed spot, and she was punctual. *A good sign,* he thought. Tardiness made him antsy. She wore sneakers, blue jeans, and a casual, bright-red top. Her shoulder-length, jet-black hair shone in the sun. It annoyed him that his pulse accelerated quickly as he rose to greet her. Julia wore no make-up but long, dangling earrings that David found very attractive.

"Don't ever come to meet me at my office! You work for the enemy." She chuckled.

She was only twenty-three and fresh out of University of Virginia, or UVA, as it turned out. David was thirty, but the age difference did not seem to matter. They were from different countries though, and Julia's background having grown up in an undocumented immigrant family—while being a U.S. citizen by birth—gave it special flavor.

"Where's your accent from?" she inquired.

"I was born in Denmark," David said, a little miffed that his accent was so apparent. "Heard about it?"

"Of course! Are you taking me for a fool? But I've never been to Europe. Oslo is the capital, right?"

"It's actually Copenhagen. But don't be embarrassed. Denmark and Norway have a population comparable to South Carolina and Alabama. And how many Danes would correctly identify their state capitals?"

David had sometimes been shocked by how little even well-educated Americans knew about geography and about other countries in general. But the U.S. was a world unto itself, an "exceptional" country and "the envy of the world" as it was sometimes proclaimed by politicians. So why bother about the rest of the world?

"So how do you like America?" she asked, as many had done before—sometimes expecting praise, he suspected. "I think the beautiful nature in this country is its greatest asset," Julia added with pride.

"I know," David agreed, "and on my to-do list is to visit as many of your national parks that I can. There is certainly a lot to be proud of in the U.S."

"And it's the richest country in the world."

"Well, it has a per capita income almost as high as Norway and Switzerland. It ranks lower if you use purchasing-power parity ..."

"What parity?" Julia interrupted.

It was an easy question to answer, but David realized that his mind was on two tracks. His left brain knew the answer and just needed to adapt the amount of detail to the situation. But his right brain was busy scanning Julia's face, her innocent brown eyes, her smile, full lips, shiny hair, and dangling earrings. The attraction was unsettling. *Focus now!*

"Purchasing-power parity (PPP) more accurately captures spending power. If you just use the official exchange rates, you miss the fact that a lot of goods and services aren't traded. A lot of those will be cheaper in poor countries...like childcare and local staple goods. PPP gives a better picture of the actual standard of living. It makes a lot of difference and means that poor countries are not as poor as it looks in the traditional statistics."

"OK, the U.S. may not have the very highest income per capita, but it's among the highest, right? But surely, it's the biggest economy of all," she asserted.

"If you are using market exchange rates, yes. But again, if your using PPP, then China actually has a bigger economy.

"I've never heard that," said Julia with a sigh. "But of course, their population is so much bigger."

Stop staring at her, look away, and keep it together, he told himself. He turned to the side, and they started walking slowly towards Lincoln Memorial.

"True, then you also have to look at income inequality, for example. The U.S. is not doing that great. But I admire the entrepreneurial spirit in this country. There's fierce competition here that forces people to innovate. And most of the top universities in the world are in the U.S."

They stopped to drink some more coffee and take in the grand view of the Mall.

Julia had majored in Environmental Studies while spreading her wings liberally across the academic smorgasbord that UVA offered. There was no academic tradition in her family, but her parents had been supportive. "They want me to live the American Dream," she noted with a smile.

They found a park bench and sat down.

"My friends at ICA tell me that the World Bank doesn't care about the environment—just about economic growth. They say that you push the 'the Washington Consensus' on poor countries. Is that true?"

David smiled, as he had heard that before. "The so-called Washington Consensus is not the official policy of the Bank but was an attempt by a British economist—John Williamson—to lay down a set of principles for successful development policies. The word 'Washington' is unfortunate because it gives the impression of an agenda cooked up here. In fact, the roots of Williamson's list can be traced to Latin America. He wrote about that in the late 1980s, and he had ten points altogether. I don't know them by heart, but the main principles are clear."

He took a sip from his coffee as he tried to remember all the points.

"It's about fiscal discipline to keep inflation in check, clearly define property rights, promote a market-economy, reduce red tape, relax exchange rates to be more flexible, free trade, and so on.

"I'm missing something about environment in that list," Julia noted.

"It's a good point and I'll get to that in a moment. But some people have taken Williamson's principles to mean a total liberalization of markets and a retreat of the public sector. I don't think that's what he meant. So, the Washington Consensus has become a politically loaded term, and for some people, it equals excessive reliance on market forces."

Julia seemed skeptical. "I don't believe that free markets will take care of the basic needs of poor people. But I also have no illusions about all public officials being honest and efficient. It's really important that civil society gets organized and influences policy. That's what ICA is about."

David nodded. "Actually, the Bank provides a lot of support through NGOs like yours in developing countries."

"That's fine," Julia said. "But I've heard about several Bank road projects that have led to deforestation and loss of wildlife habitat. What do you say about that?"

David sighed. "I can't counter all that, as I've just started. Perhaps some of those stories are true. On one of my first days in the office, I was in the cafeteria line with a road engineer who complained to me about the 'new green stuff' that was forced upon Bank staff, as he put it. He was happy that he was just building roads '… that have no relation to the environment whatsoever!'" he said. "With attitudes like that, surely mistakes will be made."

Their discussion went back and forth for several hours as they walked on the Mall, and they continued talking non-stop over lunch. David tried to explain how a market economy can handle "environmental externalities" in a smart way by using price signals, and with increasing wealth, the demand for a clean environment would rise. "So, economic growth and environmental protection can go hand in hand."

"I took a course in environmental economics, so you don't need to explain the basics for me," she stated firmly with some reddening on her lovely cheeks. "Watch out for mansplaining," she added, but she did smile.

They walked to the Smithsonian Metro station to say goodbye. It had been a much longer date–yes, it felt like a date—than David had expected, and he had a warm feeling inside about it.

"You're a pretty decent guy for someone who's working for the World Bank," she teased. "You have good values—you mean to do good. I'd say you're a Benevolent World Banker!"

Those words stuck in David's mind.

***

Julia totally charmed David. He found her smart, attractive, and a young woman with idealistic values that he shared and admired. She had made the best out of a difficult start in life. Her parents could not help her with homework and struggled with English, but Julia soaked it all up and became best in class very quickly—although she would never have phrased it that way.

The romance got off to a slow start, as they both felt uncertain about how to carry themselves. David had had flings before but never a real girlfriend for any length of time. This was something different, new, exciting, but also an exploration of the unknown in terms of culture and religion. They dated in secret, as Julia was concerned that it would be known at ICA that he was with the Bank. She was also not sure how her parents would see this young, non-Latino European. They admired all things American, but David was not that. Nor was he Catholic, which would definitely be a problem for her parents. It struck David how this labeling put up barriers for people to engage and allow their feelings to run free.

So many social compartments in this country, he thought to himself.

David was certain of his feelings for Julia but hesitated about initiating sex. Even at university, he had been cautious about engaging intimately, in spite of the free-wheeling atmosphere prevalent there. A fellow economics student, Mads, was charged with rape. According to Mads, it was all consensual, and they had been together for a few weeks before the incident.

Then, there was a nasty breakup, and as revenge—he claimed—his girlfriend suddenly charged him with rape. The counter-narrative painted quite a different picture, and a female activist group on campus quickly embraced it. Mads was mobbed to the point of desperation and left university disgraced and depressed. The police investigation was inconclusive and terminated without charges.

David's lingering sense of panic about being accused of sexual harassment crept up in an awkward way when things started to get steamy with Julia.

"Are you ok, David?" she asked, noticing his sudden cooling off.

This is totally irrational of me. It couldn't happen with Julia, he thought in anger with himself. He could not be open about his thoughts. "I'm just poor at reading social cues," he sheepishly offered. "I can interpret complex economic theory, but when it comes to reading humans, I'm often lost. Are you sure you want to have sex?"

Julia scrutinized him. "Is it me? Not sexy enough?"

"No, no, you are perfect, but you know, you're Catholic, and your parents probably are telling you that sex is a sin outside of marriage."

Julia laughed. "They would if I asked them, but I'm not." She started humming:

> *You know how us Catholic girls can be*
> *We make up for so much time ... eventually*

David recognized that from "Forgiven" by Alanis Morissette. He cracked up and pulled her to bed.

Once the ice was broken, they had sex almost every time they met. But it soon became somewhat predictable, and David was annoyed that he was the one to take the initiative each time. Julia's passive approach made asking her what she liked awkward, especially with her vague, deflecting answers.

"What we're doing is just fine," she would say. He wanted her secret desires, her dreams, her triggers. Julia got annoyed with him. "Don't try to evaluate the sex each time!" she blurted out one time.

David was embarrassed to talk about his triggers. A steamy scene in a late-night TV movie gave him an opportunity to comment on a girl's sexy lingerie and high heels. "It would be such a turn-on if you would wear something like that in bed!" It slipped out.

"Why can't you just love me as I am? Simply naked, like God created me. High heels are bad for your feet."

"I do love you as you are, but when it comes to sex, I am really dependent on visual stimuli. Those shoes are not for walking, honey. I'm sorry, it's just the way I'm wired. It's a guy thing, you know, there are surveys—"

"Don't talk about surveys again!" she snapped.

"I'm just trying to present an evidence-based argument," he retorted, but Julia walked away.

David sighed, but it was a minor thing after all. He was sure about his feelings for Julia. She fit perfectly into his life plan. Julia would be a great life partner and a wonderful mother to their children one day.

Progress on his other main goal was also ticking along. Work was intense and sometimes stressful, but he was constantly learning new things, and deep down, it was meaningful to work on alleviating poverty.

Julia had gone to bed and did not seem to be in the right mood for any exercises. *No worries. It will soon pass.*

He pulled the curtains in front of the two large windows of his little studio apartment on the third floor. It was small but cozy and he had rented it fully furnished. There was a small kitchenette with two hot plates and a microwave oven that he used frequently. The fridge was old and the freezer tiny, but he did not need much space, as he often ate in restaurants and did not enjoy cooking. There was a small couch with seats for two people and a small table in front of a TV which looked outdated. But he found little to watch except for public television newscasts, so it was not an issue. He spent most evenings at the small, dark-brown desk where he had installed a new, better lamp for easy reading. The only other item he had added was a comfortable reading chair to which he would retreat once the email inbox had been emptied in the late evenings.

He picked up the latest edition of *The Economist*. David enjoyed its crisp language, clear graphics, and liberal policy stance. Its attitude was a bit too cocky at times: "Problem X is the major issue facing mankind now, but here's how to fix it," *The Economist* loved to proclaim.

He gazed at the adorable Julia, sound asleep in his bed, and sank into his reading chair. *Life is good!*

CHAPTER 4

The Kidnapping

Could he have avoided getting captured? His contact in the Ministry for Community Development assured him that the area was safe. That day, he traveled with a driver and interpreter who knew the region. The local Bank office had insisted on adding two armed guards to his party, probably to fend off harassment from corrupt police manning roadblocks. But they would have stopped his expedition if they had serious misgivings.

He had reason to believe that the locals would greet him with approval, as the development project he was visiting was popular. Manual labor work had brought cash into the villagers' hands. Roads had been improved, wells had been dug, trees had been planted, and terraces constructed. In some villages, schools or clinics had been constructed.

He had been standing at the village meeting with the elders next to him and a semi-circle of men in front of him. He stood next to the interpreter. The guards were missing. Maybe they had gone off to the local *shebeen*? After a brief introduction, he had asked the villagers questions about the project through his interpreter. It was not straightforward.

The interpreter, Ahmad, recently graduated from the Agricultural University in the capital. His English was decent, but he had a habit of speaking for the villagers rather than simply translating. Once, the local elders engaged in a lively discussion at some length. David waited impatiently for the translation, only to be told by Ahmad that "they are happy with the project and would like more money."

David faced a dilemma. He had to build good relations with the staff of the host government, but he also had to confront issues, raise questions, and critically assess the information he received. All controversy could not be avoided. David pressed the point. "Ahmad, I can see that the man sitting next to me is very frustrated about something. What is he saying?"

Ahmad frowned but decided to deliver the message straight. "He says that payment for work is often late and that his family members have been denied work on repairing the road." Ahmad leaned in, and in a lower voice, he added: "The chief's relatives tend to get the better jobs."

Behind the project's impressive physical achievements, a complex social story unfolded and was hard to get a grip on. That would require social competence, trust, and knowledge of the local language. There was no money and not enough time for that kind of deep dive into this village's social fabric.

Then, everything changed. A Toyota pickup truck drove into the village carrying half a dozen armed men. Scarves and sunglasses concealed their faces. They had no uniforms and wore the same kind of traditional garb as the local villagers. But they also had AK-47s. Two of the men charged toward David and pulled him away. A black sack was hurled over his head, disorienting and panicking him. He was brusquely dragged away and thrown into the back of the pickup truck. The warm metal pressed against his face. His hands were tied, and the rope ate into his wrists. It was a nightmare, and he wet himself in horror.

Screams added to the frenzied commotion, orders were barked, and a few shots were fired in rapid succession. The pickup raced away on the bumpy road. It was a bruising ride, and the panic around his throat put him in a stranglehold.

But they haven't killed me, he repeated as a mantra in his head. *They want a ransom for me.*

David could not tell how far they had traveled from the village—only that he was quite sore from the ride as he was yanked off the pickup truck. Someone pushed his arm and shoulders from behind, marching him into a building with the hood still on his head. The hood finally came off, and the ropes around his wrists were removed. Then, they locked him up without a word. So, even if he could get out of his cell, he would not know in what direction to run.

His rehearsing of the dramatic events came to a halt when the guards opened the door. The same two men as yesterday. Beards, turbans, long cotton gowns open on the sides in a color that had been white once, long pants, wide at the top but tight around the legs, and leather sandals. David sat down as ordered.

The younger guard emptied some porridge-like substance into the food bowl, added a small, plastic bottle with water, and picked up the latrine bucket. He yelled something disapprovingly.

No wonder, David thought, *the stench must have been terrible,* although by now David's sense of smell was totally numbed.

At first, David had refused the food, but hunger gradually overcame any reservations. The food was usually the same, bland porridge, probably made from maize or sorghum. One day there was a spicy soup containing chopped tomatoes and onions that went pretty much straight through his stomach. He could only hope that the water came from a village pump with clean water, but it could just as well have come from a stream where cattle defecated upstream. There was no choice but to drink just to stay alive.

The daytime heat made his face drip with sweat, and the flies were plentiful. At night, the temperature became more reasonable, but the mosquitoes tortured him. His arms and legs were full of bites, and he struggled not to constantly scratch himself. Lice in his hair? Probably. He had a throbbing headache. *I must try to sleep,* he told himself.

***

They came at dawn in two Black Hawk helicopters flying low and fast. One kept hovering over the village to provide air cover. The other landed on a field at the outskirts of the cluster of buildings in the village center. Six Marines dressed in green emerged from the helicopter, agile, tough men who communicated with hand signals to secure the perimeter. Then, two of them sprinted straight to the building where David was kept prisoner.

They found the locked steel door to his cell. One Marine applied a lump of C-4 on the door by the lock, applied a detonator, and BOOM, the door flung open. The Marines burst into his cell with their M27IARs. They found David in a corner, too weak to stand up. One of the men leaned down over him, square-jawed, with black paint on his face. He spoke with a deep whiskey-baritone.

"What's your name?"

"I'm David Pedersen," he blurted out with the joy of someone who just got his life saved.

"You don't sound American," said the Marine with a puzzled look.

"I'm Danish," David yelled.

"Oh, fuck this," said the Marine and left.

David woke up with a jolt. *Damn it!* he thought. *I must stop constantly thinking about my rescue.* He marveled at the absurdity of his dream. But seriously, would the same effort be made to save him as for an American citizen? The U.S. was the only country with sufficient reach to undertake the kind of rescue that he was dreaming about. His employer would pressure them, of course, as would the Danish Embassy in Washington D.C. But would that be enough to launch an ambitious search? Pinpointing his location wouldn't be easy, and he was not the only one in danger in this part of the world.

CHAPTER 5

Clearing the Air with Julia

Six months into the relationship, David increasingly felt that Julia was The One. She was innocently pretty in a charming Amy Adams kind of way—although with black hair. He found her smart, intellectually curious to an unusual extent, and with a witty sense of humor that could dissolve tense moments in a blink. She was quick to laughter and carried a refreshing positive attitude. He had a lot to learn from her in that regard.

A few things annoyed him, so it was time to put the cards on the table. Not in a confrontational manner, of course. David disliked conflict and was jokingly known in the office as "the diplomat." Julia was also sensitive to criticism, so he had to tread with caution. He thought carefully how to minimize her defensiveness and picked a nice venue for a pleasant Saturday brunch: the Lafayette at the classy Hay-Adams Hotel near the White House.

They met in the dark-paneled lobby and entered the dining room together, where a smiling hostess greeted them. They were shown a nice window table, and a server presented them the menu, exuding experience and class in his grey vest, tie, and white shirt. Ice water was served right away. The large crystal chandeliers in the ceiling had an unusual lamp shade around them, which Julia liked. He liked the bright interior and the large windows which let in the generous sunlight. They were seated next to a grand piano, which gave some distance to the next table.

Perfect for this kind of talk, he thought.

"I'll start with the Smoked Carrot and Fennel Soup," David said. "What are you having as an appetizer?"

"I don't want to stuff myself, and they are so expensive!"

"It's my treat, Julia."

"Thanks, but I don't want you to waste money either."

"OK, let's not get stuck on that."

Julia earned very little at her NGO and lived a frugal life. David avoided talking about his own salary and did not spend lavishly–except when he gave in to his weakness for fine wines.

"What's your heart's desire, then?"

"I'd like the Maryland Crab Cake Benedict."

"Fine, I'll have the Seared Mediterranean Branzino. It comes with Fondant Potatoes, Roasted Vegetables, and Beurre Blanc. What do you want to drink?"

"Sparkling water, please. Are you having wine? It's too early for me, and I would just get sleepy."

"Yes, I'll have a glass of Chardonnay from their list. The choice of wines here is great!"

The waiter approached, they ordered, and he asked for the appetizer to come jointly with the main course so that they would eat together. When the waiter left, David leaned forward and put his hand over hers.

"I thought this would be a nice opportunity to talk about a few things." He smiled, but somehow the signals were not reassuring because Julia pulled her hand back and crossed her arms over her chest with a defensive look on her face.

"Knowing you, you've prepared a list, haven't you. What's bothering you?"

"Nothing! Why would you think—"

"I can read you, David. I may not have a PhD in economics, but I have one in reading people. What's number one?"

David sighed. "Ah good. The wine! Thank you. OK then, let's start with your phone." He pointed to her cell phone, which she had placed next to her empty plate. "You have a habit of always putting it out on the table when we meet, and—"

"I answer when my mom calls."

"But you sometimes take calls in the middle of our conversation. I'm sorry to say this, but I want to be upfront with you…I find that…rude."

Julia stiffened. "I've put the ring tone off."

"Fine, but it's still on vibrate, right? And you'll take a call if it comes, right?"

"Not all. Like I said, if my mom calls, I will. We're very close, and she calls every day. She'll get worried if I don't pick up."

"Every day! You're a grown woman with your own life now. What could you possibly talk about every single day?"

"I don't expect you to understand, but my family is different. You never talk to your father, and your mom, well, you said she calls you every Sunday. That's not enough for us!"

David took a deep breath and took a sip of his wine. He savored it and didn't want to spend their entire time lost in their emotions without enjoying the moment. He lightened his mood.

"Julia, please, why don't you just try my wine?"

Julia sipped the wine. Her shoulders relaxed. She dipped a piece of bread in the olive oil, and David smiled. He loved seeing her enjoying herself. They spent a few minutes quietly enjoying the shared wine as David cradled her hand.

When he felt that Julia was willing to continue the conversation, he said, "I can understand that your mom is very special to you, but you sometimes take calls from others, like that annoying Annika."

"Annoying? Her name is Angelica, and she's got some real issues. She had a very traumatic break-up with her boyfriend, and she has nobody else to turn to. No family, no other friends."

"I can understand why she has no other friends the way she goes about rehashing her break-up. That's old hat by now!" He had gone too far and had to back off. A server came to top up their water, so he took a moment for things to settle. "I'm sorry, that's uncalled for."

A burst of laughter from a table nearby provided some welcome distraction. *Redirect now*, he thought. "Now, I can understand that you want to help her out, and you are a very caring person, but don't let yourself be exploited."

Julia was silent for a moment and simply said, "I'll set my own limits, thank you. I also have something to say about *your* phone habits."

"*My* phone habits?" David leaned back in disbelief.

"Yes, on the phone, you're always so curt, and why don't you ever call me, you know, spontaneously, to share something exciting, or just to...well...say you love me." Julia had an adorable blush on her cheeks and looked down.

David was prepared for her defensiveness but not for a counterattack. Julia was turning things upside down, and he grasped for a way out. But it was simple really. "I call you whenever there's a need for you to know new information

… if I can't meet you at the agreed time but only an hour later, that sort of thing."

Julia threw up her hands in exasperation and raised her voice. "Listen to yourself! New information! So, I should be happy that you once established that you love me, and I shouldn't expect further conversation about that until you change your mind?"

"No, no, that's not what I'm saying." It was awkward that he had upset her and that she had raised her voice. An elderly couple two tables away looked at them with disapproval. "But we meet often and talk, so there's not much need for calling," he added in a hushed voice.

"You travel a lot and call me not even once a week. And when you're in town, we meet on weekends, almost never during the week."

"And you know why? Because I work late every day, and when I'm in the field, I'm too busy to think about my private life at all." He had gone way off script, and Julia appeared hurt. "I'm so sorry, I didn't mean it that way, I think about you a lot. Let's find a compromise here…how about I promise to call you at least once a week when I'm travelling. When I'm here, I'll call you on Wednesday evenings at ten for at least fifteen minutes, and we will continue to meet on weekends as usual. And you pick up only when your mom calls, but you'll text Annika that you'll call her back later when you are with me. OK?"

"Fine," Julia said with a tone of resignation.

David took a deep breath and waived down the waiter to order another glass of wine. He needed it. *Stick to the list and keep your cool. Shift to something positive!*

"What's next on your list?" Julia resumed.

"I don't have a list," he lied, "but I could think of something that is really positive. We have become comfortable with silence." Julia looked puzzled. "I mean we can just sit on a bench on the Mall or on my couch and read, think, feel each other's presence and enjoy life without necessarily verbalizing everything."

Julia reflected a bit. "I understand what you're saying, but I am sometimes left wondering what's on your mind. Long silences make me uncomfortable."

"But then, just break the silence!"

"Easy for you to say, but I can sense that you want quiet, you want 'personal space,' as you put it, even when we're together. So, I keep quiet."

"I had no idea you felt that way. I'm sorry, but this is an easy one to fix. Speak up, put your hand on my hand, or something, send a signal, and we will break the silence. It's just the way I am, an introvert who had very few friends growing up and grew up in a partially dysfunctional family. So, I turned inward, to books, to introspection. It's hard to change."

"Yet you try to change me?"

"No!" He lied again. "I'm just bringing up a few minor things, at the margin, that perhaps can be polished a bit to make our relationship even better."

"I also keep quiet because you've criticized me for interrupting."

"Well, you do. I just want to finish my own sentences. That is the way we talk where I'm from. There is like a little pause, a fraction of a second maybe, but out of politeness, we wait the other person out. A lot of Americans don't talk like that…they jump in, interrupt, even change the subject just like that…I find that annoying."

Julia smiled. "It's just a different culture, or maybe it's personal, I'm not sure, but we have a Finnish guy in our office, and sometimes, you've got to poke him to get a response." She laughed. "But for me, it's annoying if somebody just passively looks at you when you're talking. I'm just showing you that I'm engaged in the conversation—get used to it!"

The room was half-empty, and the conversation respectfully muted among the well-dressed clientele. The talk was not going as planned, and he hesitated to even bring up the hottest of potatoes on his mental list: sex. He couldn't think of a way to disarm that topic and remained silent.

"What's next on your list?" Julia insisted.

David confronted an easier one directly. "You have recently pulled me into several stores for some unfocused browsing, which has resulted in nothing but you looking at several pieces of clothing and even trying some on. But in the end, you haven't purchased anything. Frankly, it's a waste of time."

"I like to browse. Get your opinion on what I'm buying. It helps us get to know each other."

"When I go shopping, it's with a clear target, and I have done my research to zoom in on the best store, and I know my maximum willingness to pay."

Julia gasped. "David, you're such a nerd, and sometimes, I wonder why I love you." She moved uncomfortably in her seat. "I go shopping for inspiration, to find what I didn't know was there. This dress for example. Like it?"

She is deflecting, as expected, not wanting to address the problem. "Of course, I like it. It's colorful and fits you perfectly. But why pull me into this exercise? I have no sense of fashion."

Julia giggled. "Well, that's a true statement! You have a couple of good suits for work, but the ties, oh dear, so old-fashioned and boring, perfect for an older man! And in your spare time, I think you only have this blue shirt," she said, pointing at him.

That hurt. "This blue shirt is the most comfortable piece of clothing I own! And my ties are typical for my workplace and fit right in. Maybe they would not be appropriate if I worked for an NGO with twenty-somethings dressed in jeans and T-shirts. *So there.* And I do switch between this one…"—he pointed at his blue shirt—"and another that I really like."

Julia smiled mischievously. "And what color is that other shirt, pray tell?"

If there was a smashing riposte to that one, it escaped him in the moment. "It's a lighter blue," he offered meekly.

Julia looked like she had just scored a goal, and it annoyed him. Her phone vibrated. "It's Mom. I have to take this outside," she said apologetically.

"Give her my best regards," said David ironically as she stood up. He knew very well that Julia had never mentioned him to her parents. David picked up his own phone and started reading emails.

About five minutes later, Julia appeared and apologized profusely. "I'm so sorry, I just couldn't cut her off. A close friend of hers just got diagnosed with cancer, and now, she's worried she might have something as well. She just poured it out on me."

"Is there any evidence of her being sick?"

"Evidence? David, so typical for you to ask that. Mom is not driven by evidence but feelings—like fear."

Their food arrived. David let the situation sink in and took time to enjoy the food. Where to go next? The branzino was perfectly moist, well-spiced, and paired so well with the wine.

Julia took a bite out of her food but put her cutlery down. "Talking about shopping, which you so dislike, I went to a specialty store for lingerie called *Agent Provocateur* in New York last week. It was that dreaded girl Angelica who put me up to it." She smiled mischievously. "I would normally not spend so much money on that stuff, but you've been dropping not-so-subtle hints, and they had a sale. So, I'm wearing a racy thong and bra in black lace. I didn't put on the stockings and garter belt, but I have them in my purse. Interested?"

Damn it, she was just waiting to deliver that coup de grâce. David felt defeated and excited at the same time. He leaned forward and whispered, "Let's finish the food quickly, get the check, and go to my place, right?"

"Not so fast, sweetheart, we just got our food, and you've criticized me for eating too fast, remember? Then, there's dessert," Julia smiled triumphantly.

David had no patience for dessert, but Julia savored every bite of hers, licking her spoon suggestively as she finished the Chocolate Noir Date Cake with Ginger Ice Cream.

Things had gone off the rails for David's carefully planned talk. *Maybe I'm going about this relationship the wrong way,* he thought. *Julia is not a "project" that I can manage, making changes to reach the established goals more efficiently. If I want a future with her, I'll have to accept that she is very different from me. I have to adapt as well to make this work. But it's not going to be easy. And one day, we have to deal with her parents.*

CHAPTER 6

Rookie Mistakes

One bright Sunday morning a month after clearing the air with Julia, David went jogging on the Mall. It was pleasantly warm with a fresh breeze, and the cherry blossoms were out, enticing thousands of visitors. Spring was the best of all seasons before the humid, hot summer invaded Washington D.C. He had grown very fond of central D.C. with its impressive monuments, inviting greenery and museums. David made sure to visit at least one museum per month according to a list that he had posted on his fridge. What a cultural treasure it all was! Then, there was the magnificent Kennedy Center where he had gone several times for concerts.

After jogging for an hour, he stopped to buy water and to find a seat outside a kiosk near the Lincoln Memorial. Only one seat was open at a table where an elderly couple was seated having coffee and pastries. They were both strikingly overweight and dressed in color-coordinated shorts, T-shirts, and sandals.

"What a gorgeous day," David offered as a soft approach. "May I use this chair, please?"

"Of course," said the gentleman, turning to him with a friendly smile. "Wher'ya from, young man? Germany?"

It annoyed David that some people could detect his foreign accent right away. He was working hard to get rid of it. "Denmark."

"Oh, we know Denmark," the woman gushed. "Such wonderful people they are! We spent almost a whole day touring that city by bus...eh..."

"Copenhagen," the man filled in. "Really pretty guide that girl from Denmark," he added and winked at his wife who frowned. "Yeah, we saw everything that day, and the food was fantastic!" He finished his coffee.

"Honey, we went back to the ship for dinner. We didn't eat in Denmark." She put her hand on her husband's arm, patting gently. "You bought an all-inclusive package," she helpfully explained.

"That's right, I remember now. The food on that ship was fantastic ... steaks, hamburgers, ribs, anything you could wish for. We love to discover new countries, meet the people ..." the man added enthusiastically—"We covered a lot of countries that cruise ... Denmark, Sweden, Finland, Russia, and what was that little country next to it, sweetheart?"

"Tallinn. And in Copenhagen, we saw that great Viking ship they had picked up from the sea ..." She loaded a huge piece of a Danish in her mouth.

"Vasa," added the man.

David hesitated, but he could not resist. "I believe you are thinking about Stockholm, and that ship sank in the seventeenth century several hundred years after the Viking—"

"We met people from so many countries that trip," the man continued, undaunted. He puckered his lips a bit and averted his eyes from David, looking toward the Lincoln Memorial. "Just on our ship there were fifteen different nationalities among the crew. We've been to thirty-seven countries now. Can you believe it?"

All of them day-long stops or less with a cruise ship? David wondered.

"Lots of them from the Philippines, and I got to use all my long dresses on that trip," the woman added with a cheerful smile. She slipped her sandal on and off a bit, then looked up at the memorial, searching for something in her thoughts.

"Where are you both from?" David asked. "Somewhere in the South?"

"We're from Texas," they said in proud unison.

The man continued, "You know the best thing about traveling abroad is to get back and really feel how lucky you are to have been born here—right, honey?"

"We don't expect you to understand," said the woman soothingly with a bright smile on her face.

"Well, we'd better get going before the day is over." The man chuckled as he rose. "Really nice meetin'ya, young man. Enjoy the rest of your vacation." He gave David a hearty handshake.

"Lovely to meet you," said the woman and looked like she really meant it.

David strolled back home with an uneasy feeling. Theirs was a travesty of cultural exploration. They traveled the world, ticking off the number of countries, proudly collecting shallow glimpses of foreign cultures only to quickly retreat to their own comfort zone. But what about World Bank travel? He had little personal experience so far. But from colleagues, he had collected impressions of rushed visits overloaded with official meetings mostly in the capital, many hours of reading reports and handling emails in top-flight hotel rooms, maybe a few field visits, often heavily choreographed by the client government.

Would he ever be able to get under the skin of any of the countries that he was going to work with? If he followed a project for some years, probably yes, but there was also a rotation policy in the Bank meant to encourage cross-fertilization of ideas.

***

Stefan Holmström was a skilled, thorough World Bank economist in the Research Department. But he was also somewhat socially inept and struggled to summarize his work succinctly. He repeatedly battled with his manager with requests for extensions, claiming that "... just another six months would really improve the quality of the data." The money had run out, and it was time to deliver the results to a wider audience. Stefan's manager had given up on the researcher's ability to produce closure on his own. He consulted David's boss for advice on who might be helpful, and he turned to David whose writing he had found to be succinct.

Stefan had gathered a treasure trove of data on smallholder agriculture in Sub-Saharan Africa. Such studies sometimes gave rise to project ideas or modifications to existing projects. Potentially, they could also influence the ongoing policy dialogue with African agricultural counterparts.

Stefan was from the Swedish island of Gotland, which prided itself in annual reenactments of the Danish invasion in 1361. Swedish horsemen dressed up as Danish knights entered through the gates of the medieval town wall of Visby. They were greeted by locals in medieval costumes. A

Danish visiting journalist wrote acidly that there was "… an astounding number of nobilities but a scarcity of beggars and harlots among the locals." Stefan pulled up pictures from last summer's event to show him at their first meeting. David dodged the tease and politely steered the conversation to Stefan's main report.

David distilled the main results from Stefan's lengthy summary and wrote a one-page abstract. Stefan found it "shallow" but had to agree that it brought home the major points. Foreseeing a hard scrutiny among peers, he wanted to add more reservations and cautionary notes, but David convinced him not to. "Get out of the academic ivory tower now and spread the word," he urged. A seminar was prepared to present the results.

The seminar was a success. Attendance was high, Stefan was restrained in his time use, and many commentators weighed in with positive remarks. It was rare for seminars to turn confrontational. There could be thinly veiled jabs: "The speaker might have considered consulting previous work on this matter, which is easily available on request from my unit." Or "That kind of belief in the efficiency of market signals must be attributed to having spent too many years at the University of Chicago." There were very few jabs at Stefan. He took David out for a celebration beer after work—Carlsberg—as they could not find a Swedish beer anywhere in D.C., which David found pleasure in pointing out.

The celebration was short-lived. The morning after the seminar, Benjamin Grant's assistant came to David's office. "Benjamin wants to see you immediately in his office." Sensing that David was in for a bashing, she grinned with anticipation.

Although Grant was David's boss, they had very little personal contact outside of the unit meetings once a month.

Communication was generally via email. Grant was in his fifties, a tall, thin man with graying hair who spoke proper British English with an air of refinement. It was said about him that he had stopped reading documents and only relied on his verbal contacts and institutional memory to "wing it." One colleague suggested that Grant had the Peter principle to thank for his senior standing. Like many others, he had entered the Bank with a PhD from a reputable university (Oxford) and excellent technical credentials in the field of economics. But promoted to a management position, he seemed uncomfortable and annoyed with the budgeting process and the need to deal with personnel issues.

Grant was on the phone but waived him in. David had to endure a lengthy conversation before it was his turn. He wondered if this was on purpose—to make a point about his junior rank. Finally, Grant put the phone down.

"There's been a complaint about the invitation to the seminar you held yesterday. I got an email from Mathilda Evergreen in the newly established Transformational Strategy Unit within the Office of the President. It was addressed to me and Stefan's boss. She was upset that her office had not been invited."

David was dumbfounded. "We did our best to cover everyone with a potential interest. I have never heard of this unit. They were not excluded intentionally. And why didn't she email me and Stefan directly?"

Grant smiled. "Mathilda is a stickler for protocol. She is too senior to spend time with somebody like you or Stefan, frankly. And it gave her an opportunity to put down a marker that she's now in a position where she needs to be informed about every coffee break taken in this building. We need to be proactive before she spreads her complaint around even further."

"So, what do we do?"

"It's office politics, David. It's an art you'll learn to master to advance in the Bank—or perhaps you'll leave because you haven't. You draft an apology on behalf of Stefan and yourself that I'll forward. Express profound regret for the mishap! Include the presentation and offer a special session exclusively for her and her staff."

Really! I have to engage in this silly power play? "That'll work?"

"It's unlikely that she'll take up the offer. She'll just savor the victory."

As the days went by, David realized that it all worked out as Grant had suggested.

***

David continued to make rookie mistakes. The unit had several funds financed by Nordic donors that placed money with the Bank in their ambition to influence its activities in certain directions. It was both well-intentioned and welcome, but sometimes the donor ambitions went beyond what realistically could be expected. The Bank was a supertanker that small tugboats could not easily turn around.

A former colleague had started a study about community-driven projects in Africa, and David was designated to take over. He soon discovered that while only half the budget had been spent, the rest of the money had somehow been redirected. It would be impossible to conclude the study without those funds. It was a goose chase around many offices to trace the missing funds.

One key person, Ali, arrogantly rebuffed him and told him to "back off." Without his collaboration, David was stuck. He tried to see Grant about it, but his assistant stalled him, and he got no replies on his emails. In frustration, David contacted the Internal Audits and Ethics Department on the internal website. It assured staff members of "the utmost confidentiality" and "professional integrity." David sent a cautiously worded email to the department inquiring about how he should proceed. He refrained from mentioning names and did not accuse anyone of wrongdoing. He simply wanted advice on how to proceed in tracing the funds.

The next morning, he was suddenly called in to see Grant. He wasn't the only one—two grim-looking gentlemen flanked him at the table.

"David, this is Mr. Davidson and Mr. Kambula. They are with the Internal Audits and Ethics Department. You have filed a complaint without my knowledge. This is a serious matter. Why didn't you come to me first? You know my door is always open!"

It was the first time he had seen his boss so upset. But he really had tried to bring the matter to Grant's attention. David was stunned. He had heard the refrain of "My door is always open" several times from senior staff, but the higher up you got, the less true that was. His cautious "confidential" inquiry had triggered not only an immediate response but a betrayal of trust.

Before David had time to respond to Grant, Ali appeared, visibly agitated. David took a deep breath and decided to focus strictly on the main matter. He gave a brief summary of his strenuous efforts to trace the money flow from the donor fund.

Ali interrupted him. "There was an agreement to divert the funds to one of my studies. The funds were not efficiently used. My study falls well into the framework of our donor agreement. Nancy was acting for you at that time, Benjamin."

"Is there a record of that?" insisted David.

"If Ali says so, that's good enough for me," said Grant. "Let's not be formal about it. We're done here." That closed the meeting, as the Ethics officials seemed satisfied with that resolution.

David returned to his office but found it difficult to just pick up where he left off. He needed to vent, and to get some advice, and called Bob to check if he was available. He was, and minutes later, he entered Bob's neatly organized office two floors above his own. It looked like so many other Bank offices with a large, dark-brown desk, a small, round table and two chairs and bookshelves full of files. There was a framed canvas with Arabic text but not a single family photo or picture as was otherwise the standard. Smoking was strictly banned inside the World Bank buildings, but Bob's coat still brought a whiff of tobacco into the office.

"I guess the lesson is that somebody who is senior to you can run you over with impunity," David lashed out after describing the situation.

Bob thought for a few seconds before answering. "It's not really like that, but the Bank is a very hierarchical institution. It's collegial and informal as you move on your own level, but the higher up you go, the more you have to watch yourself. You'll probably have a good career, but make sure not to antagonize people who make decisions on promotions. At the top, it's a small fraternity, and people talk. I'd advise you not to challenge Ali. He's much more senior than you and well-connected."

"Should I be concerned that I could be fired for a thing like this?"

"Ali got his way, and he walked out feeling that he won this duel while you got egg in your face. That should be enough for him."

David was still unsettled. "I've heard stories about guards escorting people out of the building, even without a chance to collect their belongings. Is that true?"

"There could be a case where there was a suspected leak of very confidential information. Then, you would have to secure the room in order not to compromise any evidence. But otherwise, a dismissal is a rather civilized process where your manager calls you in and suggests that your exceptional talents might be put to more appreciated use somewhere else. There might be a sweetener with some financial package."

"I suppose most staff here would have a solid educational background, and with some years of experience, they could easily find a job elsewhere," David suggested.

"Yes and no. If you've published a lot and kept up to date with your field, you might be known outside the Bank and have a good network. But if you have dated academic credentials and had an operational job, you've been 'institutionalized,' so to speak. You may have mastered the internal lingo and skillfully navigated the Bank's bureaucratic maze, but you might be totally lost outside of this world. In addition, once you're out, your visa expires quickly, and you have to leave the country. Not everyone can look at the safety of returning to a place like Denmark," Bob concluded.

I left academia because I wanted something more operational, but now I'm making myself more vulnerable for the long-term, he thought. "I can see that some people might become very cautious," David noted. "But the more senior you get, the more secure your position will be, right?"

"To some extent as you build alliances. But there are limits at the top as well. We had one top guy who helped his girlfriend secure a fantastically advantageous contract when she had to leave the unit he was heading. There was an

64

uproar, and the guy had to go. There was another very senior Bank staff who maneuvered to get his brother hired and was forced out."

"So, there are some limits, even for senior management, then. But for the rest of us, isn't there some kind of appeals process if you're pushed out without cause?"

"Technically, yes, but I know of cases that have dragged on for years—you get tainted just by the process. How many managers will keenly consider you if you've been in trouble?"

David sensed that he had no other option but to swallow his pride. The recent events left him with an important lesson: *In the Bank, it sometimes matters less what is said than who says it*, he thought. He would never forget that.

CHAPTER 7

See You Soon, Julia

After almost one year together, the romance with Julia hit an abrupt roadblock. ICA could not provide her with a salary anymore. Like so many NGOs, they were dependent on grants from various foundations and individual donations. Raising money was costly and labor-intensive. Julia had expressed frustration about how much effort was invested in just keeping the organization afloat. They had lost a couple of big sponsors, and some people had to be let go.

She searched for a new job for a few weeks, but she was unsuccessful, so she decided to try joining the Peace Corps. She was grateful to quickly get an assignment in Africa. She was torn about leaving David and the U.S., but he insisted that he was supportive of her career plans. The assignment would last only for two years, and they vowed to stay closely in touch. She had to do it to get that field experience that she craved. This was the right time to do that before settling down, getting married, and starting a family.

During the past year, they'd shared endless discussions about development, foreign aid, and environmental conservation—but also about music, art, and leisure travel. David had learned a lot about U.S. pop culture, including TV shows and films. One of the few things that annoyed David was that Julia could not comprehend his ignorance about American television and movies. Repeatedly, he had to remind her that he had actually grown up in *another country*. It had its own TV programs, and the ones he liked most as a child had been Danish. Julia could not fathom that he had not watched a single *Star Wars* film. David had to counter by asking what films she had seen by Gabriel Axel or Bille August…both Oscar-winning Danish directors. Eh … none.

She tried to redeem herself. "But I watched parts of a movie by Ingmar Bergman once when I was little. My parents had fallen asleep in front of the television. I came up to get some water but stayed to watch when nobody told me to get back to sleep."

"Sorry, that doesn't count because he is Swedish."

"Oh, come on, he's a neighbor of yours! But it was a weird movie. I realized it wasn't for kids when the screen just lit up with one word in big letters: It said 'SLUT.' I rushed to bed before they would notice me."

"Well, that means 'THE END' in Swedish." David chuckled. "You know, it would be good for you to get out of this country for a while and dig into some other cultures and learn at least a bit of another language. That might put your own culture into some perspective."

"You're forgetting that I'm already part of a Latin immigrant culture and I speak Spanish very well," Julia noted defensively.

"Agreed, and that's an asset, but you have lived in the U.S. all your life with only brief family visits to Mexico. Your friends seem to all be Americans, you talk and dress like them. It's easy to take things for granted when you haven't experienced living in another country. Two years in Africa will enrich your life."

***

As David pulled up in a taxi, Julia was pacing in front of the colonial-style, red-brick apartment building where she had rented a room for the past year. The apartment had been a good place for her, as she could split the rent with two young women who also worked for non-profits. David had met them on occasion, but they had mostly spent time at David's apartment.

David came running from the nearby Metro station just in time for the taxi's arrival. "Sorry, I'm late," he said, out of breath. "I missed the Metro stop." He had been working out how he should say goodbye.

She was happy to see him. "I've already said goodbye to my roommates. They said they're coming to visit, but I doubt it will actually happen. They don't have the money."

The Peace Corps preparation had been good and reassuring. She would have their backing and guidance. But it was a posting in exotic Africa, albeit in an English-speaking country. She would be working in a rural area with a women's business development and empowerment project. Not everyone would speak English there, but she would be partnered with a local, well-educated woman. After all, this had been her dream for many years—getting out into the world and working on something that could make a difference.

They kissed quickly and got into the taxi. Julia hated goodbyes. "Mom's been gut-wrenching."

"I thought she was supportive?"

"Yes, but she wouldn't stop crying and tried to prod me into taking a large suitcase full of canned food."

"She's seen too many pictures of starving children in Africa?"

"She said she's afraid I'll be malnourished. I had to show her how much extra I would have to pay for overweight baggage."

"Your dad?"

"Pretty stiff upper lip, but he's worried about my 'adventure' as he called it. He warned me about sexual predators. But he did that when I went to college, too."

As David listened, he reminded himself to act calmly, be supportive and encouraging, and maybe even plan his visit to her on their way to the airport. Her nervousness was evident despite how she tried to hide it. He hoped that she would not cry. He would say goodbye to her at security, and she would turn around to wave at him in the escalator going down. He would smile and wave back. David knew Dulles Airport well, and it was all worked out.

"What's going on, David? You look…nervous?"

He was silent for a moment and answered with a voice that could not conceal his tension. "What's going on is that you are leaving me!" He regretted it right away.

"I'm not leaving *you*. I'm leaving for a new job. It's just two years. We'll be in touch. And you were so supportive when we discussed this."

"I…I had to be. How could I stand in the way of an independent woman…who wants to make the world a better place. But the truth is…" He swallowed hard, and she could see how he struggled to keep himself composed. "The truth is…I hate that you are leaving!"

"David! Don't do this to me. I can't walk away from this now. We agreed!" She unbuckled her seat belt to lean over and hug him tight. She kissed him on the cheek and ran her fingers through his hair, the way he liked it.

"I love you, Julia," David pressed forward, as he couldn't hold his tears back. Julia pulled out a Kleenex from her bag and dried his face. But the tears kept coming. She had not seen him like this ever before.

"I know, honey, and you know I love you too. But don't make me feel guilty for leaving. Come on! You can visit me there."

David felt like a traitor. He wanted to support her career and her independence and had decided that he would conceal his conflicted emotions about her leaving. Why hadn't he come clean sooner? That would have been more honest. His plan had fallen apart the moment he saw Julia again. His rational armor had big cracks in it.

"I'm so sorry." He sobbed. "I'm failing you."

"Stop it, David, just stop!" she begged him.

The baffled driver peered at them in the rearview mirror. "You want to stop?"

"Drive, goddammit," yelled the proper Catholic girl who had never taken God's name in vain before.

The car sped up, and they sat silently, holding each other tightly, as the taxi rushed down Dulles Toll Road out to Washington Dulles International Airport. It was a sunny afternoon with a pleasant temperature, with light traffic meandering through a suburban landscape full of new construction and shiny office buildings in glass and steel. But none of that mattered. They were alone, intensely focused on absorbing every second of their last minutes together. What still needed to be said?

The driver discreetly watched them in the rearview mirror. As they entered the circle in front of the sleek terminal building, he cleared his throat. "Excuse me. We are here. What airline, please?"

"United," Julia said. The taxi stopped in front of the United Airlines section of the terminal. They got the baggage out and faced each other.

"I'll walk in with you," David offered.

"No!" Julia demanded. "It will make it more painful. Just take the taxi back to town."

After one last kiss, she picked up her bag and entered the terminal with quick steps. "See you soon, Julia!" he called out after her. But she did not wave, and she did not even look back.

CHAPTER 8

Transfer in Captivity

David had made four scratches on the wall for each day in captivity, but he gradually lost a sense of time. His sleep was erratic, his head hurt, dehydration set in, and he could not keep the food down. At times, he was overwhelmed with anxiety about his fate, and he cried as he thought of his loved ones and how they must worry. But at other times, he could still cling to his hope that ransom would be paid or that a rescue operation would somehow find him.

About a week into captivity, he was pulled out of his cell. A black hood covered his head. The fresh wind released the smell of fried food. Propped up sitting against a tree trunk, he heard two languages being spoken. An interpreter went back and forth. Were they showing him off to determine how much to pay for the hostage? Then, they led him into a building, and removed his hood. His cell had been so dark that the lighter area almost blinded him, but he couldn't lift his arm to screen his eyes, and he bit his tongue to stay silent. His eyes adapted. A large man in a white shirt, black vest, and wide, white pants sat in front of him. He had a turban on his head that reminded David of pictures of the Taliban in Afghanistan.

"Doctor," the man said, pulling up a stethoscope. He opened David's shirt and pressed it against his heart and lungs. No doubt, this was a professional. They laid him down, and the doctor methodically checked his body. His clothes were removed, but he received a new set of traditional garb. There was no sense of humiliation…just examination.

The doctor's verdict was brief. "Drink" he said, and an aide pulled out a Coke bottle.

It was the best Coke he had ever had, and his spirit soared. His hands and feet were tied, his head cloaked with a hood, and he was draped with a tarp as they shuffled him to a waiting pickup truck. A thin blanket barely cushioned the bumpy ride. He fell into a coma-like sleep, hopeful he'd continue to receive the better treatment he felt during the examination. Not freedom—but maybe his new captors had a clear incentive to keep him in a condition to be traded for a ransom.

David woke up without a clear sense of how long he had slept, but judging by the warm tarp against his skin, the sun must be up. He needed to pee desperately and just had to let go. The pickup made its way into a mountainous landscape. After another two hours or so, they finally stopped. Doors slammed, and his hands were removed from the restraints. They led David into a building and sat him down on a chair. Finally, they removed his hood. He blinked uncomfortably in the light.

A bearded man in jeans, a T-shirt, a hat, and sunglasses sat in front of him. He was White and in his thirties. *"As-salaam 'alaykum.* That means 'peace be upon you,'" he clarified in unaccented American English. "Welcome, David Pedersen. You will be our guest here until our demands are met. If you cooperate fully, it will be a pleasant stay. God willing, you will soon return to the U.S."

David was stunned speechless at first. "Who are you? Where am I?"

"I'm known as 'The American Warrior.' You're among Allah's Soldiers in a safe place. Don't worry." He proceeded to quiz David about his capture and time in captivity. He was meticulous about details and timing and took notes in a small book.

David was put in a cell with a cement floor and iron bars covering the small window placed too high to look out from. Some daylight dribbled in, the supply of Coke continued, and he gradually could keep down the bread and hummus that was served daily. He was taken to a basic latrine when he asked for it. There were calls to prayer five times per day. This was a different kind of village.

The next day, the American Warrior burst into his cell. David tensed up, but the Warrior carried two Cokes and smiled as he offered David one. He quizzed David about his family and work. David was careful not to reveal anything that could be used against him but was eager to get some human contact.

I think this guy relishes a chance to speak English. Maybe I can get better treatment if I establish good rapport with him. When the Warrior was about to leave, David took the chance to ask some questions on his own.

"How long did you live in America?" David asked.

"Used to be a taxi driver in Detroit. My first twenty years. Then, things happened in the Muslim heartland. Many believers were killed. I couldn't stand idly by and joined the fight against the Crusaders."

"I'm not American," David was keen to point out to deflect the aggression the Warrior seemed to feel against his own nationality.

The Warrior smiled. "We're checking up on you, but we do know that you work for the World Bank, an American bank, and you are part of their global plan to subjugate our people. The Americans have sent troops to our countries, you kill with drones and airplanes wherever you choose, you attack funerals and weddings, you respect no laws and show no mercy. Why then should we?"

74

"It's not an American Bank. It's just that they have the most shares in the Bank, and they appoint its president. But we're an international organization. The staff are international civil servants and don't favor any particular nation," David clarified, much as he had done several times in the U.S.

"That's just window-dressing. You're an arm of the Western Crusader-Zionist project that is dedicated to destroying our culture and our religion," the Warrior burst out.

This was the language of militant Islamists. It was hard to make sense of the American Warrior. He had spent his most formative years in the U.S. What had turned him into a militant Islamist? But it was not unique. David recalled that Khalid Sheikh Mohammed, the "terrorist entrepreneur" behind the 9/11 attacks had a degree in mechanical engineering from North Carolina.

David wanted to avoid confrontation. He was not building rapport this way. "Tell me about Detroit," he ventured.

The Warrior took a swig on his Coke and sat silent looking down. He seemed to like remembering Detroit and after a few seconds, he continued with a calm voice. "I was a typical American teenager back then. Drank beer, smoked, chased girls, watched porn, played video games, you name it. Got in trouble for shoplifting and then assault. It was really just self-defense. My gym teacher in high school was a great guy, a Muslim. He liked me. We talked a lot, and one day, he took me to a mosque. It was cool, so I started to hang out with some of the guys there."

The Warrior looked relaxed now and leaned back in his chair. But then his face darkened. "I was bullied a lot. Hanging out with the Muslim kids got me protection."

"So, you converted?

The Warrior remained silent, as if he tried hard to remember the Detroit teenage years. Then, he continued, "I dropped out of high school and started driving a cab for a brother. I grew a beard and dressed like other brothers. That got me into trouble with some nasty passengers."

"What happened?" David interjected.

Sometimes, people refused to let me drive them when I showed up. Other times, they drank alcohol in my car, and I would stop and ask them not to. Got into a fight once, and the guy charged me with assault. He was really the one who started it. But he was White and a good Christian, so they let him go but punished me. I was so pissed, I figured I just wanted to get away."

A guard came in and whispered something in the Warrior's ear. He smirked and waved him off.

What was that about? David felt a pang of anxiety.

"I met a guy at the local mosque who was getting a group together to go to Iraq. We would be trained first before we were sent to fight against the Crusaders who had occupied the country. They wanted people fluent in English so that they could recruit new fighters in English-speaking countries. I won't spill the details to you, my friend"—he chuckled—"but I can tell you we went as tourists to Turkey first."

David was not surprised. The Warrior fit the mold of some he had read about in the *Washington Post*.

The Warrior looked at his watch and grinned. "It's funny how I found myself a successful and appreciated marketing manager, first in Iraq, later in several other countries where we fight for justice and the establishment of the Caliphate. It's the first time in my life that I feel my talents are really appreciated." He chuckled.

*He thinks of himself as "a successful marketing manager"!
How bizarre!* David thought.

The Warrior left with a greeting in Arabic.

***

The following day, David was taken into a small village square. A video camera was mounted. He had feared such a moment, as he had seen captives under duress read aggressive denunciations of the U.S., Israel, Crusaders, Zionists, and so on. Would they force him to denounce the World Bank? If so, would he read it? At that moment, the ethical dilemma seemed rather academic: *If I say crazy things, people will know that I'm forced to. But if I refuse, I might lose my head. So, I'll read whatever they give me,* he thought. He was given a piece of paper with English text, and he read in a voice that clearly betrayed the tense situation.

> "My name is David Pedersen. I work for the World Bank in Washington D.C. I'm now a guest of Allah's Soldiers. I am treated well. It is my wish to be exchanged for the following believers who have been unjustly imprisoned by infidels."

A list of five names followed, and David struggled through them. He had no idea who they were but assumed that they were Islamists who had been captured somewhere in the world by Western Powers. It was very brief, and David found some hope in that his fate would now receive a lot of attention. But he was deeply concerned that his loved ones, and his friends, would see him this way and realize that his life was in danger.

He kept his composure as he was escorted back to his cell. As he rested there it was not possible to hold up the shield of denial. *What if they don't get what they want? They'll have to show the world they are serious!* It hit him with such force that he turned on his side and threw up in violent convulsions. His body was telling him how afraid it was of death.

***

The next two days were uneventful, and David regained his composure. But then he was pulled out to the square again. The video camera was there as before, behind it, three stern-looking men with automatic weapons stared at him. A group of male villagers stood behind them, anticipating a spectacle. David was forced down on his knees, hands tied behind his back. The American Warrior posed in front of the camera, wearing a balaclava and sunglasses, recited in his clear American English, with his head lowered and turned toward Mecca:

"Almighty Allah, most gracious and merciful, whose bounties are unbounded, whose benevolence is everlasting, whose blessings are uncountable, whose being is eternal, whose mercy is unlimited, and whose love is our life, whose worship is our faith."

The Warrior raised his head and turned toward the camera, gazing into to it. His tone became harsh.

"I stand before the infidel David Pedersen who will pay the ultimate price for the insulting response that we have received from the U.S. government. You have our demands. Our offer will expire at noon Washington D.C. time tomorrow, June 5."

The American Warrior pulled out a broad sword and ceremonially put it on David's neck. It all went dark for David, and he fell to the ground. That ending must have pleased the Warrior he thought when he woke up. This would go viral on social media before it was taken down. The lust for violent entertainment was unsatiable, David knew.

***

Concerned that their hiding place could be traced somehow, they moved David again the next day. A disgruntled villager might see a chance to collect a reward and make a careless phone call. Spy satellites and drones hovered in the sky, and there was sparse vegetation to hide in.

David was brusquely loaded into the back seat of a double-cab pickup truck, his hands and feet tied, and a black hood over his head. But it was much more comfortable this way. The drive lasted about four hours on bad roads.

His new quarters were about the same as the previous ones. Only traditionally dressed guards with AK-47s wandered around the first day. On the second night, the Warrior suddenly appeared again. He brought two Cokes.

"It's confirmed," he said and looked pleased. "You're Danish, not American." As Bank staff, David travelled on a UN laissez-passer that did not identify his nationality, only his employer.

"I told you so."

"We had to check that you weren't just trying to evade responsibility for America's terrible crimes. And this is much better for us and perhaps for you. We started with the Americans and demanded they let some of our brothers free. They insulted us. They're arrogant, dogmatic people. They don't pay ransom and rarely let prisoners go. The bad thing with them is that they might swoop in with drones and SEALs and shit. But since you're not American, they won't give a damn!" He took a swig of his Coke as if to celebrate that fact.

"Now, we've opened a line with the Danish government," he continued. "Those guys don't have troops anywhere close, and they are soft and rich. They'll pay because they want their Prime Minister to appear on TV with you when you thank them."

David continued to for a way to establish some rapport with the Warrior—it might be crucial. "You know, one of my best friends at the Bank is a Muslim." It sounded like a cliché to him that he'd heard in another context. "Bob has taught me a lot about his religion, and he got me a copy of the Holy Koran. It was interesting reading, but I'm a bit confused about certain things."

The Warrior showed renewed interest. "I'll be happy to explain!"

"Well, there are passages that talk about punishing the infidels, but in other places, forgiveness is preached. To me, it's the same problem as with the Bible—you can take what you want from it."

"Hmm, this guy Bob, is he a good man?"

"If he wasn't, would I see him as a good friend and a mentor? He's the first Muslim I've come to know."

"Then, watch him closely and learn. That will be your best guide to Islam."

"First, I have to get out of here and back h—"

"Don't worry, they'll pay, and you can go," the Warrior said with confidence, stood up, and left.

***

Two days went by with no further communication. David's mood sank toward the bottom again. Maybe they would just use him as a prop in demonstrating their willingness to use violence? But he had so much left to do in life!

The next evening, the Warrior appeared, his breath smelling of alcohol as he pulled in a chair to sit down. David sat on the floor on his bamboo mat. With a big grin on his face, the Warrior fished out a plastic jug from his bag. "Try this," he offered and shoved the jug into David's hands.

"What is it?"

"It's the closest thing to entertainment you get in this fuckin' shithole of a village," the Warrior responded with a slur in his speech. He had clearly had a few drinks already. "It's fermented sorghum," he clarified.

David took a cautious sip and found the taste disgusting. But the thought of getting some alcohol into his starved veins seemed attractive, so he continued sipping.

"Do you think I could get something to read, please? It's really boring here. Do you have any books you could share?"

The Warrior grinned. "I'll check my travel library. Ha-ha. How about Voltaire?"

"You've read Voltaire?"

"Don't insult me with that look, man. As every other taxi driver in Detroit, I had a solid literary education. My teacher was Rebecca, a senior when I was a freshman in high school. She was reading Voltaire, Camus, Sartre, the whole bunch. And Frantz Fanon. Boy, that guy could write—such rage against colonialism!"

He sipped, burped, and wiped his mouth with his shirt sleeve.

"She had a French father, you know, so she could read French, but I read it all in English. That girl had the nicest tits I ever saw! I had to listen to her explaining these guys to me for hours before she would let me screw her. Same procedure every night we met. Just the sound of that language…you know, those guys have some pride, great food, good wines, brilliant writers, and the most beautiful women in the world."

The Warrior was a fanatic, but his admiration for the French showed another side of him, and he had not shed his American youthful persona entirely. The alcohol buzzed in David's head as he dared to challenge the Warrior.

"Do you really think that Allah's Soldiers and their allies could defeat the American war machine? You can annoy them, but will you ever be able to hold territory to establish the Caliphate that you dream of?"

The Warrior broke out in sarcastic laughter and took a big gulp of beer. "You're getting cocky now, eh? You've no idea what's in the making. Ha, we are working on new weapons you wouldn't believe. Think we're a bunch of turbans with AK-47s, right?" He leaned forward over David and whispered so close to him that he could smell the alcohol on the Warrior's breath. "In the labs of top universities, our guys are working on the latest cyberweapons and biochemical weapons that will strike the infidels when they least expect it!"

"But the West has its guard up," David objected. "That all changed after 9/11. Your agents will be caught."

"No, man." He smirked. "They're clean-shaven guys with Christian girlfriends for cover … they listen to rock music and smoke weed. You can't find them!" He broke out in sarcastic laughter again and took another gulp from the jug. He straightened up. "Fuck, I talk too much," he muttered and left in a haste.

A chill spread through David's stomach. Was it all just a drunken rant? Or was something like that really happening? There was a time when young Arabs went to pilot schools in the U.S. and innocently learned how to fly an airplane. Nobody suspected anything, until 9/11 happened. Could this be a repeat—only with other means? Implausible, but not impossible!

CHAPTER 9

A Jury of Peers

It was a bright, sunny day in Mandula. The usual morning rush mixed high-powered business leaders in chauffeur-driven fancy cars with imported, used clunkers that would have been taken off the road if there was an authority concerned with traffic safety. A senior civil servant took his family shopping in a government vehicle bought by foreign aid money. Shopkeepers opened their doors and chased away homeless people who blocked their entrances. Chatty schoolgirls in neat uniforms meandered among the street hawkers on their way to school.

Mavuso had a bad day. He lined up for day jobs each morning at a small market square where employers went to find day laborers at a cheap rate. But that day, few pickup trucks came around. Construction work had dried up during the recession. Depressed, he decided to spend his last money on beer. The country had a shortage of many things but never on beer.

"Gimme one," he muttered to the barman, pointing to the fridge with beer bottles. He banged the exact change on the counter. The barman handed him a bottle of his favorite local brew without a word.

The country was heavily in debt, and the budget in a record deficit. Large loans had been taken out by the government in secret, and now, the bills came due. Where had the money gone? The IMF determined that leading politicians had stashed much of it in tax havens abroad or directly spent on shopping trips for the elite to Paris and New York. It was not just fashionable hats and dresses that had been procured. No, ostentatious mansions had been bought, yachts, luxury cars, and expensive jewelry topped off the list.

Mavuso looked around to see if any of his friends would come by but did not recognize anybody. But there were more beer-drinking guests at this hour than usual, more sullen faces, more agitated conversations about the bad times.

Now came the belt-tightening prescribed by the IMF and other creditors as a condition for a bail-out, the cuts in public expenditures and subsidies. Not just a large number of "ghost" employees were fired from the ministries, but also real ones lost their livelihood. They started competing with the low-skilled labor, and tensions mounted. Gas prices suddenly jumped, infuriating truck drivers and others dependent on cheap fuel. Some fuel trucks were simply hijacked, driven to a secure place, and emptied by criminal gangs who then sold their loot on the black market.

Mavuso glanced at a group of students passing by with cardboard signs. Probably on their way to some rally. Rich kids from the university making noise in the streets—how useless!

Demonstrations against the IMF, the World Bank—what was the difference anyway?—foreign donors, and the national government, spread from the capital and into provincial cities. The national government deflected local anger by denouncing "foreign intervention in domestic affairs" and "colonial attitudes among rich country governments." The government had no desire to cut subsidies, but they were forced to by outsiders, they said.

"Hi man! What's up?" The loud greeting jolted Mavuso and he turned around in his chair.

Mavuso's friend Solomon passed by and sat down with him. Solomon was nicely dressed and liked to show off his wealth. There was a fat gold chain around his neck—a daring display, but he felt it was worth the risk as it impressed the girls and gave him stature among men. He had a small truck that he used to smuggle heavily subsidized gasoline to a neighboring country that had world-market prices. It was illegal, of course, but Solomon had a relative who worked for Customs at one of the border posts. He would tell Solomon when he was on duty, and Solomon would discreetly slip the man some notes as they shook hands at the border. On the other side, he could sell the gasoline to a contact for double the price he had paid. It was his livelihood, but now it was threatened by foreign economists who had no understanding of real life in a developing country.

Nevertheless, Solomon always put on a happy face. "Hey, man, all good?"

"All good, but no work today."

"You should come and work for me," suggested Solomon. It was an expression of goodwill—not a real offer. "But now those foreign advisors are threatening to take away my work too. It was in the paper today."

Mavuso never wasted money on newspapers, but he had heard that as well. "Who are those guys?"

"They're Americans from the IMF and the World Bank. I call them '1,2,3 and out guys.' They arrive at the airport, go to their hotel—the Royal or some other top one—and then the Ministry of Finance. They preach their free-market gospel there: 'don't spend so much on subsidies, don't control prices, pay back your loans' and all that. Then, they're done and leave! Those guys don't care one fuckin' bit about us. They just want to save the creditors' asses!"

Mavuso nodded in silent agreement and emptied his beer bottle. He would need another one, but money was tight.

Solomon glanced at his expensive watch. He liked Mavuso perhaps because his own world compared so well with

Mavuso's. And yet, they had started in the same spot once. It was obvious which one was the cleverest. He was in a hurry, always working on some new entrepreneurial idea.

"Think you could lend me some change?" Mavuso asked.

Solomon did not appreciate the request. He had enough of his own problems to take care of. Why didn't this man get a job? But it felt good to flash his money in front of a less fortunate brother. He pulled out a stash of cash and slapped a large bill in Mavuso's hands.

"Wow man!" Mavuso blurted out and flashed the first smile of the day. He gave Solomon a friendly slap on the shoulder as he rose to get the next beers.

Solomon returned to his worries. Surely, the government would not dare to abolish all gasoline subsidies, he thought. They had started, but that had already caused rioting, as it had five years ago when that was tried last time. Eventually, the government had to back down after widespread demonstrations that had progressed into looting and even some deaths. Even if gas subsidies were toned down gradually, there would be a market left. And there would be other items where price control opened up business opportunities for a guy like Solomon.

When Mavuso returned, Solomon stood up. "I've got a job to do," he declared curtly and declined the offer of a beer.

Sitting on a cheap plastic chair outside the bar, Mavuso cradled his beer and glared at the number of expensive cars passing by. "So many Mercedes-Benzes," he grumbled to himself. A rage built up inside as he watched his own mirror image in the large bar window. A man of thirty years, still unmarried, and with nothing to offer a bride. Six years of schooling with classes as large as fifty students with teachers more absent than present. Many of the teachers had bought their positions, guaranteeing them a decent public salary, job security, and little work. The better-off students could bribe them and get good grades, move on to higher studies, and get good jobs, especially if they were well-connected.

But Mavuso had no living parents and no connections to high-powered people. He was alone in this world in his tattered T-shirt, worn jeans, and plastic flip-flops. Mavuso had dreams, of course, and starting on his fourth beer, they kept growing stronger. A good job, new shoes made of real leather, and a Sunday suit for church. And that toothache had to be fixed. It kept bugging him, but a dentist was just too expensive. He was a hard worker and a good Christian who prayed to his God every Sunday for a better life. If only God would listen! It was people like him who deserved to ride around in shiny cars and impress the girls.

A large, new-model Mercedes-Benz had stopped across the street. The driver had double-parked to buy cigarettes in a convenience store. A young man eager to show off, he climbed out to display his elegant uniform for the world, and slowly walked into the store. The passenger side window was half-way down. Mavuso could hear the music inside the Mercedes blaring at full volume. He recognized the sound of Bombino, a band from Niger. They sang in Tamasheq, which he did not understand, but he loved the rocky sound. He started swaying to the rhythm of *Amidinine*, when it dawned on him: The key must be in the ignition!

Mavuso felt a sudden urge, stood up with a jolt, walked briskly across the street, jumped in, and turned the key, put it in first gear, and pressed the gas pedal hard. "This my car!" he roared as he felt a rush of adrenalin from the acceleration.

He had once driven an old, tired pickup truck for a construction company. But this car was something totally different. The Mercedes roared and shot forward like an arrow into the street. Scared pedestrians fled in panic. Mavuso wanted to get away fast, but he lost control as he tried to avoid running into a large truck. The sound of the crash was heard several blocks away.

Julia Chavez died instantly as her body was crushed between the Mercedes and a brick wall. As people quickly gathered, they saw a dead, bleeding woman pinned against a wall. It was a horrific sight that stirred great emotion. Then, they saw a man, semi-conscious from shock and impact, in the driver's seat. He crawled out and tried to get away. The situation required no explanation—not even reflection.

Street justice is swift and never hesitant. It quenches the raging thirst for retribution. There are no defense lawyers, and no time is wasted to cross-examine witnesses. But there is a jury of peers. Its verdict was instantaneous and needed no official pronunciation. Mavuso was set upon, kicked, and beaten. Two policemen came rushing. Joining the crowd in a frenzied eruption of violence, they pulled out their batons. They stopped only when Mavuso's lifeless body of pulp was beyond recognition.

CHAPTER 10

Homecoming

A letter arrived in David's office inbox. He tore it open quickly as he saw the sender's name: Maria Chavez. It was a simple card with a flower bouquet on one side and a short prayer on the back. The hand-written text read:

> *Our beloved daughter Julia was tragically killed in a traffic accident in Mandula on September 1. She is now in God's hands. We never met you, but Julia had left an envelope behind to be opened in case she would not return. We now know how much you and Julia cared for each other. It was her wish to be buried in her family village in Oaxaca. You are, of course, welcome to join. Arrangements are being made. Details later.*
>
> *Love,*
>
> *Maria and Fernando Chavez*

David collapsed in his chair, sobbing. He had thought about Julia often and had worried himself sick about the lack of any recent news from her. It had started well with short but romantic picture cards, but lately no cards, and there was no telephone service in the area where she was working. He had been looking forward so intensely to an opportunity to visit her, but work kept getting in the way. Now it was all over—over—and she was gone!

He pulled himself together, cleaned up his face in the restroom, and ventured out for a random walk on the Mall. Aimlessly walking, he only wanted to be alone with his grief. *How could people just keep working, talking, driving cars ... when his Julia had died?* He got angry and hammered away at an innocent tree trunk that offered an outlet. Could there be a mistake? Someone else got killed and was confused with her, maybe had stolen her ID? His brain was speeding, trying to find a way out—she could not be dead!

A phone call later that afternoon to her parents confirmed the details. He had to face facts. David struggled with the situation. Not going to the funeral felt like deceiving Julia. He should be there to honor her. But going would raise so many questions from her relatives and friends. It would be a visible sign that she had engaged in a relationship without telling her family. Her parents knew now, but what about others? Could he just say he was a colleague? But that would be lying, and his raw emotions would betray him. It would be emotionally overwhelming, and he would feel out of place.

The next day, David wrote to Julia's parents and apologized for not attending. He was not able to function at work. Instead, he headed home to Denmark for a short vacation to get away from it all. His boss was very understanding and authorized his leave with sympathy.

***

Strangely, landing in Copenhagen felt like he was at home— and like he was a visitor. From the airport, he took a train to his hometown, little Vannebo, a town of some five thousand people surrounded by flat, fertile agricultural land and with traditional Danish single-family houses. It was neat and well-run. The schools were considered good. While there was almost no crime, some tensions built up between older Danes and new immigrants, often from Muslim countries. Eastern European beggars had caused a stir, and a right-wing activist group harassed them at times.

His parents met him at the railway station. His mom, Merete, hugged him hard and long, and could not hold back her tears.

She was a warm, emotional woman who was horrified when David first brought up the possibility of moving to the U.S. "They are killing each other all the time in Washington D.C.," she said. Merete fed him negative press stories about the U.S. As her only child, his long absences had depressed her. She was now sixty, and years had added weight to her lower body and wrinkles in a face that carried the same warm smile that had brought comfort to David throughout his childhood.

His father, Niels, gave him a firm handshake. "Good to see you, son," he said rather flatly. He was shorter than David, a thin, sinewy man whose unusually large hands were hardened by decades of carpentry. At sixty-five, his backache rendered him immobile and bitter at times. Niels had nothing but contempt for doctors and medications, so beer became his remedy. He was not prone to weighing pros and cons but always arrived quickly to a firm standpoint from which he skillfully interpreted any new information as confirmation. It put an effective damper on the dinner conversations during David's childhood.

"We won 2-0," Niels proclaimed.

"What did we win?"

"In the soccer game against the Swedes last Sunday. You didn't watch it?"

"Those games are not broadcast in the U.S."

Niels was surprised that a country with so many TV channels did not cover milestone events like the Danish victory over Sweden in a qualifier to the European Championship. But to make up for it, he regaled David with the details of the glorious victory. David had to balance his father's description by pointing to the star-quality of Zlatan Ibrahimović.

"That guy is not even Swedish," Niels blurted out. "They found him someplace in Yugoslavia and bought him."

"Dad, Zlatan was born in Malmö, Sweden, just across from Copenhagen," David noted, and that concluded the soccer discussion.

His parents still had the same old, battered Renault. The choice of car make was a very deliberate process for Niels. German cars were impossible because of the occupation during WWII, leaving deep scars in many Danes' souls. Italian cars could not be trusted because Niels had unfortunate memories of heated arguments with Italians during a vacation trip. Niels declared British cars rust quickly without providing specific evidence. Asian cars? Such upstarts were merely cheap copies of real European ones. American cars? "Clunky gas guzzlers for show-offs." Especially worthy of contempt were Swedish cars because of the historic rivalry between the two Scandinavian states. Most Danes had moved on to a light-hearted rivalry around soccer, but for Niels, who was a history buff, it was more profound. The Swedes had "stolen" several southern provinces from the Danes in the 1600s. So, it was down to French cars.

They drove through town and out to the suburb where David's parents had made a home since his birth. The garden was well-tended, and the interior looked very much the same. His boy's room was still untouched—"David's museum," as Niels called it. It was likely to remain that way until the parents passed. David had little interest in lugging his boyhood library and other belongings across the Atlantic, although he had brought one box of his most cherished books.

The conversation around the dinner table was familiar: sports news from Niels, historical curiosa from his books on Danish history, and family and neighborhood news from

Merete. There were marriages, divorces, deaths, even a suicide, some drug use, petty theft in the generally peaceful town, newly arrived immigrants, and so on. But there were no questions about David's work or life in the U.S. He struggled to keep a straight face and not say anything about Julia, as he was determined not to cry, especially not in front of his father. It had to wait until he was alone with Merete.

"I have an interesting job now, and I have already had my first mission to a developing country," he said. His parents didn't react, so he continued. "We travel as a team of experts in different areas, depending on the type of project or study that we are working on." He continued to describe to them how the Bank delivers loans to specific projects but also as budget support for general public expenditure. "The poorest countries get grants, so they don't have to pay back."

Niels looked uncomfortable. "You are giving away money to those countries for free?"

"A developing country that is somewhat better off has to pay interest on the loan and eventually pay it back. But the terms are generous."

"How do you know it's not wasted? There was an article about that sort of thing the other day, and this woman said that people down there just spend it on luxuries and alcohol."

Merete chimed in. "There is so much that needs to be done here at home. Unemployment, people begging, and now these immigrants are pouring in. The schools are overwhelmed. We have some people now in town who don't speak a word of Danish."

David took a deep breath. He had heard it all before but not from his parents. He tried to convey just how deep the poverty was in the countries where the Bank worked. He painted a picture of a family living in a village without electricity, clean water, and sanitation. With poor schools, bad roads, erratic weather, and an insecure livelihood for subsistence farmers. On top of that, often ethnic conflicts, and at times, even civil war.

"So, things are really terrible in those countries. So, what's the point of helping them? They will only make more babies and then pour into Europe when they can't feed themselves," Niels heatedly argued.

David countered with some statistics about how things are actually getting better in the developing world. How poverty has decreased in the last ten years, how infant and maternal health have improved, how school enrollment is increasing in most developing countries, how population growth is going down as girls receive more education and have access to family planning. And finally, there was the humanitarian aspect. How could one not help these people in need? Besides, many immigrants become good citizens who contribute to society.

Merete nodded when he pulled out the humanitarian argument. David knew that she secretly made donations to Save the Children and UNICEF. She never told Niels—who would have been furious.

"We know you mean well, David, but the money is needed here at home," Niels concluded but switched the subject back to soccer.

There is never a willingness to engage in a substantive analysis of anything. Conversations jump from topic to topic like a frog in a pond of water lilies. There is simply no interest in learning new things! David thought.

"Why don't you go and see Jens?" Merete suggested as she saw David's discomfort. Jens was their closest neighbor's son and David's age. "He is still living with his parents. You used to like each other. His mom tells me he's not doing too well. I've seen a police car outside their house several times."

Having been short, studious, and in need of glasses for his myopia, David had been bullied from an early age. This made him even more introverted, so he fled to books instead of seeking out friends. Showing an interest in studies was definitely not cool, so Jens was one of the very few friends who David had made in school.

Jens was also bullied but for different reasons. He had a stutter that his classmates loved to make fun of. The teachers tried to clamp down on this, but they could not see and hear everything that went on. Jens had a lot of absences and sometimes totally refused to go to school. A speech therapist saved him from complete mental collapse and guided him to a vocational training program. He was now an auto mechanic with a reputation for professional competence and social ineptitude. His stutter was mostly gone, but he dared not take the risk of being ridiculed again. Jens was a loner, drank heavily, mostly beer, and experimented with drugs.

David hesitated as he walked up to Jens's house. He liked Jens and felt terrible about how he had been treated. But Jens did not make things easier with his indifferent demeanor that sheltered him from his peers. It had been a couple of years since they last met. What would it be like now?

Jens's parents, Peder and Anna Mikkelsen, greeted David warmly. They were not spoiled with anybody coming to visit their reclusive son. David was shown down to the basement.

A stale smell of sweat and crushed dreams became more potent for every step he took down the basement stairs. There was only one small window with a curtain pulled in front of it, and the wood paneling was dark brown. Jens was seated with his back to the stairs with two large screens in front of him. One showed a pornographic movie, the other some kind of violent computer game. The music could not have been more appropriate. It was Meat Loaf's "Life is a Lemon and I Want My Money Back." The volume was deafening.

David navigated around Jens to get his attention without startling him. Still, Jens almost catapulted out of his chair when he noticed David. "Fuck, man, you scared the shit out of me," he yelled. David motioned for him to turn down the music.

"How're you doin', Jens?" Jens had an unkept beard and long, oily hair. He was dressed in shorts and a T-shirt with greasy smears on it.

"Same sh … shit all the time."

"I hear you are a good mechanic."

"OK," he said, unsure of how to handle a compliment.

"What kind of cars do you work on mostly?"

"All kinds."

David waited him out, hoping that the topic would be engaging enough for the ball to get rolling. But there was only more silence. "Any work on my parents' Renault?"

"They sh...should sell that junk, man."

"I know, but they love that car. So many memories."

More awkward silence.

"Coming back to l...live here now?" Finally, a question!

"No, just visiting. I live in the U.S. now. In Washington, D.C."

Jens remained silent, and David looked for a new entry to conversation.

"I work for an international bank that extends loans and credits to developing countries." He was pushing it now.

"Beer?" asked Jens. David accepted one and opened it. It was a Tuborg. He noticed three empty beer bottles on the floor next to Jens and two unopened ones lined up next to the right screen. He tried changing track.

"Seeing any girls these days, Jens?" It was a delicate topic, but if there was something there, it could perhaps open things up.

"Na, they're so st … stuck up, you know?" Jens shook his head.

It would take a very special girl to be attracted to Jens. Maybe he was secretly gay and didn't dare to come out? But being gay was not a big thing in Denmark anymore.

"So, who do you see? Who do you talk to?"

"Other losers online." The answer came fast, and with a tone of resignation.

David was running out of topics to try. "I see you have some kind of game going on there. What is it?"

"GTA" said Jens.

"What does it mean?"

"You don't know?" Jens could not hide his surprise. "It's fuckin' Grand Theft Auto!" He turned to the screen and over Jens's shoulder David could see a man violently pulling out a driver from a car and speeding off. A reckless car chase ensued, and the car exploded in orange flames. David did not understand everything that was going on, but it took only a few minutes for him to be so disgusted by the indiscriminate killings with automatic weapons that he decided to leave with a short "bye." Jens did not look up.

Oh, the damage those bullies did to Jens, David thought. It only takes a single, nasty leader, a few opportunistic followers, and a bunch of cowardly bystanders who do not stand up to the taunts to create a toxic environment. From thereon, the roles of hunter and prey grow stronger and more damaging over the years. He did occasionally have nightmares of schoolyard bullying. Those memories would never quite go away.

***

Back home, David walked with some trepidation around the house to the back. The bushes had grown about a meter since he looked at them last. He looked closely at the spot, and his memory traveled back to when he was ten years old.

Niels had made several attempts to tear David away from his books and pushed him to join him when working on some carpentry project. He wanted the boy to see the good things his hands created and respect good craftsmanship. Niels had little to contribute by way of verbal advice to prepare his son for life, but he felt he had something important to show. Perhaps David would even follow in his footsteps? There was always work and decent pay for a good carpenter.

The little playhouse was meant to unleash David's hidden talents. Niels took care to show him a simple sketch, took the boy with him to get the right lumber and nails. He was disappointed that David seemed to tire easily when given a task. The boy would get the simplest things wrong, like nailing a plank in an angle when it should be straight, sawing off a piece of wood too short so that it was wasted, and struggling to get nails down without bending them. Niels berated him, and the words stung in the boy's stomach. Once, when Niels went inside to take a call, the little boy decided to show his father that he did try his best.

Niels had marked where the door hinges should be placed. When David failed to drive the screws through the holes in the metal hinges, he resorted to using the electric drill. It had a drill—a very large one—mounted already. David swiftly drilled up the holes as they were marked. This time, the holes were too wide, and the hinges could not be properly tightened.

Niels came out and took one look at the disaster before he exploded in anger. This was the last straw! This was sabotage! He had concealed his irritation with the boy the whole day, but now, he went ballistic.

"You are an idiot…a useless stupid idiot," he roared.

He grabbed the boy by the neck and shook him violently. Merete had seen it through the open kitchen window, came rushing out, and saved her helpless son from getting a beating. She had never seen Niels so upset, but she responded in kind.

"Don't you touch my son!" she yelled in her husband's face.

David ran off. With tears running down his cheeks, he ran himself to exhaustion. The world around him was blurred and unimportant now. There was only him and Niels, and the father's stinging words: "idiot … stupid." Exhausted from the aimless sprint and nauseated by the humiliation, he sank down on a piece of grass by the road. He started planning his escape from his father, but just couldn't figure out where to.

That night, Niels got very drunk. At 2 a.m., he stumbled out to the garage, found a Jerry can with gasoline and went back to the half-finished playhouse. He poured the gasoline on it and lit it with a match. An alarmed neighbor called the fire department. It was too late to save anything when they arrived. Niels was given a harsh scolding for lighting an unauthorized fire in a residential area and eventually fined.

The parents never spoke about the incident. Merete cleared up the debris and planted the bushes that now had grown taller than David. Niels kept on drinking and gave up any attempts to "straighten out the boy," as he put it. Both David and his father did their best to avoid each other from that day on.

***

Back in his boyhood room, David lay down on the bed. The whole room was like a museum, kept intact and neat under Merete's loving supervision. The plants were watered, the curtains and bed linen washed almost as often as those in other parts of the house. It was Merete's way of keeping the memories of David with her. Niels had several times suggested that they throw away or store David's "junk" and use the room for something else. It went nowhere because of Merete's fierce resistance. She rarely contradicted her husband, but David's room represented a red line for her. "It's all I've got left of him now." She sighed.

His room had always been neat. From an early age, David could not stand disorder. Shoes had to be lined up, all clothes on hangers or in drawers, his little desk had to be clean and organized. Niels had suggested that he suffered from OCD, but Merete staunchly defended him and related stories from other moms who constantly had to remind their kids to clean up.

He had forged his big life plan in this little room: getting a good education, a meaningful and intellectually interesting job, traveling the world, reading a lot of interesting books, finding a girl to share his life with, raising high-achieving children, and so on. He wanted a family better than the one he grew up in. Julia's tragic death was the most devastating setback in that grand plan so far.

It was not all bad growing up here, David remembered as he was resting. Merete had been a caring mother, cooking good, nutritious, albeit overly healthy food. She bought him clothes and respected that he hated going to the store himself to try things on. Equipped with his measurements and her own good taste, she always found him things that fit. Sometimes, she would be a bit behind on the latest fashion for children and youth, rendering David some additional bullying. But clothes were not his thing, so those stings did not hurt long.

Sunday mornings! They had been great in his early years. He remembered the cocoa drink that he and Merete would mix. It started with a rather bitter, dark cocoa powder. You mixed it with sugar, added a little cream, and worked it into a slurry with a spoon. Then, the hot milk was poured into the cup, and the mixture was stirred vigorously. Merete would spoon out a small amount of whipped cream on top, never allowing as much of it as David wanted. Her boy was not going to get fat!

It was late when Merete softly knocked on his door. Merete entered and sat down on his bed beside him. She put her hand on his forehead like she used to do when he was a child, and she came in to read and kiss him good night. "Son," she said softly, "there's something you haven't told me. I didn't want to ask when Dad was around, but … I can see it in your face, the way you move. Did something bad happen?"

"The Lid" struck David again. It was an imaginary lid on top of his vocal cords, and it would fall down on them sometimes when he was nervous. It made him mute and confused until he could compose himself. The Lid had haunted him sometimes in school when bullied, sometimes when he had tried to approach a girl. It had not followed him to Washington D.C., but now at home in his boy room, it struck again.

David breathed deeply, but all he could muster was a faint "Julia."

"So, a girl," said Merete. "Son, those things are bound to happen. She left you?"

David could not hold his tears back. It all came out. How he had found love and happiness, and everything was smooth going in his big life plan … and then … tragedy, darkness, a flailing soul searching for new meaning and something to hold on to. They talked through the night, and David felt closer than ever to his mom.

***

The following day, David darted over to the school where he had spent his first six years as a student. It was about two kilometers away—he could not get used to thinking in miles. But the route was all different now. Old houses had been torn down and replaced with much larger ones. A few had been remodeled. The gardens looked even more tended to. There was more traffic, and the cars were bigger, sleeker, with more of a mixture of makes. All of this was to be expected, but he did not expect to see the school so transformed. Totally rebuilt, it was much larger now. The schoolyard was neatly organized with basketball hoops on a green court. It had just been grass and gravel back in the day.

With heavy steps burdened by bitter memories, David approached the main entrance. School was out, and not a soul was in sight. He recalled how he had dashed out of the main entrance gate one day in fourth grade. Somebody swiped off his hat—a new green and red hat that Merete had stitched. It was so tragically out of fashion that it became a source of ridicule. But it was good enough to be stolen and handed from boy to boy in a taunting circle. "Come and get it if you can!" they hollered. They were quicker than he was, so he gave up after a few futile dashes that amused the bullies. He feared that he would have to explain to Merete why he was not wearing the hat anymore. The circus ended quickly when a teacher approached. As an isolated incident, he could have seen past it. But it was part of a pattern of taunting that frayed his nerves.

He forced himself to step around the school to the back to confront an even worse memory. Maybe confronting it right where it happened would show him that he had moved on past it. Lisa was his first lasting crush. He was twelve then, and he had joined most of the young boys in his class in secretly pining for her. There was a consensus that she was the prettiest among the girls. Even the girls seemed to agree as they established their pecking order.

Lisa had approached him one cold winter day. "David, I want to show you something behind the school. Come with me." It was exciting enough that Lisa would even speak to him, and the thought that she wanted to see him alone was mind-boggling.

As David had turned the corner, the fangs of betrayal pierced his soul. It was an ambush. Six boys stood in a semi-circle, loaded with snowballs. He froze in disbelief of Lisa's deceit. The boys pelted him with icy snowballs, and he stood there, unable to shield himself.

It was a power kick for boys who lived powerless lives. Their world was a humdrum small-town existence without purpose or vision. They had little hope of advancing beyond their fathers' blue-collar, daily grind. Now, the pleasure of attacking their defenseless prey made their adrenaline flow. They pelted him mercilessly while Lisa looked on and giggled.

Devastated and shocked, David sank to his knees and into a fetal position, covering his vulnerable head. The boys closed in, sure of their victory. They kicked him and stuffed his nose, ears, and clothes with snow. They struggled violently to force his mouth open to fill that as well but failed.

"Let's pee on him!" suggested Mads, the most aggressive of the boys who wanted to reinforce his standing as the school's alpha bully.

The bell rang for the next class. Mads and two of the boys had PE next, and that teacher was a disciplinarian who would certainly not tolerate late arrivals. Mads hurried away, and with the main instigator gone, the other boys scattered quickly, as did Lisa.

David cleaned himself up in the boys' restroom and hid there until school was over. One of his eyes was red and blue and quite swollen. His lower lip was torn, but the bleeding had stopped. He had stuffed paper in his bleeding nose. When the school emptied, he snuck out through a backdoor.

David could not see the bruises on his back from the kicks, but Merete could when she surprised him in the bathroom that evening. Maybe he had forgotten to lock the door…maybe he had subconsciously wished that she would discover how damaged he was. Whatever the reason, her reaction was immediate. Niels came running when he heard Merete's hysterical cries. "My boy, my poor boy, what have they done!" she cried.

Niels had seen many schoolyard fights, and as a teenager, he had been involved in several bar brawls. He wore his visits to the Emergency Room as a badge of honor. But Merete's wailing was not something he could handle.

Niels pressed the boy for details while Merete held him tight. It came in sputters, but soon the picture was clear enough for Niels to spring into action. For the first time ever, he called the principal to complain. He threatened to call the police, take legal action against the school, and go public in the local paper.

The next day, the principal called in "the usual suspects" among the boys known for bullying. All emphatically declared their total innocence. One expressed outrage at being targeted for that type of inquiry and engaged his parents for support. On the phone with the principal, one parent launched into a psychological theory that David was "disturbed" with "an obsessive interest in books." The school counselor should take him in for a screening. The inquiries went nowhere, and the principal washed his hands. "I've done what I can," he concluded and filed a short note in his filing cabinet.

David also tried to file away the incident, but his file was already too thick with notes. Standing in the school yard, many years after the actual events, nausea swept over him. *Why are people who are different seen as threats, hounded, and even beaten? Where does all this cruelty come from—is it innate or taught?* he asked himself. He turned back home. He cut his visit to Denmark short. His new life was waiting in Washington, D.C.

CHAPTER 11

JP

The SAS Airbus 350 left Kastrup Airport in Copenhagen only ten minutes after its scheduled departure, and David dozed off as the air pressure sank. The plane was full, and passengers often ignored the hand luggage restrictions. They complained about lack of overhead space but had themselves to blame. The tight economy-class chairs made it difficult to sleep, so he expected to get some work done instead during the eight-hour flight to Washington Dulles. The air-conditioning was too powerful, and he had to put on a sweater. As the aircraft reached its cruising altitude, a short announcement was made in a rapid but monotonous voice, first in Danish and then in English:

"Thecaptainhasturnedofftheseatbeltsignandyouarenowfreet omoveraroundthecabin."

David stood up and pulled his laptop and briefcase down. Merete had given him a folder with clippings from the local paper to read on the way back. It was a quick and generally unexciting read. Petty crime, local civic awards to people he did not know, the opening of a new supermarket, a fire with a fatality probably because of smoking in bed. But one article caught his attention.

Ida Mikkelsen and Jens Hansen, two local social justice activists, represented the Indigenous People's Liberation March for Justice. The picture of the two youngsters clearly showed them to be White with ordinary Scandinavian features. But they were now mobilizing local opinion in opposition to a dam project in Southern Africa. The catchy title read: "World Bank Drives Poor from Ancestral Lands." The Adwa Highlands Project was allegedly going to displace thousands of poor, indigenous people because their land was going to flood. The electricity would not benefit them, as it would be connected to the grid that served urban areas. Water from the dams would be channeled for export to a neighboring country.

"Those people have no accountability for their actions. They fly in and out and dictate the terms for poor people without consulting them. That dam project must be stopped, before the villages and ancestral graves are flooded," demanded Ida and Jens.

David made a note to research the project when he arrived in Washington.

***

The second day at work, he remembered the article from the local paper about the Adwa dam. It was easy to find out about the project, and the project leader was Mr. Jean-Paul Lavigne. He called Jean-Paul.

"*Allo, JP*," said a voice that was immediately recognizable as French.

David asked for a meeting over coffee.

JP countered that the subject-matter required more time and suggested lunch three days later in the Bank's cafeteria. "But look through the main project document and the annexes on the environmental and social impact assessments, the consultation summary, and the resettlement plans," he suggested. "See my assistant Angelica Cruz for the documents."

Angelica was an elegant woman in her thirties who probably spent much time taking care of her appearance—and with good results. She also used a delightful perfume that David could not help noticing. JP had not informed her about the matter, but she had no reservations about being helpful. She took David into an archive room and pointed to a large shelf full of documents. One group of documents was marked "EIA" for Environmental Impact Assessment—about a foot wide—and the "SIA" or Social Impact Assessment and the Resettlement Plans covered about an equal length on the shelf.

David skimmed the documents and realized that it would be a Herculean task to get a grip on this project. The preparatory effort had been massive. Consultations with the local population had been going on for years, and interpreters had been engaged to facilitate village meetings. Surveys documented the situation of each household that would be resettled. He needed to get JP's overview.

They met as scheduled for lunch. JP cut a fine figure in his tailored suit and colorful tie. He measured about 6'2" and looked fit, probably being in his late fifties. His beard was neatly trimmed and slightly graying, as was his short hair. His ears tilted outwards a bit more than they should, but that did not significantly detract from his distinguished look. He had a firm, dominant handshake and a pleasant smile.

They exchanged pleasantries before they picked up their lunches. They emerged together with loaded trays. JP had picked up salmon with couscous and a side salad and topped off his meal with yogurt (Dannon). He drank Perrier, of course. David went for a hamburger, a glass of tap water, no salad, and a Danish as dessert. They found a table for two in the busy, noisy dining hall and finally faced each other.

"David, you'll die young! No salad, you drink tap water full of lead and 'eavy metals, eat fat meat that 'as been destroyed by overcooking, and stuff yourself with saturated fat in pastry form. For me, I picked low-calorie fish—loaded with 'ealthy omega-3 fat—from the clear waters of a Norwegian fjord, 'ole grains, fresh organic vegetables, a lite *yaourt*, and French water with an angel's purity!"

David found this indictment hard to battle. But he had to counter somehow. "JP, that fish was raised on a farm that overloads the river with nutrients and waste. The vegetables have been sprayed several times with non-FDA-approved herbicides and picked by exploited immigrant farmworkers in California who lack basic sanitation. Your yogurt is French by name only and imported from Haiti, and the mineral water is made from tap water and labeled here in West Virginia's coal country."

JP burst out laughing. "So, Adwa dam, *oui?*"

He gave a quick project summary that had been planned for many years. The country had few assets, but tapping water and electricity for both domestic use and export was a major opportunity for poverty alleviation. Of course, it involved a dilemma. It was a hardship to be moved when the dam was filled, but people would be compensated and be at least as well off as they were before the project. Studies had been very thorough, reviewed by panels of independent experts, processed at length inside the Bank, and he considered the work solid and honest. The households to be resettled were not "thousands" but about 200 in number for the planned phase now ahead of them. The lesson from the previous phase was that compensation had been overly generous. The new houses had piped water—a novelty in this area. This caused resentment among people who had not been resettled.

David took notes. It was the kind of trade-off that was unavoidable in a dynamic economy. Some people's lives would be uprooted for the greater good. It happened everywhere. The alternative would be paralysis. The main point was that the affected population would be adequately cared for.

After the long lunch, he typed up a response to the article in the local paper and sent it as a Letter to the Editor. He never heard back from the newspaper. David asked Merete, who read the paper daily, to look out for his letter, but none was ever published.

Facts that don't fit your own narrative are just denied, he concluded.

***

JP called David on a Friday afternoon and asked if he wanted to join him that night for a glass of wine, and perhaps even dinner, to celebrate a loan approval. He had the habit of gathering a small group of colleagues to commiserate about bureaucratic frustrations as well as occasional victories in their work. Getting a loan or grant finally approved by the Board was something to celebrate.

At 8 p.m., he found JP with two colleagues in a wine bar two blocks from the Bank. JP introduced Mark from Procurement and Angela from Legal. They were both in their thirties. Angela was sharply dressed like most staff from Legal were known to be, and she spoke with a slight Dutch accent. Mark was an African-American and sported more informal attire.

To JP's dismay, David skipped the French wines and ordered a glass of red from Stellenbosch in South Africa: Thelema Merlot. He felt that wines from there and from Argentina and Chile were generally an excellent value for money but under-appreciated in the U.S. They toasted to a water and sanitation project that had been approved by the World Bank's Board and to which both Angela and Mark had contributed.

"'ave you taken the gender-awareness training, David?" asked JP.

"No, I didn't even know about it."

"Well, you will absolutely hear about it." Mark chuckled. "It's mandatory now because this place is full of male chauvinist pigs!"

"This is no laughing matter," Angela shot back. "Mark, you are an unrepentant womanizer who should be taken to a six-month re-education camp and whipped into shape by feminists."

"I could use a good whipping," quipped Mark to annoy Angela.

David could tell that they loved to tease each other. Were they perhaps a couple?

"I took that training last week," said Mark. "One guy came in a bit late, looked around, checked out the attractive lady speaker up front. Then, he walked up next to her, took a seat, and said loud enough for everybody to hear: 'I'll move up front so I can get a good look at the pretty view, ha-ha.'"

"He's just asking for it," Angela gasped.

Mark laughed. "People just froze up because this was the start of a class on gender-sensitivity, right? It was really like he was saying: 'Fuck this stupid class.'"

"What did the speaker say then?" asked Angela.

"I still don't know, but I do know it was really effective. She smiled and leaned over to him and whispered something in his ear. The guy turned beet red, stood up, and retreated down to the end of the room. And he shut up for the entire class!"

"But if he was so embarrassed, why didn't he leave?"

"First of all, his boss is Linda Harris, a.k.a. 'the enforcer.' You don't mess with her. Second, the training is mandatory. You are registered, and attendance is taken on entry, and you have to sign out at the end. Wiggling out of class is tough, and with Harris as your boss…suicidal." Mark put his hand to his temple as if shooting himself.

"What's the speaker's name?" asked David.

"Diane something…I forgot the surname. But I'm telling you, she is super-hot!" He moved away from Angela, feigning fear of physical retribution from her. Angela kept a poker face. She was determined to shut down any sexist comments.

Angela changed the subject. "I'm on a salary review committee of Bank staff that is pushing for pay equality. Women are systematically as underpaid here as in society around us. If you haven't heard about it, your unit will soon be screened for pay equality."

"I don't think there is systematic inequality in pay in the Bank," said JP. "I 'ave been acting manager several times and seen salary issues 'andled. Never 'ave we considered the sex of a person."

"JP, you're a nice guy, but you are also very naïve," Angela retorted.

"We go by education, professional experience of relevance, years in the Bank, performance evaluations, and so on. No room for discrimination."

"The people making those decisions are mostly older White men. You don't think that has something to do with it?"

"Look," injected Mark, "the Department of Labor came out with a study recently about differences in pay between the sexes. Sure, women are paid less, but that is because of choices they have made, not because of discrimination."

"What choices?" said Angela, frowning.

"Well, first of all, women tend to choose fields of study and areas of work that are less rewarding financially such as personal care and low and semi-skilled service jobs. It starts in school and even in college when they choose humanities rather than engineering. On top of that, if they have kids, the couple discovers that it's best financially if the wife takes some time off from her job. So, if you eliminate those factors, I think the so-called wage-gap disappears," Mark concluded.

Angela was not convinced. "Mark, studies show that discrepancies still persist when salaries of men and women are compared for exactly the same job—where they both have equal training and education. And about staying home with kids, why should the husband not take equal responsibility? They made the child together, so they should split the burden of raising it. But in reality, the woman is saddled with a lot more work at home. It's a trap, and it's unfair!"

The discussion got heated, with both Mark and Angela quoting studies to support their main argument. They were both well-read, and David felt like he was watching a tennis match between two skilled players who pushed their opponent to their limit. It was fun, intellectual entertainment. He had his own views, but he would not be able to serve as hard as either Mark or Angela. At times, he would call a ball 'out' when someone strayed from empirical data and injected anecdotes. In the end, the two parties agreed to disagree. Still, they left together.

David and JP appraised each other as the only ones left.

"Another glass?" JP suggested.

"Don't you want to go home to your wife by now?" David had briefly met the colorful, opinionated Eloise in JP's office and thought of her as the epitome of *joie de vivre*. She had launched a small art gallery in D.C. and had driven it with passion—and into the ground financially.

"Well, Eloise has gone back to France, I think, for good this time. She couldn't take living in the U.S. She says the people are shallow and materialistic, the coffee too weak, the vegetables tasteless, the smoking too restricted, and people are obsessively focused on their careers. The final straw was when the American 'ostess at a party put ice in 'er red wine 'to cool it off.' *Mon Dieu*, she just lost it!"

"Wow, may I offer you a cognac, just to ease the pain a bit?" David suggested.

The offer was accepted, and David waived down the waiter. He enjoyed chatting with JP who was full of stories about the Bank and saw things through the prism of somebody who had never fully grown into American culture. There was no doubt that JP would one day retire back to France.

***

The following week, Benjamin Grant stopped by David's office on his way to a meeting. "Morning, David, I have to congratulate you. We're giving you a small raise."

"Wow, that's a nice surprise. Is this the annual review?"

"Ah no, it's a special review that's been called for by a working group of women in the Bank. We took a look yesterday and plotted unit salaries against the usual criteria. It turned out that you had been entered unduly low on the scale. A slight mistake by the HR Department when they hired you. So, we corrected that."

"The study aimed to ensure that women were not discriminated against, and the result was that I got a raise?"

"Yes, you and two women. So, I guess, on balance, we had it about right. Equal discrimination, if you will," he concluded and left the office with a grin on his face.

David knew exactly what he was going to play when he got home: Joe Bonamassa's "Just Got Paid."

CHAPTER 12

The Drone and the Lifeguard

David was not sure any longer how much time he had spent in captivity, but diarrhea plagued him. The local food was impossible to get used to with the exception of tea and bread. Anything else provoked stomach cramps and nausea. The Coke supply had also dried up, and The Warrior had not been around for a couple of days.

He spent the days imagining what went on with the love of his life in Washington D.C., with his mother in Vannebo, within the Danish government, and among his colleagues and friends. What did they know? Did they think he was dead already? Was there some rescue operation in the works?

David had read about the large Islamist groupings like Al-Qaeda and ISIS but less about the "franchises" that had spread in Northern Africa, the Middle East, and East Asia. Some of them were very loosely forged bands of idealogues mixed with criminals and locals with some grievances. Ethnic conflict ran deep in Africa and could be exploited. There was also forced recruitment where youngsters, even children, were given the choice of killing some of their own or dying first. Some chose the former and were forever unable to return to normal life. It was horrific just to think about it.

It was impossible in his situation to know what really went on around him. But The American Warrior somehow enjoyed a certain status. Maybe this had saved David's life so far. Or had they just had enough of video-filmed killings for the time being for terrorist purposes? Maybe they wanted a big cash-out this time? The American government was known never to pay, but the Danish, or the Bank?

The sun was setting when the American Warrior suddenly tore the door open.

"David, get up. We're leaving!" he shouted. The Warrior was composed but moved briskly.

As David hurried out, the Warrior pointed to the sky.

"There, you see that shiny, little speck in the sky?" He waved his pair of binoculars as if that would help.

David was still not used to the outside light and did not see the speck. "What is it?"

"It's a fuckin' drone, man! A fuckin' Reaper. I've been betrayed! They know about me. Now get out into the field here with me. I want them to see you. Take off your shirt and wave. Show them your pale skin!"

"Have you gone crazy? What if they launch a rocket at us?"

"How stupid can you be? They want to rescue you so they can put on a propaganda show on TV. You are my lifeguard now."

David did as he was told, waved with his shirt, and exposed his very pale skin that would hopefully make him stand out, although he still could not see the drone. Supposedly, drones have very powerful cameras, so maybe it would work? If they saw him, the news would get back to his loved ones, his friends, to Denmark, that he was alive! He waved frantically until The Warrior yelled at him to stop.

"Let's get to the car now!" The Warrior ordered.

As they sped toward the parked car, David was horrified to see a man nailed to a primitive cross that had been raised in the little village square. He had been severely beaten. David stopped in his tracks, as he could not bear the sight. The

Warrior pulled him away with force and dragged him toward the car.

"Why the hell are you doing this?" David yelled.

The Warrior pushed him into the passenger seat of a Toyota pickup truck. With an impassive voice, he told David to fasten the seat belt. "The safety of my passengers is my first priority," he said before erupting into a hoarse, bizarre chuckle. He started the car and raced out of the village.

"Why, why?" David repeated and hammered on the dashboard as he realized that he had been let out without any restraints. He had seen the horrible images on the Internet, but seeing a crucifixion first-hand was just shattering, surreal, and nauseating at the same time.

The Warrior grinned. "Why? *Pour encourager les autres.* That guy had a satellite phone he should not have had. An informant and traitor."

"And you crucify him!"

"He confessed to ratting me out. The U.S. has put a price on my head, and the bastard was greedy."

"Of course, he confessed! Under torture, people will say anything just to make it stop. An idiot can understand that."

The Warrior turned to David and grinned. "Why don't you tell that to the fuckin' CIA?"

The Warrior drove hard but with precision to avoid the worst bumps. The car was old and battered, and the check engine light was covered with duct tape. How much longer would it hold up? What if the car stalled, or they got a flat tire?

It hit David that maybe they would fire from the drone anyway. The American Warrior surely had a big bounty on his head. The American citizen Anwar al-Awlaki had been killed by a drone, so there was at least one precedent of killing an American. Perhaps, there were others who David did not know about. But al-Awlaki had been a major thorn in the Americans' side. The American Warrior's significance was hard to know.

The car got stuck in loose sand, and they had to reverse. The Warrior found a rocky path, and they continued up the hill. David wiped the sweat from his forehead and gulped down some water. He did not like the scratchy sound as The Warrior shifted gears.

The Warrior had appeared in a mock execution video, and given his specialty of producing propaganda directed at an English-speaking audience, he should be well-known. So, probably, he was on the CIA's kill list. The "collateral damage" to David could be a secret kept from the public or just explained away as an unfortunate mistake. It was just political cost-benefit analysis. David's life might be a small entry on the cost-side against any benefit of getting The Warrior from the perspective of Langley or Pentagon. At least, The Warrior was betting on David as his shield.

"Where are we going?" said David.

"We're going to get them off our tail. It's a Reaper ... maybe the newest MQ-9. It can loiter around for up to twenty-five hours, depending on what equipment it carries and the exact model. It can fly up to 50,000 feet and reach speeds up to 275 mph. It could be equipped with Hellfire missiles and laser-guided bombs and carry a payload of up to three tons. We're talking serious stuff here."

He has done some homework, David thought, but remained silent.

The Warrior focused on navigating a particularly rocky section of the road. But he soon picked up the topic again as they reached a flat, sandy area.

"I've seen first-hand what they can do. You're yelling about a guy being punished for treason, but that's nothing in comparison with the bodies of a funeral party I saw in Pakistan. They were blown to pieces by a drone. Some idiot sitting in a trailer several thousand miles away thought they were terrorists. Just read the report by Human Rights Watch! That was the most effective recruitment video I've ever made."

The landscape was slowly changing and becoming even drier. After another ten minutes, the Toyota made a sharp turn around a cliff and backed up to squeeze into a small cave, just big enough to cover the vehicle. Presumably, they would have some cover there, but the drone could have tracked them all along. So, what was the plan?

The Warrior pulled out a satellite phone from a backpack behind his seat.

"Don't get any crazy ideas now. There're miles of desolate country around you, and you'd die of thirst or be killed. We're still hoping to cash in on you. I'm your best friend now."

The Warrior left the car, probably to link up with some collaborator using a coded message. It was risky, of course, but their location had been revealed, and he had to come up with something now. Meanwhile, darkness would give some cover. Or maybe not? Only a few minutes later, the Warrior was back. He set a timer on his watch. Then, he leaned back and closed his eyes.

"We're lying low for fifty-five minutes here, waiting for some company. Sorry, David, I've orders to hand you over to a real hardass. Just shut up and do what you're told. And not a word about our conversations—you hear me? My style is a bit different than his."

"OK. Who is this hardass?"

"It's up to him to tell you about that. My only advice is don't try to make friends with him. It won't work. I have to work with his group, although we're not on the same page about many things."

"Like what?"

"For example, his group is into what we call fighting the Far Enemy, primarily the U.S. My group isn't. We focus on the Near Enemy, the invasion of Muslim countries, and want the Crusaders out. I've refused to take part in any action targeting people in the U.S. I still have many friends there. But when U.S. soldiers occupy our lands, they become legitimate targets."

"What about civilians, then, like me?"

"I'd rather not go there, but my clout is limited. But it's OK to trade civilians for money because that's needed to keep our operations going. Not everyone is motivated by devotion to Islam. Money talks, you know. If we pay better than the National Army, a lot of guys will be happy to sign up, or, at least, sell us some weapons."

The Warrior poked around behind his seat and pulled out a water bottle. He offered it to David and then pulled out a second one. David easily drank half the bottle in one go.

"It's not hard to be better than the Army. Officers are corrupt, they often dock part of soldiers' pay, and invent 'ghost soldiers' to increase their own take. Some senior officers don't have good military training—they're just well-connected. They often treat their own guys with contempt. When they raid villages, they often go overboard and press the locals for confessions. They beat them and accuse them of collaboration with 'terrorists.' It's not like they have a choice, man!"

Seconds went by, but here was his chance to understand the Warrior better. "So, are you Shia or Sunni? And why are they so divided?"

"Ha!" The Warrior jerked uncomfortably in his seat. "You might know that it goes back to the question of who is the legitimate heir to Muhammad, right? So, the Shia argued that Muhammad appointed a relative to be the leader of the *Ummah*, the Muslim community. Sunnis disputed that and wanted another leader."

"So, they kill each other over who is qualified to be the Ummah leader. I guess they don't think about having to work with the other group."

The American Warrior smirked. "Not on the same page about many things. It's not just about leadership these days."

David shook his head, lowering his chin.

"Most of the Muslim world is Sunni, of course, and that is the main influence around here as well. We don't have Shia links, but the split is not an active issue locally. The big issue here is how to treat local infidels. Some want to convert them; some just want to fight them."

"So, this hardass, is he particularly angry at Americans? Should I point out that I'm Danish?"

"He does hate Americans, but if he knows about your *Jyllands-Posten* that published cartoons of the Prophet, then you'd be in hot water. This guy doesn't read a lot, but why don't you say you're Norwegian?"

"Not sure that would help. They gave the Nobel Peace Prize one year to Yitzhak Rabin and Shimon Peres. Of course, they gave the Prize also to Yasser Arafat the same year, but that might not be enough."

"Wait, the Nobel Prizes are given out in Stockholm, Sweden," objected The Warrior.

"True for all of them except the Peace Prize, which is handed out in Oslo, Norway."

"That's crazy. Why?"

"When Alfred Nobel wrote his will, Norway and Sweden were in a Union. He didn't explain it."

"Ok then, why don't you play Swedish, or have they done something to insult Muslims?"

He laughed. "They have plenty on their conscience. They are Denmark's historical enemies. But they keep a low profile these days. It hurts, but, if necessary, I can play a Swede."

They were silent again. The Warrior adjusted his seat back to lean down further and closed his eyes. The minutes slowly ticked by. David got restless and tense from the uncertain anticipation of the next steps. *This is surreal. I'm in a desert, in a hidden, battered Toyota pickup with a monster of a guy who could kill at the drop of a hat, who is a member of a murderous fanatical sect, but who likes to reminisce about his life as an immature teenager in Detroit. Nobody will believe this, if I live to tell it,* he thought.

There was no hope of escaping right away. But there was hope that he had been identified and that some mobile expedition could be launched to come after him. Or not. Maybe there were fifty other hostages who were followed, and he was not an American. There was a limit to how many drones could be kept flying. There would be competing claims on scarce resources. Maybe they would just focus on The Warrior.

The Warrior's clock alarm went off, and he jolted up straight. From the glove compartment, he pulled out night vision goggles that he adjusted around his head with straps. "U.S. Army issue. Great stuff." He started the car, lights off, and they rolled out, just a bit from the cave. "Did you ever see that Leonardo DiCaprio movie *Body of Lies?*"

"No. But that would be *haram* for you to watch, wouldn't it?"

"I'm very flexible about *haram*. Well, if you survive this, you should see it."

There was no time to respond. Something moved in front of them, and the air thickened with dust as it came through the open window. David rolled up. Faint glimpses of other vehicles seemed like a carousel of cars that created a big dust cloud. It made it difficult for any surveillance to follow. Suddenly, a large SUV stopped right in front of them.

Within seconds, a large, bearded man in a turban tore open the door on David's side and dragged David out with force. After only a few steps, he was pushed into the SUV and forced down on the floor. The car started moving immediately and circled around. After about half a minute, the car turned away, and the sound of other roaring engines died off.

Did we shake off the drone? Where are they taking me?

CHAPTER 13

Reaching Across the Grand Canyon

Julia's tragic death—and the traumatic memories awakened by his home visit—had unsettled David. He kept searching for a positive way forward while suppressing his memories with many hours of work. He was getting to know interesting people, but he wanted to branch out beyond the Bank. The mixture of people from various backgrounds was fascinating, but in the end, it still revolved around business too much.

He made it a habit of going into a small church only a couple of blocks from his office every day after work where he found some peace and quiet. Religion didn't drive him, but the church's serenity and dignity provided some solace. One day, he left the church at the same time as a young woman.

"You come here often," she noted.

"I didn't know I was being watched," he joked.

"Sorry, it's just that I come here often myself, so I couldn't help noticing."

"Thought I'd find some peace and quiet here."

"I hope you do. I read a bit in my Bible every time I'm here."

"I just wanted to sit down here for a minute, feel the place. Well, excuse me."

David moved around her, but from behind him, she asked, "Do you study the Bible?"

"No, but we read about it in Religious Studies in school." He turned toward a pew and strolled toward it.

"You don't have one?" she continued.

"No." Conflicted emotions flooded David as he wondered whether he'd made the wrong decision coming in there.

"Here," she insisted, handing him her Bible. "Borrow mine, and we'll meet again next week and talk about it. Please!"

David set aside his feeling of embarrassment since it would have been impolite to refuse such an earnest offer. They agreed to meet next Thursday at the same time.

"I'm Eva," she said. She extended a soft hand with a shake that would not have met the standards of an employment interview.

"I'm David," he said as he handed her his business card. He sat down to nestle into the quiet of the church, and when he opened his eyes, Eva was nowhere to be seen.

He sat and considered his personal experience with religion, which was practically non-existent. His parents had not been churchgoers, and Denmark was a fairly secular country, particularly compared to the U.S. Religion was almost never discussed in his home. But maybe there was something there that could provide some comfort?

Starting from the beginning of the Bible, the violence and brutality of life as depicted overwhelmed him, including God's devastating interventions in favor of his chosen people.

From *Genesis*, he learned that Adam lived nine hundred and thirty years and that God created the first woman from one of Adam's ribs while he was sleeping. But when God saw the evil among men, he regretted his creation and decided to obliterate it all. One exception was Noah, who received instructions about how to save his own family and a sliver of species selected to maintain life. Then, God made it rain forty days and forty nights so that everything that had lived on the ground was annihilated. Wow!

David read in *Exodus* that God brought a sequence of horrific punishments down on the Egyptians who held the Israelites captive. He sent toads, mosquitoes, and flies on Egypt in devastating waves as punishment. Both people and livestock were hit by plagues, and hail destroyed all crops. All Egyptian first-borns were killed. It was hard to understand how anyone was left at all. Finally, God obliterated Pharoah's army as they followed the exodus of the Israelites. This was not the image of God that he had heard Christians talk about.

David thought of himself as a "secular humanist" but had great respect for most religious practices. Saving souls smacked of paternalism, but establishing soup kitchens, building schools, and helping the homeless were admirable activities, often driven by religious convictions.

As he got up and walked down the aisle and approached the church entrance, he noticed that the mosaics were mostly cast in shadow with only hints of light shining through. It was later than he thought. The church visit brought him some escape from his thoughts but only briefly. As he stepped off the church steps, he wandered back toward his apartment, his mind racing with all the emails that awaited his reply.

***

As they met the next Thursday, David took pains to not sound too critical. He had only read the first five books, so he would suspend judgment. Eva defused the situation by enthusiastically talking about her volunteer work with a food bank in D.C. She talked him into joining her the following Saturday. That might provide another opportunity to meet new people, he thought.

Eva was a twenty-two year old student at George Washington University located very close to the Bank. David noted her persistent smile as she served help-seekers, engaging them with her soft voice, her caring attitude, and her willingness to listen to hard-luck stories without judgment. There was otherwise nothing remarkable with Eva's appearance. One might say that she made every effort not to look elegant. Her hair was often in disarray and had probably not seen a pair of scissors for years.

Surveys he'd read upheld that mental health issues and substance abuse were forceful drivers of homelessness in Washington D.C., but he pushed aside any judgments of people's life choices when he handled clients. Some of their sense of entitlement was awkward to witness at times. Some refused certain perfectly fine, healthy foods and went for "the goodies." But overall, it was a humbling experience and a reminder of his own privilege.

After closing up, David approached Eva and complimented her.

"You're doing a great job here. Want some coffee?"

They sat down at a nearby place, David holding a drip coffee and Eva an organic herbal tea.

"Are you volunteering because of your religion?" he asked.

"Yes, of course, that is what brings me to the food bank. I want to share God's love with everyone, particularly the less fortunate."

"What does it mean to you to be a Christian?"

"I was brought up Catholic. But with everything that this church has been going through ... the scandals—"

"I know," interjected David to save her the pain of explaining. There had been another wave of disclosures of widespread pedophilia among Catholic priests lately.

"So, we decided to leave that church behind and seek our own 'home' for maintaining our connection to God. We joined a small congregation that had sprung up where my parents live in West Virginia. They have a very charismatic preacher, Pastor John Wood. You should hear him preach!"

"I know you read the Bible a lot. Do you believe that it's literally God's word?"

"How could anybody doubt that?" Eva responded, seeming a bit flustered.

"I don't mean to put you on the spot, but there are some passages in the Bible that make me really uncomfortable."

"I can't imagine why. If you read it without malice in your heart, you'll find so much guidance in there," Eva asserted.

"I'll give you some examples. In *Leviticus*, God says that gay sex is a capital offence. Adultery should be punished with death. Blasphemous speech should be punished with stoning. In *Numbers*, there is a passage where when a man was caught gathering wood on the Sabbath, Moses asked God what to do with him. God said, 'Stone him!' Do you really agree with all that?"

"You are taking things out of context, David. God is great, he's forgiving, he's not cruel. Everyone knows that. Open your heart to Jesus, and you will see the light. Try reading the New Testament instead."

"I did that as well and found in *1 Peter* that servants should endure the most terrible conditions under their master, even if they are harsh and unfair. How is that for advice?"

Eva looked uncomfortable. "God's words can't be read like any other book," she insisted. "All of us need guidance to see the true meaning of the Bible."

They finished their beverages in silence before they walked toward her apartment to her door. Eva extended a hand and said she hoped to see him again at the church.

***

They met again the following week. Eva insisted that she was still interested in meeting David, despite his flawed interpretation of the Bible. They continued meeting at the church and took long walks together in the Mall area. David learned to avoid sensitive topics and grew fond of her genuine idealism. She had a thousand questions about him and his work, which made David happy. They were both feeding their intellectual curiosity, but he kept searching for a romantic spark. Even without that, she was interesting company.

Eva told him that she was going home to see her parents in West Virginia the coming weekend. "Why don't you come along?" she suggested. "You can meet my parents and Pastor John Wood. He'll explain everything to you."

He had known Eva for only a couple of months, and they had kept it platonic. David liked her and wanted to feel more, but there was just no physical attraction as they met. Eva had noted in passing that she found sex outside marriage to be sinful. Still, a visit to the parents could be misinterpreted. But David had travelled very little in the U.S. and never to West Virginia, so he was keen to go.

***

It was not far geographically, but culturally it was another world. The Clarksburg area was coal country, populated by right-wing Republicans. That made it interesting for David who personally did not know any Americans who had not gone to college and did not lean Democratic. He wanted to fix that. West Virginia was a solidly White, non-Hispanic state with a clear dominance of Protestants. Data on health, longevity, and poverty showed the state to be in low ranks in the U.S. Coal employment was not that high, but almost all electricity came generated from coal, and the coal industry was a powerful political actor.

They rented a car, and the ride to West Virginia was beautiful. David tried to get some advance intelligence so as not to make a fool of himself on arrival. He asked Eva about her parents.

"My parents are good Christians. They love their country and have never left it. They just don't think there is any other country worth seeing. They used to go to the Catholic church every week. But then things got out of hand with Billy." She went silent.

"Who is Billy?" said David after a long break.

"Billy was a neighbor's son. My parents knew the family. I remember Billy from school. He was younger than me, so we didn't really talk much. Billy's parents realized there was something really wrong. They pressured him to talk, and finally it all came out. A priest had ... you know ... Billy was too scared and confused to report it. He was only twelve or thirteen—something like that. For him, the priest was someone to look up to. Billy felt so guilty, saying God would punish him for his sins."

It was obviously a painful memory for Eva, and she gathered strength before she continued.

"My parents had always dismissed the stories about Catholic priests. They said it was 'the devil's gossip.' That changed when Billy came out."

"What happened then?"

Eva started crying, and it took several minutes for her to gather herself. "He killed himself."

***

Eva's parents' house was small and in some need of fresh paint. Eva's dad, Albert, had been on disability pension for the last two years, and money was tight ... black lung disease. Albert bore his yoke as a badge of honor. Coal miners had status, and they earned good money. Eva's mom, Helen, sold an assortment of cosmetics and houseware on mail order and through home parties. It sounded like a pyramid scheme to David.

Albert and Helen greeted David in such a friendly manner that David wondered what Eva had told them. They showed him around with pride, pointed to family photos, several with Eva as an adorable child. There was furniture everywhere—heavy, dark in style. The dark brown wall panels contributed to the closed sense in the dining room where a hearty meal had been laid out. The TV blared in the next room with an American football game.

It was time to eat, but first they would say grace. Albert offered David a chance, but he declined as graciously as he could, and Albert went ahead. He thought they would turn the TV off, but no one did. They held hands, and Albert thanked God not only for the food but also for bringing David to their home and wished that he would receive the guidance of Jesus with an open heart. David struggled to focus with the roaring celebration of a touchdown in the background.

The conversation was mostly a monologue by Albert, who talked about local news and people whom David could not possibly have met. His American English was occasionally hard to follow, particularly when Albert started to laugh at

133

his own jokes. Now and then, Helen insisted that he put more food on his plate.

David had difficulty following the storyline and lost focus for a while, but he abruptly paid attention when Albert said, "I thought he was goin' to Jew me!"

"Sorry, what did you just say?"

Albert looked puzzled. "You know, Jew me, take my money."

David swallowed hard. He had never heard the expression before, but the meaning was plain enough. He had not known many Jews personally. But he thought about Joseph Gold, who had come as a refugee to Denmark in the 1930s as a young boy. When David grew up, he owned a nursery in David's hometown and had treated all his customers with generosity and kindness. Thankfully, Joseph had escaped to Sweden during the war, when a German official tipped off a Danish friend that a round-up of Jews was forthcoming. Most of the eight thousand Jews who lived in Denmark at that time were able to escape. But what was the point of ruining the family dinner with such stories? He would never convince Albert that anti-Semitism was abhorrent. He kept quiet, although he felt like a coward to not stand up against bigotry.

The dinner was delicious and all home-cooked. They had meatloaf followed by a doughnut with cream filling. David made a point of expressing his appreciation to Helen, who seemed very pleased to receive such compliments. After dessert, Albert insisted that David follow him to the basement to look at his guns.

David had never taken an interest in guns and was concerned about the easy availability of weapons in America. He had never used a gun and felt awkward having to watch Albert brag with such enthusiasm about his collection. There was a total of twelve guns on display in the basement, mounted nicely on the walls. Most of them were used for hunting, and Albert went through each one of them, describing their use, their specifications, the seasons, and his most illustrious kills. Some of the hunting trophies adorned another wall in the basement, and some were on display in the dining room. Albert saved the best for last.

"This is America's rifle," he announced proudly and took down an AR-15 from the wall, cradling it in his arms like a baby. "Look at this baby, isn't she something? Got this beauty at a gun show for just $500, 16″ barrel, 30-round magazine. Just hold it!"

Albert pushed the AR-15 into David's reluctant hands. He was surprised how light it was, about 3-4 kgs maybe, without the magazine. He remembered reading about this weapon in connection with a recent mass shooting at a school. Twelve dead, twenty-six wounded, and God knows how many souls of children, parents, and teachers scarred for life? He had done his best to avoid controversy, but now, he had to say something.

"I understand that you like hunting. But why do you need this type of gun?"

Albert was not offended as David feared. He chuckled. "You know, son, we have something that you probably don't have, a Constitution, the world's oldest Constitution that gives us freedom. Freedom is how this country was built. Do you follow? And in that Constitution, there are things that nobody, not even our government or the communists can take from us. I don't suppose you know about the Second Amendment."

David surprised him by quoting from memory: "A well-regulated militia, being necessary to the security of a free state, the right of the people to keep and bear arms, shall not be infringed." He had always had a knack for memorizing things, which had caused a great deal of resentment among classmates. He had also taken some interest in the fierce gun legislation debate. David refrained from comment on freedom as a pillar of America by any remark regarding the genocide of Native Americans or the building of the colonies' economy on the backs of slave labor forced to work under inhumane conditions.

"Hmm, I guess you can read," remarked Albert, trying not to look impressed.

Eva saved the awkward situation by announcing that coffee or tea was served upstairs. There were also home-baked cookies of several kinds that Helen had made. All of them were delicious, which David took pains to point out.

Eva tried to steer the conversation onto David's arena. "David has a really interesting job. His bank gives loans and grants to poor country governments."

Her mission failed, as Albert immediately launched into a monologue about how misguided foreign aid was. "We give way too much money to those people. I bet about ten percent of our federal budget. Most of that is wasted on people who should learn how to fend for themselves, like we do. People came to this land with nothing. There were some guys running around here killing buffaloes with bows and arrows! But they created nothing—we did! God had a plan for us you see. We are God's chosen people to cultivate the land, mine the coal, and make things in our factories. That's how we built the greatest country the world has ever seen!"

David felt nauseous. The notion of a "chosen, superior people" made him think of the doctrine of a *Herrenvolk* that Hitler had successfully promoted. He had read about Manifest Destiny, but never before had he met somebody who took that seriously. He decided to focus on the easier part about foreign aid.

"Sir, according to the Department of the Treasury, official development assistance amounts to less than one percent of the federal budget."

"That can't be right. Everybody knows it's a lot more. We give more than any other nation on Earth to those poor people. Americans are the most generous people on Earth," Albert insisted.

"Well, many Americans are really generous. And in absolute numbers, U.S. foreign aid is the most substantial of any nation. That's because your economy is so large. But it is not the world's most generous nation, I'm afraid. Let's say you donate a hundred to charity, while Bill Gates gives two hundred dollars?"

"Gates, the computer guy who is so filthy rich?"

"He is quite rich, but from his own ingenuity I would say, and he's a great philanthropist now."

"Obviously, two hundred dollars is nothing for him, but a hundred dollars would be a lot for me, so I would be the most generous."

"Sir, that means we agree on something. Generosity needs to be related to your income, or the size of a country's economy. And the U.S. has the largest economy in the world, measured by using official exchange rates, that is. So, if you compare what it gives in Official Development Assistance with the size of its economy, called the GNI or Gross National Income, it's about 0.2 percent. Several other countries give a much larger share of their income per year. The United Nations target is set at 0.7 percent of GNI, but only a few countries meet that target."

Albert tightened his jaw. "Says who?"

"Those figures are from the OECD, sir. It's a globally recognized authority on international aid."

"Never heard of them. Sounds like hogwash to me."

"Sir, it's the Organization for Economic Cooperation and Development. It's an organization that groups about thirty of the richest countries in the world."

"Son, there's no limit to what the press cooks up these days. So much fake news. I still trust the local paper 'cause I know those guys. And what I hear on the radio."

Albert was obviously annoyed. He wanted to end the conversation right there and went to watch television. He sank down in his oversized chair with an extendable footstool. As soon as Albert left, Helen and Eva started clearing the table. David offered to help but was rebuffed.

"This is women's work," said Helen and suggested he watch TV.

Instead, David went outside, thinking about Albert in his oversized chair. *That is his throne, from where he commandeers a beer from his wife, offers free advice to the football quarterbacks, swears over high taxes, underfunded public services, the erosion of family values, the ever-increasing crime rate, the bloated government, the threat of socialism, the invading immigrants, and the handouts to undeserving poor*, he thought.

David went inside and made clear that he did not want to stay overnight to meet the pastor the following morning, as planned. It was an awkward, hurried goodbye.

***

As they started the long drive home, David attempted to explain, rationalize, and apologize for his part of the conversation. But with Eva, he could not hold back about her father's anti-Semitism, his abhorrence for semi-automatic weapons in the hands of civilians, Albert's refusal to listen to facts, and the complete absence of interest for David's background, work, and views.

Eva started crying. "I'm so sorry," she said between sobs. "I didn't know it would be...like this. I just wanted them to...like you. I know that Dad says some...you know, things that may not be right...but I'm so used to him going about. And he's my only dad, you know. He's been a coal miner all his life. That village is his world...and then you come with your figures and...it's like you're looking down on them! If you had only just listened and let Dad have his ways."

David took pains to apply some damage control. "Look, your dad has been a hard worker all his life. He has provided for his family while taking on a dangerous job. His health has suffered as a consequence. You've told me that he is the kind of guy who stands up for his neighbors, who is always helpful and pitches in. All that is great! But his circles are very small, and his good heart extends only to people he knows personally. He's a good father to you, but there's a huge cultural and political distance between him and me. It's like...I can't reach him with my attempts to have a real dialogue. It's like trying to reach across the Grand Canyon!"

"I want to go back," Eva insisted.

"What? You said you had to get back to school!"

"Take me back to my parents!"

This is a disaster—this is the end, he thought. David turned the car around, and they drove back in dead silence. He dropped her off in front of her parent's house.

"Eva, I'm really sorry…" She slammed the door hard.

It was a long, lonely drive home.

Fortunately, the apartment building where David lived had a guest parking slot that was open. He went up the stairs to his studio with a heavy sense of finality. It was past midnight as he sank into his little couch. A Black Chicken Zinfandel from Biale Vineyards in California provided some comfort in his misery. He found a CD with Jethro Tull and played "A New Day Yesterday." The lyrics seemed pertinent. It had been a new day yesterday with hopes of understanding better where Eva was coming from. But it already felt like an old day now.

CHAPTER 14

Stepping with Diane

After splitting up with Eva, David put any social activities aside and let work fill his life. No more visits to the church. If he was not at work, he was, at least, thinking about it. He dreamed about emails and how to compose them. Every morning, a flood of them waited in his inbox. David was issued a laptop so that he could bring work home and got into the habit of working after dinner to clear the backlog. Still, the inbox was loaded when he started the next morning.

Part of it was the frenzy to copy everyone and his brother on everything to cover your behind. Nobody could be left out, or they would bite you for being neglected. Part of it was just carelessness, such as the habit of hitting 'reply all' for the most insignificant broadcasts. Most messages required no further action. But some were useful to know about for background, and a few were urgent. Some were not urgent or important in terms of substance, but they were in terms of the sender. You had to take note of things that came from on high, or you would be sorry.

Looking at his calendar, David realized that six months had passed since he last saw Eva. This weekend should be different. Instead of going to the office, he took a long morning walk before he rewarded himself with a luxurious lunch at the Hay-Adams hotel on 16th Street near the White House. It was the same place where he had taken Julia to "clear the air" but where he had found himself upstaged. It was a bittersweet memory now that she was gone. But he was determined to confront his grief with composure.

The dining room looked just like he remembered it, with its large crystal chandeliers and unusual lamp shades, green carpet, bright walls, large windows, and waiters dressed in grey vests, ties, and white shirts. The grand piano was still there, although unfortunately nobody was playing. For a moment, he felt it had been a mistake to return here, but he fought off sentimental memories and focused on here and now. Filling his life with work was not sustainable. He needed to find a new track. But how?

He had just been served a delicious Seared Red Snapper with an Heirloom Tomato Salad accompanied by a glass of Kistler Chardonnay from Sonoma Mountain when two young dressed-up girls were seated at the table next to his. While most guests, like those who were middle-aged or were seniors wearing suits and dresses, conversed in tones fit for a library, these girls had no such inhibitions. They were dressed in chic, expensive-looking skirts and blouses with jackets, pearl necklaces, and displayed carefully manicured nails and rather too much makeup. One had a bright red lipstick, the other wore purple, matching her scarf.

"Did you hear that Melanie's back in town?" said Red Lipstick.

"Oh my God, no fuckin' way. She's in like Paris," said Purple Lipstick.

"I know her mom sent her away to like grow up or something, and she filled out papers to get to Paris on some program...she wanted to go to like high school in Paris...like in that movie you know...and her mom paid the agency she has loads of money right...and she went there, and they sent her to fuckin' Denmark!"

"Didn't she know that she wasn't goin' to Paris?" sneered Purple Lipstick.

"Yeah, but she figured it was somewhere close, right...but it takes like lightyears to get to Paris from that place ... plus, they said she had to stay and 'discover the host country!' Red

Lipstick burst out in laughter at the silliness of that notion. "But, oh my God, there's like nothing to see in that country!"

A distinguished-looking waiter approached to take the girls' drink orders, and they asked for a bottle of "champagne from California." He let that pass without correction but kindly asked for their IDs. The girls tried to look offended, and Red Lipstick huffed that she had left it in her car. Purple Lipstick handed him a driver's license. The waiter could not hide his smile.

"Ma'am, I once lived in California, and those driver's licenses don't quite look like this," he announced in *sotto voce*. The waiter stood his ground and suggested a bottle of Perrier with ice and lemon slices on the side. The deflated duo settled for this.

"That was like totally rude!" squealed Red Lipstick as the waiter had left. But she perked up when remembering her story. "But here's the best part, and you'll like totally freak out when you hear this! Her host family in Denmark had a pig farm!"

This elicited a shriek of shock and delight from Purple Lipstick. An elderly couple seated not far from them gave the girls a stern stare, and they composed themselves, giggling only softly.

"Denmark is like really big on pig farming. It's like half the population or something. Can you imagine chic, spoiled-rotten Melanie on a pig farm?" She giggled. "It was really awful, the smell, plus it's totally weird like she couldn't even plug in her own hair dryer! All their wall thingies are totally old."

"Poor Melanie. She washes her hair every day," said Purple Lipstick. "I bet she called Mom to get her out, right?"

"Oh yeah, totally. Now, her mom is suing the agency for like freakin' 'child engenderment' or something."

"That's awesome!" Purple Lipstick giggled.

"My dad talked about Europe yesterday at dinner. He said that in those small countries up there, they're socialist, so everyone must pay like almost everything in taxes. The government gives out goodies to everybody even if they're not working, so like, there's no point. The only thing that makes it OK is that everybody's poor."

That was the last straw for David, who waved down the waiter, quickly paid his bill, and stood up. He turned with a smile at the girls and said, "*Hav en god dag.*"

***

David had gained weight and felt unhealthy from sitting at his desk and in long meetings. He resolved to start working out, starting on Monday, after his unfortunate lunch that had spoiled the weekend. The Bank had an excellent facility for physical exercise in the basement of the main building. Many classes were on offer: strength, cardio, meditation, you name it.

His first was a step class. A colleague had explained that this was not a dance class but an exercise where you stepped on a small platform on risers. David vied for a spot in the back but was more or less politely chased away by arriving women who claimed that this was their territory. He ended up right at the front, close to the attractive instructor. She introduced herself as Diane. It occurred to David that this could be the very same Diane who Mark had talked about as the "super-hot" speaker in the class on gender-awareness.

Diane was a fit, shapely, mixed-race lady probably in her early thirties with shoulder-length, jet-black curly hair. She wore a tight-fitting, red tank top and matching red shorts and

144

sneakers. Her timely cues were delivered in accentless U.S. English.

The first class was an embarrassment. David could keep up with "basic left" and "basic right," but there was also "L step" and "diagonal," and other fancy moves that were all new to him. Trying to do a "grapevine," he moved the wrong way and bumped into a woman on his right and had to apologize profusely. Thankfully, she looked more amused than angry. As he was leaving after the class, Diane came up to him.

"Hello, I'm David," he said and extended a hand.

"Hello, I'm Diane," she said and met his hand with a firm shake.

She has cute dimples when she smiles, he thought.

"Thanks for the class, but I don't think this is for me."

"Look, don't give up after just one class. Let me show you something." She made him put the step back on the risers before she patiently guided him through one move after another. He was grateful but started feeling guilty as time passed.

"I'm sure you have more important things to do."

"I couldn't think of anything more important than to convince you that this is a class for you. Did you notice how many men I have in this one?"

"I saw just one other guy."

"Right, so you are a scarce and valuable commodity here. Should we have lunch?"

David could not believe that she asked him to join him for lunch on the spot. Women never took that initiative in his experience. It was always on him, and most of the time, he got rejected.

They met after showering and went to the Bank's cafeteria. Conversation was easy with Diane, and they traded information about workouts, work, and personal backgrounds. She worked in the Human Resources department and had been at the Bank for only two years. Diane was half-American after her father and half-Jamaican after her mother. She could make a perfect Jamaican accent if she wanted to, which she demonstrated. She was divorced with a young son. The ex-husband was Brazilian and had moved back there. She had sole custody of the son, but the father paid his fair share, she pointed out. Diane had lots of questions about Denmark, which was unusual. He left the lunch with a sense of excitement.

David made sure to show up at every single step class Diane was teaching. After two weeks of classes, he plucked up the courage to ask her out for lunch.

"Yes, sure," she said, "but why don't we go to some place outside the Bank?"

There was a natural air of healthy confidence about her. She was taller than David and put on heels after class which made it even more apparent. Her makeup was sophisticated and not overdone. Short skirts looked good on her, and she could show off her shapely legs with confidence. Her brown skin had the tone that Scandinavians dreamed about when they paid for charter trips to southern destinations. Many ended up like lobsters after the first day of reckless tanning and had to retreat into the shade with peeling skin for the next few days. But Diane had the perfect color naturally. He envied her in that regard, while he realized that his white, unattractive skin was sometimes a social asset. Discrimination against people of color was surely there.

David's immediate physical attraction to Diane was gradually underpinned by a sense of growing emotional engagement. He could feel it every time they met, only to retreat into doubt over the potential of their relationship when they had parted. Discreetly, he inquired about her social life, but he did not get past sweet anecdotes about the precocious young son and some comments about her ex. How far could he push the envelope?

***

Work left little time to pursue romantic interests as demands on his engagement kept exceeding what he could deliver.

A new computer system was introduced across the Bank. A confusing plethora of systems had popped up over the years, and often, they did not speak to each other. Standardization across the Bank was lagging, and the IT staff struggled to keep up with maintenance.

Smart, well-paid consultants had the magic solution: a new system that would replace everything old, outdated, and inefficient. There was just one problem. The staff had to be retrained. Convincing them was not the issue—it was not like staff had a choice once senior management had signed off. But the top brass was eager to sell the changes as evidence of progress and technical sophistication.

Another group of smart, well-paid consultants was engaged to handle the upgrade. They produced flashy videos and emailed messages with smiling people who marveled at how easy the new system was to implement. Productivity would increase so much that staff would be able to cut down on overtime and stay out of the office on weekends. Better work-life balance! Win-win!

What better way to sell the new than disparaging the old? Staff were told that their current systems were embarrassingly outdated and inefficient. Data could be lost

147

irretrievably, and the Bank would be seen as a pitiful laggard among international institutions. Counterparts in developing countries would be laughing at the backward Bank. The message was pumped out in town halls and in brochures and emails to staff. David wondered how such a disastrous set of systems could have been accepted in the first place.

Training started and was oversubscribed. Everybody wanted a seat at the table and feared being left behind. There was not sufficient teaching capacity, however, and when a part of the system was implemented, many staff had no previous experience handling it. Complaints mounted; frustration rose. In response, trained "champions" of the new system were placed across units.

David attended a training session for the new travel booking system, but he was stumped the first time he tried to do it on his own. He was used to simply calling an in-house agent who expertly booked his flights and a room at one of the Bank-approved hotels. That system had worked perfectly fine, but now, it was not good enough.

The "champion" was a pleasant lady in her thirties by the name of Laura. The trip went from Washington Dulles Airport via Frankfurt, Germany to Nairobi, Kenya and back the same way. Nothing difficult there! When the system asked for the airport codes, it did not recognize NBO for Nairobi. Laura managed to find a way around that after a few minutes. But when the two flight legs were entered, the system declared the route "not authorized."

Laura tried to go via LHR, London, but the system was frozen on "not authorized." She found no work-around and called a "super-specialist" who connected from Chennai. He fixed it somehow, and the booking could continue. It went fine until the very end when the system announced that "travel cannot be concluded before departure." That seemed both reasonable and irrelevant. Laura and David went over the dates, and they were correct. The "super-specialist" was called again, and a new voice answered after a long wait. He was equally puzzled but consoled them.

"Don't even try to understand this system, just find a work-around. I can show you an override. There is so much work still to be done to get this up and running properly, but senior management is very keen to get started."

Unfortunately, waiting for the "super-specialist" had taken so much time that the booking had timed out. There was no "save" function, and everything was irretrievably lost. Laura was kind enough to do all the entries this time, putting the heralded training aspect aside, and after a bit more than one hour, the trip was booked.

Later that day, the president's office issued an all-staff message to celebrate the successful launch of the travel booking system. Back-slapping all around.

***

During the next two months, David and Diane continued to meet once a week for a quick lunch or a coffee in the cafeteria or sometimes a place close by. One day, she suggested they meet for dinner after work. "A lunch will not give us enough time," she said. That sounded promising to David.

He picked a small, cozy restaurant in the Adams Morgan district, famous for its nightlife. He was nervous about it and had even gone there to test the food and check the wine list. It was diverse enough for most palates. One table in a corner provided a bit more privacy, so he booked it.

David arrived much too early and walked around the block several times to mark time and calm his nerves. Was this the first step in taking their relationship to a new level? Nothing had been said explicitly about that, but the chemistry was there. The physical attraction he felt was obvious, but she was so much more. Smart, with a good sense of humor, and with a positive outlook in general, she shared vignettes of her life with openness and listened as well. She had questions, she was intellectually curious, and she had good values. What more could one ask for? But why would she be interested in pursuing a serious relationship with him?

He returned to the restaurant five minutes early and checked his pale appearance carefully in the men's bathroom. *Manage your expectations now*, he thought.

Diane stunned him by appearing in a stylish, v-cut black dress, red high-heel sandals, and black stockings. She wore a pearl necklace, matching bracelet, and long, dangling earrings in the same style. Diane extended a freshly manicured hand with bright red nails and smiled. "You must be David," she joked, smiling.

David felt a rush of attraction but also a sense of being overwhelmed by the social demands of the situation. She was out of his league, and she would quickly realize that. The two gentlemen sitting at the closest table had been loud when they walked in, but they turned silent and looked unabashedly at Diane.

She defused the situation with pleasant small-talk, and David found his footing. Diane quickly decided on a salad, declined a starter, and ordered a glass of Sauvignon Blanc from the Marlborough region in New Zealand. David found it hard to concentrate, his brain looking for suitable subjects to bring up in the conversation. He resorted to ordering exactly what he had tried during his "training" visit: Mahi-Mahi and a glass of Catena Alta Chardonnay.

It was the same waiter, and he smiled in recognition at David. "Welcome back," he said with a knowing nod.

The pressure on David subsided when Diane kept asking him about his background, family, and Denmark. They had covered some of that already. Home territory calmed his nerves, and he was flattered by her interest.

"I mentioned to you another time that my dad is a carpenter and admires people who work with their hands. Nothing wrong with that, but he never took an interest in my choice of study and work. He never asked any questions about it, and he never had much respect for academics in general. University just made people snobbish," he said. "You know, he didn't even show up for my PhD graduation ceremony!"

Diane extended her hand over his and squeezed it. "I'm so sorry to hear that."

"Unfortunately, he was injured in a work accident. Disability pension works fine in Denmark, but it left him bitter. He still does a little hobby-type work on the side, and I don't think the tax man knows much about that. Denmark competes with France and Sweden for having the highest taxes in the world, so it's tempting to cheat. The extra income buys him beer, I guess, and he drinks plenty nowadays. His temper can be very explosive."

"Was he ever abusive to you or your mother?"

"Never physically. But psychologically, yes. He never gave my mom the appreciation she deserved. She would praise me when I came home with good grades. But Dad said it was important never to brag. He did have an interest in Danish history though. That's why he's so mad at the Swedes and refuses to go there."

Diane declined desert, so David felt he had to as well. He had set his eyes on the ice cream, but that was for another day.

Standing outside the restaurant, the moment became awkward again for David. But Diane took him by the arm, and they started walking. "A taxi for you? Or I can walk you to the Metro station?"

"I'd like to see where you live," she responded.

David hesitated. "You have your son to take care of. Don't you need to release the babysitter?"

"Josh is at a neighbor's apartment. I have a friend who lives close by. Another single mother with a son about the same age as Josh. So, he's on a sleepover."

David's head was spinning. He was walking home with a gorgeous woman who had just made clear that she was free to stay for the night. And this was after dinner number one. Sure, they had known each other for more about three months, but they had only met in connection with work. This was different—it was their first real date.

Fortunately, he had tidied up the studio a bit before leaving because he liked it that way, not that he expected company. There was red wine but, otherwise, little on offer for drinks. Fortunately, it turned out that Diane was not interested in drinks.

As soon as the door had closed, she turned around and gently pushed him against the door. She kissed him deeply with an intensity that caught him off guard. His heart raced as she started to unbutton his shirt. As she ran her fingers across his chest, his perspiration made her stop.

"David, I want you to take a shower first," she said.

"Of course," he said awkwardly, as if caught in a compromising situation. But he had been perspiring on the way home in nervous anticipation of what was to come. He went into the bathroom, undressed, and got into the shower.

It was his quickest shower ever. As he stepped out, he realized that Diane was standing there, still fully dressed, but holding his towel.

"Let me dry you." She went about her task very methodically, not missing any spot on his body.

They kissed again with sweet intensity, and he pressed his body against hers. Still standing, they explored each other's body. Her elegant, red nails very gently scratched his penis until it was rock hard. He pushed his hand up her dress and cautiously massaged her.

Grabbing him by his erect penis, she pulled him out to the bed and pushed him down on his back. She pulled her dress over her head, got into the bed, and straddled him just below his erection. Still wearing a lacy, semi-transparent bra, black stay-up stockings, and elegant heels, she lifted herself onto his pole and embraced him with her warm moisture.

No need for more foreplay, David noted.

Diane leaned over him, kissed him hungrily, and grabbed his wrists in a dominant posture. He felt her grinding him slowly, while he lay still in awe over her overpowering sexuality. *I am not in charge here*, he realized with a sense of elation. The movement of her perfectly shaped breasts was mesmerizing. Now and then, she leaned forward to give him a hungry French kiss. He wanted it to last forever but was soon swept away by an irresistible wave of lust.

"That went quickly, but we aren't done yet," Diane said with a mischievous smile. She let him catch his breath for a couple minutes, but then rolled off him. She sat down on the edge of the bed.

"Honey, I want you on your knees and your tongue on my clit." Her tone was casual as if saying, "Pass me the salt, dear."

It was a simple instruction, and David got into position. Diane was wearing an open-crotch panty in red lace. He was not new to cunnilingus but had never found it particularly appealing. Suddenly, he found it thrilling. She grabbed his hair and guided him firmly to the right spot and delivered instructions along the way to her climax. When her body was completely relaxed, he climbed up into bed.

Nothing needed to be said.

CHAPTER 15

Why Do Some People Have So Much Cargo?

It was Friday evening again, one week after David's exhilarating first real date with Diane. Unfortunately, she was busy that whole weekend. David left work early to catch up with JP. He was a guy with "convening power" as the jargon went, and often gathered a group of mostly younger colleagues on Friday evenings. Older ones tended to rush back to their neglected families, but the younger crowd was keen to socialize.

This time, David had convinced Bob to join them. It was not easy, as Bob was quite busy organizing a Muslim Association at the Bank. They had met for a quick coffee the same morning. "There's a sense of growing Islamophobia in this country," Bob complained. "I can't say I'm surprised as we read and hear so much about the damage that Islamists can do. But those militants are not representative of our faith. We need to stand up and explain ourselves to the world!" David made the winning point that the Friday meetings could be a forum for that type of message.

They had gathered in JP's favorite wine bar where French wines were *de rigueur*. It was a cozy place with dimmed lights, comfortable couches in red velvet, and colorful, fluffy pillows.

JP quickly introduced David, then Carmen from Environment, Sushmita from Agriculture, Jürgen from Procurement, Donald from Infrastructure, and Ruben from Legal. Everyone seemed to know Bob already, the veteran he was.

155

The waitress came around, and JP ordered a first round of tapas and two bottles of Medoc from the Bordeaux region. "A blend of Merlot and Cabernet Sauvignon," he informed the table reassuringly. He often hosted a table but expected others to pitch in at times.

"'ow many of you went to the guest lecture by Jared Diamond today?" JP asked. Only Bob and David indicated they had.

"This is sad," said Bob with a serious face. "You're too busy to listen to a great thinker on development. The Bank offers generous opportunities for us to inform ourselves, but we are knee-deep in emails and chasing deadlines. So, we miss the big picture! What drives development? What stands in the way? We need to take a step back at times to consider what we're doing."

Several colleagues looked uncomfortable. "I didn't have time," said Carmen defensively, "but I've read his book on *Guns, Germs and Steel.*" David and Sushmita also indicated they had read that classic book. "I was really impressed by that one. Is that what he talked about?"

"Basically, yes," Bob continued, "although it wasn't a lecture about the book itself. Diamond has that wonderful ability to sweep across masses of data and somehow tie it all together to a holistic...eh..."

"*Weltanschauung,*" suggested Jürgen with a smile. "German has a number of great expressions that other languages don't seem to be able to capture as accurately. Like *Schadenfreude.*"

And some expressions, we would rather forget, thought David darkly, such as *Endlösung der Judenfrage* (Final solution to the Jewish question). But more constructively, he added, "I think 'world view' and 'epicaricacy' work just as well."

"So, for those who 'aven't read the book, or who 'ave forgotten it," JP continued, "the starting point is that a guy in New Guinea asked Diamond: 'Why do White people 'ave so much cargo?' Meaning, 'ow did you get so rich and produce all that stuff that we see unloaded from ships and airplanes? Diamond took some twenty-five years to think about that one. Then, 'e produced a brilliant narrative about the geophysical and social forces that 'ave shaped the modern world. 'e starts 13,000 years back, so it's a thorough review of 'istory."

"It's a great starting point because it really takes on the fundamental question about why some nations are poor and others rich. Is he suggesting race has something to do with it?" Donald asked suspiciously. David knew that Donald had come as a refugee from Zimbabwe as a child.

"No, on the contrary," interjected Sushmita. "Diamond reiterates that biological differences among people are not the explanation for current differences between societies. Instead, he focused on how their environment shaped their historical arc."

"Let me try to point out the main factors, or 'ultimate causes' as Diamond puts it," Bob filled in. "Food production evolved differently among people depending on the wild varieties that were available. Another basic factor was the domestication of animals as food and use for agricultural production. Just think of the importance of the horse and the oxen in plowing. And on the basis of food production, you had the emergence of writing and technical innovation, including steel and weapons development. Unless you have a surplus of food, everyone is bogged down in farming.

"What about the germs mentioned in the title," Ruben asked.

"Diamond points out that humans with domesticated animals were the first to be exposed to disease emanating from them. But then they developed immunity toward those diseases. This became crucial when Europeans colonized areas where the population didn't have the same immunity. The impact on them was devastating. Have I captured the essence of Diamond's *Weltanschauung*?" Bob asked with a quick look around the table.

"It all sounds sensible, but it leaves a few things out," Sushmita added. "I personally find Jeffrey Sachs's 'poverty checklist' as he calls it, very useful. He agrees with Diamond on the physical geography: landlocked countries with a high disease burden and natural disasters are obviously disadvantaged. But he adds things like poor governance, especially corruption, bad economic policies—like barriers to trade, throttling of the private sector—and cultural factors."

"What does he mean by 'cultural factors,' then?" asked Donald.

"One example I remember from his book *The Age of Sustainable Development* is female participation in the labor force. Obviously, that can make a huge difference in the economy if you tap into that resource."

"One more thing comes to mind," said Jurgen. "I went to a seminar with Hernando de Soto a couple of years back. He talked about his book *The Mystery of Capital*. I was impressed with the way he had done his work on the role of property rights. Basically, the theme was that without secure property rights, poor people have little leverage to get out of their trap. He had collected a lot of empirical data from Latin America about that."

"I think that applies everywhere," Donald added for reinforcement.

The wine arrived, JP checked the labels and nodded. He made a little show of his tasting by first looking at the color against the white tablecloth, swirling the minute amount poured by the waitress, noting the "nice legs" of the wine, then pushing his nose aggressively into the glass and inhaling demonstrably. "'mmm, *merveilleux*...nice blackberry and black currant on the nose..." He took a sip, and his smile brightened. "Aahh...nice complexity, elegant style, smooth tannins, lively acidity, and again the dark fruits—lingering finish..." He put the glass down with a serene expression as if he had just reached Nirvana.

They all burst out laughing. "Stop the snobbery, JP!" said Carmen. Stick with 'full-bodied' or something believable. I know you're very French, but just cool it."

JP feigned resignation. "So much is lost on you people." He sighed and attacked the tray with nuts and chips that came with the wine. After chewing down a mouthful, he resumed the conversation.

"Well, Diamond would probably respond that 'e agrees that 'e 'asn't given the complete picture. 'e came through as a 'umble man. But 'is narrative is still pretty powerful. And it manages to explain a lot without messing with race."

"I read the book recently," Carmen interjected. "Diamond writes in a final chapter that cultural differences may be important. He speculates about why, for example, it was Europe that colonized Africa and America, not the Chinese. He thinks that the decentralized power structure of Europe allowed for more competition and experimentation. When one colonial power, such as Spain in Latin America, started profiting from the colonial trade, other powers were keen to get in on the action. Britain, France, Portugal, and the Netherlands started to compete in the colonial race. But in China, the centralized power structure blocked such ventures. It's fascinating to think how different the world could've been otherwise."

"Wow," David thought, *imagine Latin America full of Chinese, the official language being Chinese...and of course it would not be called "Latin" America, then.*

"Maybe it's because of my legal background, but I have a somewhat different perspective on what matters for economic development," said Bob. "Some of our colleagues are deep into what governance means for development. They have come up with a system of scoring the quality of governance, you know how well institutions work, the level of corruption, and so forth. There are important connections between that and the level of economic development. Outside of the Bank, there's a really good representation of an institutional approach in *Why Nations Fail.* Has anyone else read it?"

None had, so Bob keenly continued. "Those authors explicitly reject the geographic theories proposed by Diamond. In addition, they also argue against cultural norms, religion, and such, as explanations of differences in wealth and income. They also dismiss what they call the 'ignorance hypothesis,' that is, the theory that rulers simply don't know better. They argue that elites are simply pursuing their own narrow interests and are in fact implementing policies that are rational given their mindset. What they arrive at is a theory of institutions as the key factor in explaining social progress."

"I could think of some good illustrations of that hypothesis," David added. "Think about the stark differences between North and South Korea, East and West Germany, for example. Clearly, it's not geography or ethnicity that explains the differences. It's a social organization. And the rulers in the poorer countries are not simply stupid. They have an agenda that they have decided is beneficial to them.

160

But in a democracy, you can't pursue a narrow, corrupt policy for very long, or you'll be voted out of office."

"Hang on," said Carmen, "maybe it's my background in environmental studies, but I don't think we can throw out the environmental factors. Clearly, the quality of soils, the amount of rainfall and how regular it is, the type of crops you can grow, what draft animals you can use, and so on, all that is important for food production. That, in turn, is the basis of supporting all the categories of non-food producers that society needs to develop. We should be open to a combination of factors, not just look for the ultimate one."

"OK," Bob conceded. "Let's not reduce everything to a single factor. But there is something important for us as aid professionals in the theory I talked about. If those authors are right—I think they're called Acemoğlu and Robinson—then we can't assume that 'good advice' will do the trick. We would be asking them to go against their own incentives. So, when analyzing why a country is failing, we need to find the rationality behind that. It's in somebody's interest, usually some kind of elite, that things are organized in a certain way."

"I've come across that in practice," Carmen agreed. "We looked for biodiversity projects in an African country. We found some areas that definitely were hot spots from a scientific perspective. But when we brought the plans to the central government, they rejected all the ones that were located in provinces where the political opposition was strong. When it came to making decisions, they simply had a different rationality. It was not about science; it was about political gain."

"I can contribute another case," Sushmita added. "In one country where I worked, we developed a scheme where farmers would sell their raw cashew nuts on the world market through a clearing house we wanted to set up. That would give them access to much better prices than what was offered domestically. But the single processing plant for cashew nuts in the country lobbied the government through private connections. The head of the plant was a cousin to the Minister of Finance. So, the scheme was stopped, and the domestic monopoly for buying raw cashew nuts continued."

"One more thing comes to mind about the need to understand the political economy," said Bob. "Acemoğlu and Robinson dig deep into colonial history and come out with a fascinating narrative. The early colonizers in Latin America went there to extract quick profits. They basically plundered the indigenous people's riches. They massacred the Aztecs and the Incas. In North America, the early colonizers had a similar idea—take Jamestown in Virginia as an example. But they didn't find the gold they dreamed of. They couldn't enslave the locals to do their dirty job. They had to actually make a living themselves. Out of that grew more inclusive political structures and the embryo to modern democracy. In the South, the business model was extraction by a small, powerful elite. That didn't give rise to the same dynamic economic development as in the North. I think that is a fascinating narrative," he concluded.

"So, what's the conclusion for us?" Ruben inquired. "If the maintenance of misery is rationally based in the preferences of the elite, what hope is there of positive change? There's a risk that we fall back into defeatism here."

"It's not all depressing," Carmen objected. "Look at the longer-term perspective. The march forward of democratic institutions this past century has been really impressive. The Soviet empire has crumbled, for example. Some of the authoritarian leaders are still in place in the former Soviet Republics, but some nations are setting out on a new course."

"For me," said Sushmita, "the bottom line is that effective aid has to be informed not only about natural conditions in a country but also about the political economy. This will make us more realistic and modest—but ultimately more successful—when delivering aid. And we should be more upstanding and courageous in backing away from projects and programs that don't work."

"Easy to say but try to tell a Country Director and his staff that their program will be slashed to a minimum of emergency aid because studies have shown the country to be hopelessly corrupt!" Donald objected. "Let's be honest! We have our own vested interests in this game as development professionals."

A lot of interesting perspective here, David thought. But there's a real risk we leave this debate pessimistic about what can be done, given all the constraints we are facing. Let me throw something out here. "There's a short-cut available out of the theoretical maze about what works in development. Have you read the recent work coming out of the Poverty Action Lab at MIT? Their approach is straightforward: Let's look at what works! Let's test our hypotheses with Randomized Controlled Trials. This has been the gold standard in medicine a long time, but we aren't doing it."

"But we have a whole department working on evaluations," Ruben objected.

"We have lots of evaluations, sure, but the analytical perspective is more 'before-after,' and that's not good enough," David continued. "I think we should go home and write up a proposal for an RCT in relation to a project that we are working on. There are Trust Funds that could finance that kind of work. If we can't do this ourselves, we can at least study and incorporate evidence from RCTs in our work," he concluded.

Several colleagues nodded in agreement, although it was clearly not a task that all of them could undertake.

"How do you figure RCTs could be applied to our work?" Bob asked.

"In very general terms, let's take a community development project with a large scale. Map out fifty villages of about similar size in a region. Randomly pick half of them as 'treatment' villages and the other half as 'control.' Deliver aid in some form to the treatment villages—cash transfers, water & sanitation, agricultural extension, impregnated bed nets against malaria, etc.—and follow up on how a number of observable parameters of development evolve over time," David suggested.

"It sounds really complex and expensive," Bob objected. "The evaluation budget attached to a project is often very limited."

"That's why we need to collaborate with academic researchers and mobilize funding from Trust Funds to augment the usual Bank budget," David argued. "I'll get to work on that tomorrow!"

His colleagues wished him good luck but also indicated that they were too busy to venture into such a project. They ordered more tapas, and Donald offered to pay for that round. "My turn," he volunteered. There was a lull in the discussion before they regained focus, but the conversation drifted back to the lecture of the day.

"Another factor that Diamond mentions, and that I think is really important not to forget, is about powerful individuals," Sushmita remarked. "One example that I had never heard about before, but found in Diamond's book, is that Hitler was nearly killed in a traffic accident in 1930. Imagine that!"

"No," Donald objected, "I don't think that is a compelling argument. Hitler was a skillful demagogue, but he gravitated to the top of the political structure in Germany because of the historical context. Germany had lost the First World War. Its economy was in shambles. In addition, the Allies humiliated Germany with a peace deal that had them pay enormous reparations to the winning side. Of course, this caused a lot of resentment. That prepared the ground for Hitler. Don't you agree, Jürgen? You're the German at this table."

Jürgen looked pained by the question. "Look, it is a very delicate subject for me. The Germans have really confronted their dark past like few other people. I grew up learning about the horrors of the Nazi area—no excuses. But if Hitler had died in 1930, someone else with his agenda could very well have emerged and taken the reins. Anti-Jewish sentiment was nothing new, and the depression sharpened social conflicts. The bitterness against the Versailles Peace Treaty was widely shared. Runaway inflation broke the economy. There was a thirst for a 'strongman,' somebody who could resurrect the German people's dignity. Individuals play a role on the margin, but they don't really determine the course of history."

The tapas arrived, and the discussion broke up into pairs and triplets. The wine loosened their tongues, and the ambient noise had increased around them to a level where it was hard to keep a single discussion focused. Inevitably, the focus drifted from academic references to the frustrations of the day: the unreasonable email load, the most recent directives from senior management, rumors about people leaving, gossip about office romances—some innocent and some inappropriate—and the next missions coming up. David loved these informal gatherings, and he did not relish the thought of going back to his empty studio.

David left at the same time as JP, and they strolled a few blocks to the Metro station where JP would catch a train out to Bethesda in Maryland, where so many Bank staff had found a home. They parted at the Metro, and David continued wandering home in deep reflection on the evening's discussion.

He saw several homeless people on the way. Mostly, they just sat on a bench sometimes smoking or drinking. Some would lie down in a heap of clothes, often with an overloaded shopping cart next to them. He started thinking about Eva and the soup kitchen.

"Hey, man, can you spare some change?" The scruffy man extended a welcoming hand to receive his change. This was not development theory any longer, it was give or not give? David donated money through GiveWell, a non-profit charity assessment organization that carefully checked the efficiency of aid delivery. But individual giving?

It was just outside a liquor store. *A poor choice of venue.* He felt ambivalent. After all, there was a social safety net. Shelters, social workers, soup kitchens, food stamps, and temporary cash support if one had children, and unemployment benefits if you had worked. But some people would refuse to go to shelters where they could not smoke, drink, or use drugs. Some could not stand the noise and the rubbing against the idiosyncrasies of other homeless people. Some feared for their safety. There didn't seem to be a solution to the issue, no matter how hard the city government and NGOs worked on it. He decided not to extend financial support when in D.C. In a developing country, he would have done it, knowing that their safety net caught very few.

He arrived home. It was too late to call Diane. He turned on his laptop and started going through the forty-three emails that had accumulated since he left office. At least, it had been a good discussion—the type that made it so interesting at times to work for the Bank.

A clear analysis of what drives development and what hampers it is essential. It's the starting point for designing effective aid. We all walk around with an implicit development model, but how often do we take time to question it? he thought.

CHAPTER 16

Reality Check

The wild ride in the SUV lasted for some two hours, although David could not keep time very well. He was lying on the floor with his hands cuffed behind his back, a black sack over his head, and somebody's feet on his back. His fear grew as the ride went on. "A hardass" was the Warrior's description. What did he mean by that?

The car stopped, and David was brusquely pulled to his feet and led into some building. He was pushed down to a lying position and left there. After a few minutes, a door opened and the sack over his head was torn off. The Big Man again, grinning in triumph. He let out a long incomprehensible tirade.

David shifted his position and noticed two more people in the room—two teenage boys, with big, innocent eyes looking with fascination at the prisoner. The Big Man had no uniform, but he had a long whip in his right hand. He gave David a sharp rap on his left arm. The strike was so forceful that it tore through his clothes and skin.

When reading stories about torture and beatings, David had wondered how he would hold up in that situation. As a teenager, he had read Orwell's powerful novel *1984* and for a long time struggled to suppress horrific thoughts about torture and in particular Room 101—the place where tailor-made horrors were delivered to finally break the victims. Now, images of those horrors descended on him like a giant, poisonous spider that wrapped its legs around him. Would he be able to maintain his dignity?

The reality check came with a brutal answer rather more quickly than he would have liked. Once he felt the sharp, burning pain in his left arm, he could not help thinking about the next one. *A kick to the head and I'll be brain damaged for life*, he thought. *Maybe he wants to kill me! But if I live, I'll be carted back to Denmark to live the rest of my life in a home for disabled. I'll be a vegetable. I'll lose Diane, I will lose my dignity, my job…*the horrific thoughts spiraled through his brain like a tornado, and panic constricted his throat.

The second blow landed on his back and tore into his skin. He had never felt such pain. David pleaded. "Please! Stop!"

Thankfully, he had no secrets to spill and no friends to betray. But that also meant that he had nothing to offer his captors—no bargaining chip to please them—unless they could trade him for ransom. He had to confess to himself that he was not able to stand up to a beating. It felt like his dignity was all gone after a couple of forceful blows.

The Big Man grinned with delight. The infidel was squirming at his feet after only a couple of warm-ups. The teenagers' eyes lit up. The Big Man was their leader. When they grew up, they too could be in charge, they could beat an infidel into submission and watch him squirm. Not to mention what they could do to infidel women! Unspeakable things that could not be done to a Muslim woman. But the infidels were different.

The Big Man kicked David's arms and rib cage until he heard a cracking sound that delighted him. He handed the whip to one of the teenagers. Unsure where exactly to hit, he went for the legs. But David did not move and said nothing. It spoiled the fun.

The Big Man turned to the blown-up photos on the wall from Abu Ghraib in Iraq. He gestured and explained, and the teenage boys listened and soaked up every word. The door opened, and a man with an AK-47 spoke with urgency to the

Big Man. He scurried out of the room, yelling instructions to the boys.

An overpowering pain in multiple places consumed David's body. Every breath inflicted pain on his left side. Broken ribs from the kicks? There was a dull, persistent ache in his left arm. His hands were still cuffed behind his back, but he could at least wiggle his right arm. Not his left.

There was a call to prayer from a nearby mosque, and the boys turned toward Mecca, kneeled down, and prayed. Once done, they had lost their momentum and looked searchingly at each other. After some discussion, they simply sat down in a corner where the daylight fell into the cell and picked up a book.

The Koran, David thought.

The Koran's famous "Sword verse" says: "When the sacred months are over, slay the idolaters wherever you find them. Arrest them, besiege them, and lie ambush everywhere for them." But it also continued: "If they repent and take to prayer and render the alms levy, allow them to go their way. God is forgiving and merciful."

That is the part I hope they remember, David thought.

CHAPTER 17

The Yellow Cactus

After the first night together with Diane, he wanted to see her every day, but she put up limits. She worked long hours and had a young son to go home to. Diane made no secret about occasionally seeing other lovers. David was jealous, but her pushback on any discussion about that was quite firm. He decided to just focus on his incredible luck of having any time at all with her. The way she would just naturally take charge during their erotic playtime fascinated him. It was a blow to his self-image, but with a great pay-off. There was a lot more than great sex involved. While Diane was in some ways very different from Julia, he recognized the same kind of deep feelings from his time with her.

David dug into work to suppress his daydreams about Diane. There was a replenishment of the Nordic Fund for Equitable, Inclusive, and Sustainable Transformation (NFEIST) with the Bank. Now, he could apply for a grant to undertake the Randomized Controlled Trial study of community development grants that he had conceived after the discussion about "why some people have so much cargo."

David had read up on several RCTs and the work of MITs Poverty Action Lab. He had also identified a potential full-scale project that was in the making in Kenya. It would have the money for preparation and implementation, but not to undertake an RCT on top of that. The paperwork was extensive, but the potential reward could be high, and he applied for $500,000. Unfortunately, that was the cap for any application. If the first stage went well, he would apply for more to make it a long-term study. He consulted Bob in finalizing the application, and he enthusiastically gave his support.

***

Two weeks later, he was greeted with a curt memo declaring that his study was "ineligible." David was baffled, as he had carefully followed the guidelines for application. The decision was signed by a Mr. Salovsky. He called his office. The assistant informed him that Salovsky was in a meeting and took a message. He never returned the call, nor did he answer any of David's emails, so David set up an appointment with Salovsky at the first opportunity his assistant could find—a full week later. However, when David appeared at the agreed time, Mr. Salovsky had embarked on a mission. The assistant refused to book a new time, claiming that she could only do so with the boss's agreement. Clearly, he was being stonewalled. David wanted to resolve things on his own if possible but went to his new boss, Muhammad Mahmood, to complain.

"Salovsky is known to be a difficult chap," said Muhammad. "He is very senior and well-connected. I doubt you will be able to get anything out of him. It may not be to your advantage to challenge somebody like him." With great disappointment, David put it aside but vowed to look for new opportunities.

***

There was a knock on his door. He was surprised to see Diane with her son, Josh, in tow. "Sorry to barge in, but it's 'take your kids to work day,' and Josh really wanted to come. I thought you might like to meet him."

David rose to greet them. "Of course, welcome, Josh." Josh extended a hand and shook David's with a firm grip while looking him straight in the eyes. "Nice to meet you," he said casually.

This guy will do well in job interviews, David thought. "So, Josh, how old are you now?"

"I'm seven years, three months, and four days old," he responded without hesitation. "How old are you?" he added quickly, still looking straight at David.

A bit taken aback, David said, "I'm thirty-three."

"If you tell me your birthday, I can figure it out for you more exactly," Josh offered.

David glanced at Diane, but her straight face made him suppress his laughter. This was a serious guy!

His boss appeared in the doorway.

"Hi, David, oh, sorry to interrupt..."—he gave a quick look at Diane and her son—"...but there's an urgent meeting that I need you to attend on my behalf." David was often dispatched to meetings that his boss preferred to bow out of.

"We were on our way," Diane said with a smile and took Josh's hand, which he seemed not to appreciate. "It was good to see you!"

"Have a nice day," Josh added politely.

He was obviously raised well.

David received a file and a few quick instructions and went on his way.

***

On return from the meeting an hour later, David found a voicemail from Diane. Josh was joining another mom and son for the rest of the day, and she suggested they meet after work at a coffee shop a few blocks from the Bank.

As they met, David remarked on Josh's precocious behavior. She smiled. "I know, but with Josh, you mustn't laugh about it. He gets very upset if he thinks you're making fun of him. He does really great in his studies but doesn't read social cues well. It gets him into trouble, and it's exhausting to be the only parent at times. Please come around and play chess with him sometime. He refuses to play with me. 'It's too easy to win,' he complains."

"When I was seven, my mom bought a chess board and asked Dad to carve simple wooden figures so that I could play. I got chess books from the library, but I didn't have anyone to play with."

"That's so sad."

"I still enjoyed playing through famous games described in literature by myself, and I thought of myself as pretty good. That changed one day. At a university party, I met another PhD student. He was doing theoretical physics. A pretty reclusive guy, but when somebody mentioned chess, he perked up. We found a chess set in the apartment where the party was and started playing. He opened, and I did a standard Sicilian defense. But after just a few moves, he looked at me with some sympathy and said, 'I'm sorry, but this doesn't look that good for you.' I thought he was psyching me, so I just laughed. But he looked very serious and said, 'I'll give it seven or eight moves.' I really tried my best, but seven moves later, I was checkmated. Totally creepy!"

"Wow, did you play again? You could've learned a lot from that guy."

"Unfortunately, he disappeared to finish his dissertation at Princeton."

"Funny, that's where I went for my bachelor's degree."

David froze and faced her. "You…you went to Princeton?"

Diane frowned. "Of course, why not?"

David bit his lip. "I'm really sorry if I sounded … you know, surprised, but it's just that you've never mentioned it. Look, I know you're really smart, that's not new, but it's a pretty exclusive place academically."

"I've learned to hide it. Some people find it intimidating, especially men."

"That's ridiculous!"

"It is! But it's real." She laughed at her memory. "I moved to New York City right after graduation. At a party in Manhattan, this cute guy had bragged about going to Fordham. He really tried to impress me. When we came back to my tiny apartment, he was visibly keen, so to speak. So, we stumbled into bed, and I was on top, of course, and he looked up and saw my diploma. He just froze, and I could feel how the blood drained out of, hmm, him." She chuckled, but quickly got serious. "I shouldn't be laughing. He didn't recover and…well, he just left and never called me again."

"What a story! I'm glad you didn't bring this up on our first date. I would never have made it home with you," David noted with an awkward attempt to smile.

"Honestly, David, at that first date, you were just ashen in your face when we met at the restaurant. I was afraid the evening would end with me doing CPR," she teased.

I must be able to laugh at myself, he thought. He hugged her tightly and whispered in her ear: "As I recall, mouth-to-mouth worked just fine."

They kissed, but then she changed the subject. "I want to bring you to a meeting that should be interesting," she said. "There are many things that I want to explore with you, but

175

you have to be open and prepared to do things that you never thought you could do."

"Sounds ominous."

"Not at all, just be trusting and open. Nothing will be forced on you."

After a quick latte, they left and took the Metro a few stops into the SE section of D.C. He had studied the crime maps of Washington D.C. and decided to limit his exposure to safer areas. Diane seemed perfectly fine with walking from the Metro to a rather run-down building nearby.

A tall, dark man stood by the gate. There was no sign indicating that a particular activity was going on in the building.

"Hello, Diane," he said with a smile.

"Hello, Richard. This is my guest for the evening. David, show him your ID please."

Richard took his ID and scanned it in comparison with a list of names in alphabetical order.

"The blacklist," whispered Diane in his ear.

"OK," said Richard and issued a guest card to David. It had a logo on it that read "The Yellow Cactus" and an artistic rendering of the same. He had to pay a $10 entrance fee. Diane paid only $5 as a member. They descended to the basement where some twenty-five people had gathered.

"Richard is an off-duty police officer, and he runs the security detail for these meetings. There will be a series of short presentations soon. Some of them may seem a bit weird to you, but try to suspend judgement."

The audience looked very "normal" to David—like accountants or teachers dropping in after work. Several had suits and ties and others less formal business dress. A few in jeans and T-shirts. Two women deviated in their leather pants, leather jackets, and purple hair. Bikers? Another couple had their arms covered in colorful tattoos. A male couple entered and sat down next to David.

They look like they could be colleagues from the Bank, he thought.

The first talk was delivered by Joe, a portly, balding gentleman in his fifties dressed in jeans and a T-shirt. His special interest was rope bondage. After a brief review of the history of this practice, Joe was keen to demonstrate the basic knots on two models, one male and one female, both treated equally. There was no nudity, and the models were dressed in casual street clothes. Joe emphasized safety.

"As a top, you are responsible for the safety of your bottom. Never leave them unattended in bondage." He also demonstrated some tie ups suitable for beginners and releasable in a second. The tone was very factual and a bit dry. Disregarding the subject matter, it could have been a talk about home fire safety.

The second talk focused on sensual body oils. A rail-thin woman with red hair in her forties—Amanda—explained how she manufactured erotic oils in her own kitchen from basic ingredients. She seemed quite passionate about her subject matter.

"You can make something that is just perfect for you and maybe make some money this way," she assured the audience. Several samples were passed around for sniffing. One in particular had a delightful, flowery fragrance. David glanced at Diane, but she shook her head.

"It's good, but I already have better stuff at home," she whispered.

A young woman dressed in stylish office clothes delivered the third talk. A lawyer perhaps? She introduced herself as "Anita."

"I'm a proud feminist, and I am here to speak in defense of masochism," she started out to David's amazement. "Masochism is a label applied to many things, and often in a pejorative manner. There's a history of psychological analysis that portrays it as a sickness. Interestingly enough, some of the early work on masochism was concerned primarily with male submission as a 'perversion.' The idea of female submissiveness struck these gentlemen as totally 'normal.' Women were seen as naturally masochistic!"

There was some laughter in the audience. Anita took a sip of water and then continued.

"Freud saw the masochist as a victim—somebody who was not willing or able to stand up for himself. The truth is that many men—successful, normal men can find relief in masochism. But recognizing that takes courage to escape from under the protective mantle of the macho image. Masochism means you have to trust somebody deeply by showing them your vulnerabilities."

Diane pinched his thigh as if to say: "There now, did you get that?" And David was listening attentively at every word from this articulate young woman.

"Now," said Anita, and her posture tightened with engagement, "to the females in this audience I want to say this. Don't be bothered by the lectures from the purist ivory towers that claim female masochism to be a betrayal of the struggle for empowerment. We do want respect and equal pay for equal work. We want reproductive rights and the right to choose. We're not selling out to the patriarchy and not giving in to bullying."

There was some murmur indicating agreement in the audience, and Anita flashed a smile at some friends in the front row.

"On the contrary, a healthy B&D relationship is as much based on the guidance of the submissive as of the dominant. A good scene caters well to the desires of the dominated within the safe, agreed boundaries. There are life-style practitioners, of course, but most of us have a day-job and go about our business as most people in mainstream culture. But we allow ourselves to explore, to fantasize, to take calculated risks, to seduce and be seduced, to play and to pretend. At the core, it is about sexual pleasure—not humiliation."

David absorbed every word of this verbal *tour de force* from this articulate, young woman dressed as a lawyer. He turned to Diane who pulled him closer and kissed his cheek.

The fourth talk was introduced by a tall, overweight gentleman—Mark—dressed in a huge diaper and tank top. As he proceeded to show various adult diapers, David turned to Diane and whispered: "How long will this go on?"

She flashed a big smile, took his hand, and pulled him up to leave. Richard stamped his card as they left. As they walked back to the Metro, she asked, "Were you shocked?"

"Not really. The first guy made a lot of sense. He was obviously knowledgeable about rope bondage, and I don't find anything strange about that if it is consensual. It just seems really constraining and complicated and probably not for me. The oils, well, nice fragrances can be sensual, and massage with oil can be great. Then, the diaper stuff…no way…that is just not sexy. Is it about escaping back to childhood? But the woman—Anita—she was something else! I've never heard such an articulate defense of masochism."

"I've not heard her speak before. But there's a book that I'll lend you. It's written by Anita Phillips—another Anita. It's called *A Defense of Masochism*. Not an easy read, very philosophical, but eloquent, I think. She writes about masochism as "...a very intelligent perversion.""

They trolled along in silence as that line sank in.

"I was surprised how 'normal' people looked in that meeting. It could almost have been a PTA meeting!" David laughed.

"Well, did you expect a freak show? People who have erotic fantasies don't look any different, although they might dress up at times. Sure, there are lifestyle doms and bottoms, but most of these guys will go home, cook dinner, and read to their children like everyone else."

"OK, but did you recognize anyone?"

Diane stopped, grabbed his arm, and faced him with a stern expression. "David, I will never out anybody, including you. If you recognize somebody from another context but haven't been properly introduced, you don't show it. Discretion is very important. There are some high-ranking members in this association who would lose their jobs, their security clearance, and more if their sexual preferences became publicly known. There are a few who openly represent this community, but most of them just want to be left alone."

David regretted his question and looked for a way out. "Another thing, why did Richard stamp my card when we left?"

"When you have two stamps, you can apply to come to one of the Yellow Cactus play parties. But you still have to attend an orientation session first. There's a certain etiquette you need to learn. Just so you know, there are other special interest groups that are into other things as well. Like tickling, hypnosis, needle play, golden showers…"

"You must be kidding! Tickling?"

"Well, to each his own. As long as it is consensual and among adults, why judge them?"

"Your ex-husband, did he join you for these meetings?"

"He did, several times. Carlos had several strong fetishes and was really fascinated by rope bondage. But there were also problems with him. First, he wanted me to exclusively play with him. Then, he wanted to make me a switch."

"A what?"

"A 'switch' is a person who can alternate between being dominant and submissive. That's just not me. I'm not wired that way. I'm dominant, period!"

David had secretly wondered if he could ask her to be submissive. Better not try that. Besides, it seemed so strange to him—a believer in the equality of women—to ask somebody to be submissive to him.

"You said he wanted exclusivity, but you didn't want that? Weren't you married though?"

"We were, and I did love him then. I didn't really want the marriage, but his visa was running out. Marriage was his ticket to a green card and later citizenship. We had quite a simple civil ceremony with two witnesses. That was all, but it wasn't fake. Most people exchange vows and promise monogamous love until death do them part. But you see, I never promised Carlos that, and he did not promise me that either. He had a roving eye and made no apologies for it. So why should I?"

Diane made clear that there would be no sex that night, but she invited him for a "shopping trip" the weekend after next. "Don't masturbate until then," she sweetly advised.

David came home to his studio all fired up with fantasies. Something new and exciting was happening—he wasn't quite sure what. He put on a CD with Andreas Vollenweider's *Trigon* and turned up the furious saxophone solo so loud that a neighbor started banging on the wall. But David was euphoric and beyond caring.

CHAPTER 18

Mission to Swabania

The plane arrived four hours later than scheduled at the international airport outside the capital of Swabania. Passengers descended the stairs and crossed the tarmac to the arrival building. It was hot and humid with no breeze to mitigate the feeling of a wet blanket wrapping around his body. The poorly lit tarmac smelled of airplane gasoline, and a jet plane revved up its roaring engines for takeoff.

JP had talked David into joining his environmentally focused mission to Swabania. "It's important that you get exposure to different kinds of missions—that you broaden your experience. I know you care about the environment, so here's a chance for you. Come with me!" he had argued.

The immigration line was short, but only one officer handled non-citizens, and the lady behind the raised counter was meticulous and in a bad mood. She was seated behind glass, making it hard to hear what she said, so she resorted to barking orders. "Return ticket!" This poor country seemed anxious that nobody would enter to stay behind and become wards of the state. Stamps were entered on all the right papers, and she dismissed David by loudly yelling "Next!"

The customs control consisted of a large X-ray machine where everything had to be fed through. Whatever it was they were searching for, it was unlikely that it would be caught. The two operators were busy trading stories and did not look at the computer screen as David's checked luggage, hand luggage, and jacket were all slowly passing through the humming beast.

Before he could pick up his luggage, a porter swept it all up and dashed toward the exit. David insisted on carrying the

183

computer bag himself but had to tear it from the porter's hand. There was no need for a porter, but it was an informal employment scheme that David empathized with.

At the exit, he handed over his duly filled, lengthy, and detailed customs declaration. He had declared under penalty of harsh jail punishment and bankrupting fines that he did not carry illegal drugs, weapons, pornography, liquor in excess of one liter, merchandise for sale without an import permit, or literature dedicated to the violent overthrow of the government. The officer took it and waved him through without sacrificing even a split second to look at the form.

The World Bank Country Office was supposed to have sent a driver, but David could not see anyone holding a sign with his name when he came out from customs. But there were plenty of willing drivers at hand. He was quickly encircled by young men. "What hotel, sir?" "Good car, air condition!" "Fast car!"

David avoided the fast-car guy and went toward a man who carried some kind of official-looking badge. It may be meaningless, but most of the others had no ID. Nobody had a uniform that identified them as taxi drivers. Free market indeed.

He plowed through the throng of young men out to the parking lot in front of the terminal with the porter and the driver. A third helper suddenly appeared and grabbed the small cabin bag. The two porters seemed to know each other. At the car, the two porters lined up to be paid. U.S. dollars were widely accepted, and David was prepared with small change. It had been a very short walk, and he extended a dollar bill to each one of them. They declared that only one dollar would be an insult and asked for two each. It was late, he was tired, and outnumbered. Why argue?

"What's your name?" he asked the driver. Maybe it was just silly, but he wanted to establish some rapport if he could. He carried an expensive computer and phone and cash worth a lifetime of hard work for most people in the country. Credit cards had limited use outside the best hotels, and travelers' cheques were cumbersome and expensive to cash. So, he had to carry enough cash to see him through two weeks. If he could appear as a friendly person and not as an arrogant rich White, perhaps he would be safer.

There were stories of taxi drivers robbing their passengers and of ambushes set up along the way from the airport where other gang members took over the ride and stripped the visitor of everything valuable. Occasionally, things got out of hand. It was rare, but fatalities had been reported. David shifted uncomfortably in his seat, but this was part of the job.

"I'm Joe, sir." That was unlikely to be his real name, but the driver was probably tired of repeating a longer, indigenous name to foreigners. "What hotel?"

"Hilton, please."

"Best hotel. Very expensive."

It was top of the line, and one of the few in Swabania approved for Bank staff. Just saying the address would identify you as somebody with deep pockets. He asked Joe about his family, and Joe was clearly proud of his wife and three children. He even handed over a set of pictures that he kept in the car. David leaned back in his seat more relaxed and volunteered a story about his own wife and two small children. Humanizing stuff.

After a five-minute ride, they were stopped at a police checkpoint. The police officer shone a bright light directly into Joe's eyes and ordered him out. Joe complied without saying anything. A conversation ensued in front of the car. David opened the window. They did not speak English. Joe pulled something out from his pocket and handed it to the police officer. Joe returned to the car, started it, and got waived through.

Joe was silent. "Did they demand money?" David asked.

"Yes. Airport is good ride. They say pay. If don't, they find wrong with car. Write big ticket. Or feel pockets. Pull money."

They drove on in silence. As they entered the suburbs, Joe spoke up again.

"Sometimes, police no pay. Then, we pay!"

It was well-known that public servants in Swabania sometimes went without pay for long stretches. This would fuel a wave of bribe-taking. It could hit not only police but any kind of permit that needed to be issued. Inspectors of all kinds made surprise rounds and noted with concern some deficiency that would potentially close down the restaurant, the construction of a house, the operation of a service business, and so on. A small envelope with "encouragement" to the inspector eliminated the issue efficiently. If it was successful, it was hard to pull back from such a lucrative practice. They became cemented into routine and tended to escalate unless met with firm resistance, such as violence. An organized protection racket emerged as one response. No wonder small businesses had a hard time flourishing. Larger ones could better afford to pay themselves, free from harassment.

Joe looked at David in the rearview mirror and smiled. "Sir, not to worry. You are White. Police want no trouble with you."

The first suburbs were clusters of informal settlements— slums. New arrivals from the countryside flocked here, hoping to get a bite out of the tempting urban apple, but few were lucky. The houses were heaps of whatever building material could be gathered, begged, borrowed, or stolen. They approached a major crossing, and the signals were clearly red, but Joe just slowed down to watch traffic and then sped up to avoid a collision.

David sat up straight and scanned the cross streets. "You don't stop for red lights?"

"Robbers here. You stop, they rob!"

Fortunately, there were no more traffic lights until they entered more of a middle-class neighborhood. Joe was still watchful and kept the engine running, prepared to take off immediately if needed. Further toward the city center, the scenery changed again, as did Joe's driving. At a well-lit crossing in an upscale neighborhood, with security guards visible in several of the entrances to shiny office buildings, Joe turned off the engine.

"Save petrol," he explained. He continued to save petrol at every crossing until they reached their destination. They arrived safely at the Hilton, and David rounded up the payment, hoping it would cover the police bribe as well.

In his room that night, he tried to call Diane but could only leave a message. It annoyed him that he was unable to go shopping with her as they had planned the previous weekend, but the mission dates were moved at the request of the Government of Swabania, and he suddenly had to leave.

***

The next morning, a red-eyed, sleep-deprived David met up with JP in the hotel's posh cafeteria. JP was in a cheerful mood. He had persuaded David to join him on this exploratory environmental mission to Swabania. The country was extremely poor but rich in biodiversity, according to reports from Western scientists who had dutifully catalogued its riches since colonial times. With new political stability in the country and new donor money, it was possible to look for ways of harnessing the potential for environmental protection coupled with tourism development. Perhaps there could be a project funded with a grant from the Global Environment Facility?

The Bank had a marginal involvement in the tourism business traditionally. It was seen as something for the private sector to capitalize on. One had to be careful of not overextending the public sector. But there was a need for an institutional framework that provided comfort to private capital. If investors feared sudden confiscation, pervasive corruption, and a deficient infrastructure, there would be no capital flows coming. In addition, foreign investors may have little concern for actually protecting the environment rather than building massive blocks of hotels that spewed out sewage over sensitive coral reefs. Hence, JP had been tasked to lead a mission to start the long-term efforts at updating the resource inventory, stimulating an institutional framework for sustainable tourism development and market the results through an international donor conference.

Most operational Bank staff avoided such "small potato projects" if they could. The way to build a career in the Bank was to take big chunks of money in a nice package to the board. Large-scale budget support was the best way, as it did away with some of the nitty-gritty, maddening details of a more specific investment project. Those invariably brought out vicious inter-ministerial rivalry, not to mention special interest groups within the Bank. But if you fed the Ministry of Finance with a massive financial injection, you could get by with general descriptions of the healthy economic impacts spreading like a chocolate sugar high in a starved body. That's how you collected gold stars in senior management's master ledger.

While it was not his area of primary expertise as a development economist, David had a genuine interest in the environment. He also enjoyed going on missions with JP who was full of stories about the Bank and about life in general. If there was a decent restaurant in the country, JP would know.

After breakfast, they made their way to the Ministry of Tourism, only a short walk from their hotel. The reception area was empty, and no signs indicated where the Minister might have his office. David hastened down a corridor and found a janitor. He asked for "Minister" and repeated this a few times. The janitor smiled and showed three fingers.

They approached the most impressive-looking doors on the third floor. A young official greeted them, expressing regret that the Minister of Tourism had been called away for "an urgent meeting." His English was halting, but an interpreter appeared with some delay. They were joined by a British woman, Margaret Huntington, who apparently served as an advisor to the Ministry. This was not surprising, given the beehive of donor activity that had sprung up in Swabania. It was impossible to keep track of all the initiatives, and delegations kept bumping into each other at the few hotels that foreigners found to be of acceptable quality.

Few bureaucrats spoke fluent English, and with the centralized bureaucracy, there was little appetite for risk-taking and initiative. Hence, everything was guided from the very top, and the few qualified staff that the country could muster spent a great deal of their days seeing foreign delegations. In addition, some of the most qualified public sector staff were recruited into much more lucrative jobs with foreign donors or NGOs.

JP introduced the mission objectives, which, of course, had been communicated well in advance and agreed upon by the Swabania government. As a general starter, he asked the counterpart official for his overall assessment of the tourism potential. While the translator conveyed this, Margaret leaned forward.

"We don't want mass tourism. This must not be a new mecca for sex tourism like that dreadful Thailand."

David and JP exchanged glances. The interpreter came back with the young official's response.

"You are welcome in my country. Now, we can develop. If we get money, we know what to do. Many people are waiting for new money. The Ministry needs new cars, Toyota Landcruiser best."

They waited for more, but that was apparently the message. Margaret explained. "What my counterpart is saying is that we don't want a lot of foreign consultants and donors to pervert the process. It must be built on a genuine, local stakeholder consultation."

And here she is talking on their behalf, David thought. *The irony seems to escape her.*

Margaret laid out her vision eloquently. "This country needs eco-development based on small, local initiatives. There is rich biodiversity here and a large number of endemic species. There's no charismatic megafauna, but the bird life is spectacular, and there are some rare species of monkeys and amphibians."

Margaret folded out a large map of Swabania. "There are mountains covered with undisturbed rainforest and a few small, decent beaches—but unfortunately not much marine life to attract visitors. The few coral reefs have been demolished by dynamite fishing and dredging for a new harbor. It's probably the World Bank's fault," she added with a frown.

"The Bank is not involved in that 'arbor project," objected JP. "It's funded by the Chinese."

"Well, then why aren't you?" she snorted. "You should be there to put a stop to that madness."

Damned if you do damned if you don't, David noted.

The Minister never appeared, and the mood was low as JP and David went back to the hotel to prepare for the next visit.

"Our British friend 'as cornered the market for advice to the Ministry. But we 'ave many more contact points."

"How many foreign tourists were there last year?" asked David.

"Nobody's really counting, but the best estimates I 'ave seen say one thousand, maybe two thousand."

"But that's nothing! And now, they fear mass tourism! Why would that suddenly appear when the airport only takes small planes on a short runway, and there's only a few hotels that maintain international standards in the country?"

JP shrugged his shoulders. "People like Margaret are out to preserve the *pristine nature* above everything. But there 'as to be both new income and conservation."

***

The next meeting was with the Ministry of Nature Conservation. Unfortunately, they were not on speaking terms with the Ministry of Tourism. That could be a dilemma for the drafting of a national plan.

There were twenty-two ministries, and they were a major employer in the capital. The Ministry for Foreign Affairs occupied a new, impressive building in the capital's center. The Chinese built it. They had lobbied the government to give up their ties with Taiwan, and now, they were richly rewarded. The Chinese had also begun the construction of a new presidential palace to further cement ties between the People's Republic and Swabania.

The Permanent Secretary, Francisco Rodriguez, was on site and on time. He turned out to be a surprisingly young man, speaking fluent British English. Fresh back from years at Oxford University, he had returned to rejuvenate nature conservation in his native country. His enthusiasm was evident, and he seemed well-briefed. Rodriguez took them on an impressive tour of the country's biodiversity assets. He handed them a list of suggestions, including an upgrade of the only national park, an updated biodiversity inventory, training of staff, engagement with the emerging private sector, community outreach, and so on.

They had just gotten a jackpot! "Rodriguez is our man," gushed JP as they left.

***

That evening, JP and David had dinner at a small, well-run family restaurant. The cook came out and discussed what was on offer. JP took command in the discussion about what to prepare, and the long wait turned out to be worth it. Unfortunately, the wine selection was such that they settled for sparkling water.

"I 'ad an interesting meeting with American environmental NGOs before I left on this trip," JP recalled. "Sometimes, people like me are used as an 'environmental alibi' for the Bank. You know, we are often marginalized in internal discussions. The chairperson often calls upon us at the very end of a meeting, signaling an implicit pecking order. Plus, I'm often dismissed as a 'troublemaker' when I insist on respect for the rules about environmental impact assessments. But when environmental NGOs come to the Bank, we are trotted out like a shield to defuse the situation."

"Hmm, what was the meeting about, then?'

"Well, there is a review process again about 'ow we do EIAs from various angles. The NGOs want to weigh in, of course. They want environmental protection at all costs. Management 'as moved from ignoring and stonewalling them as they did when I first joined the Bank. Now, there is an attitude of 'let them come with their demands so that, at least, they can't shoot us down in the press for ignoring them.'" He stopped to taste the fish sauce, and his face broke out in a satisfied grin. "*Merveilleux!*"

"But aren't some of the NGOs quite reasonable and in fact, working with the Bank in various field projects? I've even met some former NGO staff who are now our colleagues. They seem very competent and driven—at least the ones I've met."

"True, but some of the environmentalists on the outside are dogmatic. They want to tear down the Bank. Some of them 'ave no sense of the desperate need for poverty alleviation. They would rather 'ave an untouched museum of nature where a small elite of enthusiasts wouldn't be bothered by regular tourists. Some of them romanticize the traditional life of poor, indigenous people. But many of them actually want a more modern life. It's their choice to make, I think," JP concluded.

"Maybe we can find a way to balance the eco-vision with development of commercial tourism. Of course, we are only here to contribute to the legal and institutional framework, but we could also try to get money from the Global Environment Facility for an investment program along the lines proposed by Rodriquez," David suggested.

***

The next morning, they traveled to the national park a few hours outside the capital as Rodriguez had suggested. All the legal steps in creating the park had not been fulfilled, and lawyers within the country could not agree if the park had the protected status of a national park or of a conservation area that was much more vulnerable to exploitation if such interests would arise. David promised to engage Bob at HQ to review the documents. Bob was his trusted mentor for many things including legal matters.

Unfortunately, Rodriguez could not join them, but he sent an assistant and a driver. The young man, Rodrigo, looked like he was sixteen and spoke little English. But he was critical in finding the national park since the road became increasingly bad as they left the capital.

After an hour on bumpy roads, they turned into a field.

"There," said the young man, "the sign."

There was a metal pole shaped like an inverted L where the entrance sign to the park had once hung. The sheet metal had presumably found a better use, but the rusty pole was still there. They drove in the lowest gear possible over rocks and fallen tree limbs on the barely discernible road up to the park building.

There was no telephone line to the park nor any other form of working communication, so it was not a surprise that nobody greeted them. The young assistant dashed out to collect the staff, which he said numbered about a dozen. He had been to the park before to deliver payment to the staff.

JP and David surveyed the dilapidated site. The building was in terrible shape. The roof was leaking, some doors were off their hinges and had been placed next to the opening, only one toilet flushed—with some hesitancy—and there was no material for interpretation of biodiversity. A dusty logbook revealed that the last visitor had been there six months earlier—a professor of botany from the U.S. There were nominal guest quarters for a half-dozen people, but there

194

were no signs that they had been recently occupied. Some beds lacked mattresses.

Outside, cattle and some horses grazed on what was supposed to be protected land. They presumed that this was in fact the main source of income for the national park staff, as the visitors were so few, and payment of salaries from the Ministry were unreliable.

The young assistant appeared triumphantly with the Chief Conservation Officer, a Mr. Goncalves. He seemed genuinely happy to greet visitors. He described in his own language what the park needed, and the eager assistant translated, while adding his own views now and then.

They drove back from the park with a sense that it would be easy to improve upon the dismal state of this potential crown jewel in the country's biodiversity. As darkness fell, they had to slow down to avoid potholes and stray dogs and cattle.

"We need gas," the driver noted as the red light lit up on the dashboard.

Fortunately, they could reach a gas station with only a short detour. As they drive up the hill to the tiny town, the sun was setting and silhouettes became sharper. At the top of a hill was the single pump gas station that would save them. The attendant sat leaning against the pump, slowly smoking a cigarette.

***

After an intense week of visits, calls, and report writing, the framework for a program took shape. The list of needs was long, but the budget would be the constraining factor. They put it all in a summary aide-memoire to be agreed to by the main national counterpart in the Ministry of Planning. Unfortunately, nobody was available to meet them at the agreed time, so they had to leave the documentation with an assistant to the Minister. They would follow up from HQ.

At the end of the mission, they met with the Minister of Tourism who actually showed up. He apologized for his previous absence and clarified that he had been at a United Nations conference in New York and then a Donor Forum in Paris for the past two weeks. No wonder he did not have time to meet the Bank delegation. The Minister reviewed the aide-memoire and had only encouraging comments. The project could open some financial flows to his country. They were leaving on a high note.

"Gentlemen, are you going back to Washington, D.C. now?" the Minister asked as they made their way toward the door.

"Yes," JP confirmed.

"I have two sons in that area, and they really like it there."

"Studying?" David inquired.

"They've graduated now, and honestly, I don't think they will ever come back," he sighed. "There's really no future for them here."

JP and David exchanged sad glances but said nothing. David left with heavy steps.

***

David arrived at Dulles International Airport about an hour after the scheduled ETA. Few passengers queued in the arrival hall, so he sailed through immigration. This time, the officer even added a friendly "welcome back" after a couple of perfunctory questions.

David ignored the unofficial taxi operators who often hung around in the international arrival hall and approach passengers with an offer of a "cheap ride." At least, they were not as pushy as the hustlers in most arrival halls in developing countries. He got in line for the authorized taxis and did not have to wait long for a cab. He gave the address and settled in. The driver had a typical South Asian accent, and a small flag on the dashboard confirmed it. There were also two small pictures of a smiling young man and a girl.

"Your children?"

"Yes! My son is now twenty-two. Studying engineering. He'll be very successful." There was no doubt about his pride.

"And your daughter?"

"She is seventeen, and she will also go to college before marriage."

"What do you think she will study? Engineering as well?"

"Oh no, not engineering for her. I haven't decided yet."

What now? Stand up for women's equal rights? That would be the honorable thing to do. But it would be passing judgment on ingrained cultural attitudes. He would just be seen as another White person with a "colonial" attitude. David slumped a bit in the back seat as the rain pelted the window in streams. *His daughter will have to manage her own rebellion—if that is what she wants.*

CHAPTER 19

Shopping with Diane

Back home again, David met Diane, as agreed, outside the Bethesda Metro in Maryland. But instead of going down the stairs, Diane led him to a parking lot where a rental car was waiting. On the drive out to Gaithersburg, Maryland, she laid down the rules for the day.

"We are going to a place that I know well called 'Fantasies.' They have an assortment of interesting gear for people who are into Bondage & Dominance. I want to push your boundaries a bit. Of course, you'll have definite, hard boundaries, but they may be more flexible than you realize now. We'll explore that together and see how far you can go."

David adjusted his position in his car seat. Again, she was in charge. He had been to sex stores before, but with her, he could not be sure how this would end. It was exciting though! It was a short car ride. As they stopped outside the store, Diane laid out the rules.

"We go in together as a couple. I'll allow you to pick five things for me to wear, and I'll pick five for you. We decide on our own picks. Sounds fair, right?"

"So, there is equality in this relationship after all," teased David.

"Of course. For example, I'll pay half the bill, you the other."

She did not wait for any discussion about that and went to the store. The entrance was low-key and with a small sign only. The windows were covered with blinds that prevented anyone from seeing customers or merchandise inside. A sign warned of "adult material" and barred anyone less than eighteen from entering. They were greeted by a voluptuous, tattooed lady in her forties, fully dressed in black leather.

"Hello, Diane," she said with a smile as they entered. "What have you brought in today?"

David felt like he was on display as the latest prey caught by Diane. But the lady burst out in a hearty laugh and squeezed his arm gently.

"I'm just kidding! We'll fix you up with some good stuff, right? I'm Hanna."

Diane found her number one pick, a face mask in black leather. "It's a beginner's mask," she clarified. It doesn't obstruct your vision and won't be hot. But it'll help you to take on a different persona—it's something to hide behind when you slip into your role."

David liked the idea. For a short while, he had joined an amateur theatre group founded by students at the Copenhagen University. He was fascinated by the "improv" sessions when each new person who stepped in could redirect the scene and everyone else had to play along. It went really crazy sometimes, but the agreed format made crazy totally legitimate. It was hard to really let loose for David, and after a few sessions, he quit. But with Diane, he was willing to try everything.

"Your turn," said Diane.

David got oriented, as the store was large and confusing at first. He drifted toward the lingerie section and looked through an impressive collection of nylons. He found a pair of black ones with a backseam. Nylons had always fascinated him. It started in his early years when he found his mom's pantyhose in the laundry pile. Something about the smooth feel and the luster of the fine texture made for a titillating experience. He even tried them on, but looking at himself in the mirror, he quickly removed them and felt ashamed. No, he was not a cross-dresser.

Hanna asked if he wanted stockings with a "Cuban heel," but David didn't know. She showed him a pair, and he agreed that would be great. One down, four to go.

Diane had no problem finding her second pick and put a tiny, black nylon thong for males on the counter. It was medium, and Hanna produced a tape measure to check David's waist. He got the feeling that she enjoyed this little "scene." Thankfully, there were no other customers in the store.

David's second pick was a given, as the stockings required a garter belt. Hanna suggested a black, lacy set with four straps, and it was added to the pile.

It was Diane's turn, and she pulled out a set of wrist restraints. She took her time to try out several pairs on him in front of a mirror. He found the situation increasingly erotic. The pair she settled for was adjustable and a softer kind that was nice to your skin. They also had a hook to allow them to be linked together, if needed. David's pulse increased as the items were gathered and his imagination accelerated.

Another customer entered, and David ducked into the lingerie department again for cover. It was unlikely that anyone he knew would show up, but he felt embarrassed. He did feel excited about being there with Diane. She would push his envelope but not beyond consent. He found the shoe section and weighed a pair of six-inch pumps in his hands.

"What's your size?" he asked.

"Eight. I won't be able to walk in those, but I could wear them in bed. If you go down to four inches, I could stand firmly and actually walk on them. It depends a bit on the type of shoe. Stability can be important in some kinds of play." She left the rest to his imagination.

Hanna appeared now, having dispatched the other customer. "If you are into trampling..." she started and laughed at David's puzzled look.

"We won't go there—for now," said Diane and waved it off. Hanna retreated.

At David's suggestion, Diane tried a pair of five-inch sandals in red. The impact on David was instantaneous as she took a few steps and showed off her legs. Her calf muscles tightened, and her buttocks firmed up under the tight skirt. She became even taller and towering, more powerful, and dominant. It was a buy.

Next, Diane selected a set of nipple clamps. She explained to David that these were fully adjustable and perfectly suitable for a "beginner" like him. David was not entirely sure, but he knew better than to second-guess her.

It was logical that David's next item would be a sexy bra to match his previous choices. Hanna allowed Diane to try them on, and she pushed David into the fitting room for them to decide together. After testing three, they found a great match and a good fit. The style was exceptionally low-cut, just baring the nipples, and in a semi-transparent style that was not far from what she had worn on their first date.

Diane's final pick was a blindfold. David could not hold back his alarm at that choice. It may seem innocent, but to David, it represented a severe punishment—being unable to watch her. It would be a great turn-off.

"Please no," he blurted out.

Diane glared at him. "You know the rules. It's my pick..." Diane put both hands on her waist in a posture he had seen his mom use when she scolded him as a child. "But if it's really important to you, I will allow an exception for once." She put back the blindfold and went for a perforated gag ball in red with a black leather strap to be tightened around the head. "This is what you get for speaking out of turn." It was her fifth item.

David hesitated with just one pick left. He would like to see her in so many things. Bodystockings, corsets, panties, high-heel boots, long gloves ... But a set of large hoop earrings charmed him. He could never explain why those were sexy—they just were. He put number five on the counter, and Hanna rang it all up. But she could not help putting in an extra plug.

"We have a special deal on floggers and riding crops this week," she announced.

Diane flashed a broad smile at David who looked a bit intimidated. "We are well-equipped in that department already," she reassured them both. She snapped out her credit card and asked Hanna to charge her half.

David had pulled out cash, as he wanted to avoid any trace on his credit card. He was not sure why he was concerned, but somehow it offended his sense of privacy to leave a trail.

Diane pulled David aside and told him to put on the thong she had picked, and he went back to the fitting room.

Diane drove on the way back as well and hummed with the music on the radio. With her eyes on the road, she extended her right hand and massaged his crotch gently. David groaned as he felt the tight thong straining against his erection. He had heard the song before but couldn't place it, as his brain had closed down everything but its rewards system.

"You're the right kind of sinner to release my inner fantasy..." she hummed. "Honey, do you want me to stop?" she asked. Her voice was sweet, her eyes still firmly on the road, and a mischievous smile on her lips.

"No! ... aaahhh ... but you're driving me crazy!"

"Take out the wrist cuffs," Diane ordered.

She pulled off the main road and went into the parking lot of a small park. There were only a few people there, and they were too far away to see what was going on in their car. She told him to turn his back toward her and pulled his arms back and cuffed him. "Lean back." She unzipped his pants and wiggled out his stiffness into freedom. He was breathing heavily.

"Diane, please, you can't do it here!"

"I'll be the judge of that."

The whole visit had been erotically charged, and David's excitement level was already blinking red. It took just a few strokes of her soft hand before he let out a guttural roar as he felt an irresistible, warm wave of relief sweeping over him.

"This is when you say, 'Thank you, Mistress,'" Diane instructed with a naughty smile. She uncuffed him, handed him some Kleenex, and he cleaned up while she drove. "Clean the dashboard good. It's a rental," she reminded him. She hummed again.

As his brain regained normal functions, it came to him: it was Pat Benatar's "Heartbreaker" she had been humming.

It was clear to David that Diane was taking him into a new realm of erotic adventure—one that he could never have envisaged for himself before meeting her. But there was so much more than exciting sex. He felt good about meeting her for an innocent coffee in the cafeteria where they might exchange reviews of books they were reading or talk about U.S. current events or a movie one of them recommended. Sometimes, she asked his views on parenting her young son. Things just clicked with her. They had different interests, of course, but there was a lot of common ground, and there was definitely *chemistry*—that inscrutable but necessary ingredient in a successful relationship. She was a lot different from Julia, but he had come to recognize the same sense of profound engagement and joy. Another adjustment to his life plan was in the making, and there was no way he could stop it.

***

They returned the rental car and got a short ride back to the Metro. David looked for ways of prolonging their time together and insisted on walking with her to her apartment. "For protection," he insisted.

"Of you or me?" she responded. But she hooked into his arm and started walking.

"How long have you been playing as a dominatrix?"

"I always had an independent, even tough, streak in me. My two older brothers would tease me a lot, and I learned to stand up for myself. They played a lot of pick-up soccer, and I joined them, playing with boys. When they hit on me, I gave as good as I got. On more than one occasion, I ended up kneeing a persistent stalker in the groin. The message worked, and they left me alone after that. The next step when I was about fifteen was for me to initiate conversations and flirting. Some boys would immediately go overboard, but I learned to coach those situations."

"So, when did you first have intercourse? I hope you don't mind me asking."

"I was fifteen. It wasn't great. We were both nervous. But he was cute, my age, and I liked experimenting sexually with him. When he didn't want to do something, I threated to tell my older brothers that he had sex with me. That got him into line!"

"Wow! That wasn't very nice of you—a real power trip."

"Yes, I'm not proud of it, and some years later, I apologized sincerely to him. He just laughed and said it was the best introduction to sex that he could have asked for."

They strolled in silence for a block, and David was unsure how to continue. She made a preventive move. "David, I'm not going to let you interrogate me about my sexual history and every boyfriend or playmate I've had. My ex-husband was obsessed about finding out every detail, and I had to put a stop to it."

"Sure, I would never dream of pursuing that line," David lied.

They stopped outside the entrance to her apartment building. David could not contain his curiosity.

"You have this long experience over many years. And I can tell that you are exceptionally good at what you're doing. Do you ever…eh, charge for playing?"

Diane slapped him so hard with her right hand that he jumped back from her, holding his burning, red cheek in his hands.

"Is that answer clear enough for you?" Her composed sarcasm added more sting to his cheek.

"I didn't mean to imply that you're—"

"Don't dig your hole deeper now," she interrupted. Diane raised her hand again, and he bolted away from her. She turned around, entered the access code, and marched through the door without saying goodbye.

Deflated, David took the Metro home. He had no idea she could flare up like that. But maybe it would wear off just as quickly? He started composing an apologetic text message but struggled to find the right tone. Maybe it was best to let her cool off first? Should he send her a longer email instead? Maybe sending flowers would work better? As he debated various options, he forgot to get off to switch trains at Metro Center station and had to backtrack. He had to figure out a way to fix this!

That evening, he took both an Ambien and a large glass of his favorite Cousiño-Macul wine, the top-of-the-line Lota. It was a combination against good advice. He found Joe Bonamassa's "Sloe Gin" on a CD and put it on. The sophisticated red wine was a long way from a drink of Sloe Gin, but the lyrics about loneliness seemed appropriate.

CHAPTER 20

Free at Last

The early morning light shone through David's tiny cell window. Several vehicles came roaring into the village, followed by bursts from automatic weapons. There was screaming and yelling.

A few minutes later, the door to his cell burst open, and a young man in a military uniform entered with his weapon at the ready. He halted when he saw David, stunned. Then, he turned around and yelled something. Three more soldiers pushed into the small room. One of them knelt down to David who was lying down on his mat, unsure of the situation.

"OK?" the soldier inquired.

They had uniforms; they were not Allah's Soldiers. *They must be with the National Army or maybe some local militia,* he thought. Their uniforms were torn and dirty, but the important thing was that they had them. They had finally come, and they could be his ticket to freedom!

"OK!" he blurted out, suddenly energized by the situation in spite of his lingering pain from the beating. But what if they thought he was a White Warrior among Allah's Soldiers? They might simply shoot him.

There was more shouting, small arms fire, and a distant explosion. An officer now appeared. His uniform was crisp and clean. He wore a sidearm, but no other weapon.

"Prisoner?" he asked with a thick accent.

"Yes, prisoner." A powerful wave of relief swept over him, and he started crying.

The officer barked an order, and not long afterwards, a young man in a uniform with a red cross armband appeared and proceeded to check his body. He spoke no English but seemed to know what to look for. David screamed as he touched his left arm, his ribs, and his back. The medic gave some instructions to one of the soldiers who quickly left. The medic opened a small box and took out a large, white pill. He held it up in his open hand.

David decided to trust him and took it. He was immediately offered some water from a flask. Whatever it was, he needed to get rid of the pain.

The soldier soon returned with a big duffle bag marked with a red cross. The medic took out a large pair of scissors and carefully cut open David's shirt. He removed it so that any wounds could be visible and treated. The medic did not bat an eyelid as he went over the wounds from the whipping, cleaning them and putting compresses on them. He had probably seen much worse.

One of the soldiers got agitated as he saw the whipping marks on David's body and unleashed a long tirade before leaving the room in a hurry. Perhaps out to exact revenge?

The medic took out a splint and applied it to David's left arm. He secured it with a sling around David's neck. The medic and a soldier carefully lifted David up to a standing position, and the medic pulled down David's pants to inspect his lower body. The teenager had whipped him a couple of times over the legs but without much conviction. There were only bruises.

The officer returned. On his command, two soldiers supported David as they lumbered out of the building. The bright sunshine was brutal in David's eyes, but he could see that in front of the building, a group of some twenty villagers were seated. They all looked very frightened and were sitting down with their hands in zip ties on their backs. The officer took a menacing posture at the periphery of the encircled men. He yelled at them and waved his pistol in the air.

David could not understand a word but imagined that the officer was asking for information. But had they even known about David?

It was apparent that the officer did not receive the information he was looking for. In frustration, he simply shot the man closest to him in the head. He tumbled over, bleeding profusely. Some villagers cried in anger and fear, but there was nothing more they could do. Some were mumbling to themselves, perhaps praying. He thought he heard the words *Allahu Akbar*. The villagers were not cooperative. The officer yelled another order and one of the villagers was lined up against the wall and unceremoniously shot.

Pour encourager les autres, once again, David thought. Both sides of this struggle abide by this thinking.

New yelling, new questions, but only cries and murmurs from the villagers.

The officer turned to David. "Tell me who kept you prisoner! Tell me who beat you!"

If the hardass Big Man had only been there, David would gladly have given him away. But then, he realized that the two teenagers were actually among the seated prisoners. He met the pleading gaze of one of them. He was silently pleading for mercy while the other one was too afraid to look at him. They were so young.

If I give them away, they might shoot them or, at least, beat them severely. But if I let them go, they might become full-fledged warriors among Allah's Soldiers, David thought. Either way, lives were in the balance.

209

The officer watched his gaze like a hawk. He marched over and readied his gun at the head of the youngster staring at David.

"No, no, not him!" David blurted out.

The officer lowered his gun but kept yelling at the villagers.

Only a few steps away from the circle of villagers, two soldiers pulled out two frightened, screaming women from a hut. They dragged them behind a small, brick house, and there was more screaming. This agitated the villagers, and some of them tried to stand up. They were quickly beaten down.

This is no way to win hearts and minds, he thought bitterly.

A soldier with a large backpack with an antenna came up to the officer, and they talked briefly. The officer grinned and pointed to David who had sunk down to the ground in horror during the killing spree. Two soldiers pulled him up and guided him to a jeep where he was put next to the driver. The officer later joined them in the back seat, and they started to navigate out of the village. The sight of merciless killing weighed heavily on David, and he leaned over to vomit outside the car.

The painkiller must have been strong, and David felt the pain receding, replaced by a pleasant brain fog. Where were they going? The driver seemed not to understand English, but the officer yelled, "Back to base now."

After a few kilometers, the jeep and a following truck with soldiers entered a paved road, and the speed picked up. After about an hour, they reached an Army post with the national flag hoisted high on a pole. A tall radio antenna on a hill at the edge of a dusty field towered over several guard posts surrounded by sandbags. Military vehicles were parked outside. They drove straight into the compound and descended from the vehicle.

David was offered one of those ever-present Cokes as they sat down in a sparse conference room. A senior officer with three stars on his shoulders entered and greeted David.

"Welcome! You are now the guest of the National Army, 22nd Brigade. We have received some information about you." His English was cultured, with local and British accents. David began to feel more hopeful. "Please confirm your name."

"David Pederson. I work for the World Bank in Washington, D.C., USA."

The officer nodded, unsurprised. A soldier came with a camera and took several pictures of David. He was also asked to pose next to the smiling officer. Things got even better from there. He was given the chance to shower under a bucket that had been propped up behind a curtain. A soldier delivered new clothes and a pair of flip flops. There was a tiny mirror in the improvised shower, and David recoiled at his own image. His beard had grown long and wild, his hair was long and unkept, his eyes red and swollen, and the weight loss was written all over his body. He had aged ten years in—what?—maybe two months' time.

David was desperate to get in touch with Diane and his mom. He had thought about them both in agony and dreamt about them being distraught. *They must be suffering so much*, he kept thinking. But the base only had a radio connection with other Army units and no civilian telephone service.

***

There was a small airfield next to the base, and the next morning, a small, civilian airplane landed. Two gentlemen in civilian khakis stepped out. David was given a ride out to meet them.

"Mr. Pedersen, great to see you alive! I'm Roger Brownstone from the American Embassy."

"Hello, I'm Mateo Lopez from the Bank's Country Office. I have warm greetings from our president who is keen to meet you as soon as you are able. How are you feeling? Are you in a condition to travel?"

"It's great to be alive—and free! Thank you. Yes, I'm foggy from the pain killers, and I don't move well, but I really want to get back. Do you have a phone I could use to call the U.S. and Denmark, please?"

"Sorry, we can't get any coverage out here, but we'll arrange it as soon as we get back. The flight is only an hour."

He yearned to make those calls, but it just had to wait. "Well, I don't have any luggage to check in," quipped David, and they all laughed. "Let's go!"

***

The small plane landed at the capital's international airport in bright sunshine. A car drove up to the plane, and David was driven directly to a clinic used by the international diplomatic corps.

The doctor checked his vitals and did a quick check on his medical status. "Your heart sounds fine, and your lungs are clear. You are dehydrated, and we'll put you on a drip right away. You probably have a fracture on your left arm and on some ribs. We'll do some X-rays. Clearly, you have lost a lot of weight. But you have been imprisoned for a short time only and should recover quickly on that account. You need to leave a stool sample for analysis. Intestinal worms and giardiasis are common in the area where you were picked up.

We'll draw some blood for a simple analysis right away. You should also see a trauma counselor and perhaps a psychiatrist. We can offer some basic lab analysis here, but you should have a more thorough checkup when you get home."

David asked Mateo again about a phone, and this time, he was given one that could make international calls. He asked to be alone and dialed Diane. He took some deep breaths to compose himself for the call. After several failed attempts, he got through.

"Hello," Diane said.

Suddenly, his composure was gone, and he opened and closed his mouth without being able to speak. Tears started flowing, but no words.

"Hello, who's calling please?" she said. "Hello."

The sound of her voice ripped apart the mental shield that he had grown during captivity. *I could have died, I could have lost her*, he realized with brutal clarity. He had to support himself against the concrete wall and slowly slid down to the ground, clasping the phone with both hands.

"I ... love you," he pressed forth with all his effort.

It was her turn to cry, and for several minutes, they exchanged sobs and fragments of sentences about love ... longing ... relief ... agony that was now over ... and when he was coming home.

He had to take a long break and gather himself before calling his mom. He was more composed this time, but his mom dissolved in tears. It was a long call on a poor line.

***

David was hurriedly flown back to Europe in an ambulance plane accompanied by a nurse. He was brought to a medical center close to the Frankfurt am Main Airport, where he had changed planes so many times. He got a thorough medical checkup with extensive blood work.

A representative from the Danish Embassy showed up at the clinic to welcome him on behalf of his home country. He also arranged a Skype call with David's parents.

What David saw shocked him. His mom was in tears, of course, but so was his father. He had never seen his father cry, but he was barely able to speak.

"My son, my son ... we thought you were dead ... You look so thin, you poor thing," his mom sobbed. "So many people have been asking about you, praying for you, and supporting us."

David had planned to tell them that he was going back to Washington D.C. as soon as possible. But seeing them both so emotional, he gave in to their pleading and heard himself say, "Of course, I'll come home—as soon as I'm able to travel."

Another Skype connection was arranged, and the gracious Prime Minister of Denmark inquired about his health. She suggested that they meet in person once David had fully recovered. David could not help asking the questions he had thought about so much: Was it true that they had negotiated for his release? Had they launched a search? Had they paid?

The prime minister smiled. "Just don't worry about those things. Enjoy your freedom. The only thing I can tell you on record is that no money was paid. The rest will have to remain a secret."

***

The Embassy kindly arranged his trip home to Denmark. He asked them to keep his return secret, and this was agreed.

On arrival at Kastrup Airport, a group of journalists flocked around him as he emerged from customs. They shouted their questions at him, but he could only capture snippets of them: "... feel to be back ... torture ... exclusive interview ...parents ... World Bank ... a book ...TV ... terrorist ..." They yelled at him and held microphones close to his face.

Flashes blinded his eyes for a moment, and he stood still in confusion before he guided ahead with the help of two police officers. His parents pushed their way through toward him, and they embraced.

"Careful with my ribs!" he yelled. It made for good front-page pictures.

When they finally got on the road in his parents' battered Renault, his father gave an excited account of what had happened when news broke about David's kidnapping. "The Foreign Ministry sent a rep home to us and kept our courage up. He said they had news about you, that you were treated well, but the negotiations were secret. Somehow, the story leaked to the press, and all hell broke loose. We're so proud of you standing up to those bastards! A lot of people reached out to us, even people we had never seen and a Muslim neighbor too."

"Watch the road, Niels," yelled his mom, as his father kept turning to David who was seated next to him.

"Calls every day, many visits, flowers, hot meals, chocolates, many bottles of Gammel Dansk—you name it. So many people remember you and wish you well. The local paper had several articles with interviews with your friends."

"What friends?"

"There were, at least, two girls who said they had been your girlfriend in high school. One was really pretty, Lisa something, I don't remember. And many former classmates were also interviewed. We didn't know you had so many friends."

"You know I never had a girlfriend before university. Even then, it was only for a short time."

"I'll show you the articles. We've saved them all," his father declared, waving his hand, as to show David his folder with clippings. "The mayor of our town wants to hold a celebration for you."

David was more furious than tired. How did people dare to feign past friendship with him? Bullying scenes from school flew through his brain, and he wondered which of the bullies had claimed to be his buddy. And the so-called girlfriends? Was it the same deceitful Lisa who now took another round with him to get fifteen minutes of fame? He wouldn't put it past her to go on TV and cry in a chic dress about her nearly lost former boyfriend.

They arrived home, and David went to his room—his museum—and slept for ten hours. As he woke up, he went to the kitchen and found his parents sitting at the table, sorting through newspaper clippings about himself.

He sat down, and his father peered at him. "Look at this, son," he said proudly and pointed to a full-page article in the local newspaper. Anything written there had unquestionable credibility with Niels.

There it was in plain text: a classmate calling David "a fantastic friend," a math teacher recalling that he was "the most talented student I've ever had" and a professor at the University of Copenhagen regretting that David did not want to pursue an academic career. "He would have gone far, but he was impatient to find applications of economics—he

216

really wanted to get out there and combat poverty." The article also noted that he had been recruited by "the prestigious World Bank, a leading development agency."

His father could not refrain from reading that line out loud. He beamed as he turned to David. "Son, I've thought a lot about this. I got so afraid we had lost you. Then, people started telling me what a great guy you are ... the good work you do. It got me thinking. I haven't really ..." His father kept moving his hands like he was washing them. "I haven't given you credit. I haven't been fair to you."

David could see sincerity written across Niels' face. He had never expected that statement.

His mom pulled his father's hand on top of David's. They both stood up and hugged, just hugged each other hard. "Careful with my ribs!" David reminded him, and his father moved his arms to his shoulders but kept hugging him. It hurt, but David didn't want to let go. He had never hugged his father like that—it was surreal.

After they finally sat down, his father brought out a bottle of Gammel Dansk and three glasses. "Now, tell us everything," he insisted.

And this time, his parents listened without objecting.

***

On return to Dulles Airport, the Bank had arranged a special reception for him. As the plane door was opened, an immigration officer and a Bank representative from the president's office greeted him. They escorted him out before all the other passengers. All formalities were handled without his direct involvement, and he was given a new suit, shirt, tie, and shoes. He got some help dressing with his cast, but in the end it all fit, so they had done their homework, he noted.

He soon found himself in a massive SUV with tinted windows driving in toward D.C. at an illegal speed. They totally avoided the gathered press.

A colleague from External Affairs in a flashy suit and tie slipped him a speech. "David, we're taking you straight to the Bank for an important event this evening. It's very important that you keep strictly to the text we've given you. You'll meet the president, and he doesn't like surprises, remember that. Do you understand what I'm saying?" He paused to elicit some confirmation that David was taking it all in.

"OK," David intoned.

The flashy suit smiled. "Great. We know you've been through a lot, and your time to tell us all about that will come. Several news media have inquired about interviews, but we have turned them down to protect your privacy. We've prepared some appropriate remarks that can be shared with the media. But never talk to the press directly and alone! Whatever you say could be distorted to fit their preconceived narrative about you and the Bank. But we're here to help you get the right message across." He looked searchingly for confirmation, but David kept quiet.

"David, this is a great opportunity for the Bank to get its message out, not just about how much we care about our wonderful staff, but also about our good work in general. The spotlight will be on us now for a few days before the sharks move on," he concluded.

On arrival at HQ on 1818 H Street NW, he was escorted through the main entrance and on to a reserved elevator to the 13th floor, an honor usually accorded to a minister on his way to signing a loan agreement with the Bank on behalf of his government. Stepping into the hall on the top floor, he was greeted by the president of the World Bank himself. A man of tall stature, with a natural radiance of confidence and authority, grey carefully combed hair, and a broad smile. The handshake was long enough to give the official photographer a good chance of capturing the event.

A small podium had been raised about a foot from the main floor. It had a large Bank logo on the front. The head of External Affairs introduced the president and expounded on the president's personal, relentless engagement in David's release. Then, the president himself took the stage. He was in his element, known as an eloquent speaker and someone who enjoyed the spotlight and the stature his position accorded him. He took his time to paint the background to today's event.

The president let everyone know that the Bank had spared no expense or effort to get David released. A task force had been gathered with representatives from all corners of the Bank to work on this challenging task. Members had been recruited with an equal number of women and men, and minorities were well-represented. In fact, the task force chair had been an African. The Bank's impressive network of contacts in the region had been tapped into. A position paper with respect to kidnapped staff members had been elaborated—but in great secrecy. The results of this cutting-edge analysis would forever remain under lock and key but could be made available for the benefit of other organizations on a select basis. Small exploratory delegations had been sent to West Africa, as it was not clear even in which country David was held. The Bank did not explicitly take credit for David's release, but implicitly all these efforts must have borne fruit as David was now back— albeit looking pale, very thin, and with an arm in a sling.

David was touched to hear about how the Bank had rallied for him, but he quietly maintained the impression that the

National Army had stumbled upon him during a raid against Allah's Soldiers.

David was invited to the podium, and he opened the speech he had been given. It was an awkward moment. Of course, he was grateful for everything that had been done. Of course, he wanted to thank people. But couldn't they have given him some time to find out what had really happened, assess the situation, and then articulate his own response? Apparently, there was a rush. The pressure was overwhelming. The podium was ready, the microphone on. The lights were focused on that single point in the large room, where he was expected to deliver an emotional tribute to everyone who had worked for his release. He was cornered. He started reading:

"I have regained my freedom thanks to the generous, and persistent efforts of many people. Some are here today. I want to thank the president of the Bank for his personal involvement in securing my freedom. To all of you, my dear colleagues, I want you to convey my heartfelt thanks for everything that you have done for me. The thought of my wonderful family and all of you is what kept me alive during those difficult, horrific days in captivity among brutal terrorists who have no respect for life and liberty.

I also want to extend my sincere thanks to the U.S. military, whose intelligence gathering, anti-terrorism training, and aerial support was crucial in securing a successful outcome.

Last but not least, I want to thank the Government of Banatu and its National Army for their courageous and timely intervention at a moment when my life was in imminent danger.

Thank you, and God Bless you!"

David skipped "… and God bless you." There was thunderous applause, and not an eye was dry in the audience. The representative from External Affairs was beaming, and

David suspected he would list his organization of this event as "outstanding" in his personal evaluation form at the end of the fiscal year.

The president immediately took the stage and delivered an announcement.

"It's timely that the Bank has just concluded the negotiations for a record loan to the Republic of Banatu. This path-breaking budget support loan will set a new standard for the Bank's activities globally. It is the fruit of diligent work by the Bank's dedicated staff in constructive engagement with the counterpart government. The loan is based on the premise that development will only be successful if based on the priorities of recipient governments. The time for restrictive conditionalities and petty micromanagement of development aid has passed."

There was more applause and cheers. David left the podium. Several people whom he did not know approached him and embraced him spontaneously. He tried to protect his ribs as best he could. Bob and JP pushed through the crowd to greet him.

"Please know that many Muslims have prayed for you," Bob told him as he held David's both hands in his.

"Let's celebrate with some champagne after this," suggested the smiling JP.

But where is Diane? David kept thinking.

He was a rock star now in the circus of flashy news pieces, rumors, and speculations that lasted a few hours before the media searchlight found a new focus. The text of his speech had already been disseminated to the media through the efficient External Affairs office. It was embargoed until the time expected for the speech. The picture of the Bank's smiling president and David achieved wide circulation.

221

David excused himself early. A Bank car took him the short route back home. He realized that he did not have a key to his own apartment. Luckily, the building supervisor was able to help him. He welcomed David home and had lots of questions. David deflected them, got the door opened, and went straight to his bed where he collapsed.

He woke up to the ring on the gate phone. It was Diane, and he buzzed her in. Wrapped together in a tight bundle of limbs, they cried softly before they fell asleep.

CHAPTER 21

Debriefings

The reunion with Diane had been tearful but deeply satisfying. Day by day, things started to feel more normal again. After two days of rest, a physical exam at the Bank, and a consultation with a psychiatrist, he wanted to get back to work. External Affairs also wanted him back before the spotlight on him was turned off. As soon as he showed up at work, he was given a warm welcome by many colleagues who came by to see him.

A series of carefully orchestrated media events had been arranged. David's role was to read a brief statement of gratitude toward the Bank, the U.S. government, and the Government of Banatu. Then, the media-trained young staff took over and eloquently delivered slick PowerPoints with bullet points promoting the perspective of the Bank's management.

The message was upbeat. Lending was at a record level. Client governments reported great satisfaction with the Bank's pull-back on conditionalities. The administrative budget for staff had been restrained, and staff benefits were cut to show the Bank's frugal face. "It's important to counter the image that Bank staff are overpaid fat cats," a colleague from External Affairs told David. "It isn't true, but appearance is reality these days," he added glumly.

Several journalists called and asked for interviews, but he declined on the advice of External Affairs. "We will handle the messaging," he was told. But he did secretly take up an offer for a debriefing with Amnesty International.

Amnesty's office was located on Pennsylvania Avenue in SE D.C., and he took a taxi outside the Bank office. "Do you work for the World Bank?" the taxi driver asked.

"Yes."

"I hear you make a load of money, and I'd love to work there. But I just don't know anybody who could get me in."

The belief that you got to work for the Bank through personal contacts was one that David had met before. "I didn't know anybody at the Bank before I joined."

"Eh...so why did they hire you?"

David inhaled deeply. "I'm as baffled by that as you are."

The driver was silent, but they got stuck by a long red light, and he peered at David in the rearview mirror. "Any ideas how I should prepare talking to the Bank?"

"A PhD in Economics from a good university and experience from work in a developing country might help," David suggested. That marked the end of that conversation.

***

A short, dark-haired woman in her thirties greeted him in the Amnesty International lobby as agreed. "Hello, I'm Angela," she said with a welcoming smile. She was plainly dressed and had a pale complexion that betrayed endless hours of office work.

She was a senior researcher specializing in West Africa. They went upstairs and meandered through a maze of cubicles where people were still busy working in the early evening. The air was a bit stale, perhaps from the dogged determination of ambitious, dedicated staff who were up against monstrous violations of human rights.

I admire them, but it must be depressing to work here, David thought.

They sat down at a large table in a silent conference room, and Angela introduced a colleague. "Mike works with me on West Africa and has a lot of experience debriefing people who have been through traumatic experiences. Could you please start by simply giving us an overview of what you went through. We only have a very general picture from news media and the Bank's press releases."

David had prepared a timeline with key words and went though it in an orderly fashion until he got to the "reality check" that he had experienced being beaten. The words would not come out as the memories flashed through his brain. He did not want to remember his sense of capitulation, his helplessness.

"This must be hard for you," Angela intervened. "Why don't we take a short break?"

David just nodded and went to the bathroom. He looked himself in the mirror and saw a tired, sad face with black shades under the eyes. His eye infection was still not completely gone, and his body ached whenever he did not feed it enough pain killers. More composed, he returned and got some water.

"I'd like to continue." He went on and covered the beating, the soldiers' entry, the questioning of the villagers, the killings, and the probable rapes that had occurred.

Angela showed him a folder with a large number of pictures and asked if he could identify anyone. He saw a face he recognized without a doubt. "That's him—the officer who commanded the scene when I was taken out of the cell and released."

"That is Major Adeoye, and he is under investigation for a series of human rights violations. We are building a case about him and others to send to the Prosecutor of the International Court of Justice in The Hague," said Mike. "It would be helpful if we could record a sworn statement from you specifically on his involvement. Would you be willing to do that? Would you be willing to testify before the court if it comes to that?"

David reflected on the repercussions. He would become a potential target for retaliation, and perhaps, the Bank would object to his involvement. The Board Director for Banatu would be furious. Would he be protected? So many unknowns, but there was only one possible answer. "I would be happy to contribute to the truth coming out about these human rights violations."

***

The CIA—also known as The Company—let David know that they wanted to have a talk. David was hoping that he would get to visit their HQ in Langley, Virginia, which he had seen pass on the TV screen many times. He was met as agreed in the Bank's reception by a young man who showed him his ID, checked David's, and escorted him to a car just outside.

"Did you bring a cell phone?" he asked.

"No, I was told not to," said David.

His escort nodded and showed him into a windowless van. There was a black screen between him and the driver's seat, so he could not follow where they were driving. They drove a short stretch, and he emerged into a parking garage. This could not be Langley. He was accompanied through a guarded metal detector with meticulous scrutiny. Belt, pen, shoes, glasses, jacket, and watch, it was all fed on a tray through an x-ray and carefully assessed by an operator. They passed through several doors with coded locks and cameras. At one door, he had to place his right hand on a reader, which approved his fingerprints for entry.

I'm in their database, he thought.

The interview room was quite sparse with a table and three chairs. There was a large, dark mirror on one wall, and he assumed it was a one-way window that allowed for surveillance. A video camera was placed on each side of the table, one very close to where David was asked to sit. There was a microphone on the table, probably for the benefit of the observers behind the glass.

The two agents rose to greet him. "Mr. Pedersen, welcome! I'm Ed, and this is John. We have some questions for you. Water?" There were three bottles and three plastic cups on the table. His interviewers had no pens or paper but looked at small iPads in front of them. They both had earpieces as well. "It should only be a short session. Don't worry, we can take breaks when you need them."

David was bursting to talk about the egregious human rights violations he had witnessed when the army had freed him, but Ed cut him off. It was not their concern.

Instead, they showed David a set of pictures and asked him to identify anyone he could recognize. He flipped through a number of photos on a tablet, and the American Warrior was very easy to pick out. He was asked to review many other pictures as well but could not recognize anyone.

What had they talked about? What was his demeanor? Any bragging about his achievements and actions? Any discussion of future plans? Did he mention any contacts in the U.S.? There was no end to their interest in details. Apart from being tiring, David did not like the tone in some of the questions. They seemed to be fishing for signs of sympathy for his captors.

"Look, it's not like we became best friends—there's no Stockholm syndrome here! He talked a lot with me. He was simply bored with the lack of action. He was in hiding and wanted to get back to a place where he could use his talents. He liked speaking English, and I was the only one who could understand him and his background. There were things he missed about the U.S. He told me he did not support any operation in the U.S. where he still has friends. Clearly, he was frustrated with the local leadership and their use of excessive violence against any resistance. He wanted to win people's confidence, their 'hearts and minds' if you recognize the phrase—yes?"

The CIA officers did not smile in recognition. "How did he plan to do that?" Ed asked.

"By treating people better than the National Army, for example. I saw first-hand how brutal they can be against the villagers. When I was dragged out of the cell—"

"David, answer the question. We are not concerned with the Army here. The Army is our partner in the hunt for terrorism. We train some of their best officers here in the U.S. and even teach them about the Geneva Convention."

David struggled to stop thinking about all the violence he saw in the name of rooting out terrorists. He pictured villagers lined up against the wall and unceremoniously shot. "Well, for example, the locals are often frustrated by corruption. The judicial system favors the influential and the rich. It's extremely slow. The police are incompetent, and when the army appears, they often interrogate, jail, or even execute locals. That, on top of the general poverty and lack of public services, is an excellent breeding ground for a movement like Allah's Soldiers."

John and Ed never commented directly on his responses. They only continued with their questions. But there was a slight nod, indicating that they were not surprised by this description. They must have heard it all before.

"So that prepares the ground. But what exactly do they do when they enter a new community?"

David's mind filled with the memory of the officer standing in front of him yelling, "Tell me who beat you!" He clasped his jaw and brushed some sweat on his upper lip.

"They start by eliminating the most oppressive guys. Often by public executions to make a point. Then, they gradually clean out the corruption. A new type of court is installed with some representation from locals, and it goes to work and makes very quick decisions. Feuds that have festered for years are resolved. Thieves are caught, and their right hand is cut off, sometimes both if the crime is more serious. The women are told to wear veils and dress conservatively. Alcohol is banned. This is painful to some but popular with many others."

David asked for a bathroom break and was ushered to a toilet—with a camera mounted in the ceiling. He returned to continue.

"The exact measures vary from place to place. Sometimes, there is a conservative culture in place, and they move swiftly to tighten it. Sometimes, there are lots of infidels, and they are coached to gradually accept the Sharia Law. When the situation has stabilized, they go for the next phase."

"And what is that?"

"For example, schools for girls are closed down. Instruction in school becomes focused on memorizing the Koran. The dress requirements become stiffer. The local imam is sent packing unless he's really cooperative, and a more doctrinaire is installed. Music is banned, and dancing becomes a serious crime. Professional women are confined to their homes. Local girls are forced to marry fighters who sometimes use them as disposable sex slaves. It goes on like that, and any opposition is rooted out. That said, there is some local variation, according to the Warrior."

"When he spoke about this process, what was his perspective."

"He was definitely in favor of a mild form of Sharia. To him, that meant fighting corruption, efficient courts, conversion to Islam. But he thought that girls should be allowed to go to school. They too could become good fighters for Allah, he said one time. He even talked about the Kurdish women fighters with great respect."

"Why was he so open with you?"

"Maybe he thought that I was going to be executed so nothing of what he said would come out anyway. Or he was just so frustrated with what he felt was an overzealous perversion of the kind of Islam he wanted to see. 'Not everything here is what I signed up for,' he said."

With the American Warrior thoroughly analyzed, they proceeded to question him about his last place of captivity. He told them about the beating but he could not bring himself to reveal how cowardly he had felt. His mind flashed with the memory of the gun pointing at the head of the youngster staring at him but could not bring himself to tell that story either. They were not really interested in what he had gone through, only how he could deliver information useful for the manhunt.

"We have come across cases where prisoners, especially when held for a longer period, chose to convert to Islam. It may be a tactical measure to get better treatment. Did that apply to you?"

"Not at all."

"Have you read the Koran?"

"Yes, I was interested in better understanding this religion that seemed to give rise to so much intolerance. What I found were very contradictory statements. Some called for violence against infidels, but others emphasized how merciful and forgiving Allah is. It's a bit like the Bible—you can cherry-pick and find support for most things."

His interviewers exchanged glances at that last statement but made no comments.

"Are you religious?"

"I'm a secular humanist. I believe one can be good without God."

The interviewers appeared to be winding down, so David took the opportunity to ask some questions.

"Can you show me where I was held? And what happened to the guys who were with me when I was kidnapped?"

"Your interpreter was held for a week but then released, possibly against some ransom. His government won't tell us. He identified the exact place where it happened. I'll show you."

"I know exactly where I was kidnapped, but I don't know where I was taken. What about the guards who came with me?" David insisted.

"No trace of them. Perhaps they were complicit. Or, if they resisted, they might have been shot."

Ed pulled up a map on his tablet and turned it so David could see. A red dot signified the place of capture and a small tag next to it identified the village: Yanyawa. He remembered that name. "And where was I taken from then on?"

"We got a drone sighting of you and the American Warrior here," said Ed who pointed to a blue dot: Doguwa. It was just on the other side of an international border. "It seems that you were picked up by Allah's Soldiers and taken to one of their base villages. The border crossing made it more difficult for the Banatu National Army to follow up any lead. You were found by the National Army here." He pointed to a green dot on the Banatu side of the border: Rumi.

"Were you looking for me or for the American Warrior?"

"Our mandate is to safeguard American citizens and the security interests of our great nation. We never comment on sources and methods," said John sternly.

"So, I was not on your radar even?"

Ed was more forthcoming. "You must understand that at the time, four American citizens were missing in this vast region. We were also searching for some high-value target Jihadists. As for the National Army, they were looking for more than 600 abducted schoolgirls from several different schools. Everyone had their plates full."

David took a deep breath and hesitated. *Would they be interested and take him seriously?* He decided to test. "So, are you interested in capturing the American Warrior?"

John and Ed chuckled. "What do you think? Look, it's not like we're asking for advice here," John lashed out. He looked at this watch.

Ed glared at David. "What do you have in mind?" John seemed ready to leave, but Ed signaled to him to stay.

"I'm obviously not here to tell you guys how to do your job. But I spent a great deal of time with this guy, and a few things came out in those talks. Especially when he was drunk on local beer."

"He was drinking alcohol?" said Ed in astonishment.

"He had a very pragmatic view with respect to *haram*, and he was clearly bored with waiting so long in that little village for his marching orders. There's a certain vanity to him, he wants to be seen, heard, and understood. He doesn't like the crude image of Jihadists that prevails in the West. He wants to explain to us why the fighting in the Middle East and Africa is going on."

"So what? He can just make another video then," John scoffed.

"No, hear me out. It's true that the Warrior has reinforced the crude image of militant Islamists by his own videos of captives—including me. He even used a sword to feign my execution–which still haunts me. But there's another side to this. Suppose that he was given a chance to be interviewed by a respected, Western journalist and give his perspective on the so-called war on terror. I'm sure you have a number of journalists in your pocket already…"

John frowned at that statement, but Ed smiled. John leaned forward. "You're suggesting we hand a megaphone to a terrorist?!" he blurted out.

David decided to ignore the comment and continued. "One more thing. He had a French girlfriend once, and she left a big impression on him. He has a weakness for pretty women, and a particular weakness for anything French. So, there's the formula for getting him out of the woodwork, to make contact, and to reveal his position. What you do then is not my business."

John made a dismissive gesture, but Ed stared straight at David. "Thank you for sharing that," he said.

"There's one more thing," said David, although he wanted to leave. John had stood up, but Ed, who seemed to be the senior one, motioned him to sit. "I leave it *entirely* up to you to evaluate if what I'll say is of any importance," he stressed, looking straight at John. "But one day when the Warrior was drunk, he bragged about a new wave of modern Jihadists. They are not dressed in turbans and waving AK-47s. No, they work undercover as westernized students in the advanced labs at top universities in the West. They are cyber-security experts, biochemists, and so forth. That's the next wave."

"Nothing we haven't heard before," scoffed John.

"Did he mention any specific universities?" asked Ed with a stern face.

"I'm not sure, but I don't remember any."

"Try to remember exactly how he put it," Ed insisted.

"It's just what I already said." David sighed.

They finished, and John shook his hand without a word. "Thanks for coming in," Ed said. "Here's a card with a contact number. You can leave a message there if you can think of anything at all that might be of interest to us. Mention the code that is on the card, and the message will get to me."

David was escorted out by the same man who took him there and felt a profound sense of relief as he got out of the car on 1818 H Street NW. Now, he needed to get the kidnapping ordeal out of his system. He had to refocus on his professional mission to combat poverty and to pick up where he left off with Diane. His love for her had only grown during his time in captivity. She was his "family" in the U.S. now.

CHAPTER 22

Prioritize!

The quickest way to recover from his ordeal in captivity was to get back to a normal working life again. Emotionally, he experienced much greater swings than before his kidnapping and oscillated between passionate affection for Diane and fear of losing her. He continued to see a psychologist once a week as a useful safety valve for his frustrations. David dropped the more potent pain killers and rapidly gained weight. But it was challenging to adjust, and he was more overwhelmed than ever before. Diane, Bob, and JP were all trying hard to be supportive.

David met up with JP in a cozy wine bar that had "decent wines," as JP put it. That is, it specialized in French wines. David ticked off JP by asking for a California wine: Seghesio Home Ranch Zinfandel. JP intervened and offered to pick up the tab if only David would change his order to a nice, full-bodied red blend of Merlot and Cabernet Franc from Saint-Émilion with subtle dark fruits, firm tannins, and a long finish.

"JP, open your eyes to the fact that there's excellent wine from the U.S. as well. Remember the famous tasting in 1976 in Paris when two California wines beat out a set of French wines. The wine experts were all from France, but the tasting was blind, and they didn't know they were comparing French and Californian wines."

"I do remember," said JP with a tone as if he reminisced about a deceased friend. "The tasting was organized by a gentleman by the name of Steven Spurrier, from England, of course. It was the kind of trickery that we 'ave come to expect from people on the other side of the Channel."

"Come on, JP, the Hundred Years War is over. And so is the time of condescension toward Californian wines. There are hundreds, no, thousands of wineries now all over the U.S. Even around here in Virginia and Maryland, there are some great ones."

They got their glasses, and David went straight to the point. "I feel overwhelmed. No matter how many hours I put in, it's not enough. All these meetings, the constant inflow of emails, the demands to review this, review that, the red tape, asking for permission, clearances, filing reports on tight deadlines, reminding people that they should have delivered something yesterday, finding qualified consultants at short notice, making sure you follow all the procurement rules—"

JP held up his hands. "*Assez*! You just need to prioritize. Me, I'm not stressed. *Pas du tout*. First rule: delete all emails you get from management! I've done it for years. Never got caught. They send you requests but then forget about it. Don't remind them! Second rule: make a list of ten things you want to accomplish for the day. Stick to it!"

David sighed. "I don't think I can get away with not attending to management requests. You are well-established, highly regarded, your boss protects you, and most people know you're really weird and can't be bothered."

"Not weird, *mon ami*—just principled. You try to make everyone around you 'appy, but it's impossible. That would be the day chicken 'ave teeth!"

David laughed. "I don't think that's an English expression. But I'll test your approach for a week. Cheers!"

"There's one more thing," said JP. "You're a young man with a profound dedication to development. You're intellectually curious and a rigorous researcher--I've read you dissertation."

"You must be kidding! That makes you one of a handful of people." David laughed.

"My point is that you should think about your career. Look for a position within the Research Department! It's got some great people, serious thinkers who penetrate the core issues of what drives development, aid efficiency, the role of governance, and so on. You would thrive there."

"It's just the opposite of what I've been thinking," David objected. "I left academia in search of something more hands-on and applied. That's what attracted me to the Bank."

JP frowned. "This is exactly what makes me sad. Young, talented minds from great universities enter the Bank and become institutionalized. Grey bureaucrats who learn to master the intricate processes to churn out massive loans, the bigger the better for their careers. With increasing general budget support, we 'ave mostly given up on guiding development."

"You're exaggerating, but that's what our client countries want," David noted.

"*Bien sûr*! But development aid is not a popularity contest!" JP threw up his arms and argued with such heat that a couple at the next table turned to look at him. JP looked embarrassed and sank into his chair.

They silently emptied their glasses. "Let's not try to resolve those issues here and now. I need to focus on getting through the next few weeks and get back to normal life," David concluded in a low voice and stood up.

JP rose and put both hands on David's shoulders and looked into his eyes with a smile. "*Mon cher ami*, I'm 'ere for you," he said and turned to leave.

***

Equipped with his ten priorities, David arrived early the next morning. He fired up his computer and found thirty-seven new emails, although he had emptied the inbox the night before. Only fifteen were left to process when the boss's assistant peeked into his office.

"Muhammad wants you to represent him at a meeting. Here's the file."

"OK, when's the meeting?"

"It's already started. He probably finds it too boring to go to but says our unit has to be represented."

"Damn, I have no background to this. How can I represent the unit?"

"You just have to show up. And read the background paper on your way there," she added gleefully.

The meeting was on the 12th floor in a rarely used conference room. It took five minutes to find it. The room was packed. He nodded in recognition of some colleagues and found a seat in a corner, far away from the speaker. The speaker was already on slide twelve. It was cluttered with an overabundance of bullet points in small fonts.

David glanced through the background paper. It was fifty-four pages long plus annexes. There was no summary up front, the language was flowery and long-winded, and he encountered something approaching a statement of purpose only on page three. The formally dressed speaker went far beyond his allotted time. His English was fluent but heavily accented. Unfortunately, he made it a theme to speak about the importance of creating "a critical mass of expertise." But in his accent, it came out as "a critical mess," which created some muted amusement among colleagues.

There were several peer reviewers. David discovered to his horror that Muhammad was listed as one of them. Now, time was of the essence! He scrutinized the paper's structure, underlined key passages, and jumped from paragraph to paragraph, focusing on the introductory sentence. Sometimes, he had to read the whole paragraph, but the text was not that information-intensive. He also listened closely to the other peer reviewers.

The chairperson surveyed the room. "I don't see Muhammad here. Do we have someone from his unit?"

David had to acknowledge that. "Unfortunately, Muhammad was hastily called to an urgent meeting. He sends his regrets and the compliments to the author. I'm David Pedersen."

The chairperson nodded to go ahead, and the author smiled.

"First, let me congratulate the author for his production of a very thought-provoking piece." (Code for: the paper challenges common sense.) "Let me also echo the pertinent observations of my fellow peer reviewers..." (Polite agreement was always welcome. It diffused tension and was part of the ritual.) "...in that the language could be somewhat tightened to make the presentation more succinct." (This was standard editorial advice and almost universally justified).

David scanned the room, took a sip from a water bottle, and continued. "The aim of the paper is commendable..." (It was motherhood and apple pie and so vague that nobody could disagree.) "...and it pursues a line of reasoning that is a testimony to original thinking." (It's unsupported by logic.) "Its conclusions would deserve a more prominent display up front to further enhance its structure." (The conclusions are buried in a morass of jargon). "With some further work toward finalization, it could become a helpful contribution to this important debate." (When no genuinely appreciative adjective was appropriate, the code term "helpful" was thrown in for cover.)

It was probable that most of his colleagues had read between the lines. First, that he had not read the paper thoroughly, but they had all been in the same situation and forced to wing it. Second, he did not think highly of the paper. The speaker, an outside consultant, thanked the participants profusely for their constructive comments.

David rushed out of the room. He had lost an hour and a half of his day already.

***

David turned to his list of priorities, but the phone rang. He should have looked at the call screen but was expecting a certain call and lifted the receiver eagerly. It was not the person he expected.

"Hello, I'm Jonathan Robinson, an intern with the Educational Media Knowledge Management Group in Austin, Texas. How are you today, sir?"

"Fine, thanks, how can I help you?"

"Nobody at External Affairs picked up, but the switchboard said you're an eminent expert on Africa."

"That's flattering, but an exaggeration, I assure you. Do you have a question?"

"Yes, we're making a booklet and video about Africa and all its problems. You know, there's so much goin' on there, like wars and tribal stuff and—"

"Could we get to your question, please?" David glanced at his watch.

"Well, it's like this. We'd like to know …"— Jonathan ruffled some papers—"how much of Africa is unfit for human habitation," he intoned.

David took a deep breath. "Jonathan, what's fit or not for human habitation depends on many things, primarily the technology and level of economic resources available. It is not a given number that remains static over time."

Jonathan was silent for a moment, pondering the bad news. "So, couldn't you give me…maybe not an exact number but an…interval?"

"Let me explain in another way, then. Have you been to Las Vegas?"

"Of course, yeah, it was really cool."

"Right. Now, imagine that in the early 1800s you had come to the spot where Las Vegas is now. That was before even the first fort was built there, there was no irrigation, and no railroad going through. Assume that you would have had rainfall data, and it would show that you could expect maybe four inches of rain per year."

"Hmm, it would be hard to grow anything there. I wouldn't have settled there."

"Right, so if you look at a map of Africa, you might conclude that given conditions today, large parts are not suitable for human habitation, but that is an ever-changing number. Think about how oil and gas have transformed some desert countries. Also, I think it would be important to focus on how to build good institutions that create an environment for economic growth and poverty alleviation. When Botswana achieved independence in 1966, most people saw it as a basket case. A big desert mostly with a poorly educated population and little infrastructure. But they built sound, democratic institutions, and harbored their wealth of diamonds in a responsible manner. They added cattle ranching and ecotourism as important sources of income. It's a positive, complex story that deserves to be told."

Jonathan stayed silent for a moment. "A *complex* story. Nobody wants that … they want easy numbers. I'll just tell my boss you weren't willing to give me a number. Thanks, and bye."

"Jonathan, listen to me, there's an important lesson to be learned from your question—"

The disappointed intern had hung up.

David returned to his priority list. There was a knock on the door, and his boss came in with a tall woman in her thirties in a stylish dress. "Let me introduce Ms. Hicks to you. She is keen to learn more about the exciting work you are doing with the Bank."

Clearly, Muhammad wanted to get rid of her and took the opportunity to dump her on an unsuspecting but diplomatic underling.

"Hello, I'm so pleased to meet you. Thanks for taking time to see me," she said with a beaming smile. Her makeup was a bit overdone, but her perfume was pleasant. Ms. Hicks sat down by the small, round table, and David joined her. "I have worked as a campaign advisor to Senator Davies, but I'm now looking for new challenges. I thought the Bank looked interesting."

"I'm glad you think so. Could you please tell me more about what particular interests you have and your work with the senator?"

"As you know, Senator Davies is a leading defender of Second Amendment rights, small government, low taxes, and personal freedom. He is also known for cautioning against the fostering of dependence among the poor, both as individuals and their countries. I think the Bank might benefit from the perspectives that somebody like me could bring to the table."

"I see. You are intent on influencing the Bank's policies, then."

"Of course. But let's start from the beginning. When did the Bank start? What's the difference between you and the IMF?"

David got a sinking feeling in his stomach. The lady had not done her homework and was now on a mission to correct the Bank's misguided policies. That may not be well-received by Bank staff, coming from somebody who lacked experience from developing countries. Clearly, she had some connection at the top floor to be able to barge in like this. He painstakingly went through the Bank's main historical events, explaining its purpose and structure. Ms. Hicks took notes and expressed a surprised "oh" at times. But she soon lost interest.

"You are obviously not American," she remarked. "Is there a quota for people like you to come here and learn and then rotate back to your own government? Does your government pay for you?"

"No, I'm paid by the Bank. I am not linked to my national government at all. I'm Danish, but it doesn't matter."

David could tell from Ms. Hicks's body language that she had determined that this bank was not for her. She stood up, shook his hand firmly with a big smile.

"Thank you so much for your time, Mr. Patterson, I hope you find the time to look around our beautiful country while you are here. Ours is a country that never took a penny of foreign assistance," she declared with pride. "Have a nice day!"

I guess she forgot about the crucial French assistance during the Revolutionary War, David thought.

Annoyed with the lost time, David was anxious to return to his list. He logged in to his computer, but it froze. The usual tricks of Ctrl+Alt+Del and rebooting did nothing to solve the issue. He called the IT department.

"Your call is very important to us, please stay on the line, and your call will be answered in turn. This call may be monitored or recorded for training purposes. Did you know that most issues can be resolved online? Please visit our webpage…" It droned on.

"My computer is frozen!" he muttered between clenched teeth.

After a ten-minute wait, a technician answered. Judging by the accent he had been hooked up with the service center in Chennai. Arjun had a friendly voice and proceeded through a checklist of questions. He concluded quickly that the problem was so serious that David needed a technician on site to deal with the desktop. He transferred the call to the local IT department in D.C.

"Your call is very important…"

Twenty minutes passed, while David read a project document to use time efficiently. The call timed out, and he had to get in line again. Finally, Elena answered with a Russian accent. She scheduled a technician visit the following day. All was not lost. Several offices were available, as colleagues traveled all the time. Before he had a chance to move his papers to an empty office, the phone rang.

"Hi, it's Philip with External Affairs. We're putting together a brochure about the Bank's success stories. We're countering the negative press that seems to be coming out about Africa. Can you send me a blurb of a max of 300 words about 'Breakthroughs in African Natural Resources Management?'"

"Wow, you want something meaningful to be said in three hundred words about that gigantic topic? When do you need it?"

"Well, it was due last week, but the first two guys I asked didn't deliver. So, now it's down to you. You have until 4 p.m. today."

David's fuse blew. "Damn it, you expect me to boil this down to almost nothing and deliver it instantly, and without the context of what this publication is about, how it will be used, and what the target audience is?"

"No, no, don't take it like that! There is a Concept paper, a Briefing Paper for senior management, a Targeting Strategy for Dissemination, and so on. I can send you all that, but it's about fifty pages, and there's not much time for you to read it. Look, I tried another guy earlier today, but he told me to fuck off."

"Then, my answer is the same!" David hung up, fuming. It was not the first time that he had been asked to perform quick tricks with unreasonable timing.

***

David needed fresh air. Often, he resorted to picking up a box with lunch from the cafeteria and eating it while processing emails. *Not today*, he thought and ventured out. A new sandwich shop had opened up a block from his office. The shop was almost empty as he entered.

The attendant immediately yelled, "What can I get you?"

"I'm here for the first time, so let me take a moment to check the menu," said David. He read through the large sign posted above the counter. "Please give me the number 8 sandwich on rye bread to go with honey mustard, no onions, and leave out the pickle, thank you."

"Number 8, white-wheat-or-rye?"

"Rye bread, please," David repeated.

The attendant had already sliced open a bread that looked white, but David didn't bother to correct it and watched quietly as the sandwich was built at impressive speed.

"Mayo-mustard-ketchup-salsa?"

"Honey mustard, please," he repeated.

"Here or to go?"

"To go," he repeated.

The attendant wrapped the sandwich in paper, pulled out a bag, and slipped in a large pickle. He handed the bag to David while turning his face to the next customer and yelling, "Next!"

David took the bag and went to the cashier to pay. He found a park bench in Lafayette Square opposite the White House a short walk from the shop and sat down to eat. But first, he had to remove all the raw onion rings.

***

Back in the office, David logged in to the system from the next empty office and found the computer to be in working order. He took on the next priority, to remind a colleague, Martin von Regt, of a missing Environmental Impact Assessment that was crucial for the finalization of board documents for a community development project. But the colleague continued to be unresponsive.

He decided to check with the boss's assistant, who knew Martin personally. Was he sick maybe? She did not look up as he approached and stood in front of her cubicle. She continued typing. "Excuse me, have you heard from Martin lately? Is he alright?"

"Let me finish this letter for Muhammad first, then I'll answer. I'll call you." It was her usual style and aggravating, but she had the full support of Muhammad and was untouchable. If she reported him for "creating a hostile working environment," he would be in trouble.

He returned to his office, and the assistant called for him after ten more minutes. She did not bother to come to his office, but simply yelled from her station. He went out to her cubicle.

"What is it you want?" she pressed.

David explained, and she smiled. "David, you're obviously not clued in. Martin is in the country office of Bawana. They're preparing frantically for a visit by the president of the Bank and his entourage. Their operations are paralyzed. They don't respond to anything. Nothing can go wrong when the president descends on them next week. Once the president leaves, they can breathe again." He gave up on Martin and the EIA–for now.

Then, a batch of boxes arrived. Finally! A publication that had been in the works for months had now been printed. It was seriously delayed because of a blockage in the printing office. They had to go outside to a commercial printer for an expensive rush job. A separate firm handled the cover, and he had approved it months ago. Now that publication could be put on the tables the next day for a conference at the Bank, where it would reach a large audience.

Excited, he tore up the first box and pulled out a copy. It read "Case Studies of Community Development in Anglophobe

Africa." Fuck! He had approved a title with "Anglophone," of course. He checked his own copy. It was correct. Furious, he tore open the next box, and the next, and in all of them, he found the same disaster. Five hundred copies straight to recycling!

At the end of the day, David had crossed out four of his ten priorities. Dejected, he reached for the phone. He asked if JP would join him for a drink after work. "I need a glass or two after this day, and some better advice from you, my friend." JP agreed on the condition that David would give French wines the appreciation they deserve.

CHAPTER 23

Mission to Tanaland

After two months back in the office after his release from captivity, David's strength returned enough to go on a mission again. Bob helped him through his network of contacts to find a mission he could join. Bob's work as president for the Bank's Muslim Association had made him a well-known but somewhat controversial figure.

David joined a mission to Tanaland, where he was asked to contribute to a project-implementation report for a National Land Titling Project, or NLTP. The Country Office mostly prepared it, led by a young talent, Simeon Ngozu. Management wanted somebody from outside the project team to review their report, which included a field visit.

More and more work was being done locally rather than in Washington, D.C. The client dialogue was easier, and local staff were generally better at navigating the local Byzantine bureaucracy. But it could also be harder for them to take on a contentious issue and stand up to their national counterparts. Some of them were likely to be former colleagues, and they could even be relatives. As the Bank paid better than the government, there was sometimes friction between local Bank staff and their former colleagues. There was also friction at times between local Bank staff and better-paid HQ staff. It was not just about pay but also about decision-making power. All that had to be carefully navigated.

Simeon was in his thirties and a cheerful man with a beer belly. He was the Bank's leading man for the project. The technical work had been done by the Ministry of Land Use Planning, but much of the community outreach had been contracted out to an NGO. Simeon suggested they start by looking at the results in the field.

Together, they drove out to meet a community leader, John Otieno, in the slum on the capital's outskirts. Otieno was tall, thin, very dark, and flashed a bright white smile as they shook hands. They set out by foot from the project's modest HQ into the project area.

"John, I've read the briefing papers about the project, but I'd like to know how you evaluate progress so far," said David. He was well aware that Otieno had an incentive to embellish the project results, as his NGO was dependent on projects like this one.

"Let me give you some background," John started. "In this area, people drift in from all over the country to find jobs in the city. There was a time when the government simply tried to keep the informal settlements out. They saw it as illegal incursions on what was mostly state land. Some years ago, there were even campaigns to 'clean up' with bulldozers and police!"

He talks to me like I don't have a clue, David thought. There was a thorough background description in the documentation he had read on the plane. "That must have caused a great deal of resentment," David suggested.

"Of course, there were riots! The government slowly realized that this was a process they could not stop—they could only regulate it. They also realized that the people moving in were contributing to economic growth. But there wasn't a good system for registering property and providing ownership security. There is still some resistance within government about land titling, because the old system gives more opportunities for them to make backroom deals with rich people." He glanced toward Simeon.

David noticed his glance. *Maybe these two are not on the same page politically?* he thought. *Simeon has relatives with senior positions within government. Perhaps they had even been involved in the slum clearance controversy or corrupt deals?*

"What attitudes do you meet from people in this area?" David asked.

"You think it's easy building trust in our programs after such treatment? They come from rural areas across the country and tend to cluster according to tribe, and there's sometimes friction between them. Most often, the women traditionally don't have a strong standing when it comes to ownership and inheritance, but in our modern law, they get equal treatment. So, it's a women's empowerment project, you might say."

Simeon was keen to weigh in. "Since there used to be no record of ownership, disputes broke out, and people didn't feel safe to invest. That has changed now that people have clear title to their land. What they build on feels secure. You'll see a lot of improved roofs, new windows, and so on."

"Another factor that contributes to success is that the city is now providing better infrastructure, electricity, piped water, and drainage to the houses. Roads are also slowly being improved." He looked to Simeon, who nodded. "Although there's much left to do," John added.

"Yes, I've looked at those figures, and the progress is impressive. But there's still an issue about counterpart funding. The government has been late in paying its share of those costs," David noted.

Simeon shook his head. "It's a major headache, and I spend a lot of time in government offices to fix that. You can see from the report that there's some improvement in the last quarter."

David decided to drop that topic for the moment and bring it up when he met the relevant government officials.

Their walk continued. "I see a lot of latrines. I didn't see that as listed as a part of your project?" David asked.

"Strictly speaking, no, but because we have built good community connections, we could also bring in an NGO that specializes in sanitation. They have a campaign to promote communal latrines," Simeon noted, "but the funding comes from another project."

"That's great if you can use the same communication channels for multiple initiatives. Now, once property rights have been formalized, can the owner use it as collateral—" David asked.

"For loans? Yes, and that's a really important impact of the project," John inserted and grabbed David's shoulder to turn him around. "Look at that house!" he said, pointing across the street. "The owner has borrowed to buy three sewing machines and now operates a small-scale tailor shop. She could do that because she has title to her house. Let's talk to her!" He went up to the door and knocked.

A short, rotund woman in a red apron answered the door. She smiled brightly at John, and they exchanged a few words. But then she noticed David and turned serious, straightening her apron with both hands.

"Please tell her this is not an inspection!" David blurted out.

John translated, and the woman flashed a big smile. She waived them in. The two ladies behind their sewing machines immediately stood up and peered at the unexpected guests. John must have cracked some joke because they all started laughing. The mood relaxed and they were shown around the very modest room. There were bundles of textiles and some finished products hanging on the walls. The shop owner proudly pointed out some of them, and John translated bits and pieces but couldn't keep up with her.

The lighting was poor and the room hot. A small table fan was broken. "How reliable is electricity here?" asked David.

John chuckled. "It's not! You would be lucky to get through a full day without any blackouts. Sometimes, it's off for a whole day."

The shop owner was eager to hold up a dress before David. John laughed and translated. "She's asking if your wife would like this."

Once you established rapport, the conversation with locals could turn very personal at once, in David's experience. Questions about wife, children, how old he was, etc. just spilled out. The assumption was generally that a man of his age would be married and have a few children. "I'm sorry I'm not married," he said with regret. *She'll be wondering what's wrong with me.*

The lady could not hide her disappointment. But she was not giving up. "Girlfriend?" she tried in heavily accented English.

David cracked up and capitulated. "OK, how much?" It was not a dress that would fit Diane, but it didn't matter. They settled for a small sum, and David refused her change. They left on a high note with the pleased shop owner continuing her sales pitch.

"Well, that was heart-warming to see her enthusiasm and the good work they are doing," said David as they gathered in the street.

"This is what makes my work here meaningful," John added. "When you see change for the better, even if it comes in small steps."

"Who is driving this change?" asked David. He had a good idea from his briefings but wanted John's perspective.

"It's a coalition," John responded. "The government helps with surveying of land, registration, and all the legal stuff. A World Bank loan funds the whole thing with some matching government contributions. It also funds community outreach so we could get local leaders together from different tribes. Once the elders agreed, people were willing to collaborate. We trained community-outreach workers who went from house to house and explained the process."

"How did that work out?" David asked.

"Most people here can't read or write, and there are different languages involved, so it was not an easy sell. Confidence in government is not high around here. But our NGO has the right experience."

For a moment, David thought about Julia, working in a community trying to make a difference, and he felt a knot building in his stomach. *I can't be distracted now by thinking about her!*

They meandered around in the slum with a trail of curious kids in tow, and David could clearly see the difference between areas that had clear title and areas that had not been touched by the project. That applied also to some of the most recently established areas on the fringes of the urban area. Otherwise, age could have been a confounding factor. This was anecdotal, but the statistics in the implementation report gave good support.

They went back to the very modest project office, and John pulled out reams of data sheets from the archive. Local maps covered every inch of the walls. The furniture looked worn, but there was a fresh smell of soap from the recently scrubbed floor. "This is our ongoing assessment of progress," he explained. "We have a small evaluation unit advised by the Bank that keeps us honest." He laughed. "This is the main input for Simeon's report."

"What about legal enforcement of property rights?" David asked. The gap between carefully worded laws and regulations and their effective implementation was often glaring.

Simeon flashed a big smile. "I'll be honest, it's still problematic. The courts are inefficient and sometimes corrupt. But we're making progress even there, with the help of another World Bank project that is about reforming the judiciary."

They spent the rest of the day pouring over maps and data sheets. There was no doubt about John's enthusiastic engagement in the project. Simeon was more reserved, but he knew his numbers, and David left the office impressed. "John seems like just the right guy to lead this type of effort at the local level," he noted to Simeon as they drove back to the Bank office. "What we have seen here is impressive."

"He's critical to its success. It's all easy in economic theory: clearly defined and enforced property rights are fundamental to development. But the trick is in implementation, establishing trust and procedures that aren't too costly. That's where his leadership comes in. I have spent a lot of time with John and his team to build rapport. The fact that I'm based here has certainly helped."

It was not the first time that Simeon had hinted that local control and leadership was essential. "On that note, frankly, your boss at HQ seems to think that you are a bit stretched here at the Country Office. Do you feel that you have sufficient capacity even in the next phase when the project will expand?" David inquired.

"Oh yes!" Simeon blurted out. "We've established good links with the lead Ministry and the NGOs. Remote control from Washington wouldn't help... eh, I mean I don't mind that you're coming out to check on things, but we can certainly keep running the project from here."

It would not be David's decision, but he would be asked about his impression on return. He was not so sure that Simeon applauded his visit.

***

Simeon had invited David to visit his home that evening. It was the first time he had received that kind of invitation by a local colleague. He was greeted by Simeon and his wife, Hanuni, a short, energetic woman with a perpetual, warm smile, dressed in bright colors.

"Hanuni is a teacher at a high school in the low-income neighborhood that you have seen today," Simeon explained.

As they sat down for a home-cooked meal in their modest but tastefully furnished apartment, David asked Hanuni about her job.

"I love that some students are so motivated. Not all, but especially the girls realize that education is the ticket to the future, to income, and some independence. That's why it's so sad to see the girls who get pregnant and are kicked out of school."

"They are kicked out?" David didn't hide his distress and leaned back.

"Yes, the view of the school administration is that the girls have committed 'a sin' and should be punished. Unfortunately, teenage pregnancies are common. The girls

256

are poor and are tempted by sugar daddies who will not accept using protection. In addition, most girls here have no clue about contraception and reproductive health. They have no agency!" she concluded and gestured in exasperation.

"Is this at a public school?"

"Yes," Hanuni confirmed.

"With private schools, we can't do anything, but I know the Bank has an education program here for the public schools. I'll have to check with my colleagues in that department, but perhaps this is something they could bring up with the Ministry. There is a lot of emphasis on girl's education, so this should interest them. I'm afraid that's all I can say at this point, but I'll get back to you," he promised.

David enjoyed the delicious meal that Hanuni had prepared. A large plate with a maize meal dish was placed in the middle of the table, and they all served themselves portions to go with a meat stew and a salad of tomatoes and onions. Hanuni kept asking David if there was anything else he needed. Ketchup? Don't Americans use ketchup with everything? More salt? He tried to assure her that nothing was missing and that he enjoyed the meal.

"Another issue," Hanuni continued, "is that we have excellent teachers, but some shouldn't be there. It's not a secret that the school administration is corrupt, and some people buy their teaching job. It's a safe government job, relatively well-paid, and you can skip attendance if you have the headmaster's support. Some male teachers harass girls they find attractive. Some girls come to me and complain, and I talk to the headmaster, but he doesn't want to listen," she concluded with resignation.

Simeon suggested another beer, but David declined as graciously as he could. He could not remember having had more than one beer per day since he left university. Simeon had no such constraints.

"But aren't there some alternative schools they could go to, with better teachers? It's a big urban area," David inquired.

"There are private schools, and some of them are much better, but they are expensive. One school is managed by a U.S. foundation. It's not expensive, but students have to take a test to qualify. This is seen as elitist, so many people here are angry with them and want to close it down. Some are against foreign foundations running schools. There are rumors that they provide sex education, and this has alarmed many people."

"We are dealing with a lot of conservative and outdated views on women here," Simeon argued. "Actually, women themselves have a lot of ideas that must strike you as odd. For example, surveys show that about thirty percent of men here believe that a husband is justified in beating his wife if she is disrespectful to in-laws. But the percentage is even higher among women!"

"Yes, even for a woman to go out without her husband's permission is seen by many women as a legitimate reason for a beating. So, we are battling the attitudes among women as well as men," Hanuni added.

"What about female genital mutilation? Is it still practiced?" David asked. WHO has estimated that about 200 million girls and women live with FGM. Simeon and Hanuni looked at each other. *Perhaps it was too delicate an issue?* David thought.

"It's not really talked about much, but it's not often done in urban areas where the level of education is higher. But in rural areas, old habits die hard, and people want respect for old traditions," Simeon noted.

David felt strongly about FGM, and he had to push away recollections of the horrific images he had seen about the subject. This fear of female sexuality—he could not understand it. To rob young girls of the chance of a healthy life and the pleasures that consensual adult sex could bring. What if Julia or Diane had grown up in that environment! Oh no, he mustn't even touch that thought. But he could see that the subject matter was painful also to his hosts, so he ventured into neutral territory.

"Simeon, what meetings are planned for tomorrow?"

"Well, I have a meeting with the Local Planning Commission, but I think it would just bore you. I have some more project-related data to show you, so you can just read those, and we can discuss later."

"I'd be very interested in meeting with the Local Planning Commission," David noted dryly.

"Hmm, very well, then, but I'm warning you those guys can be very long-winded. Let's leave together from the Bank office at 9:30." Simeon looked unhappy.

Hanuni brought in dessert, which defused the tension. It was delicious, which David made sure to point out. Hanuni beamed when she received the compliments, and the evening ended on a relaxed note.

***

In his hotel room that night, David summarized his impressions. The documentation showed that the NLTP project had made real progress, and he added this one to a collection of signs of progress that he had come across over the years. He needed more information about the local capacity and the project's requirements in the next phase to come to a recommendation about future project management.

The conversation with Hanuni had left him sad. He could think of no more important effort toward development than girls' education. New schools had been built, and attendance was up. But here it was sabotaged by old-fashioned ideas that punished the victim while letting the guilty party off the hook. It was maddening, and he couldn't do anything about it except bring attention to the problem when he returned to D.C.!

***

The next morning, David found his colleague Antonio in the hotel cafeteria. A well-respected macroeconomist, he was known for his jokes—not all of them politically correct—his love of good food, and his positive approach to life in general. A balding man in his late fifties, he had been in the Bank for twenty-five years.

"Antonio, it's not my business, but I was worried about what I couldn't help observing two nights ago in the bar. I saw you from the dining room, and you were walking around to the row of working girls at the bar. Be careful. Last month, a consultant was fired on the spot in this hotel. A friend of mine was on that mission. It was led by Jenny Wolf."

"I know her...tough cookie!"

"The story is that Jenny wakes up at two in the morning by party noise next door. She bangs the wall, but somebody bangs back and yells on the other side. She got furious and went out and banged on the door to the next room. She didn't give up until somebody opened. The consultant—I don't know his name—appeared half-naked, very drunk, and aggressive. Behind him were two more-or-less undressed girls he had picked up from the bar. He was fired on the spot."

Antonio laughed loudly. "What are you suggesting, David?"

260

"I'm not moralizing, but beware of the risks."

Antonio took his time to calmly finish his coffee, orange juice, and toast. Then, he leaned forward toward David with a broad grin on his face. "We're trying to convince the government that they need a currency reform. They claim that the black market is only in isolated pockets of criminal money traders. My argument is that the black market rate is widely known and much more separated from the official one than they acknowledge. Hence, I sampled eleven women and asked for two prices for a particular, well-defined service, in U.S. dollars and in local currency. The pattern was marvelously consistent."

David wasn't sure if Antonio was making this up on the fly. "Several reasons could explain why the rate was so consistent. A pimp monopolizing the trade?"

"It's more like a cooperative with semi-independent operators. They keep an eye on each other, enforce barriers to market entry—one new girl was sent packing down the stairs the other day. Undercutting in price is frowned upon, and information travels well. It's just a competitive equilibrium."

"OK, Antonio, but your sample of eleven is not that impressive. Where else do you collect empirical data?"

Antonio grinned. "I visit money changers, but they are illegal and suspect strangers. There's also the risk of getting robbed and beaten. The thing is that variance in the black market rate is surprisingly low. And with low variance, the sample size needed for reasonable accuracy is modest. For example, if all Chinese were observed to be of exactly equal length, you need only measure one to estimate their average, right?"

David laughed. It was vintage Antonio, who emptied his glass and then took the opportunity to get back at David.

"I'm not moralizing, but I actually saw you in conversation with a working girl at the bar the same night. Be careful!" he said with a mischievous smile.

"Antonio, you probably noticed how short that conversation was. The young lady snuggled up to me as I was getting a glass of red and whispered, 'Honey, what part of a woman's body interests you the most?' I whispered back, 'Honey, that would be the brain.' That's when she darted away."

Antonio chuckled, but when a female colleague showed up at the table, the topic had to change. Miranda was in her forties and recognized as a clever econometrician. She sat down to join them.

"Good morning, guys. I had an interesting meeting yesterday at the Central Bank. I brought up the black market exchange rate, which seemed to be a delicate subject. The Bank has published estimates, but I don't see the empirical underpinnings, Antonio. We need some rigorous analysis on the black market rate. I've read some interesting articles about dynamic-adjustment models that we could use. How about we engage Professor Brookfield at MIT? He's expensive but a great econometrician!"

Antonio smiled mischievously. "Brilliant idea—if you can get the budget for it."

Good luck with that, David thought.

***

Three days later, the mission was over for David, and he checked out of the hotel. He paid and turned around to pick up his computer bag. It was missing! He had left it in a chair just three meters from the reception counter. It was a punch to the gut. The work computer, several important documents, a personal calendar, and some cash in an envelope was in that bag. Fortunately, he had his passport and wallet on his body. But he needed to get a police report about the theft. He got a taxi to the nearest police station.

A small "Police" plaque by the door was also translated into a local language. It looked closed, but he persisted banging on the door until somebody opened it. A young officer in a green uniform opened it.

"Yes?"

"I'd like to report a theft, please."

The officer opened the door somewhat reluctantly and let him in. It was apparent why he did not want to be disturbed. A soccer game was on the TV, the volume on high, and the entire staff seemed entranced by the game. The officer ordered the only female employee to handle the case. Presumably, she was the lowest on the totem pole. And what did women understand about soccer anyway?

The young lady smiled kindly and gave David a blank sheet of paper. "State your particulars."

"Should I write the report?"

"Name, passport, address, what crime…"

David sighed, took a seat, and tried to ignore the audience's roar as one team scored. He listed his stolen items and asked the lady to come back. She perused the sheet, looked puzzled, and took it to an older male officer. He read it before he walked over to David.

"Welcome, sir, sorry for your loss," he said with a kind smile. "We are not crooks in this country. When you go home, please don't think about this."

The officer's kind demeanor was not matched by his efficiency. Once he found the form after a lengthy search, the headings of the one and only Incident Report had to be copied by hand onto a blank sheet of paper. The copying machine in the far corner had stacks of folders on it and must have been out of commission for some time. David could barely hide his exasperation.

The succinct narrative that David had written caused the officer some problems. He wanted some context. "Why visit our country?"

It would have been impolite not to answer and add irrelevant details, so the report grew longer. In addition to frequent glances at the soccer game, the officer annoyed David by peeking at his cell phone. Then, he realized that the officer was checking the spelling of some words. "The thief (or thiefs) took …" the officer checked the plural and found it to be "thieves."

David shifted back and forth in his seat, watching the time. It took more than half an hour for the Incident Report to be properly written. He was asked to read it and sign in the designated spot at the bottom.

"Is there a working copying machine here?" David asked, nodding toward the impressively large Xerox machine from yesteryear.

"Need copy?" The officer looked confused. "We have report now."

"Yes, but I need it to show my employer that I have properly filed a police report. It's also required for insurance purposes."

"No copy machine here," said the officer with regret.

"May I please take the report with me to my hotel? I'll get it right back to you."

This was a request out of the ordinary. The officer rose and talked to the most senior colleague. Without taking his eyes off the soccer game, he waved off his younger colleague with a curt phrase. Returning to David, the officer smiled. "You make copy. Come back."

David rushed out with the report in hand. It was not easy to find a taxi, and he started to sweat in the brutal sunshine as he stood by the roadside to wave down a car. Finally, a car stopped, and a young man leaned toward him. It was not a registered taxi, but the kind of car that the Bank warned staff to avoid. But he was desperate and gave the hotel name and jumped in.

The car had seen its best days. The seat was sunken in and uncomfortable, but it was a short ride. The inside panels were gone on one side, with the wiring sticking out. There was a big crack in the windshield. The "check engine" light was on. The engine died at every red light as they stopped. The seat belt was stuck. But after all, the young man drove with care. He was also an entrepreneur of sorts.

"After hotel, where you go?" he inquired.

"Back to the police station. Can you wait for me, please?"

"Of course! Then to airport?"

"Yes."

"I give you good ride. No robbery," he assured him.

"That's very reassuring," said David, struck by the absurdity of the conversation, but impressed by the young man's business acumen.

The receptionist recognized him and was happy to help. He returned from the copier with a concerned look. They were almost out of ink, and only about three quarters of the page was legible.

"This police paper, no good," the receptionist argued, incorrectly.

"Any other copier available?" tried David.

"In manager's office."

The line behind David had grown long and impatient. He was sweating in the insufficient air-conditioning and from the awareness that time was ticking away.

The manager's pretty secretary delivered the perfect copy with a smile. David rushed out to the car and found the young man waiting as promised.

At the police station, a new shift had entered. A bewildered officer received the report and reviewed it. It was difficult to fathom why a foreigner showed up with one of their own reports in hand, duly stamped by his station's registrar.

"How you got this?" he demanded.

It was not a suitable time to explain. "Thank you so much, and congratulations on your win in the soccer game!" He hurried out to the waiting car. The ride to the airport was about an hour. As he calmed down, his eyes fell on a small handwritten sign, taped to the dashboard. It read: "Business in business."

"Excuse me, why have you posted that sign there?"

"It's my car, my business. I need money. But brother, sister, friends, all want free ride. I say 'no!'"

"Hmm, do they all expect you to give them free service?"

"Of course, they say 'you rich, make good money.'"

David had read a recent Bank report on the struggles of the country's small businesses. Entrepreneurs were stifled by red tape and by the informal pressure to share the fruits of one's labor as soon as any surplus was accumulating. The burden was especially heavy on the first-born son. The sisters had other burdens, of course, such as caring for elderly parents or parents-in-law and other relatives in need.

They reached the airport in good order, and David paid the young entrepreneur handsomely. "Good luck with your business!"

David rushed into the terminal, only to find that the flight was seriously delayed due to "operational reasons." He found a seat in a bar and rewarded himself with a beer. Wine was prohibitively expensive and of poor quality in Tanaland, he had found.

"A brewery is the safest investment in any developing country," JP had stated without irony. *I can understand why*, he thought. Further delays were announced, and David ordered some food at the bar. A middle-aged, balding gentleman in a rumpled suit sat down next to him, took off his jacket, and wiped the sweat off his forehead. He ordered a double whisky on the rocks and swept it as does someone who does not care about the subtleties of carefully crafted spirits—only about hastening its dulling impact on one's senses.

"You can't fuckin' trust anybody in this bloody country," he declared to anyone who might care to listen. Only David seemed to have noticed. The gentleman ordered another round. David tried to look busy checking his phone, but it did not stop the man from leaning over toward him. "She screwed me out of a crapload of money!"

It was an embarrassing situation, and David tried to de-escalate it best he could. "What happened?" he inquired, careful to not react and just listen.

"I came here to look for her, you know, Ikhlas! She was supposed to come to me, and I sent her money for the ticket.

I even paid for her mom's eye surgery—several thousand dollars! So, I got worried when she stopped writing. Came last week. Went to her school where she was teaching. They never heard of her! Showed them her picture, and the headmaster laughed at me! Said it was an actress famous around here. Just look at her!" He wiggled out a crumbled photo from a pocket in his jacket. The woman in the photo was very attractive, the pose seductive. He had been hooked.

"I've met somebody here called Ikhlas," David recalled. "She said it means 'honesty, integrity.' It can be a man or a woman, actually. A bit ironic, isn't it? How long did you have this ... eh ... conversation with her ... or him."

"Two fuckin' years! First, all about her dreams, then her love, then about money, more and more money. I felt so sorry for her, she was poor, her mother was goin' blind, and one thing after another, I just had to help. I wired money via Western Union." His voice trailed off, there were tears in his eyes, and he slumped down on the bar counter, covering his face with his hands.

"I'm very sorry. Most people in this country are very poor, and they desperately look for ways to have what you and I take for granted," David volunteered. "Unfortunately, yours is a story I've come across before. But don't judge everyone in this country after this unhappy experience. Most of them work hard to make an honest living."

David's argument barely impressed him. All David could do was to make sure none of them missed their flight out.

268

CHAPTER 24

Strip Search

Four months back from captivity, Diane suggested that David had recovered physically enough to engage in some more advanced play. He arrived early to their meeting place, and he sauntered around the block several times to avoid standing around and perhaps arousing suspicion. It was not the wealthiest part of D.C. Diane arrived on the dot. She marched right up to him and gave him a long, sweet kiss.

"I'm so glad you could find the time to see me." She giggled, well-knowing that nothing could be more important on his list than seeing her.

Diane entered a combination on the basement door, and they descended. There was a changing room with a toilet and shower to the right. Beyond that was a red door. They sat down on a small couch.

"Now that you have recovered, it's time we take our sex to the next level," she declared. "This is a great place for playing. It belongs to a friend who owns the house. She rents it out but only to people she knows well and trusts."

David offered to pay, but she waived him off.

"My treat," she smiled.

"Now for the scene today," she continued, "imagine that you are arriving in a new country where a female customs agent will check you for drug possession. Obviously, you'll have no alternative to complying with a thorough search."

David had speculated what she would spring on him this time and had run through a hundred fantasies. Now that he knew, he felt a nervous excitement building in his stomach.

"Well, that opening is not too difficult to imagine, but I've never done this kind of role-playing. And I'm not a great actor."

"What I'm looking for is not so much an Oscar performance as obedience and attention. Focus on how your body feels. Focus on watching me. I'll guide you through every step. Don't think about it as theater—just fun, erotic play. Now, pick a name for yourself."

"What's wrong with my real name?" said David, puzzled.

"Nothing, but this is a scene where you should allow yourself to act out, to do and say things that aren't a part of your regular persona. It will help to set your imagination free. Think of a name that's not attached to any particular person who you've met or even read about."

"How about Rex? I draw a complete blank for that name."

"Fine then, Rex it is. Now, let's agree on safe words. You know about those?"

"Do you think I haven't had any experience at all with this?"

She laughed. "Well—"

"Yeah, I watched an instructional video where they used 'yellow' and 'red.'"

"That works. Yellow will mean that I will ease back. But red means 'stop right now'! Never hesitate to use those words if you need them. I'm good at this, but not a mind reader. One more thing. Don't try topping from the bottom when we are in the scene. I know your hard limits, as well as some soft ones, and I respect those."

"Not sure what you mean."

"Some submissives, or bottoms, try to interfere in the middle of the scene to make things just right for them or make new demands," Diane explained. "It can break the rhythm and spoil the atmosphere. It's like asking to rewrite the script when the play has started. Try to just go with the flow. Think of it as dancing, and I'm leading."

"I don't like the word 'bottom,' but 'sub' is OK. I don't know that I could do this with anyone else, but you're a natural. I'll just follow your lead. In a way, I'm the one being pampered by this. You turn me on, keep me excited, play to my fetishes, relieve me of my responsibility and the pressure to please you. That's what has been worrying me during vanilla sex."

Diane smiled. "Honey, there will be plenty of opportunities for you to reciprocate the pleasure. It's just that I'll be in control of that as well. And don't forget that it's a turn-on for me to watch your excitement and to feel that I'm in charge."

"Should I call you 'Mistress'?"

"Of course. There is no need to add a name to that. We'll keep my name out of the scene as well."

"Eh...one more thing, please," said David with some hesitation. "I like when you are dominant. But I don't like to be humiliated. The difference is important to me."

"Absolutely! But tell me more where you want to draw the line. I'll respect that."

"Well, I've seen some videos where the dominatrix calls the sub terrible things and makes fun of his penis. That's a big turn-off. And please don't yell at me."

Diane leaned closer to him and let her right hand run gently through his hair. Just that light touch was arousing to him. "Our play has nothing to do with slavery and humiliation. I'll control the scene without yelling. But I'll practice some

271

'tie & tease' where I might remark that you'll be just out of reach. I'll make you desperately horny, but deny you release—until I decide it's time. I'll watch your reactions carefully. We'll get better and better at this kind of play as we practice. And we'll have a debriefing afterwards."

Rex took a thorough shower. He entered the anteroom in office clothes, but under his pants, he was wearing the tiny, tight thong that Diane had bought for him. Behind the desk, he found the dominatrix dressed in a Customs Officer uniform complete with an official-looking cap.

"Passport," she demanded.

Rex handed over an imaginary passport, and the Mistress pretended to study it.

"We have received a tip about an incoming delivery of contraband. Hence, all passengers are subject to search. I'll have to frisk you." She stepped around the desk and proceeded to thoroughly pat him down.

"Don't try to resist! Put your hands on your back." There was a click as the handcuffs came on. "You are hiding something in your pants." She unbuckled him and pulled down his pants. "Oh, that's a nice little thong there," she purred and let her hands caress his straining erection. "A bit tight though, isn't it?" She remedied that by slowly pulling the thong down to reveal his rock-hard erection. "Bend over for a DRE."

"A what?"

The officer pulled on a latex glove on her right hand with visible delight, added lubrication, and then provided a hands-on answer to his question. She took her time and seemed to enjoy having him in that helpless position. No contraband was found, but his prostate received a careful massage. The officer proceeded to check his pockets and triumphantly retrieved a small bag with white powder. "Aha, here we go! Cocaine!"

"It's not mine!" Rex objected. "You must have planted it."

She smacked him hard on the butt cheeks for that accusation, until he apologized. He was uncuffed, stripped of his last clothes, and taken into the dungeon. "This is where you will confess," she declared.

Only large, white candles lit the dungeon, many on tables and some hung from the ceiling. Various tools for B&D play adorned the red-brick walls. Soft, dreamy music played in the background. *Probably by Deuter*, he thought.

The officer locked his wrists into leather cuffs before she hoisted them up above his head. Rex had to stand very straight and could watch his naked, helpless position in a mirror on the wall in front of him.

"Prepare your confession," the customs officer commanded. Then, she disappeared.

The scene sent his imagination racing.

***

The Mistress entered the dungeon in a long, silky black gown. Now, she wore red lipstick, rouge, blue eye shadow, and the hoop earrings he had bought for her. He could not see her shoes, *but the heels must be very high*, he thought, as she stood in front of him in a towering posture.

Her hands went down his chest, teasingly running her long, blood-red nails lightly across his skin. His breathing accelerated, and his penis tightened again. As she ran her fingers across his body, everything was now an erogenous zone. She was so close, yet so untouchable. Her hand moved down to his crotch and pulsated gently to provoke a forceful response.

The Mistress circled around him to inspect her prey. "A very spankable butt," she noted approvingly and gave it a few hard slaps with her hands in between her caresses. Her nails scratched his back ever so lightly, putting his nerve endings on fire.

She came around to his front and tugged at his nipples. They stiffened under her touch, and she gradually increased the pressure. The Mistress pulled out a set of nipple clamps. They were the ones they had bought together. He felt an almost electric connection running from his clamped nipples down to his groin. Rex was on fire now and strained against the cuffs above his head. If she would only give him some good, long strokes, he would come in seconds.

But she did not. Instead, she took a step back and slowly slipped out of her silky gown. The Mistress was stunning in her black, lacy panty and bra set from *La Perla*, the shiny nylons with backseams tightly held by a matching black garter belt and the red five-inch strappy sandal stilettos with metal heels. Rex was restless with his handcuffs above his head. He strained to come closer to her, to stroke himself against her. Anywhere! But she was just out of reach with a teasing smile.

A display of whips, floggers, canes, and paddles on the wall opposite Rex drew some tingles throughout his body, some of fear…others of anticipation. There was also a St. Andrews Cross, a large, metal cage, and a bench with leather restraints for ankles and wrists. For another time, perhaps? But this Mistress played close to her sub, maximizing his sensual play rather than sensory deprivation and captivity. The Mistress took her time, in agonizingly slow motion, selecting the right tools. She returned with swaying hips and a black leather flogger and a riding crop.

The first throws of the flogger tails landed only gently on his shoulders. He was glad that she was avoiding his spinal cord area and neck but proceeded down to his buttocks. The lashes gradually became harder. As she watched his reactions, he was nowhere near pronouncing a *"yellow."* *Algolagnia is weird,* he thought. *This is a world apart from the whipping I suffered in captivity. They meant to hurt me, she means to excite me, their bullwhip scarred me, her flogger caresses me. But some people won't see the difference and would find this sick.* He wanted to beg: "harder," but that might be "topping from the bottom," so he kept quiet. And harder it got. It stung, but in an exciting way.

She stopped the lashes. Her hand caressed his burning bottom. "Nice and red," she noted with approval. "Are you ready to take back the accusation that the cocaine was planted?"

Rex did not want her to stop. "That plastic bag, with whatever it is, is not mine."

"Hmm, it seems I have to work a bit more to refresh your memory, then," she concluded. The Mistress tugged on the nipple clamps, and it burned in an exciting way. Then, she removed the nipple clamps carefully, instructing him to breathe in first and exhale strongly when she took them off. The impact was lasting as she rubbed her fingertips on the nipples, and they stiffened even more as the burn intensified.

She lowered the handcuffs above his head and uncuffed him. She found the cuffs that they had bought together and pushed his hands behind his back. She switched to a riding crop in black leather.

"Stand with your legs wide," she instructed.

He felt very helpless and exposed as she gently tapped on his cock and balls. Now and then, she paused to gently run her nails or a finger across his body. He was amazed at how such tiny but precise stimuli could excite him so much. Just looking at her was an injection of erotic visuals. He begged for release.

"I will continue to punish you and deny you any release until you confess," the Mistress declared. "Get down on your knees," she directed.

He was instructed to show his appreciation by worshipping her body with his tongue and kisses, starting with the heels, then the seams on the back of her stockings, up to the tops. She guided him to a comfortable, soft carpet in front of a sofa where she sat down, crossing her beautiful, long legs. The play continued with Rex in every conceivable position, kneeling, laying down at her feet, being gently poked by her high heels and stockinged feet.

Once, she pulled him by the hair and placed his face very close to hers. She smiled brightly and formed a kiss with her lips. But she stopped just short of planting them on his mouth and instead pushed him away. How close, yet so far! How tempting and seemingly inviting, but so firmly superior in her control. She was playing with his mind like a toy!

He was forbidden to touch himself, of course, as she was in charge. But finally, she gave permission. "If you confess to cocaine smuggling, you are allowed to release on my stockings."

"I confess!" Rex blurted out. He got on his knees and frantically worked himself toward a climax. But it was hard to switch right away from holding back to letting go. For a moment, anxiety crept into him. He could not possibly fail to finish now! Perhaps he was simply too excited, and his penis too numb from all the stimulation?

The Mistress had seen it before and smiled. "Relax, let me take charge."

First, she pulled him up to stand in front of her and gently took his penis into her mouth. It was sensational, and Rex jolted with excitement. Then, she had him kneel before her, and he focused on letting go. She leaned down, and her gentle strokes made him race to that point of no return, where the dam would burst. Rex moaned loudly of relief.

"As a first-time offender, I'm willing to let you go with a suspended sentence," she said with a smile. As Rex finally crawled up from the floor and into the large, comfortable sofa, she placed his face right where she wanted it. "Now, put your tongue to good work," she purred. "You know what to do by now."

He did.

CHAPTER 25

Kangaland Revisited

Bob approached David with a request to join a supervision mission to Kangaland. That was where David's field experience started and where the friendship with Bob had begun. It would be the second time he visited that country and its now well-established Community Development Project.

Arriving back to Kangaland, he was struck by how much had changed. The airport was much larger, and the immigration control was streamlined. The foreign currency form was no longer handed out but integrated into a much-simplified customs declaration. His laptop still had to be registered, but the format was simpler. He saw no armed guards, and the staff had neat civilian uniforms.

Two gentlemen from the Ministry of Development enthusiastically received them and drove them by bus to their hotel. The hotel had been renovated and now had running water at all times. There was fresh paint everywhere, and the restaurant was much upgraded.

It was nice to see Jemal again. They had been in touch via email, of course, but there had been long gaps in their conversation, and David had not been available for any of the intermediate missions. Jemal was a great guy, but communication was not his forte, and most information had to go officially via Jemal's boss to the Team Leader for the project.

The next morning, they set out in a Toyota Landcruiser to visit a project that the Bank had financed. The road out of the capital was new, financed by the European Union. They passed a new railroad being constructed with British aid. But the unimproved road was increasingly bad, and they had to slow down. The village they were visiting did not have a road, so the last half hour they walked. Approaching the village, some kids could see them and came storming toward them full of curiosity.

Jemal translated that they kept asking, "Who are you?" and "Give us some candy!" He laughed, a bit embarrassed. "When I was their age, I thought that White people always had a lot of money and candy in their pockets."

They reached the edge of the village, and they were clearly expected. A group of elderly men were gathered on a piece of flat land. A single chair made of rough wood and with a leather seat and backrest stood in the middle. Jemal pushed David to take a seat there. It was awkward, but apparently, it was what they wanted. Jemal stood next to him and began to address the crowd. Seated on the ground, wearing a grey blanket and with a large stick—looking almost biblical—an old man with a long, white beard, spoke for the community. He was surrounded by other old men, the younger ones standing in a semi-circle in the back. There were no women.

David waited for the old man to finish. Finally, Jemal translated the long welcome speech in a rather curt summary. "We thank our president for this project. The president is our leader. You are welcome here. We have seen many improvements. We have new trees, new terraces, water stays better now in fields. The new wells have good water. Now, we need a road to the village. A school for our children."

There must have been much more in the speech, but he could inquire about that later. Tea was served for him, and only him, in a metal cup. It was really hot, so he dared to drink it. He had to in order not to offend. It was worse with the plate of porridge with a hard-boiled egg on top that was put in front of him. Obliged to take a bite, he used his right hand, not the left. David was left-handed, but he had been cautioned by a colleague that this hand, in many countries, was earmarked for other, more personal uses. Jemal continued to provide him bits and pieces of translation.

Jemal gave his own speech in the local language, which was apparently well-received.

David would have to ask about that later. "I have some questions, please," said David.

"Of course, you can ask anything you want."

"The trees that I see planted over there, who owns them?"

"They belong to the village," Jemal clarified.

"Please just ask them," David insisted.

Jemal smirked but translated.

There was a lively discussion. Finally, Jemal turned to David. "They say that the Ministry will tell them what to do with those trees."

David had many more questions, and the dynamics continued to play out. Short, specific questions, translations, long discussions among the elders dominated by just a few, short translations that contained some answers, but also deflections and empty rhetoric. After half an hour, Jemal reminded him that they had another stop on the way home and could not linger. It was dangerous to drive after dark. Pleasantries and thanks were exchanged.

David asked if the village had a latrine, but Jemal shook his head. "There is plenty of land here, so you can choose any bush," he suggested.

They continued to the second stop. Only two hours away, it was in some ways another world. A forceful woman who exuded self-confidence ran the very poor, small village. She received them outside her simple hut. The conversation dynamics were much livelier this time.

Jemal relaxed, as did the village head. A veteran from the liberation war, she had become a high-ranking officer in the army. She wore pants and a shirt in military fatigue style. Her answers were crisp. In response to David's questions, she pulled out a ledger with handwritten notes. She had the data on project achievements: wells dug, terraces constructed, trees planted, an improved village road, fertilizer and hybrid seed delivered, labor engaged, salaries paid and so on, and she knew her stuff, impressing David.

They systematically moved around in the village to see physical evidence of what the village head had talked about. They were met with smiling faces and curious children everywhere. *Here is proof that aid can give results on the ground*, David thought. The infusion of cash for village labor had also been substantial.

The mission continued for a week with several more field visits and formal, long meetings with government officials in the capital. At the end of the mission, their counterparts in the Ministry had arranged a party. Cheerful collaboration replaced the suspicion he had met the first time he came to Kangaland. As they drank beer together and listened to local music, Jemal was keen to tell him that he was going to a semester-long course in Agricultural Engineering and English in another African country. David suppressed his smile at the memory of how Jemal had been so indignant about the suggested need for 'capacity building' the first time they met. Once the first colleague arrived back home and talked about his experience studying abroad, it was easy to recruit the next batch.

The visit was particularly gratifying in comparison with his very first mission for the Bank. He left in a very different mood this time as he watched the fields of Kangaland disappear from his airplane window.

***

David had close to the maximum sixty days of vacation saved and would lose any excess days. He added some personal days to the mission. He needed a break. Hence, he flew from Kangaland to Sawatini where he had never been. It was an island off the coast of Africa with beautiful nature but a troubled economy, a despotic regime, and widespread poverty.

David arrived at night in a chaotic airport where aggressive taxi drivers competed for his attention. No orderly taxi system existed, and he ended up in an unmarked car that had seen better days. The back seat was totally worn out, and the seat belts stuck halfway.

The driver protested when he tried to put on a belt. "I'm good driver," he yelled. He turned off the ignition at each red light to save on gas. They arrived safely at the hotel.

Usually, David's trips were overloaded with tasks, but now, he relished a chance to just discover things as they unfolded.

The hotel where David stayed was one of the city's best and most expensive. It naturally drew the city's large begging population. In some poor countries, the authorities cracked down on beggars, and in many, the extended family served as a compassionate safety net in hard times. But in many poor countries, the increasing mobility from rural to urban areas loosened family ties and created huge holes in the social fabric. Social capital diminished, begging became more widespread and sometimes aggressive.

The begging here took on a particular heartbreaking form. Guards with batons policed the immediate area at the hotel entrance. But as he turned the corner, he was no longer protected. A group of children spotted him and descended on him like a swarm of locusts. Yelling "Give me money," "Mister, hungry, hungry" in broken English. They surrounded him, tugged on his clothes, and stretched their thin arms up toward his face, cornering him. His guilt from his privileged world became unbearable when a young girl was deliberately pushed to the front to show off her malformed face. She had cleft lips, and one side of her face had large burns or maybe a severe skin disease. Whatever it was, it was gut-wrenching, and David felt nauseous. It was as if the crowd was telling him, "Look here, you cannot say no to this girl. If you have a heart in your body, you will give what you've got now!"

The situation was unbearable and he reached for the change in his pocket, but a memory struck him. Another time in another country, he had seen a White couple coming out of a fancy hotel to meet a similar group. They panicked and resorted to throwing candy and a few dollar bills around them to escape. The ferocious fight that broke out was merciless. An older, strong boy was the most triumphant as he knocked down his weaker competitors. The couple retreated to the hotel, visibly shaken. He wanted to avoid repeating their mistake.

"I'm so very sorry I can't help you all, and if I give some of you money, there will be a big fight," he said but the shouting drowned him out. Retreating slowly to not trample anyone, he made it back to the guarded area, where the security guards quickly dispersed the children. He had to retreat to his room to compose himself. Years of working in poor countries had numbed him, but this sort of confrontation was still shocking.

I can't help these kids directly, he thought, *but, at least, I can help to bring money and knowledge to this country so that they can feed their population better. Some of my colleagues are working here to put all of these kids in school and provide clean drinking water and medical care.* Yet, he could not escape a profound feeling of insufficiency and frustration in the face of such abject poverty.

***

David had emailed JP about his trip to Sawatini, as he knew that country well. JP responded promptly and suggested he should pay a visit to the local Bank office and see Pedro Garcia, an old friend of JP's. "'e knows the country well, and 'e's got a great sense of 'umor. If 'e has time, 'e'll show you around."

Garcia answered the phone right away when David called. He explained his impromptu visit and asked for advice about things to see. Pedro suggested they meet the following morning in his office at 8 a.m. "I'll arrange for a Bank car. Even the registered taxis are not really safe here. We use our own cars whenever we can. Be ready at 7:30 a.m. please. The driver will have a uniform and a badge."

The next morning, the room phone rang at 7 a.m., and David raced out of the shower to pick it up.

"Mr. Pettersen from World Bank?" a heavily accented voice inquired.

"Yes, who is this?"

"World Bank driver, sir. Please come."

"But I was told the pick-up would be 7:30," David objected, feeling caught off guard as he stood there wet from the shower.

"Sir, traffic very bad. Please come."

In haste, David got ready and descended to the lobby. A short man in a dark suit rose to greet him. "Please come," he said and grabbed David's briefcase.

"Hang on," David blurted out. "May I see your badge, please?"

"Ah, badge in car, please come," repeated the man. He looked agitated now. Something was not right.

"Why aren't you wearing a uniform?"

"Ah, uniform is cleaned, sir. Please come."

David refused to let his grip go of the briefcase. "Security!" he yelled.

Two guards by the door immediately approached. His driver went for the door but was stopped. An agitated discussion followed in a local language. The suspect was pushed into a room where the loud confrontation continued. David sat down to see if he could be of help later. The Duty Manager approached David.

"Sir, we apologize for this incident. That man is an imposter. Most likely he would have taken you for a ride to his friends waiting in some garage where they would have separated you from your valuables. Perhaps nothing more than that, but still not a pleasant experience."

"I don't understand how that man could know who I am and that I was going to the Bank office."

The manager sat down with him and spoke in a low voice. "This is what troubles me. I suspect somebody in the reception informed him that you had checked in on a Laissez-Passer identifying you as Bank staff. The routine then is that there is some kind of a meeting the next morning at the Bank office. It happens all the time."

"What happens now? Do you need a formal statement?"

"The guards watched him approaching you. The police here are very good at extracting confessions, so I don't think we need anything more from you," he smiled.

It was an unsettling experience, but his thoughts were interrupted by a uniformed young man who approached him. "Mr. Pedersen?"

"Yes."

The young man held up his World Bank badge. "I'm ready to take you to our office when you so wish."

They arrived at the Bank office after only fifteen minutes. Pedro welcomed him to his office. He inquired about JP and a few other colleagues. Then, he apologized that he had so little time. A new meeting had been called in the morning, and he had to attend. In the afternoon, a mission from the Bank would arrive to the office, and the evening was booked for a family event.

"I'm really sorry, but I just don't have any time to spend with you until tomorrow evening," he explained. He offered a good country map and some quick advice on things to see.

David thanked him and took the same car back to the hotel.

***

David cut the visit to Sawatini short and headed back to the airport in the evening. He had found a flight to another beautiful island off the African East coast, Marasca. Its biodiversity was legendary. He checked in to the modest airport hotel and reviewed his options. While transportation was underdeveloped and the tourism infrastructure only nascent, he found a three-day excursion out to the most prominent national park.

After a short flight, he checked in to a rustic, very clean lodge just outside the gates to the park. Local guides offered tours, focusing on both animals and plants, and he marveled at the different species of monkeys and the amazing variety of plant life in the rainforest.

One evening, he ran into a group of botany students from UC Berkeley, sitting in the hotel bar. When pressed, David admitted working for the World Bank.

"You guys are just killing the rainforests," one of the students blurted out.

"Name me one organization that provides more financial support to biodiversity conservation than the Bank," David challenged him. There was an uneasy silence around the table.

"You support biodiversity conservation?" A girl with bright red hair, tattooed arms, and a nose ring looked unconvinced.

David pulled up his laptop, and fortunately, the WiFi worked fine that evening. He displayed a set of publications and project reports and soon had an eager crowd around him. They had hard questions and were not easily swayed, but the mood gradually changed.

"Damn it," said a tall long-haired boy with Jesus-looks, "I've been demonstrating against the Bank, the IMF, and the military-industrial complex. Now, I feel like buying you a beer."

Everyone laughed, and the evening proceeded with a thoughtful discussion about what economic development really should be about.

Toward the end of his week on the island, he sauntered around the capital. He sweat from the pounding sun as he navigated his way, running into only a few tourists. A palace that had housed the nobility for centuries towered over the city on a hill. The view lived up to its reputation, and David raised his camera to take a picture.

"*No, no monsieur,*" a voice called out. A uniformed guard approached him, looking agitated.

"I'm sorry, is photography not allowed here?" David asked.

The guard realized that French was not the right language of the moment. "Come," he said and went ahead of David toward a small tent on the edge of the hilltop.

Seated in the tent were two serious-looking, uniformed gentlemen. An impressive ledger lay in front of them. The older of the two men smiled and greeted him in French. David responded in English. The officer switched to English.

"Sir, you must have permit before taking picture," he announced with careful dictation.

"I'm sorry. I didn't know. How much is it?"

The gentlemen smiled. "There is no cost. You must apply."

David was used to all sorts of permits and fees being required when visiting sights of interest. Maybe there was no official fee but a small note of "encouragement"?

"*Passeport,* please," said the senior officer, extending a hand.

Usually, David did not carry his passport with him, only a photocopy. But there was no functioning safe in his hotel room, and the clerk at the reception had left the hotel that morning. It turned out to be fortunate, as his passport was scrutinized for every possible detail. All the data were entered by hand in the impressive ledger.

"So, if there is no fee, can I take my photos now?" David asked.

"*Monsieur*, permit ready tomorrow."

"Hmm, but is there any reason to believe that my application will be denied?"

"*Non monsieur, pas du tout!*"

David was at a loss. Maybe some "encouragement" was needed after all? He fished out a local bill with about a five-dollar value and placed it on the table.

"Would this help to expedite the process?"

The smiles on the faces of the two officers vanished quickly. No doubt, they were offended by such a blatant attempt at compromising their integrity.

"*Monsieur*, permit *gratuit* ready tomorrow."

Feeling ashamed, David got out of the tent. With the guard on his tail, he did not dare to take any photos and resolved to return the next day.

***

The hotel dinner that night was delicious but provoked a most unfortunate digestive reaction. He spent most of that night in the bathroom.

The next morning, he ordered some Coke from room service—"no ice please"—and spent most of the day in bed, recovering. Going out was too risky with his unstable stomach.

Having rested a full day, he felt better the second morning. It would be the last day on the island. The view from the palace hill was the best in town, so it would be worth it to walk there in spite of the heat.

Sweating and panting from the uphill walk, he arrived at the permit tent. "I'm here to pick up my photo permit, please," said David, extending his passport.

It did not take them long to find the entry. The senior officer turned to him with a look of regret. "*Je suis désolé…*permit expired yesterday!"

Stunned, David retreated downhill without any photo of the grandiose view. As an economist, he was used to looking for the rationality behind even the most surprising human behavior. "What are the incentives at play?" was the textbook question. A fee or a bribe would have answered that. Employment creation was a driving force behind some regulations, but that effect would be achieved also with open-ended permits. If some cultural behaviors cannot be explained with Western economics, what does that mean for development aid?

CHAPTER 26

Race Matters

Gradually, David found himself writing less original work, and reviewing the work of others more and more, sometimes in circles of reviews. It bothered him. "Palimpsest" was a word he recalled encountering in Orwell's *1984*. It signified a manuscript that had been scrubbed clean to fit an updated version of politically correct history. In the Bank, it was a high-profile document that went from department to department to accommodate a never-ending string of changes to satisfy refined sensitivities and special interests. After several rounds, little of the original text could be traced. Sometimes, the process reached its end only when a senior official put a determined footprint across the text hard enough to make the ink stick. At other times, the document died a silent death in some archive, having been scrubbed of most of its original content.

The project documentation for the "Makanana Port Project" in Leonia was unusually lengthy and displayed a notable talent for circumlocution. Granted, some of that was pro-forma stuff that had to accompany any project document at this stage. Other years, senior management led initiatives to "reduce paperwork" or "streamline for efficiency," and the forms were simplified. Of course, this resulted in a countermovement some years later, when "a holistic approach," "enhanced structure," and "attention to detail" were celebrated by imposing a number of specific requirements on project documentation. The Bank was in that phase now, and it weighted down the document.

Leonia was one of the poorest countries on Earth and ravaged by a civil war. Incorporating some of the rebel leaders into a unity government had achieved a peaceful settlement. Donors were eager to award the new regime a flying start. A consortium of donors offered to help with infrastructure improvements, including a full-scale upgrade of the dilapidated Makanana Port.

David skimmed through the project documents and was struck by the level of ambition. With only an ordinary budget allocated for the preparation, the team was suggesting going much beyond the port itself and into the country's general economic planning. Every single aspect of the port's repercussions on the economy would also be analyzed in detail. It read more like a macroeconomic master plan of development for the entire country. The text was also a bit disjointed, giving the impression that different team members had put in their wish list without a final reconciliation process.

The review meeting started at eleven. There were about fifteen people in the room. The chairperson was a stern-looking gray-haired woman with an Eastern European accent. She did not introduce herself, assuming that everyone knew her.

"Mr. Johnson, you have five minutes to present the project. Then, I'll call upon our three peer reviewers. I'll lay out a few key points for discussion, and we'll stick to that agenda. We have ninety minutes."

The team leader, Alex Johnson, laid out the grand scheme. "The Makanana Port Project is the key to Leonia's future development. We have a historic opportunity to contribute to this ground-breaking scheme that can enhance the livelihoods of a population that has suffered so much in the past ten years." He continued to read key passages from the main document, describing the type of installations foreseen at the port, the surrounding infrastructure plans, and the expected downstream benefits. After the allotted five minutes were up, the chairperson simply cut him off.

"Thank you, Mr. Johnson, we've all read the documents. I now call upon the first peer reviewer, Mr. Odinga."

Mr. Odinga, who had experience with port projects elsewhere, started by cautiously praising the documents for their "comprehensive style," and "impressive attention to minute detail." "It's a very ambitious agenda," he continued. "The suggested 'study of the port's direct and indirect downstream effects on the prevailing unequal gender power-relations' would seem to be methodologically problematic. What impact will it have? Is it relevant? Aren't there more direct interventions that could enhance the women's situation in Leonia?"

Alex was supposed to let the reviewers finish, but he jumped into his defense right away.

"You're missing the point! This is a holistic project that aims to capture the full set of synergies emanating from this catalytic port project. This is a once-in-a-lifetime opportunity to map out a full-scale assault on the constraints that keep Leonia from developing. If we neglect the role of women, we turn our backs on half the population!"

The chairperson broke in. "Mr. Johnson, this is not the time for rhetorical exuberance. Nobody's turning their back on women. But this project cannot do everything."

Alex looked entirely unconvinced but kept quiet, and Odinga was allowed to finish.

"Our next peer review is Mr. John ..."—she searched for her reading glasses but didn't find them— "do I read that right? John Wayne?" She could not stop herself from muttering, "May God forgive his parents!"

Muffled chuckles came from the back row. Mr. Wayne was a senior macroeconomist in the Leonia Country Office. A young man to David's right leaned over and whispered,

"With a name like that, can you imagine booking a table at a restaurant or a hotel room? Either they hang up on you, or they give you the very best."

Mr. Wayne was not present, but he had sent three pages of comments, which the chairperson's assistant placed before her. "In summary, Mr. Wayne thinks that the project should be more narrowly defined. He advises against the ambitious macroeconomic model for the country that's suggested. He doesn't think there's a sufficient statistical basis. He recommends a simple partial analysis of the port and its links into the transport sector."

The third peer reviewer dealt with environmental impacts. She expressed concern about the extensive dredging that could be foreseen. "What about the impact on the coral reefs and the local fisheries?" she asked. She also suggested that the impacts of climate change should be assessed.

Alex objected. "Climate change! You're talking about something that might become important in a century, if even then!"

The peer reviewer from Environment kept her cool. "The port must be designed with a very long-term perspective. Sea-level rise and intensified hurricanes are already happening. here's also increased risk of flooding from upstream rainfall. Some of the planned infrastructure is located on a flood plain—even using old data. Frankly, it's not an ideal place for a port."

"Then, why this location?" the chairperson intervened.

"There's already a small port there," Alex volunteered.

The young man next to David leaned in and whispered. "The prime minister's relatives live in that area and could make a fortune off of land deals."

The reviewer continued, "There's also excessive groundwater pumping in the area for commercial agriculture and industry which leads to the ground slowly sinking. This adds to the long-term risk of inundation that could impact the port's links to the rest of the country."

Alex threw up his arms. "Listen, I can't deal with all of that, I have a tight schedule to do this. It has to go to the Board within six months, or else…"

Everyone in the room knew what he meant. Bringing projects through Board approval was a way to collect gold stars. It may have been Alex's first project as a team leader. But why had he not been given better advice? Or had he refused to listen? The contradictions were puzzling: over-extensions in some areas, but a refusal to deal with other things that were of relevance. True, some colleagues thought of environmental issues only when they had to.

The chairperson laid out an agenda for the discussion, and others were given a chance to comment. It only served to reinforce what the peer reviewers had stated, and to avoid repetition, David decided to leave it at the written comments he had sent before the meeting.

The meeting did not end to Alex's satisfaction. The chairperson handed out advice that sounded more like orders. She demanded that Alex see her in person in two weeks to ensure that project documentation had reached "greater maturity."

David stopped by the men's room on the way out. After he came out to wash his hands, Alex was standing next to him. Without looking directly at David, he said, "They just can't deal with a Black man who thinks for himself!"

David thought to respond for a second. Discrimination against Black people was real. But from David's perspective, it was not a matter of race at all in this case. David had read the documents with similar reflections to the peer reviewers, not knowing that Alex was Black. But if he said that, he would only come across as another White bigot who was denying racism. It was awkward, but an idea sprung to mind.

"Alex, do you know James Robinson?"

"I've heard about him. One of the few Blacks who has made it to senior adviser in this racist bank."

"I suggest you should have a word with him about your project. He is very experienced and senior, but an approachable guy I have learned from first-hand."

Alex looked unconvinced, but after a brief pause, he said, "I might try that. He'll understand my perspective."

***

David went for lunch. He would normally just pick up something in the cafeteria and read emails while eating. But today, Antonio, the colleague he met in Tanaland, invited him to a lunch in a posh restaurant very close to the Bank.

David approached Antonio's table and was introduced to two colleagues: Denzel, who was based in D.C. and worked on water and sanitation projects, and Akuada, a strikingly well-dressed Black woman who worked in the Bank's country office in Tanaland. They exchanged pleasantries and impressions from the working day.

The waiter took their orders. Akuada held up a glass close to the waiter's face, saying, "I believe I'm entitled to a clean glass."

The glass looked fine to David, but there might have been something on it, and the waiter apologized and quickly arrived with a new one.

"Akuada means 'a girl born into a wealthy family,'" quipped Denzel.

Akuada looked embarrassed. She kept adjusting her expensive-looking necklace and golden bracelets.

Denzel drifted into criticizing the staff at the Ministry of Water and Sanitation in Tanaland for their inefficiency and corrupt practices. "There's just no work ethic around there. I can say that because I'm Black, but you guys"—he nodded toward Antonio and David—"you'd be called racists!"

"Rubbish, you a' not really Black," objected Akuada with a clear British accent and pronouncing every syllable carefully. "A little bi'd told me that you were raised by your White mothe' in New Je'sey. You don't even know who your fathe' is, hence, you don't know if he was Black."

"Look, I do know he is Black, or was. I don't know if he's still around. He kind of lost interest when my mom started turning her attention more to me than him. At least, that's what she told me."

"How typical fo' a Black man," Akuada blurted out.

Antonio and David looked at each other in shock. If either of them had said *that*, the label would have been obvious. David had seen the figures from the U.S. Census Bureau. Among mothers raising kids solo, there was a significant over-representation of Blacks, but one could not raise that as a White person.

"You can't tell me that I'm not Black," said Denzel, clearly offended. "I've always been self-identified as Black. And I was always treated and *mistreated* as Black as a kid. In school, I was mobbed by Whites, Latinos, and Asians, but accepted by Blacks. That's who I am. Period!" He rose quickly and went to the restroom.

Akuada re-arranged the napkin to cover her expensive skirt, then leaned toward David. "Denzel is idolizing his absent fathe'. He craves an identity that really isn't his. He is a shade da'ker than you two, but that is utterly insignificant. You should see him with the locals. He is as keen as mustard but still like a fish out of water. He is bloody patronizing them, whilst thinking he's one of them."

"Wow," said Antonio. "How can you even work together?"

"It's how I make a living, how I can be independent as a woman in my country. All progressive ve'biage notwithstanding, there's a lot of sexism among the so-called 'brothe's.' As a woman, you have to wo'k twice as ha'd as a man, and as a Black woman even ha'de'!"

Denzel returned from the restroom, looking tense. Akuada dug up a report from her Gucci bag and handed it to Denzel. "The repo't your asked fo'! Done and dusted!"

"Ok, thanks," said Denzel, looking surprised. "It's finished already?"

Akuada frowned. "Well, not everyone in Tanaland is inefficient," she ridiculed.

Antonio tried to defuse the situation with a funny story about a failed date. He was divorced but apparently trying to remedy that situation. Food came, and they all enjoyed it. David thought about bringing up the morning's discussion and asked them what they thought, but it would be too sensitive. Then, Akuada took a call and stepped away from the table.

Denzel leaned into the table. "That bitch can be so aggressive," he confided. "She thinks that she knows everything about Tanaland because she's from here. Worse, she makes herself the spokesperson for Africans in general. The truth is that she's from a very wealthy family, grown up with servants, expensive boarding school, college in England, and all the rest. Her father is a high-ranking military officer. Of course, she doesn't want to hear about high-level corruption."

They waited for the food. "Antonio, you're a Harvard-man, is that right?" said Denzel.

In any conversation with Americans lasting more than fifteen minutes, the question, "Where did you go to school?" was likely to appear. David had come to understand that the college years branded an individual for life, gave them prestige—or not—as the case may be. It was the underpinning of personal identities and fierce rivalries.

Antonio grinned. "No, I'm an MIT-man actually. But Harvard is an OK school if you can't get into MIT."

Akuada returned with apologies.

Denzel smiled and proposed a toast to Boston. "Well, I spent some great years at Harvard."

"Whe' you got in because of affi'mative action," interjected Akuada. She smiled, but David could tell that there was a serious undertone, and Denzel looked hurt.

"That's so much bullshit! I earned that spot."

"Of cou'se, you did, but will you not admit that sometimes it's convenient to be classified as Black, although you live a life of privilege?"

"You should not be talking about privilege," Denzel burst out. It was getting ugly now. "As a Black man, you have to work harder than anyone else to prove yourself!"

David searched for a way to defuse the situation. "Hang on, both of you identify as Black, so I'm sure that you can find a lot of things to agree on. Reparations for slavery, for

299

example. I sympathize with the idea, given the heinous crime against humanity that it was. But I'm just not sure how it would work in practice. What's your view on that?"

"Reparations!" Akuada snorted. "Slavery was ho'rific, but it is ove' since a long time back. The real victims a' dead, but the current generations should not lock themselves into victimhood. Besides, they a' mostly better off in the U.S. than they would have been in Africa. A' you suggesting people like Denzel should get money because his dad was Black and several generations ago one of his ancestors was traded from Africa to America? Should he get a fifty pe'cent cut because his mothe' is White? What about people who a' 1/16th Black? Whe' does it end?"

She glanced around the table but nobody offered an answer. David felt awkward as his attempt to defuse the situation had blown up.

Akuada was on a roll. "If a lot of money is directed only to Black people, do you think racial relations will be bette' o' wo's?"

"Don't be silly," objected Denzel. "It shouldn't be individual payments. I'm talking about structural changes to promote Black entrepreneurs, improve Black education, invest in schools, affordable housing in Black areas, justice reform, better policing, all those things. I'm talking about combating structural racism. I'm talking about teaching kids about Critical Race Theory. People need to understand that racism is not limited to personal attitudes—it is something that is embedded in society across sectors."

"So, who should pay?" Antonio asked. "All taxpayers, or just White people?"

"For practical reasons, all taxpayers will have to contribute, even if it means some Black people will take a hit financially. Morally, everyone who was involved in the slave trade bears a responsibility. In principle, even Black Africans who were complicit," Denzel concluded.

"What a' you talking about?" said Akuada through clenched teeth. "Africans complicit?"

"Calm down, Akuada, you know as well as I that the slave trade was made possible to a significant extent through cooperation with African tribes. Slavery was not invented by the White man. It had deep roots in tribal warfare. The White colonizers were hunkered down in coastal forts. There were few of them, drunk and sick from tropical disease. Do you think they ventured into the bush on their own? No, they depended on a chain of delivery of slaves from the uplands. They fed on the old tribal rivalries and encouraged them. But who do you think ran that supply chain? Some of your ancestors, I'm sure!"

This was too much for Akuada, and she hurried from the table. Denzel threw up his hands in a resigned gesture.

"Some people can't face the facts. Black men like Henry Louis Gates Jr., another Harvard-man, have written about this. Have you read his *Life Upon These Shores: Looking at African American History*? There are other studies that more fully document what I've just said. But she can't stomach a frank discussion about it."

"OK," said Antonio, "some Africans did collaborate with the slave traders. I've read about that too. But surely the main moral burden lies with White people who organized the trade, made it lucrative. Without that demand, the supply would have been much more limited. And pretty much everybody in Europe was involved, I think, even the Danes, right, David?"

"I won't deny it," said David. "Denmark was not a big player, of course. But there was some colonialism in our history. There were Danish forts on the Gold Coast, Ghana today, that engaged in slave trade in the eighteenth century. There were also colonies in the Danish West Indies in the seventeenth and eighteenth centuries."

"So, Denzel, shouldn't the Danes also be paying reparations? They built some of their welfare state on the backs of Black slave labor, right?"

"Look, I'm not sure where to draw the line. In practical terms, the Danes are doing a great job already funneling generous amounts of aid to Africa directly. I don't see the Danes sending money to the U.S. Treasury to hand out to Black communities," Denzel concluded.

The food arrived, and Antonio asked to have Akuada's portion bagged so that he could take it with him. True to form, he wanted to steer the conversation in a more light-hearted direction. "David, shouldn't you also pay Britain and Ireland for all the pillage, plunder, and rape the Vikings inflicted upon them?"

"Impractical, my dear friend. Besides, the Vikings were not colonizers and organized as slave traders. OK, they were not great diplomats. Their English wasn't very good either. So, negotiations sometimes went haywire, especially since those guys had filled themselves with mead and eaten hallucinogenic mushrooms before the battle. That's how we got the word 'berserker' into the English language. When diplomacy failed, they sometimes got violent. And when the enemies' men were killed, it was natural for the Vikings to take care of the women and children. They would have been worse off if left behind!"

Antonio and Denzel burst out laughing. "David, that's the poorest excuse I've ever heard for plunder, kidnapping, and brutality! I know you guys have stopped all that, but the worst of your gene pool still lives among British soccer fans.

You have a lot to answer for," said Antonio and slapped David's back gently.

The conversation drifted to more innocuous subjects as they finished their food and paid. David went back to the Bank. Apparently, the idea of reparations for slavery was not only controversial among White people.

***

In the Bank's lobby, David was approached by an acquaintance he recognized. Mike was a young, energetic American who had done some short-term consulting for David. On that basis, he had recommended that Mike should apply for a permanent post that had been advertised.

"Hi, David, I'm just out from an interview with HR."

"How did that go?"

"As expected, I guess. As a White male, you're really at a disadvantage when trying to join the Bank. They made no bones about it. They're looking to hire more women and people of color. I can understand why, but it's tough to be up against that personally."

"I'm sorry if you feel discriminated against, but the fact is that the Bank hires some White males as well. And because of history, it's still the largest single group, I think."

"Maybe, but that's all changing. Working here and with people like you was rewarding, but I need a more permanent job and will look elsewhere now."

"It's the situation for quite a few consultants of all races and gender. But don't give up, keep doing good work, and you'll be noticed."

"You know what really got to me was when that interviewer said they're trying to recruit people from 'underprivileged groups' as she put it. "Well, shit, man, my dad was a sawmill worker in northern Minnesota who cut his hand so badly it had to be amputated. He became dependent on opioid pain killers and died of an overdose at age forty-two. My mom never recovered from that and became an alcoholic and lost her job as a janitor. I worked through community college as a waiter and got a transfer to University of Minnesota. With stellar grades, I got a good package from Cornell—still had to borrow a lot, of course. It took me six years to get my PhD in Economics because I had to take breaks to be my mom's caregiver. I'm still up to my ears in debt, but they just plaster the label 'White male' on me and assume that I'm privileged!" he snarled.

All David could offer was "I'm really sorry to hear this about your parents. Those labels are superficial, but unfortunately, they are becoming more and more important. They are based on good intentions about equality, but they hide the individual and promote tribal thinking. Still, the Bank hires some White males, so don't give up! They just make an extra effort to look at other candidates."

They shook hands, and Mike hurried through the doors out from 1818 H Street NW.

David climbed the stairs up to his office. The issue of race could not be dodged when working on development in Africa. He tried to be observant of his own behavior and language in order not to offend racial sensitivities. Most of the time, it seemed to work, and he had forged some productive relationships with Black Africans. When he was met with negativity or rudeness, his default assumption was that it was not racially motivated. Although, at one time, walking in the U.S. in a Black neighborhood, somebody yelled, "We don't like White people" right behind his back. That hurt!

In the U.S., sharpened identity politics did not only empower voices among minorities, it also provoked a backlash of White nationalism and even domestic terrorism recognized by the FBI as an important threat. Just looking at the demographic trends instilled fear in some conservative Whites. They got organized to protect their privileged position in society. In the long run, would democracy hold for these tensions?

Within the Bank, there was now much focus on counting the representation of various groups in each department. Managers were given targets and told they would be accountable if they were missed. But the labels established to further "diversity" hid so much *individual* diversity themselves. His meetings this day had illustrated that. So how could a "fair" system actually be implemented?

David did not have all the answers and turned to more practical matters. He had deadlines to keep!

CHAPTER 27

Are Things Getting Better?

A special branch at the Bank trained staff working in the public sector in developing countries. Some courses took place in Washington D.C., and David got an invitation for the closing dinner for one of them.

There were many round tables in the large atrium where the dinner was held. He spotted an empty seat and asked if he could sit down. The gentlemen on each side nodded. As David reached for the menu card, the gentleman on his right leaned forward to him.

"I see you work for the Bank," he said and pointed to David's ID clipped to his coat pocket. "I want you to know how much I resent how you interfere with our domestic development policies and projects. You come with your conditionalities, your audits, and your cookie-cutter recipes for development. We Africans are proud people. You should just hand over the money that we have earned as compensation for past injustices and let us take care of it."

This could be an unpleasant dinner, he thought. "Hello, I'm David Pedersen," he said, extending a hand to the gentleman.

The gentleman was a bit perplexed but realized that he had not introduced himself. "Hello, I'm Mr. Katinga, Permanent Secretary, Ministry of Development," he said, managing to produce a smile.

David turned to the left and introduced himself. The gentleman on the left had already started on the appetizer and was absorbed in that endeavor. "Hello, I'm Nelson Bandulo," he said and extended a hand. "I see that you are with the Bank," he said and nodded at David's ID.

"Yes," admitted David and prepared for the next onslaught.

"Well," said Nelson with a puzzled look, "I don't understand you people. I mean, you don't seem to understand how much corruption and mismanagement there is in Africa. You just write checks but look the other way!"

For a moment, David figured he had been set up. But a second look at the two as he pushed his chair back made him realize that the two gentlemen were sincere—just totally on opposite sides of the argument. David pushed his chair a bit further back and had them shake hands.

"Well, gentlemen, it seems like on the one hand we are dictatorial colonialists who arrogantly impose our policies on developing countries, but on the other hand, we are irresponsible spenders of taxpayer money that is captured by corrupt elites. So, which is it?"

The puzzled gentlemen restated their respective positions, and a lively set of back and forth exchanges took place. It continued during the main course and the dessert. At coffee time, the positions had converged a great deal. David mostly held back and let them fight it out.

Nelson summarized. "I guess we agree that there has to be accountability for funds. We want money to be spent well, and taxpayers in rich countries have the right to know how money is spent. But resources should be guided by the will of the people in developing countries."

"Sounds like a balanced view, and one that the Bank could support." David smiled. The two gentlemen also smiled and thanked each other for a good discussion.

After some final words by the dinner's host, the large atrium emptied, and David went up to his office to deal with some emails. The balancing act that Katinga and Bandulo had highlighted was real, and it was likely that the Bank went too far in either direction at times. It was a reminder to him to search for a sensible middle ground in his own work.

***

David was asked by External Affairs to make a presentation at a conference in Utara in North Africa with the title "Development Progress in Africa." Since it would gather mostly NGOs, the speech could be delegated all the way down the pecking order to David. The presentation would be prepared by External Affairs to ensure adherence to official policy. An independent foundation sponsored the conference. David had never heard of it, but apparently, they had plenty of money. The sponsor wanted donors to meet NGOs and activists for a constructive dialogue. The invitation noted that in spite of setbacks, the share of extremely poor was decreasing globally as was infant and maternal mortality. Indicators of school enrollment, and vaccination rates also pointed in the right direction. Meanwhile, surveys of popular opinion in many countries revealed a pessimistic outlook among a majority: things were getting worse, in their view.

A Swedish medical doctor, Lars Roslund had become the poster child for a well-documented, cleverly popularized optimism about development. David had seen some of his talks on YouTube and marveled at Roslund's ability to break down complex arguments into simple illustrations that stuck in people's minds. Roslund was invited as the keynote speaker.

External Affairs provided him with a standard PowerPoint with fifty-five slides highlighting the Bank's achievements as "the premier development institution" it was. Too many slides, in David's opinion, as he went through them. In addition, several were overloaded with data and invited a comment he had heard many times during public presentations: "I know you can't read these fonts, but…"

David dreaded standing in front of his peers saying comments like that, so he noted which sections he'd consider skipping at the podium.

***

It was the usual departure from Dulles Airport. There was no free upgrade to first class available this time, but Business class to Paris with Air France was not a bad deal. You could count on good wines. Arriving to sit next to him was a tall, obese gentleman who introduced himself with a crushing handshake clearly meant to establish who the alpha male was.

"Sven Andersson, Volvo Trucks."

"Hello, I'm David Pedersen, World Bank."

Sven scoffed. "I've read about you people. You're probably an economist on your way to some poor country. They don't need more economists. They need engineers!"

David sighed. As a World Banker, he was used to being attacked but rarely so immediately and blatantly when flying. His silence provided an opportunity for Sven to continue.

"Do you know why people are poor?"

David did not have time to answer until Sven disclosed the secret.

"It's about transportation! Those people can't get anywhere and can't sell their stuff because the roads are fucked up, and they don't have transportation! And do you know who makes the best trucks?"

This time it appeared that Sven really wanted to hear David's answer.

"I suspect the answer you wish to hear is 'Volvo.'"

"You're damn right!" Sven exclaimed and hit the armrest with a hard slap to reinforce his point. That settled the discussion about poverty for Sven, who brusquely stopped a passing air hostess and commanded two vodkas with ice. "Make sure it's Absolut," he added. Sven put on his headphones and reclined with an expression of contentment.

David sighed and sank into his chair. This belief in a silver bullet for development was not unusual, although usually presented in less ridiculous terms. The lack of interest in hearing opposing arguments was also a common refrain. A more sophisticated expression of this mindset was called "special interest pleading" inside the Bank. David had been to meetings where specialists from various sectors fought over resources, each one genuinely convinced that their own expertise was more crucial than others.

***

David flew via Paris to the capital of Utara, a long drive from seaside resort where the conference was taking place. On arrival, he picked up a rental car in the airport, a small, white Toyota that smelled "new car." The road from the airport was in excellent condition—as roads frequently used by the national elite tend to be. The drive was about four hours, so he stopped for coffee about halfway to the conference venue.

Waiting at the table for his order, he picked up the conference files. There was also a file with a country briefing and his clearance to travel. It had required a last-minute dash to the Country Director's office to get the clearance, which had been stuck for days somewhere in the pipeline. This was a frequent and annoying problem. He found a security briefing for Utara and started reading it.

"Car jackings have become frequent in Utara in the last two years, and rental cars are often targeted. The main road south from the International Airport has received significant attention by armed gangs. The common mode of operation is for one car to overtake you. Then, it will start to slow down, while blocking any attempt by you to pass. A second car will appear behind you, and they will try to force you to stop completely on a road stretch without habitation."

The coffee and cake arrived at his table. *Gosh, this sounds terrible!* He continued reading.

"It is advisable to avoid being boxed in. But if confronted by armed men in front and behind, it is advisable to cooperate fully and without delay."

"Damn it!" he said out loud in frustration, "avoid being boxed in!" This advice was not very comforting. He should have read this before arranging the rental, but the briefing was a last-minute arrival.

On the road again, he kept looking for suspicious cars, and it was a nerve-racking ride all the way to the conference hotel. Nothing happened, but he decided to turn in the rental car as soon as he could and pay the one-way charge.

***

The hotel was popular with tourists, and the beach was marvelous. Arriving in the evening, he met several people he had encountered over the years, bilateral development experts, academic researchers, NGO reps, and some journalists.

He met the United Nations Development Programme speaker who growled, "I don't understand why the Bank was given more speaking time than UNDP." It was a perpetual and petty rivalry, and David wanted no part of it.

The conference had a formal opening with a long-winded welcome speech with an official who struggled with his reading of a bland text. But everything changed as Dr.

Roslund entered the stage and started with his famous juggling act. After that entry, he held the undivided attention of everyone in the large banquet hall.

Roslund had worked as an MD in Africa, often in very remote, tough environments. Villagers nearly killed him at one time when they objected to his taking of blood samples. Later on, he taught medical students about international health at the famed Karolinska Institute in Stockholm. Roslund was struck by their pessimistic and outdated comprehension of realities in the developing world. From there on, his pedagogic toolkit took shape, and he tested a cleverly tailor-made version on the audience.

Quick polls in real time showed that this particular group was more well-informed than the general population. But there was still some tendency to signal agreement with the more dismal statistics among the options that the speaker showed. He celebrated progress in girl's school enrollment, access to clean water, electricity and cell phones, increased literacy, and much more. Roslund also pointed to decreasing malnutrition, HIV-infections, emissions of sulfur dioxide, the extinction of smallpox and so on. The bottom line for Roslund was this: Things are getting better in the world!

When the ovations died down, David went for a coffee in the hotel's foyer. Sushmita Devarajan was an environmental writer and activist from a think-tank in New Delhi who joined his table with a cup of tea.

"Hello, David, good to see you again! So, what did you think of the doctor's lecture?"

"Well, Roslund plays a significant role in public education about development. His latest book is a brilliant piece of pedagogics. His data is the best available, much of it from the World Bank, and I agree that there are many positive trends that we should take note of."

"We must not take all the statistics at face value," Sushmita remarked. "I know from experience that data coming out of national statistical offices is sometimes based on very weak information and sometimes dressed up for political reasons. For example, if deforestation is increasing in my country, perhaps I don't want to flag that for the world. And if your career within the government depends on your region showing good data, there will be a strong temptation to enhance reality."

"Good points, and there's one more thing," David added. "Behind the statistics is a more complex reality. Take for example the encouraging figures on school enrollment. That's great, but the quality of instruction is sometimes quite low." He put down his coffee—it was bitter and lukewarm. "I was in Tanaland recently and learned that pregnant girls are kicked out of school. Sexual harassment is also common according to one teacher I met. The first would be caught by enrollment figures, but the latter would fly under the radar."

Sushmita nodded and reached for a napkin. "Much instruction is still focused on rote learning—not on critical thinking and analysis. Another point that I found missing in his presentation is absenteeism. Several World Bank studies about teacher absenteeism in developing countries are just shocking. The same goes for attendance of doctors and nurses at clinics, especially in remote areas."

The noise level was rising, so David struggled to focus in order to avoid becoming distracted. "There's also the issue of student attendance once they are enrolled," said David. "Conditional Cash Transfers have contributed to better attendance. But then the next question is: does better student attendance improve learning outcomes? The evidence is not compelling. National surveys and some international comparisons of proficiency in math, reading, science, and English prove this."

Sushmita nodded, but there was another issue she wanted to bring up. "There's the question that Roslund didn't talk about, but we must ask ourselves: how much of these improvements are because of foreign aid? I doubt foreign aid has an important role at all."

David contemplated how to comment on that. "I don't agree with your last point. Aid has made a crucial contribution to disaster relief. But more generally for development, I won't be able to assign a percentage to it. In some areas, it's been critical ... take the agricultural research that led to improved seeds that fueled a revolution in agriculture, and the fight against HIV for example. And for general economic growth, foreign donors have put pressure on developing countries to adopt more market-oriented policies, so that's been important."

David waived down a waiter and managed to get a bottle of water instead of the coffee.

"So, my point is that the World Bank and others have been driving policy changes through its dialogue with client countries. Better policies have allowed the private sector to flourish and international trade has opened up."

Sushmita was not convinced. "If we take the most celebrated example of poverty alleviation in recent years—China—it's clearly not a product of foreign aid and free market policies. The Deng Xiaoping reforms starting in the late 1970s unleashed some markets, but there's been tight state intervention along the way."

"My view is still that it was capitalism in disguise that lifted hundreds of millions of Chinese out of poverty," David argued.

Other conference participants interrupted them to chat, exchange business cards, and share stories.

The representative from USAID was waxing lyrical about her pre-conference trip around the country. "David, you must take the opportunity to see a bit of this fascinating, beautiful country," she gushed.

She rattled off a list of "must-see" places, and he realized that he had not even thought of anything but the conference. She pulled out a country guide from her purse and lent it to David. The jet lag was setting in, and he excused himself from the group.

Back in his comfortable hotel room, he made himself some tea and took some snacks from the minibar. There was a comfortable reading chair and a small table next to the King-size bed. There was even a tiny balcony from which he could look out over a beautiful park. The sound of slowly moving traffic filled the air, and noise from a restaurant filtered up to his fourth-floor outlook. The smell of grilled meat was unmistakable, and he went in to get some more snacks.

David changed his ticket online and delayed his departure one day. He could use his weekend freely anyway.

***

The next day, he ventured out during the lunch break in search of an agency that could provide a guided tour up-country. A block from the conference venue, he found a small office with tempting posters of various exotic destinations that could be reached at deep discounts. A short man with a friendly smile and an uncomfortably warm suit approached him and greeted him in French.

"Good morning," said David in English. "I'm afraid my French is not very good. Would English be OK?"

The man's smile only got broader. "Of course, sir, 'ow can I be of service?"

"Do you arrange guided tours at all? I would be interested in a full-day tour tomorrow. From here to the international airport. I have to be there by seven."

"Of course, with pleasure, sir. 'ow many in group?"

"It's just me."

The man's smile vanished. "Very sorry, sir, not possible. Minimum two persons."

"What's the charge for two persons, then?"

"For two, $200 plus tourist tax, airport fee, and tips to driver."

David reflected. He could go with the group bus to the airport at no personal cost, but he wanted to take the chance to see a bit of this interesting country. "I'll take the tour and pay for two, then."

The man looked puzzled. "Maybe English not good, sir. Two people minimum. You are only one, *oui*?"

"Indeed, but I'm paying for two. It's my only day left in your country."

The man now looked sad. "Sir, you not understand. Two people, two!" He held up two fingers for emphasis.

They went back and forth a few times, but the vendor did not budge. He seemed to think there was a language problem, or perhaps the customer was simply dim-witted. Defeated, David left the office and sank down on a park bench nearby. After a few minutes of recovery, he marched with determined steps across the street, where a larger travel agency had its office.

A well-dressed man with thick glasses and dark hair approached him with a welcoming smile.

"I'd like to go on a guided tour tomorrow from here at 8 o'clock in the morning for a drive through the country and all the way to the international airport in the capital. I need to be there at seven in the evening. Would that be possible?"

"Of course!" The man gestured enthusiastically and pulled out a sheet of paper. "Your names, please?"

David gave his name and asked for the price.

"The price for three people minimum is $300 plus tourist tax, city tax, airport fee and tips if you wish. Coffee for driver is good."

It was a lot of money for a day. "I'll take it," said David and pulled out his wallet.

"Names of people in group, yes?"

"It will only be me, but I'll pay for three."

The man looked like a bee had stung him. *"Mais non, Monsieur*, not possible! Against company policy," he clarified to settle the matter authoritatively.

David was usually very composed, but he lost his cool and raised his voice. "For God's sake, I understand you want a certain number of passengers to make it financially worthwhile. But I repeat, I'M PAYING FOR THREE!" he yelled and hammered the counter.

There was a sudden rustle in the back of the office. An impeccably dressed gentleman in a three-piece suit rushed to the counter. He gestured to dismiss his junior colleague. With the broadest smile of the day, he leaned toward David.

"You pay three, *oui*? *S'il vous plaît, Monsieur*, sign 'er."

***

David returned to the conference. The afternoon featured a series of rather predictable presentations. Everyone touted their own brand, multilaterals, bilaterals, and NGOs. There was little real exchange of views. A French-speaking representative of UNDP blasted through an overload of PowerPoints at a speed that sent the simultaneous translators panting. His English was fluent, with a carefully curated French accent, but it was a matter of pride to him to speak in his native language. That was his right, but it meant that eighty percent of the audience had to pick up their headphones and listen to a translation in English at furious speed.

It was striking how different speaking styles could be. An American almost always started with a joke. They went on according to the mantra: "First tell the audience what you're going to say, then say it, and finally remind them that you've said it." David had adopted that style.

After a training session in public speaking at the Bank, David had nailed a small note to his wall. It read: "Don't expect the audience's attention span to last more than seven minutes." There were studies to prove it. With that in mind, he set out to redraft his presentation. He wanted to reach this particular audience of mostly youthful NGO reps. But would they even listen?

After completing an outline of keywords rather than complete sentences, he called Diane and Bob for advice. It was still afternoon in the U.S. Diane cheered him on but suggested to make it even shorter and more personal. "Speak from your heart," she advised.

Bob was more reserved. As an old hand at the Bank, he could foresee a negative reaction from senior management if unfavorable feedback trickled back to HQ. "There are likely some journalists at the conference," he cautioned.

David opened a bottle of Bougène Émotion and chuckled as he stumbled across Van Morrison's album *Inarticulate Speech of the Heart* on his phone. That set the tone for the late evening as he continued outlining his speech.

CHAPTER 28

Speaking from the Heart

On the last day of the conference, it was David's turn to give the first speech. The Congress Hall was packed with some 300 participants, mostly youthful NGO representatives. "The old guard" sat in the front row with seasoned staff from donor organizations and several journalists from newspapers and radio stations. Only one TV camera represented a national station.

The chairperson gave a very short, neutral introduction of David, and a sense of tense expectation permeated the hall as he approached the podium. Scattered boos arose from a back row.

"Ladies and Gentlemen, the topic I was given, 'Development Progress in Africa' is not really possible to do justice in half an hour. I do come with a carefully crafted PowerPoint presentation, but I will leave that for you to read on the World Bank's website. It's already posted there as of this morning." A murmur spread in the hall. Was the speaker deviating from the script? "Let me instead speak directly to you on a more personal note. No slides!"

Some laughed, and some even applauded.

"Right before traveling here, I attended a dinner at the World Bank in Washington D.C." David recounted in brief his discussion with the two African gentlemen on opposing sides of their critique of the Bank.

The first salvo against the Bank drew cheers and "hear, hear" from some in the back. But they quieted when the counter argument was unleashed. As he went on, laughs and nods of recognition arose among the audience. He had their attention—for now.

"So, how can it be that the Bank is both a part of an evil empire that serves to enslave developing nations into the orbit of brutal capitalism, and an irresponsible ATM with no understanding of corruption and mismanagement?"

It was a rhetorical question, of course, but he paused for effect and to let that sink in. Some chattered in the audience, but no one dared to voice a reply.

"This illustrates the dilemma that we are facing—all of us, even NGOs—when promoting sustainable and inclusive development. All of us come with an agenda. We have goals and guidelines. We have a responsibility to produce results to show the people who pay for our work. But we also need to listen respectfully to our clients and adapt to local priorities."

A few young people held up handwritten cardboard signs reading "WB hands-off Solania," "Water, food, energy should be free," and "Forgive all debt." Solania was a failed state with no functioning government and a raging civil war with an Islamist militia in control of most of the countryside. It was in arrears to the Bank and IMF for many years, and there were no Bank projects there. Apparently, the Bank was still seen as an enemy.

"I've come to the conclusion that in the big scheme of things, foreign aid only plays a minor part in development."

This got the attention of several jaded listeners. Wow! Was he downplaying his own institution? Most participants were engaged in some form of development aid themselves, although a few thrived off finding faults in others' work. Was the speaker attacking their own work?

"Much more important is the quality of governance, global trade, investment, and migration. The Organization for Economic Cooperation and Development tells us that Official Development Assistance is approximately $200 billion per year. Remittances from migrants have now reached more than $600 billion per year according to the World Bank. Total exports from developing countries are at about $8,000 billion per year according to the UN trade organization."

A young man rose in the back and yelled something in French. David couldn't make it out and let it pass.

"These figures are apples and oranges, but that gives you some perspective. Global figures also hide tremendous variation among countries, but my point here is that we should sometimes step back and look at the big picture. Aid can still be of great use particularly in the poorest countries, and it can be of critical importance in a disaster situation. But it takes good institutions at the receiving end to make it effective."

A couple of participants to the left in the auditorium had heard enough and marched out right in front of the podium holding a sign—high for effect. It read "Close the World Bank."

"The World Bank publishes a set of governance indicators every year. They document six dimensions of governance quality, and there's a striking correlation between the level of economic development and the quality of governance. So, in my view, we must continue to insist that some conditions are fulfilled as we provide aid."

The noise level in the hall rose, but there was still a palpable sense of engagement.

"Other indicators published by the World Bank assess the business environment. It matters a great deal for economic development if it costs half the average income to start a company as in low-income countries, or just four percent as in high-income countries. It matters if it takes ten or two hundred hours to complete the export documentation for a shipment abroad, as it does in some countries."

He drank some water. It was hot, and the fans mostly wisped around the warm air.

"Some of you believe that we should simply push for a massive increase in development assistance. You're right to point to the glaring inequities in the world. But look at the facts. In 1970, the UN General Assembly—with a few dissenters like the U.S.—agreed on a target of 0.7 percent of Gross National Product to be given as aid from rich to poor countries. In reality, only a handful of countries have reached that goal. It is simply unrealistic to pin our hopes on a change of heart on that account."

He could see that some journalists in the front row were scribbling furiously. It was fodder for distorting headlines that could sell more papers. He could almost see it: *World Bank says: "Give up on aid."*

"Many of you detest globalization, but it's a major reason that you can buy inexpensive goods. Globalization has even lowered the cost of services dramatically. It's hard to discern those benefits, but easy to see the people who have been outcompeted. We should be doing more to compensate those who are losing while not giving up on globalization."

Globalization had few fans in this audience, and lively discussions erupted in several places. A few more left the auditorium, and David had to wait until most of the noise subsided. His fan club was shrinking.

"In developing countries, you can more easily see the impact of lifting people out of poverty. The Asian Tigers led the way, and China has become the prime example of successful poverty alleviation. It's an example of historic proportions. More globally, Dr. Roslund already made a good summary of the progress we can see if we take a step back and look at history. I'll not repeat that."

Several audience members had picked up their phones and were texting or reading from them. But most still looked his way.

"While we should celebrate economic progress, I must make a couple of important caveats. First, there's been enormous environmental costs to this ascent from abject poverty. Second, there is a political cost. I mentioned there are losers in this process, and they are bitter. In Western democracies, they are showing their discontent by voting for populists who promise to turn the clock back and keep the foreign competition out. They promise to fight 'deindustrialization' when in fact output from the manufacturing industry kept on rising or remained the same. Sure, there was outsourcing, but the major reason for shrinking employment in rich countries was automation."

A few NGOs had heard enough and stormed out. He could see a new sign saying, "Stop globalization." He switched tack.

"Migration is a force that we should not fear, but welcome and manage more generously. Remittances from migrants are already about three times greater than the flow of development assistance and growing fast. The other side of the coin is that the rich world actually needs immigration to balance its labor force with its aging population."

There was scattered applause for that statement. David gave a few select figures to illustrate his point but felt it was generally accepted in this forum and did not dwell on it.

"Let me say a few words about climate change. This is the world's greatest externality and a big part of the environmental costs of development that I mentioned. Market forces alone will not be able to tackle this effectively. But if governments correct the price signals, markets will respond with efficient solutions. Put a price on greenhouse gas emissions! Market forces don't have to be our enemy. They can be our friend."

Some booed in the audience but some applauded.

"I'm happy to see that the World Bank has understood the challenge that climate change poses. It has learned, it has changed, and lending to adaptation and mitigation of climate change has become central to the Bank's mission. I'm not here to boast about it because we are only one of many forces that contribute."

Some bilateral representatives gave him a thumbs up.

"The support we provide developing countries to adapt to climate change is not charity, it's not even aid in the traditional sense. It's rather reparations for the damage that the rich world is inflicting on the poor due to past greenhouse gas emissions. And even though China is now the greatest emitter, there's a historical burden that the rich world should carry."

He needed to change tracks in order to keep the audience's attention.

"Let me say something personal to you, young activists. As a young man, I read apocalyptic books about rampant overpopulation and how we are running out of resources. Perhaps you have read newer versions of the same pessimistic themes. This has led some people astray to fight for a dictatorial eco-regime that forces the world onto the 'right path.' This is a dangerous thought! This is not a time to put the brakes on economic development when hundreds of millions are still without electricity and decent water and sanitation!"

A lively discussion erupted in the back of the room. Some shouted but David could not make out what they said. A young man rose with a clenched fist and yelled, "Civil disobedience is the only way forward!"

David continued. "As a young man, I blamed capitalism for the world's ills and wanted it replaced. But as I studied the candidates for replacement, I realized that partial fixes were better than a wholesale replacement. Most of you in this hall are young, idealistic activists who are out to fight poverty and contribute to sustainable, inclusive development. There's no task more important than that, and I wish you well. But you should spend less time clamoring for unrealistic alternatives, and fighting against the IMF and the multilateral banks, and more time on adjustments to the market-driven system that has lifted mankind to historical heights of welfare."

There was scattered applause as he concluded. Many were surprised at this short, personal speech without PowerPoints. It broke the mold. David felt drained, but clean. He had spoken from the heart. The chairperson opened the floor for questions. There was a microphone placed in the middle of the auditorium, and people eagerly lined up to speak.

The first was a journalist. "Mr. Pedersen, I was intrigued by your statement that foreign aid is of no importance. Should the World Bank be dismantled?" he asked with a smirk.

"I didn't say that, only that quality governance, trade, private investment, and migration are more important as drivers of development. There is still a special role for aid."

A young man took the journalist's place. "How can you defend giving millions of dollars to corrupt regimes?"

"The World Bank is owned by governments and has to work through them, most of the time. We do our best to make sure that the money is well-spent and don't just give it away without checks. Our rule about auditing is one thing that often gets us into discussions with the client countries. And we do back out if corruption is blatant and can't be fixed."

"Was your speech really cleared by the World Bank?" asked a third person to some laughter.

"No, I just spoke more personally since this is a conference mostly for young people who want to make a positive difference. I was trying to reach out to you."

"How can you defend the Monamasa Project?" a young activist with long, blond hair and Santa Claus beard charged.

"I'm sorry. I don't know about that one, so I can't comment."

"You're denying any responsibility for the mass eviction of poor peasants, innocent women, and children!" he continued.

"As I said, I don't know about the project, but I can tell you that the Bank has very strict rules for compensating people. I can't take responsibility for every single Bank project." The questioner stormed away, cursing.

A young girl made her way to the microphone and faced him. She glared at him, crossing her arms over her chest. "I've read that you guys make millions in tax-free money. Doesn't that bother you when you travel to poor countries?"

"We don't make millions, and let me explain what 'tax-free' means in this case. If you're American, you do have to pay tax, but you get compensated for that. If you're not American, you don't have to pay tax, but you are paid less."

The girl looked unconvinced and turned away with a sour look on her face. The next questioner spoke in heavily accented English, but his question was clear. "Why do almost all your projects fail?" he inquired.

"What is your evidence of that?" David asked.

The questioner looked stumped. "Everyone knows that…I mean I've read that so many times …"

David sighed. "The Bank has an independent system for evaluating projects. Please take a look at the Independent Evaluation Group's website and see for yourself. It explains the ratings and methodology. You can study a treasure trove of data and reports if you want. But also remember that the Bank is a 'lender of last resort,' so we take on projects in very difficult circumstances."

The next speaker was an older woman in colorful clothes. "The ten richest men own more than the poorest three billion people. How can you defend a system like that?"

"I don't," said David. "But focusing on wealth redistribution will only get us so far. We should focus on elevating poor people's productivity so that they can help themselves. Poor people are often trapped by poor public services and regulations that prevent them from running successful, small businesses. So, let's focus on reforms in developing countries!"

There was some unrest among the audience and many had lost interest. The chairperson thanked David with a few platitudes and closed the session.

A young man raced up to David. "Your speech surprised me. It was like you were talking directly to me. I'm that young man who's very pessimistic about where the world is going. Capitalism can't be trusted, but I don't see any better alternative. I'm majoring in ecology, but maybe I should try some economics as well? Could I have your email, please?"

David smiled, recognizing himself as a teenager. "I can't advise you without knowing a lot more. But here's my card and do email me. For starters, go to the library and get the book *Factfulness*—it will cheer you up and inform you. Then, add Andrew McAfee's *More from Less*. He will convince you that there are constructive forces at work in the economy. It's not all about development, of course, but you'll get acquainted with a liberal economist's worldview. And get a subscription to *The Economist* if you can afford it."

To his surprise, several other young people rushed up to ask for cards. If only one of them had seen fit to question their own received wisdom after his speech, he would be rewarded.

CHAPTER 29

The Perils of Spyware

On the flights home from the conference, David felt a sense of normalcy. His nightmares of captivity had become much less frequent, and his loving relationship with Diane was flourishing. He had not felt so good about his personal life since he was with Julia. The thought of likely never becoming a father weighed on him, but he would have to accept that. A Byzantine bureaucracy burdened his work life, but the sense of contributing to something meaningful was still there. Some results in the field inspired him as did personal encounters with hard-working counterparts from developing countries. Best of all was to meet poor people who had been impacted in a positive way by Bank activities.

He returned to Washington D.C. with some apprehension. Would he be hauled into some big-wig's office and given a dressing down because of his free-wheeling speech? He checked for media articles during the stopover in Paris. The big media guns had ignored the conference, but some smaller papers had produced critical as well as appreciative mentions of David's speech. As usual, some journalists cherry-picked to fit their preordained narrative. But thankfully, Dr. Roslund had stolen the show.

Arriving at Dulles airport, he called Bob, who had a great network of contacts in the Bank. "Hi, Bob, just back. Have you heard any noises about my unorthodox speech at the conference?"

Bob chuckled. "Do you really think anyone upstairs is paying attention to you? They have their hands full now with the mother of all reorganizations. All the labels are being moved around, units are consolidated, others are split up according to a revolutionary formula handed down by supersmart, Armani-wearing, MBA-types from McKinsey & Co."

David thanked him and spent a calm day working from home and catching up on emails.

***

The following Saturday, David begged Diane to play again. It had been more than a month now because of his mission and her intense work. He needed it, and he knew she also liked it. But he also grudgingly accepted that she played with others as well. Both men and women—he could not ask about it in detail. She had made that very clear. But she also had no problem with David pursuing other love interests.

David very much wanted to find the right woman and start a family. But he could not conceive of giving up his relationship with Diane—it had everything except exclusivity. It was unlikely that he would find a new partner who would accept having Diane in the picture. It was also very unlikely that he would find somebody who could recreate the erotic vertigo that Diane mastered. It would have to be one or the other.

They spent time together with no sex at all, but with rewarding exchanges about everything from the most profound to the most mundane. They leaned on each other for moral support in times of adversity. He had met her precocious son again and liked to play chess with him and discuss books he had read. *Don't focus on the one thing you can't have but just enjoy what you have,* he kept telling himself.

Diane responded promptly. "Think of a great scene! We can meet on Sunday. I'm free the whole afternoon."

David's mind went spinning. The basic outline for the start of the scene was that he would be put in a situation of vulnerability—she would have some leverage on him. There was no end to the scenarios that one could think of to kick off the scene. It was only a prelude—a framing of the fantasy that later developed more according to her script than his. That, of course, was part of the excitement that he would not know where she would take him once she had established control. He was still secure with his safe words and the mutual agreement on boundaries.

He read in the *Washington Post* about a company that had installed spyware on staff computers. It had revealed that some spent hours on company time surfing on porn sites. Heads rolled, and the CEO declared a "zero tolerance" policy for porn watching during company time. "That's what weekends are for," he quipped to the interviewing journalist, somewhat unfortunately. He called back with a "clarification" later, but the quote went viral, and the CEO had to resign in disgrace after receiving death threats on social media.

***

They met outside the dungeon as agreed and hugged and kissed like lovers do. Diane entered the secret code, and she pushed the door open. They shared a glass of wine first, agreed on some details in the scene and then headed for separate showers.

David changed into office clothes and became Rex. He knocked on the door to the anteroom to the dungeon. It looked like a regular office and was used as such.

"Come in," she said, and he opened the door and stepped inside the office. She was dressed in a pinstriped jacket, a just-above-the-knee matching skirt, and a silky, white blouse. Subdued make-up, unremarkable earrings, and a pearl necklace, and three-inch pumps. No stockings. "Have a seat," she added and pointed to a chair in front of her desk.

"Why this sudden meeting and so late in the afternoon?" Rex asked.

"Rex, I know you worked on the Task Force for Enhanced Productivity. So, you'll recognize this report." She waved a thick document in front of him, without actually showing him the cover, but it was a good prop. "Let me quote: 'Our working group recommends the installment of adequate software to monitor responsible working habits among staff in order to enhance productivity and optimize company cohesion as we take the next steps to maximize shareholder value.' Remember that?"

"Of course, I was on that task force," Rex willingly confirmed.

"Well, as a result, our IT department installed spyware on staff computers across the company. As Head of HR, I get weekly reports. Including about you, Rex."

"Well, it wasn't meant to apply to the most senior staff ..."

"Our CEO decided otherwise, so spyware is compulsory, except for him, of course."

Rex was still confident. "Look, several people have access to my computer. My assistant could have been surfing when I was out. She knows my password. It's against the rules, but everyone does it."

The head of HR chuckled. "Really, Melissa, a devout Evangelical Christian, age sixty-three, would have surfed on porn sites for BDSM? Really! Is that the best excuse you can think of? Remember, we have keystrokes, we have data on the time you spent on each site. Are you saying good old Melissa spent thirty-seven minutes watching 'The English Mansion' a femdom website on June 27?"

David almost burst out laughing at the thought, but he had to stick to his role. "Eh...well OK, I did look at that website, but only because I was actually looking for a house over there. And then this just popped up. And once you're in that loop, new windows pop up all the time, and you can't stop it."

"Listen," said the head of HR and leaned over him. She pulled his neck hair hard and forced his head back to expose his throat. He felt very vulnerable now. "Enough excuses. You have broken your own rules. This is grounds for dismissal, and you know it. You have a choice: submit to my punishment or you'll be fired."

"Couldn't we work out some deal...I mean a small envelope to compensate for your arduous work?" Rex suggested in a pleading voice. He tried to lean back, but her grip was tight, and she leaned even closer to him with a piercing glare in her eyes.

The Head of HR raised her right hand to slap him, and Rex recalled another time when she actually hit him after their shopping trip. "No, please," he said. "I take that back! I would never imply that you would take a bribe. How can I atone for my transgressions?" His voice trailed off.

"Start by stripping naked and then face that wall and wait for me."

Rex rushed to comply as ordered. The sheer anticipation of her return sent his fantasies spinning and built his excitement. It seemed like an eternity before she clicked her sharp heels against the hardwood floor. She cuffed his hands behind his neck, then came the gag ball. His submission was total now, her power firmly established, but so was the trust they had built. There was nobody else in the world who he could play with like this. The outer world disappeared, as did any sense of responsibility or guilt.

She turned him around. The Mistress looked stunning. Her hair in a tight ponytail, the large golden hoop earrings he had once given her embraced her face beautifully. Her lips were as blood red as her nails, and she had added a touch of blue eye shadow above her long, archly curved eyelashes.

The Mistress inched her nails with very gentle, slow scratches across his chest, stomach, and down to his crotch. She bruised his nipples gently and seemed pleased with his responsiveness. She guided her sub into the dungeon and to the St. Andrews Cross. She fastened his wrists and ankles in leather straps.

He was facing outward and noticed her long, black gloves, which left her fingertips bare. She had a black choker now instead of the pearl necklace. The leather corset pushed up her breasts and just barely covered her nipples. Her leather skirt was very short, and there was a hint of lacy stocking tops and a garter belt as she bent down to fasten his ankle cuffs. The heels had grown to five inches, but she still moved with grace. She was a fetishist's dream, and Rex maintained a full erection without the slightest direct touch.

"Look at yourself in the mirror," she commanded and pointed across the room. There was a full-length mirror on the wall, and he was perfectly placed to see himself in it. There was only candlelight, but there were many of them. Voyeurism was another kick for him. The cavernous dungeon had the perfect ambiance for B&D play.

The Mistress took her time to select the right tools from the wall with an impressive collection of disciplinary instruments. By not-so-sheer coincidence, she ended up with his favorites: a short riding crop and a long flogger.

She put the crop to work with gentle taps strategically placed to keep him fully excited but avoiding numbness. His nipples also got some loving attention. Her tempo was slow and deliberate, to allow him to feel every stroke. There was a flowing sequence of stimuli that made for unpredictability and excitement.

Rex was allowed down to the floor to engage in some leg worship and to show proper respect for his dominatrix. Then, he was pulled up again and turned around on the cross. Securely fastened, it was time for him to pay for his office transgressions. The flogger landed on his bottom with increasing intensity. Now and then, the Mistress stepped up to slowly run her nails lightly down his back and buttocks. He bristled under her touch and groaned with pleasure.

After exacting a fair punishment for his rule-breaking behavior and obtaining a sincere promise from Rex never ever to watch porn again, she let him off the cross. She had him standing in front of a mirror with his hands tied behind his back. Then, she surprised him by pulling up a chair beside him. She pulled out a new toothbrush and opened its packaging. She wet it with her lips, and with a mischievous glance at her helpless sub, she very carefully let it slide up and down his shaft.

"Hello, corona," she purred and let the brush gently, gently run across the surface of the tip of his penis. It was electrifying, and he almost lost control. "Wait for my permission," she reminded him sternly.

"Hello, frenulum," she purred, and focused the soft, teasing brushstrokes on the delta on the underside of the penis below the corona. Rex recalled a biology textbook describing this area full of nerve endings as 'a source of distinct pleasure.' How true it was!

"Please, please," he begged under his gag.

And the benevolent Mistress gave the green light, and it took all of ten seconds for her gloved hand to bring him to climax. She made sure to finish the job properly. Released from his shackles, Rex stumbled into a large bed in the dungeon. A profound sense of relaxation came over him. This was his catharsis—his total escape into another persona.

The Mistress soon returned to him, now completely naked. She cuddled up to him, and they kissed passionately. When his heart rate had returned to normal, Rex went for a quick shower. He returned fresh to even the score for his Mistress.

David had learned something new about toothbrushes and the perils of spyware.

CHAPTER 30

Kafka's Return

Coming back from the play with Diane, David opened the door to his studio and closed it behind him. He was shocked to find two men standing in his kitchenette. One of them took a quick step behind David to cover the exit. The other took a step forward and motioned him toward the sofa.

"Mr. Pedersen, take a seat."

Dumbfounded and scared, David sat down. The two men were tall with muscular builds, buzz cuts, and stern faces. They wore suits, ties, and plastic gloves, like a dressed-up version of the torpedoes he had seen in American gangster movies.

"Who are you?" David managed to get out after scanning the scene.

"That's classified. All you're allowed to know is that we work for the U.S. government. However, you're not allowed to discuss this conversation with anyone. If you do, it will result in serious consequences. We have some questions to ask you."

"Look, I'm exhausted, and I've had my debriefing with your government already."

"Mr. Pedersen, it's in your own interest to cooperate. Obstruction of justice is a serious crime in this country."

David got furious and stood up, and the men instantly stood up and closed in on him. "Don't threaten me! I want a lawyer!"

There was a moment of tense silence, and David sank down on the sofa, suddenly out of energy.

"Mr. Pedersen, you're not under arrest and have no right to a lawyer."

"So, what's this then—detention? Am I free to go? Do you have a warrant to enter my home? I want to talk to my Embassy!"

There was a condescending smile on the lips of the taller gentleman, who now leaned forward to David. He spoke in a low, firm voice that David found intimidating.

"Mr. Pedersen, you don't seem to understand. Terrorism law gives us extraordinary powers, including entering your home. We may keep you if we want, here or at a venue of our choosing. We wanted to make it more low-key by seeing you here. The fact that you're a foreign national provides no protection—on the contrary. Do you think that your little socialist banana-kingdom would come running to save you? Now, let's not waste any more time with theatrics." He motioned to his colleague who opened a thick folder with a black cover.

"Mr. Pedersen, are you a Muslim? You have studied the Koran carefully."

David sat up straight. *Unbelievable,* he thought, *is this what it's all about?* He remained silent.

"Mr. Pedersen, refusal to cooperate will result in serious consequences."

Let's get this over with quickly, David thought. *They might be gone in five minutes if I just answer these nutty questions.* "No, I'm a secular humanist."

He noticed a recording device on the coffee table now. It had a small camera and a microphone. There was a pile of his books on the table. The Koran had been picked out, but not the Bible that he had borrowed from Eva. Sowell's *Marxism:*

Economics and Philosophy had been picked out, but Milton Friedman's *Capitalism and Freedom* had not. He could see *Permanent Record* by Edward Snowden, but not Michael Hayden's *Playing to the Edge: American Intelligence in the Age of Terror*. It was a somewhat selective selection.

"I have studied the Koran just as I have studied the Bible. It doesn't mean I'm religious, I just want to understand."

"Understand what?'

"Why some men find the inspiration to live peacefully and with generosity among his neighbors, while others find inspiration to commit murder—and they all draw from the same book."

"You underlined one passage in chapter 2, verse 103 that says '... woeful punishment awaits the unbelievers.' Is that your conviction?"

"No! I just underlined something that I found significant as an expression of unfortunate intolerance. You will find a hundred phrases underlined in that book. Some of them are about forgiveness, mercy, and generosity. Don't pull this out of context!"

"What is your relationship with Mr. Muhammed Hassan of the World Bank?"

Aha, they are after Bob now, David realized. "He is known as 'Bob' and is a colleague of mine."

"In your conversation with Mr. Hassan, has he ever expressed sympathy for Islamist jihad?"

"Well, the concept of 'jihad' had many meanings, but if you're trying to pin terrorism on him, that would be totally ridiculous!"

"Mr. Hassan has provided financial support to a number of Muslim charities that are under investigation by federal authorities. Did he at any time ask you to contribute to such charities, and did you at any time provide financial support?"

Muslim charities? Bob supports several Muslim orphanages—could that possibly be a front? I did give him some cash once, but that can't be traced.

"No," David said firmly.

Is it possible that Bob is part of a sleeper cell, like the Illegals Program that Russians had organized some years back? The words of the American Warrior came back to him: "They are clean-shaven with Christian girlfriends; they smoke and drink … you can't find them." Bob had no beard and a Christian wife, he was a chain smoker, but only of tobacco as far as he knew and he didn't drink alcohol. *No, I'm getting paranoid*, he thought.

The questioning took on a repetitive rhythm. The questions became more and more detailed and bizarre in David's view. He got upset, revolted, and shut down. When he refused to answer, there was an escalation of threats. So, David gave in and started to answer. After about half an hour, the men— who David thought about as No. 1 and No. 2—closed their files and looked at each other. They seemed to agree. No. 1 went out in the hallway outside the apartment, probably to make a phone call. After only a few minutes, he returned. Signaling with two fingers, he nodded to No. 2, who pulled out a new file from his briefcase.

"David, we're satisfied now that you are not a Muslim sympathizer. We apologize if our questions may have offended you, but they were necessary to establish your credibility. You have suffered greatly while in captivity among Islamist Jihadists, and we will give you a chance to join in our struggle against them." No. 2 spoke in a soft, personal tone now, and even attempted a smile. But it failed to reassure David, who was still fuming.

"Hence, we are ready to engage you as an informant to closely follow the next moves of Mr. Muhammed Hassan, aka Bob. You'll carry this recording device at all times. It cannot be turned off, and we will always know where you are. The microphone is sensitive, but we have ways of filtering out the voice we are looking for. You will seek him out as much as possible."

No. 1 turned to David. "David, it's important that you inquire about making contributions to the charities that Bob supports. Find out as much as possible about them. Inquire about his views on the Muslim attacks on Western targets. Imply that you want to better understand the rage of Muslims against the West. Tell him that you found interest in Islam during your captivity. Don't go overboard but encourage him to confide in you. We know that you have been colleagues for many years, and he'll trust you."

"We will be in touch when we want a verbal report," No. 2 added. "The recordings will be automatically uploaded when you are in proximity to our equipment. Rest assured, that we will always know exactly where you are!"

No.1 smiled and added, "Normally, patriots do this kind of thing for free, but since you are a foreigner, we are allowed to sweeten the deal with a monetary incentive. The payment will be determined by the quality of reporting. We could be talking about several thousand dollars if we get what we want—tax-free, ha-ha," he chuckled.

David had read about people being recruited as informants. Some had even sued the FBI over the retribution they had faced when refusing to cooperate. But if they were from the FBI, why didn't they just say so? He recalled an article in the *Washington Post* about sixteen different intelligence agencies. It could be one of them. Or maybe this was some consulting company that operated as guns for hire, giving the government agency convenient deniability if things went awry? It was also well-documented that the government used undercover agents in engaging with suspects to supply them with fake weapons, unusable bombs and so forth. Would that be the next step?

"I'm not interested in becoming a paid spy," David asserted. "I've answered all your questions truthfully. But I'll absolutely not become an informant for your fishing expedition. There's no way that Bob is some kind of terrorist or even sympathizer."

No. 1 looked annoyed and chewed his gum faster as he leaned toward David. "David, we've extended a generous offer to you. I'm very sorry that you so arrogantly dismiss it. So, let's switch gears here. You don't seem to understand that you've got no power here—none! We can easily d-e-s-t-r-o-y you. We have your personal computer search history and a constant tap on your keystrokes. We know everything about Diane and your perverse interests. Such things could unfortunately leak into the public domain... In fact, we know everything about you."

No. 2 took out a set of photos from his folder. The first was a picture taken inside David's apartment. *They've been here before.* The second was a photo taken in the World Bank cafeteria when he had lunch with Bob. *Damn it, they have access to the Bank!* Then, there was a copy of an email from David to Diane, and even more chilling, a transcript of what should have been an encrypted, erotic message from David to her. A rage percolated in his body at this violation of privacy.

"I've never engaged in any sexual activity that wasn't between consenting adults!" David exclaimed.

No. 1 resumed. "If you're not sufficiently embarrassed by the sick stuff you are doing, then consider the possibility that law enforcement receives an anonymous tip that you've taken a strong interest in child pornography. And when they check, they'll find your hard disc full of nasty stuff. You'd be left with no friends. Your family would disown you. Your cute playmate would leave you. You'd be fired on the spot and then subject to a very long judicial process." he chuckled.

No. 2 filled in. "You'd have plenty of time to sweat even before the trial. Condemned to a lengthy prison term, you'd soon be somebody's bitch. I'm sure you know how pedophiles rank on the internal prison totem pole."

"I detest child pornography and have never watched it," David managed to let out. But his voice was shaky, realizing what a total collapse his life could face if he was not able to please these tormentors.

"Well…your version would be hard to prove if the word got out that the government had found it on your computer, wouldn't it?"

A numbing realization sunk in. This was totally against his core ethical convictions, but he had no choice but to play along. He could figure out a way out later.

No. 1 summarized. "We are done, for now. I repeat that you are not to mention this meeting to anyone under any circumstances. Any hint of a contact with your Embassy, ACLU, or other ideologically biased organizations will be observed by us in a manner you won't be able to detect. I don't need to remind you of the severe consequences for doing so. Have a nice day!"

David sank down on the bed in a sense of Kafkaesque powerlessness. Was this how Joseph K in *The Trial* had felt? He too had been visited by two strange men one day. They had not arrested him formally but had given him notice that he had been charged by an obscure court, for reasons that were secret. Once word got out, Joseph K was unable to focus properly on his work—as a successful banker just like David, no less. Gradually, Joseph K's life withered away. One day, K was picked up by two men, and he was expecting them. They stabbed him to death, and the book's last line was, he remembered this clearly: "It seemed as though the shame was to outlive him." It would be the same for him if they planted child porn on his computer!

He went to his bed and covered himself with a blanket in a futile attempt to hide himself from the world. *There must be a way out of this hellhole*, he thought. But how? Lying in a tight fetal position, he mentally considered the possibilities. He was tempted to get up and set pen to paper or use his computer to organize his thoughts. But these dark powers might read every key stroke, and even his scribbling on a paper might be photographed by hidden cameras. The only place he could hide was inside his brain.

First, there was the possibility that some department in the gigantic CIA complex had a different idea than the professionally correct debriefers he had met. They had been satisfied to find out about the Warrior. But this department wanted to engage him on an offensive against perceived threats.

Second, there was the possibility that this was not the CIA at all but the FBI or one of the other governmental intelligence organizations in the complex web of the anti-terrorist machinery. Lack of coordination among them, and even a certain competition, would not be a novel feature. The 9/11 Commission had documented that.

Third, there was the possibility that this was some kind of freelance group, perhaps with a contract to one of the intelligence organizations. Perhaps ex-military with experience of combat in Iraq or Afghanistan and a personal hatred of Muslims or anyone with the slightest sympathy for them. If your friend had been blown up by an IED, you had a legitimate grudge.

Fourth, it could be a prank. Maybe they had no connection to the government at all. Perhaps they had read an article about him recently. They simply hacked into his computer and found emails to and from Diane. Maybe they videotaped the whole thing and would later put it out on YouTube and rejoice as the clip went viral. No, they had shown him evidence of a professionally conducted surveillance.

In any case, he most likely had no way out to an honorable life. He got up and searched for something to dull his senses. His head hurt from thinking very hard. David had no liquor at home but found three bottles of red wine and picked the most exclusive one. It was a top-end Catena Zapata from Argentina, a full-bodied, dark fruit wine that he had saved for a special occasion. *It won't get any more special than this*, he thought with a frown as he opened it. But as he let the first sip swirl around to enliven his tongue and palate, his brain went back to consider the worst-case scenario. He drank the expensive Catena bottle faster than he had ever finished one in his life. Then, he collapsed on his bed.

***

The sunlight in his face woke him up the next morning. He had not pulled the curtains, and the studio was in bright morning light. David found Tylenol and took the maximum recommended dose, plus a little more. His neat, orderly life was falling apart.

His first thoughts went to No. 1 and 2. They had probably planted some surveillance equipment in his apartment. He wanted to call Diane and Bob but did not dare to. In George Orwell's *1984*, there is a "telescreen" in everyone's apartment. It cannot be turned off, and it picks up everything you say. It was used to broadcast incessant propaganda from Big Brother. There was no telescreen in David's studio, but the creeping feeling was that everything he did and said might be observed. Perhaps they had put something inside his TV?

He examined the TV and realized that he did not have the right tools to unscrew the back of it. He unplugged it, turned it around, and covered it with his bedspread, although he felt childish about it. He searched all the light fixtures for possible cameras or listening devices. His phone was, of course, suspect, and he took out the battery, realizing that he would soon have to put it back again. He disconnected the landline telephone and the computer. What else?

He had seen surveillance equipment installed in the ventilation in some detective movie. Standing on a chair, he could not see anything unusual in the ventilation screen, but it would require a screwdriver to really check. He would have to get one. He checked under the coffee table and the desk—nothing. He recalled another spy movie where a hidden microphone was planted in a flowerpot. David had only one, rather miserable looking, plant. He emptied the pot in the sink and combed through the soil. Nothing!

It was futile. He could not cut himself off from the world. He looked up a section in Edward Snowden's book *Permanent Record* that he had marked as particularly scary and found it on page 326: "...once America's spy agencies had proven...that it was possible to passively collect all of your communications, they started actively tampering with them... Now they were capable of winning total control of your whole device, including its camera and microphone. Which means that if you're reading this now...on ...a smartphone or tablet, they can follow along and *read you*."

David, pull yourself together! he thought. *This is not 1984. This is America, a democracy with strong institutions, free speech, and civil rights. I may not be a citizen, but I still have rights. There must be a way out of this Kafkaesque hell.*

CHAPTER 31

Agent Provocateur

David got to work the day after the shattering home invasion by the two secretive men, conflicted with the dilemma he faced. They had forced him to betray a colleague's close friendship for the sake of saving his own skin. David headed to Bob's office to see if they could meet for lunch.

As he approached the door, two people were raising their voices in there. It was out of character for Bob to yell, so he hesitated knocking. But people were passing by, so he felt compelled to knock.

Bob opened the door and looked surprised at David. "Oh, it's you! Well, my friend here was just leaving, weren't you?" he said and nodded to his visitor.

The visitor, a tall man who looked Middle Eastern, nodded and left in silence.

"Come in!" Bob said with a waving gesture. "What can I do for you?" His usual smile appeared in his face.

"Sorry if I'm coming at a bad time, but would you have time for an early lunch today?"

A shade of concern passed over Bob's face. "Sorry, I've got to sort something out urgently, but I can meet you after work at 8 p.m." He sighed. "The work with the Bank's Muslim association is taking a lot of my free time these days. It works fine inside the Bank, but now, we have external interests trying to influence us. Never mind, I shouldn't be talking to you about this, my friend, sorry!"

David left with a sense of misgiving. He had never heard Bob so upset. And who was that man? He had a visitor's

349

badge on his jacket. Was Bob involved in a secret controversy with other Muslim groups? After all, Bob had become a spokesperson not only for the Bank's Muslims and had appeared as a public face of Muslims in news articles and even once on local TV. Was he under pressure to support things he did not believe in?

***

They met outside the Bank's main entrance, and at Bob's suggestion, they strolled to The Exchange Saloon on nearby G street, which was a popular waterhole for Bank staff. It was not ideal for a private conversation, but they managed to find a table with some privacy. David was acutely aware that he carried a recording device and felt lousy about it.

"I'm so glad to see you looking more and more like in old times, David. But your captivity must have been a harrowing experience that has left its mark long-term. I want you to know that as a friend, I'm here for you."

"Thanks, Bob, that's great to know. I'm still trying to figure out how these people, you know they call themselves Muslims, can share the same religion as somebody like you."

"The people who kidnapped you are simply bandits. Some of them masquerade as believers, but they have caught on to a perversion of Islam. Just like there are good Christians and crazy Christians, we have the same problem with some Muslims."

They ordered food and drinks. Bob would find it odd if he brought up too many questions at once. They talked about his kidnapping in some detail. But as they got back to his captors' worldview, he made another push in a low, discreet voice.

"Do you also believe that there is a Jewish-Zionist conspiracy to control the U.S. and ultimately the world?"

Bob burst out laughing. "David, that kind of talk is just nonsense. Propaganda! The Jews are about two percent of this country's population. They have outsized influence because they are well-educated, well-organized, and often successful financially. The situation in other countries varies a lot. There's no conspiracy there."

"But Zionism, then. Surely, you are critical of Israel, right?"

"I don't think that Israel is treating the Palestinians right. I'd like to see an independent Palestinian state on the West Bank including Gaza. The occupation is illegal, and the settlements are in violation of international law. In fact, most countries would agree with me. The U.S. administration is either not talking about it or calling them 'unhelpful' and such vague things. It depends on who is president. But all that is separate from what I think about individual Jews. I've worked with several of them in the Bank. I respect them, and they respect me."

David kept probing, but whatever he tried, Bob kept coming back to his diplomatic attitude. Then, he recalled another point from yesterday's interrogation.

"What about the charities that you support? Please tell me about them!"

"I've been sending money for several years to three orphanages. One is in Lebanon, one is in Yemen, and the third one is on the West Bank. I have come across them through relatives in Lebanon and other people I've met over the years. I've visited all three to check that they are well-run."

"What do they teach the children in those orphanages? Are they like *madrassas*?"

"They're not religious schools. The orphanages provide a safe home for the kids. Then, they go to different schools outside. It varies depending on what is available, and who's willing to accept them without payment. And when the kids get older, they can have a say in the choice of schools."

David kept pushing with more questions but got nothing that could be seen as incriminating. He left, feeling vindicated. Maybe this would work out after all. *Those guys will realize they are barking up the wrong tree*, he thought. That left an ethical dilemma: if Bob was innocent, how could he continue to spy on him without letting him know? But he was ordered to always carry the recording device. David considered a way to get around that. He just had to tell Bob!

***

David usually jogged on weekends and every other Friday, as this was a free day thanks to a compressed schedule the other workdays. When Friday arrived, he put on his shorts, T-shirt, and jogging shoes. Bob kept the same schedule. He knew where Bob lived and that he attended the Washington D.C. Islamic Center mosque on L Street NW. Bob could walk different ways there, but one route was the most likely. He remembered that Bob talked about never taking calls on a Friday when he was off, so he would not carry his cell phone. Maybe they tapped his as well, and his house could be under surveillance. The Bank office was not safe either, as they obviously had access to it.

If they caught David without the recorder, he would blame it on having no pockets and not expecting to talk to anyone. His usual jogging ground on the Mall was conveniently closed for a demonstration. David had to jog back and forth several times on one block before he saw Bob walking alone toward the mosque. He had come around the corner from a direction that David did not expect, so he caught up with him only a block away from the mosque. It was risky, but he felt a burning urgency to go through with his plan.

"Hey, Bob, fancy meeting you here!" he yelled. Before Bob could say anything, he whispered close to his ear, "I'm forced to spy on you! Be careful!" He pulled back, noticing Bob's stunned face and said loudly, "Great to run into you, Bob!" and quickly turned away.

***

That evening, the media were filled with the news that a lone gunman had targeted a mosque in Washington D.C.. Seven people were shot dead, twenty-six were wounded, but the White gunman, twenty-six, had put up his arms and surrendered to the police once they arrived. Apparently, he trusted that they would treat him fairly. Unharmed, he was keen to lay out his motive for the attack. A local TV station gave an account.

"I wanted to kill as many Muslims as possible," the gunman had stated. "Those people are invading our country illegally and have lots of babies. They are trying to take over the country with their *sharia* law. They want all women to stay home and cover themselves in black sheets. I've been to Afghanistan and Iraq to serve my country, so I know. They hate us, so we should hate them back. I'm a good Christian, and most Christians secretly stand behind me."

David called Bob's number. If the phone was tapped, he could only pray that Bob did not in any way comment on their meeting earlier that day. But the massacre had happened at Bob's mosque, so he had to find out if Bob was unhurt. To his relief, Bob answered right away, although it was a Friday.

"Bob, are you OK?"

"I'm not hurt, but I'm deeply shaken. I had left the mosque when it happened."

353

"That's a relief, but let me express my sincere condolences for this terrible attack. It's an act of terrorism!"

"Thank you for your compassion, David. It is a bitter day for me and for my Muslim brothers and sisters. This is part of a spiral of hatred and violence that has grown over the last few years. Muslim extremists have their share to answer for. They've ruined much of the goodwill that ordinary Muslims like me have earned through persistent work."

"What will the local Muslim community do now? Will there be revenge? The gunman claims to be a representative of 'good Christians.'"

"That's so much nonsense! Sounds like he wants a religious war. What's needed now is a gesture of goodwill from religious and political leaders of all faiths. They need to meet publicly and condemn this violence. They should do the same if there's a gunman who invokes Islam as his driving force. Excuse me, others are calling."

David ended the call and breathed deeply. He could have lost a great friend and mentor that day! *Terrorism follows me*, he thought darkly.

***

The next morning, No. 1 and No. 2 helped themselves into David's apartment. "We listened to your conversation at The Exchange. You're too timid in your approach. Don't let Bob's friendly face fool you. He's hiding his true colors. That's what these people do—they are trained liars."

No. 2 pulled out a big photo of a man from a folder. "You'll insist on going with Bob to his mosque next Friday to show your solidarity with the victims after this incident. The man in this photo is named Aziz Amin. He'll tell you that he's one of the massacre victims' brothers. He's starting a collection for the deceased families. You'll contribute generously with a personal check. Here's an envelope with the money to cover that. You'll strongly encourage Bob to do the same. That's the first step. Amin will take it from there," he concluded with a confident smile.

The men left as quickly as they had entered.

***

Next Friday evening, David accompanied Bob to the vigil that had been arranged to honor the mosque shooting victims. The mosque was still cordoned off by police as a crime scene. The vigil was held in the street just outside the mosque, and hundreds of people participated. The media presence was massive, and the police department had mobilized a sizable force to prevent any incidents. Much like Bob had suggested, several religious leaders were in attendance, all proclaiming their solidarity with the victims, and their condemnation of the heinous massacre.

Aziz Amin knew his act. As he made his rounds to collect money for the new Solidarity Foundation, he crossed paths with Bob and David. His grief over his lost brother was palpable. David handed over a check as instructed. David suggested to Bob that he should consider contributing, as he had been told to, but he found it hard to fake any enthusiasm. Bob insisted on wanting to know more about the Solidarity Foundation before committing. Amin was happy to oblige and invited them over to his apartment the following day.

***

They met in Amin's modest D.C. apartment the next day. It was not the low-key information meeting about the Fund that they had been promised. Amin had pulled together several relatives of the killed and injured victims. Pictures of the victims and some photos from the crime scene had been blown up and posted on the walls around the group. Amin suggested a minute of silence to honor the victims and everybody bowed their heads.

Amin gave a short introduction about the Solidarity Foundation, and solicited contributions which he said would be given to the victim's relatives. Bob was moved to offer some cash, but Amin refused the cash, saying that he was only authorized to handle checks. He promised Bob a full account of the Foundations finances and referred to the website which he said contained complete background information. Grudgingly, Bob wrote a small check.

Having collected a bundle of checks, Amin turned to future activities. The discussion gradually became more excited and militant under Amin's skillful guidance. One after another, the participants declared that "thoughts and prayers are not enough this time." Something had to be done to counter the elements of extreme Christian violence against Muslims.

"I know who these people are," one man volunteered. "Seven of us were killed. Let us look for seven of them! The gunman is from a Christian militia. I have names and addresses!"

There were loud expressions of support from several of the gathered, and shouts of revenge were heard. Bob rose and objected strenuously, but several of the massacre victims' agitated relatives drowned him out. David recorded it all but was starting to feel sick. It was a trap. Amin was an informant, and he fueled the fire. Gathering the aggrieved relatives was a clever strategy. Two of the most agitated men declared that they had military experience and were ready to use it. That Christian militia should suffer as they had suffered.

As chaotic plans for revenge were thrown around, Bob pulled David up, and they left in a hurry.

Bob had not said anything incriminating—on the contrary. But here he was in a setting where incriminating statements were thrown around. Both of them were present and would be implicated. If a tape like that were played for a jury, how could you credibly argue that you were not in agreement? Bob was shouted down, and editing of a tape could cut out any mitigating evidence anyway. On top of that, maybe the handing over of money to Amin had been recorded. Amin's money could be forwarded to an organization labeled as "terrorist" by the U.S. government. "Exhibit one, Your Honor!"

As they came away from the apartment, Bob stopped and turned to him.

"David, this could be a trap. Amin could be an *agent provocateur* working for the FBI or something. He was fueling the flames all the time. That other guy who talked about having names and addresses. I've never seen him at the mosque. Stay away from those two! Some of the other men I know. They are good people, but they are being manipulated now that they are upset and grieving."

David returned to his apartment. He found a Super Tuscan, *Antinori Tignanello* in his wine cupboard. It did not provide solutions but some comfort at least. "Wish You Were Here" by Pink Floyd played on his CD-player, and he longed to be with Diane. He tried to organize his thoughts. *What are the options?*

Things were getting too hot for David. He was pushed into something that could end badly for him. But pulling out of it would probably be worse. There was only one person in the world with whom he could share it all in confidence.

***

No. 1 and No 2 woke David up the next morning, as they had let themselves in. He received new instructions. A small group of Islamist militants would conduct a planning and training exercise the coming weekend. They would gather outside the north exit of the Vienna Metro station before they traveled in cars out to the Shenandoah Valley. They would meet at a farm owned by a Muslim leader. Amin had prepared the ground for David's participation. He was met with some suspicion, but Amin had played up a story of his conversion to Islam in captivity and argued that he had the money necessary to finance the purchase of weapons.

"You will write them a check for $10,000 from your checking account to show them your support. Make it out to the Solidarity Foundation for the Victims of the Mosque Massacre. We will generously reimburse you."

"I can see what you're doing," said David. "You want to implicate me to the extent that I can never get out of this and have to play along with you."

"You are not as stupid as you look," said No. 1. He coughed and quickly went for a glass of water in the kitchenette. It helped, but he had to wait a couple of minutes for No. 2 to emerge from the restroom. "We'll be keeping our eyes on you," No. 1 reminded him as they headed to the door.

CHAPTER 32

Tom

Tom Sipowicz closed the door to his spacious office in the Department of Justice building on Pennsylvania Avenue in Washington, D.C. It was 7 p.m., and he looked with resignation at the pile of files that he still had to go through. His wife had divorced him, and his two sons had left the home a long time ago and were busy with their own careers. They blamed him for the divorce and had told him more than once that he had been a neglectful father, too wrapped up in his successful, but demanding, career.

Tom was fifty-five, 6'3", with graying hair and a face that betrayed his long working hours. Born on a dairy farm in Wisconsin, he was a first-generation college graduate, a brilliant student who aced his undergraduate studies at an inexpensive in-state college, went on to law school, and transferred to Yale Law School after two years at a Midwestern law school. After a few years in the private sector, he had made the choice to dedicate the rest of his career to public service. The pay was not great, but he truly enjoyed the sense of working for something he believed in.

As he put in some files in his office safe, he checked the personal telephone that he kept there. It had only one number programmed. There was a message. He logged in to the encrypted messaging app ProtonMail.

"Your offer for a free cruise to the Bahamas extends until 10 p.m. this evening. Please respond YES to indicate your interest. Press STOP to unsubscribe from this offer."

It was all code, but he knew exactly what to do and, smiling, responded YES without hesitation. "Departure from Miami or Tampa?" was the next question. He picked Miami, knowing it would be a park near his office.

At ten minutes to 10 p.m., he gathered his papers and hurried out of the building. Three blocks from the office, the poorly lit park was deserted at this time at night. He lit a cigarette and waited, happy about the surprise rendezvous.

Diane appeared on the dot in a long, grey overcoat, boots, fake glasses, and a blonde wig. They always met with great discretion. With his high-level security clearance, Tom was obliged to report any romantic relationships to the DOJ for clearance. He was afraid that Diane's polyamorous and unorthodox lifestyle would be considered a "security risk."

Diane showed him a note with the text: "If you brought your phone, put it in my Faraday bag, please."

Tom glanced at her in surprise but took it out and dropped it in her bag without a word. There could still be eavesdropping through a directional microphone in the vicinity, but a small fountain was splattering, which would make any sound recording difficult.

"I need your help," she said. "I've never asked you for anything like this, and I don't expect it to ever happen again. But you are the only one I can turn to in this case."

"I'm listening." He made an effort to hide his disappointment. It would not be the kind of meeting he had hoped for.

"I have a close friend, let's call him K since I know you're a fan of Franz Kafka, and it seems appropriate in his case. He wanted to come himself, but I refused because he might expose you. He's pressured by an obscure Islamophobic group claiming to be associated with the U.S. government to conduct surveillance on a high-profile Muslim colleague. When he refused to collaborate, he was threatened with planting incriminating evidence on his home computer. After reporting only innocuous results, he is pressured to provoke illegal activities. Some people want revenge for the killings at the mosque in D.C."

Tom took a deep breath. He had followed the mosque killings closely. "A remarkable and tragic story! Why doesn't K just go to the FBI?"

"Look, have you followed the court cases against the FBI where the plaintiffs argue that they have been threatened with retaliation if they don't inform on their fellow Muslims? There has also been a string of cases where FBI informants and undercover agents have allegedly encouraged or assisted radicals to prepare for violent actions here in the U.S. I don't know what is true, but K doesn't trust the FBI."

Tom sighed. Of course, he knew about those cases, rather more than what was in the *Washington Post.* "The political pressure from on high is tremendous within this administration. We have to nail these terrorists, or heads will roll. No more 9/11! So, some agents may go out on a limb to get a gold star. They could be contractors for some intelligence agency, while the government can maintain plausible deniability. They could also be rogue guys, some kind of private militia that has appointed itself to uphold patriotic values and go after Muslims. The number of hate crimes against them has increased dramatically."

"You're in a very senior position to, at least, have a look at this."

"This sort of issue is super-sensitive. DOJ is swarming with political appointees who are ideologues rather than lawyers with professional integrity. They are arrogant because they have White House backing. Can't this wait until after the election? It's only a month from now! There's, at least, a chance that we will get a complete change of leadership then."

"I'm sorry, but this is really urgent. K is going nuts. I'm giving you a handwritten note here with some particulars of this case, including K's name and address and a detailed description of the two secretive persons who have harassed K. Let me also give you this bag."

Tom took the bag and asked, "What's in it?"

"K said that the first time they came to him they were very careful and wore gloves. But now that they feel he's working for them, they have let their guard down. There's a glass in a plastic bag that K secured after the latest visit. The person he calls No. 1 drank from it, so it should have some good prints."

Tom peered into the bag. "And the other small bag?"

Diane smiled. "Men have their peculiarities," she noted. "The other guy, No. 2, went to take a pee but missed a bit. You've got his DNA in those swabs from the floor. One thing I forgot to write is that he's also got a deformed left ear, maybe from boxing. It will be easy to see if you're going through pictures. The rest is in the note."

"OK, I'll see what I can do. Just because it's you. But, K, is he—"

"You know better than to ask," she interrupted and glared at him.

"I'm sorry, it's none of my business. Just couldn't help myself." He leaned back and held up his hands in a defensive posture.

"Tom, you must know that this isn't some kind of emotional blackmail from me. I have the deepest respect for you, and that will not change, no matter what. This is a very risky business, even for you. I will understand if you say no. But I also know you as a man of great integrity and passion for upholding the law."

"Thank you for saying that and for confiding in me. I've told you many times that I'll be there for you if you need me, so I guess it just happened. Let me take that note, please. I'll be in touch the usual way."

As Diane left, Tom stayed for a few minutes to ponder his options. Of course, he wanted to help her. K was probably a lover of hers, so in a sense, a competitor. But if Diane cared, then he cared. There was another aspect as well. If a rogue operation sustained itself on the fringes of government, or if this was a freewheeling Islamophobic movement that was willing to provoke violence, it had to be reined in. It was not his job *per se,* but as a career lawyer who had taken an oath to protect the Constitution, he certainly felt obligated. He knew the people who should be alerted.

***

Diane trusted Tom. They had met ten years ago after Tom's divorce. He would go to bars to drink and look for women. He found out about the Yellow Cactus and started going to their meetings. At one introductory session for members only, he met Diane in full dominatrix regalia. Watching her in action, he felt an immediate attraction that was too strong to hold back. He just went up to her.

"I place myself in your hands," he said.

"It's a place you have to earn," she responded with a big smile. They started meeting for quick lunches, just to talk. After getting to know each other rather well, they started playing. It all responded to some inner need that Tom had never known about—or dared to recognize.

After two weeks of anxious waiting, Diane's special phone lit up with a carefully coded message from Tom. They met in the same spot as last time that evening.

"I had to do a lot of careful digging and call in a few favors," Tom started in a hushed voice as he leaned closely toward her. "The two mystery guys have been identified. Both ex-military and listed as consultants for the security industry. They work for a small company registered in McLean, Virginia. It was easy with the fingerprints that were good quality. We were lucky with the DNA, as that guy had a conviction for rape, so he was in the database."

"That's a great start that we know who they are!" Diane exclaimed and could not help raising her voice as she turned to peer at Tom closely. "But can you act on that information?" she continued in a lower voice.

Tom took out a cigarette and lit it. He puffed with quick drags on his cigarette as he kept looking around. But there was nobody else within earshot.

"Not now, it's just the tip of the iceberg. There's real substance here—explosive stuff. Unthinkable things are happening under the surface of our well-polished democracy that we hold up as a beacon to the free world. But there's a definite limit on how far I can push this within the current administration."

He took a deep drag on his cigarette and let the smoke out slowly with a troubled look on his face.

"If I go any further with this now, the result will simply be that I'll be fired, along with a few other confidantes. They can bury this thing if they want to put out smokescreens. The capacity for disinformation is frightening now...I haven't been able to determine what level of high-level support this secretive organization has. But K has to assume that they are for real and dangerous."

Diane sighed. She stood up and started pacing back and forth as she shuddered at Tom's words. "That sounds frightening! But surely, the talk about our proud democracy is not just empty blabber. The system has a lot of integrity. Congress may be divided and pretty paralyzed right now, but the judiciary is solid. So, even if this administration wins the next presidential election, there is a solid part of this country that would celebrate if the truth would come out about these sorts of activities. We still have a free press."

Tom was silent as the seconds ticked away. "I can agree with most of that. But things have changed in the last few years in a manner that I didn't think was possible. Things that we read about in the developing world, corrupt practices, disinformation, blind loyalty, a machinery for mass-producing lies to feed the Internet, you name it. Of course, we have to stand up to it, but I fear many of us will just be swept away."

Tom paused for a moment, and Diane reflected on the enormity of what he had just said.

"There's another side to this," Tom continued. "With a good outcome of the election, I might be in a totally different position within the department. Obviously, I can't reveal any details, but there have been solid discussions about...well...what might happen for me personally within a new administration."

"That sounds really exciting, but I realize that's confidential. So, what's the next step?"

"If K is pushed any further by his handlers into a group planning illegal and even violent activities, the FBI could hit him on the other cheek. There are reports of a conspiracy to commit crimes in revenge for the hideous mosque killings in D.C. The FBI has infiltrated those circles. From what I know, they don't have a clue that he is acting under duress, and it may be hard to prove that he is. Best he gets out quickly before he is caught in the crossfire."

"I'll talk to him, but where would he be safe? The organization that is on his back seems to be quite professional."

Tom scoffed. "Safe? He'd be safe in North Korea."

"Don't joke about this!"

"I'm sorry, but there are very few places, really tight dictatorships, which would be totally safe from extradition. In addition, there's a number of countries without an extradition treaty with the U.S., but most of them are poor and could be penetrated or have governments that can be leaned on."

"What do you mean by 'penetrated or leaned on'?"

"Consider two cases. First if this obscure organization—I don't even have a definite name yet—goes after him hard for 'defecting,' they could simply send a hit man to get K. Second, there could be a lot of unofficial pressure exerted if this organization is able to get the support at the top level of the U.S. government. Or the FBI could drive the case from their perspective. The administration has great discretion to slap punitive tariffs on imports. There are also lots of bilateral collaborative agreements regarding the military, intelligence, science, culture, and so on. What if one day there were suddenly "problems"? Maybe the prime minister's children are attending Harvard and their student visas are suddenly canceled. I could go on…"

"Tom, I get the picture. But if K is in a country with integrity, wouldn't they stand up to U.S. government pressure and let the judicial process run its course? Even if they have an extradition treaty? I read about a case where our president called the prime minister of a small EU country and asked for the release of an arrestee. But he was told that the prime minister couldn't interfere with the judiciary."

"Well, there's still the possibility that the U.S. will bypass the normal judicial route. Working with the country's intelligence service, they could pick him up. An unmarked plane would be sent from here. The host country would be happy to get rid of him, given the serious accusations. It could be kept quiet. A rendition could be arranged to a dark prison somewhere in a cooperative country. A confession could be secured, if you know what I mean, and then he could face a trial, or just be kept in prison."

"I thought all that had stopped! The black prisons, renditions, keeping people without trial for years..."

"Officially, yes, but who knows? We still have Guantanamo. Lots of empty space there now. I'm not saying it *will* happen, because K is a small fish after all, but it *could* happen."

"Are you telling me our justice system is falling apart?"

"Not at all. Most people in this country will go along with their daily lives without any problems. Only the ones who engage in activities that get them into trouble with the government could face these consequences. Hypothetically, a powerful non-governmental organization could reach out on its own—like an international mafia. But the number of people impacted is so small that most people won't care."

"But isn't that how the system starts fraying—at the edges? And if these things are done with impunity, the repressive measures could grow."

"Perhaps, but I'm still talking about things at the margin. Of course, another 9/11 would completely change the political calculation..."

They were both silent as they speculated about what was happening to their democracy.

"Can't this wait until the election in two weeks?" asked Diane.

"If tomorrow a number of people are killed in a coordinated operation carried out by militant Islamists in revenge for the mosque killings, then K is in very hot water. The laws about terrorism are draconian. The calculation is easy. If you have a possibly catastrophic outcome for yourself, you need to take precautions, even if the risk that it happens is small. I'd tell K to get the hell out now!"

CHAPTER 33

Exit, Voice, or Loyalty?

Diane set things in motion with a coded message delivered by a taxi driver who read the message on David's intercom. Without giving the address, it referred to the place where they had met for their first date. He went there after taking several different Metro trains to shake off any followers. He left his phone and the recording device behind in his apartment. They met at the agreed spot and marched from there to a hotel nearby where Diane had secured a room.

She did not tell him more than what was absolutely necessary in order to protect her source. David suspected that it was one of her lovers with a strategic position within law enforcement. He would better not ask.

"The FBI is on to the group of Muslims planning a revenge attack for the shooting at their mosque in D.C. You have been observed in meetings where violent actions have been planned, and you have contributed financially. It could be difficult to prove that you have been forced to participate. We have identified the two mysterious guys, but we don't have evidence to show how they have blackmailed you. It's time for you to get out!"

David systematically went through his options. The dilemma reminded him of Hirschman's classic: *Exit, Voice, and Loyalty* that was in the small book collection he had brought to the U.S. He could make a quick exit and leave it all behind. Or he could speak up, raise his voice in public, rush to the office of the *Washington Post* and spill the whole story—but who would believe it? And he would be hunted down like an animal. Or he could hunker down in coward loyalty to his oppressors and give them what they wanted.

But he was pressured from two sides now. David's face had lost its color when he grudgingly put his realization together.

"Diane, you know I can't just sign off and remain here! I'll have to go into hiding, give up my career, and worst of all, leave you!" His voice was barely audible and he buried his face in his hands.

She tried to console him. "David, I love you. But please understand that my life is here. My son, my job, my lovers, and friends. I can't give all this up. But maybe you can hide in secret, and I could still come and see you. Things may change here, and you could return one day."

After a teary, conflicted night together, he had made his decision. The choice was exit. His ambitious life plan was in shreds. He felt like he was standing on the edge of a cliff with his tormentors rapidly approaching. Looking down at the river beneath him, he was not sure he would make it without drowning, but, at least, there was a chance if he jumped.

David took out pen and paper from the desk in the hotel room and wrote two letters by hand. The first was a letter of resignation addressed to his manager. He wrote that unforeseen personal circumstances forced him to immediately terminate his contract with the Bank. He expressed his appreciation to his manager, his colleagues in the unit, and the entire Bank, which had offered him the opportunity for professional growth and fulfillment while pursuing the noble cause of poverty alleviation. In spite of the caveats, he could write those lines with sincerity. Further communication would be handled by his legal representative, Mr. Edward Robinson, of Robinson, Becker, Doolittle, and Gold.

The second letter was a power of attorney made out to Edward Robinson of the said firm. Edward was a long-time friend—and he suspected also a lover—of Diane. Diane vouched for him and argued for the benefits of handling further matters under attorney-client privilege. David gave Robinson full powers to enter his apartment, put his personal belongings in storage, terminate his lease, sign for and receive any payments on his behalf, and hold them until further instructions arrived. David counted on being able to retrieve his savings with a debit card from scattered locations and to sell his shares online from an untraceable place.

They went through his escape plan one more time together.

***

The next morning, he went home very early, and he made sure to talk on the phone with Diane about his Cancún vacation plans. He was going for a short vacation, as he felt stressed by work, he explained. He assumed that the phone was tapped. With only a vacation bag packed, he got a ticket to Cancún with a return in three days.

He checked in at his hotel in Cancún with his credit card to leave a trace. David wrote a few glib greetings from his email account addressed to Diane and programmed them to be released irregularly during the next three days. He left the phone in the room with the charger plugged in.

He went straight back to the airport. There was a direct flight to Madrid, so he bought the ticket with cash shortly before departure. The flight manifest would leave a trace, but it would be too late to stop him. As the plane left Cancún, he felt relieved, but also incredibly sad. He kept gazing at a hard copy picture of Diane he kept in his wallet. He found "The End of a Dream" by Evanescence on the airplane playlist and had a good cry to it.

On arrival in Madrid, he bought a new smartphone. Within the EU, it was easy to move around freely. There were good, fast trains, and he could spread his tickets around several different train companies to make tracking more difficult. He had enough cash to make his way to Denmark. Would that work? He had no idea, but he wanted to make it more difficult to find him.

He called his neighbor and friend from school, Jens. When David came to see his parents after his release from captivity, he had also met Jens. They had a surprisingly good talk. Jens had met a crazy hacker girl, Nina, with some social skills, and he was gradually coming out of his shell. He had fixed her motorbike, which was apparently the best way for a guy to impress her. The relationship with Nina had transformed Jens. His stutter was gone. He was keen to tell David how much he had appreciated his support during the trying times in school. He had declared that if David ever needed his help, he would be there.

That time had suddenly arrived. Jens took notes when David called but asked no questions. He just closed the call by repeating, "I'll be there for you, David."

Jens and Nina met him at the Central Station in Copenhagen when his train arrived from Hamburg. Jens was a new man now, shaved, showered, and dressed in clothes that Nina must have picked for him.

Nina drove the rental car well, albeit too fast. With her cool biker outfit in black leather, heavy flat boots, and multiple piercings, she reminded David of Lisbeth Salander in the *The Girl with the Dragon Tattoo*. Just the kind of girl that Jens needed to knock him into shape.

David shared only the most essential information. He needed to get away for a while, as he was "burned out." He wanted to be alone in a remote place and chill. It was important that nobody knew where he was. The two of them did not bat an eyelid. None of them was interested in probing that further, but they were keen to help. David stayed the first night with them in Nina's apartment in Copenhagen.

Jens surfed the Internet and found a remote cottage for immediate rent near Skagen on northern Jutland where David could blend in. The rental was arranged under Jens's name.

They went shopping in a nearby town on the way and stocked up with cans of soups and beans, and—at Jens's insistence—a good supply of chocolate pudding. All you had to do was to add water and stir. "You can live on just that for a year," he explained with some pride. He knew. They also got an ample supply of Carlsberg and Tuborg. David tried to pay them, but Nina waived him off.

"We are financially comfortable," she assured him. "You are our guest now. Jens has told me that you were one of the few who never teased him in school."

"Thanks for saying that. I'm impressed that you are 'financially comfortable.' So, what is it that you do?"

"I approach companies and offer them better cybersecurity. They often don't know, but I show them some vulnerabilities and help patch them up. It pays well these days."

"What if they say no?"

Nina smiled. "I always come with my homework prepared. I hack in before I talk to them. When I show them the results, well, nobody has turned me down."

Nina's cheerful rendition triggered ambivalent feelings in David. Nina was probably a good hacker, using her talents to shield companies from sabotage, theft, or blackmail. But wasn't there an implied element of blackmail in her approach? More seriously, it made him think about how his own privacy had been violated, his reputation threatened, and his whole life uprooted because of high-tech capabilities.

They arrived late at night to the cottage but found the key as promised in a lock box. It was a nicely furnished house with two bedrooms and a cozy family room with a fireplace. The furniture was all in light wood and elegant, minimalist, Danish design. There was a fresh soap smell in the house, and everything looked clean and neat.

They sat down for beers and prepared a simple meal of pasta, tomato sauce, and shredded parmesan. Nina was a vegetarian, so Jens had become one as well. Jens was keen to talk about his new life with Nina. David shared few details about his, and they respected his secrecy. They realized they were talking to a person going into hiding. David had never imagined that he would one day feel such gratitude toward Jens and count him as a trusted friend.

CHAPTER 34

A Dramatic Turn of Events

I could just disappear here, David thought.

Skagen was once a quaint fishing village whose fabulous beaches, magnificent light, and rustic fishermen had inspired a whole school of painters. The Skagen Painters—a group of Scandinavians—had been active toward the end of the nineteenth century and had mastered the art of painting *en plein air*. Skagen was no longer primarily a fishing village, but it was easy to see why this area had captivated painters.

Jens rented the cottage on David's behalf so that he could quietly slip into the community without any legal trace. Keeping to himself, he bought food online using one of Jens's credit cards. He reimbursed him later once a secret account in the Cayman Islands had been established where he could stash his savings and withdraw money without a trace. The cottage was well-equipped, and he enjoyed the feeling of personal safety. If somebody encountered him, he looked like any other Dane. It was also an area that attracted single souls in search of solitude, so he fit right in.

With its vast resources, the FBI would eventually find him if it was important enough. But they would have to go through the official channels—*Politiet*. That would mean due process, a chance to state his case, and probably years of negotiating a transfer to the U.S. in case it ever came to a request for extradition.

It was different with the secretive group that had pursued him with the dubious claim to work for the U.S. government. Their style was more like that of a free-ranging militia. Clearly, there were also examples of intelligence agencies moving into "dark ops." What if those guys really wanted to shut him up for good? But would they care as long as he was quiet?

During the first weeks, David thrived on the solitude—the hours of reading fiction for pleasure and even poetry at times—while listening to his favorite music as loud as he wanted without anyone complaining. He was able to order top-flight wines through a local wine store. The long walks along the coast were refreshing even in harsh weather.

He even started to write a book, based on his career at the Bank. But after finishing more than a hundred pages, he realized that very few people would be interested in reading it. *Too dry, too didactic, I would have to fictionalize my story*, he thought and put it all away. Writing fiction was not what he was trained to do.

Admittedly, he missed the fundamental sense of working with a purpose, collaborating with dedicated development professionals in poor countries who labored with high spirits in spite of little reward. He also missed seeing the encouraging results on the ground, the collegiality among peers, and the intellectually stimulating seminars and discussions.

But the heaviest item of all was the loss of Diane. The few indirectly delivered messages they exchanged only served to remind him of a painful emptiness in his new life. His isolation was both a shield from enemies and a growing curse that ruined his sleep. Just looking at a picture of Diane could make him cry helplessly. He would wake up some nights and start planning a secret return to the U.S. One night, he dreamed that he had entered Canada onboard a Danish fishing boat. He snuck across the border to Maine and traveled by bus to Washington, D.C. He made it all the way to the door of Diane's apartment before he woke up in sweat, confusion, and disappointment. Those nights he drank too much.

He tried to counter his loss by enumerating what he did not miss, starting with the Bank's daily avalanche of emails, the Orwellian language acrobatics to placate innumerable interest groups, the dealings with lethargic, corrupt institutions in developing countries, and the erratic commands from senior management. At various times, they urged staff to bust silos and work across disciplines, but then to focus on their specialist competence, develop long-term holistic solutions, but then ensure quick wins by going for low-hanging fruit, focus like a laser beam on top priorities, but then to think outside the box, lift their game, but then to return to basics, launch flourishing transformative initiatives, but then to streamline, pay attention to details, but then to take a big-picture approach, take risks, but then to be accountable for mistakes—and other original ideas cultivated at short-term retreats with expensive consultants. Every new president or high-level appointment brought a fresh crop of brilliant ideas to the fore to be fed to the increasingly numbed and sometimes openly cynical staff in the trenches.

David stepped out to seek some solace with company and a glass of wine. Jesper, the jovial café owner greeted him in his favorite bar. It was housed in an old, attractive half-timbered house that also contained a wine store.

"Hello, Michael, what can I get you today?"

Nina had arranged a passport and driver's license in the name of Michael Nielsen, one of the most common names in Denmark. That was David's new identity.

"Were you able to get hold of that Uruguayan Tannat that we talked about?"

"Sorry, my distributor says he can't get it. But I have something else for you: a fully loaded super-Tuscan!"

The bar TV showed CNN, and there was suddenly a face that David recognized. His stomach tightened as he stared at the image. The news anchor excitedly described a sensational SEAL operation in Beirut. A jihadist militant whose *nom de guerre* was The Preacher had been killed. Another militant called The American Warrior had been captured. He was in critical condition, but now treated at the American Ramstein Air Base in Germany. Unfortunately, a Lebanese journalist had been killed in the raid, although he had not been a target. Two Lebanese security guards had been wounded in a shootout, but they were in stable condition.

The news cut to a recording from the Pentagon where a spokesperson summarized the event. "The Preacher, whose real name was Timothy Baker, met the fate he richly deserved yesterday. Mr. Baker was given the best start in life anyone could possibly get, to be born in the greatest country the world has ever seen. But he betrayed his country and turned to terrorism. The same applies to the American Warrior, whose real name is Timothy Williams and who will be brought to the United States to face justice if he survives. Let our enemies know that the United States will pursue them as long as it takes and wherever it takes to eliminate or capture them."

A clip from the White House Press Office followed. "The American Warrior has been a target for years. How did you manage to track him down?" one journalist asked in an excited voice.

"We never comment on sources and methods," the press secretary responded. "But the President has declared that we will not spare any effort to neutralize those who threaten us. Next question."

"The Preacher was a U.S. citizen. So, who decided that he deserved the death penalty?" asked another journalist. "Has his case been tried in a court of law?"

"As the President has made clear, those who place themselves outside of the law by resorting to terrorism should not count on mercy. Next question."

David stood frozen by the bar. *What did he feel? Jubilation that the Warrior was captured? Yes, he was a terrorist. But could somebody like him have a moderating influence, at least when it came to terrorist actions in the U.S.?* The Preacher? It sounded like he had been a propaganda instrument much like the Warrior. Now, Islamist militants would retaliate.

The U.S. administration celebrated the raid as a significant win. Few Americans would worry about how the decision was made to kill a citizen—if he was labeled a terrorist and it happened far away. A trial against the Warrior would also be a good media opportunity. He flipped through all channels to get more information.

Did they set a trap like he had suggested to the CIA? No, it was presumptuous to assume that.

Jesper suddenly returned. "I'm sorry it took me so long. But here's the wine!" He poured David a small amount to taste. Then, he got a look at David's face and stiffened. "Christ, what's happened!"

"It's a long story. Keep the bottle for me, please. Now, there's something else I need to do."

***

It took him two days to find what he was looking for. An article in *Berlingske* quoted *Le Monde* that conveyed information from unidentified but reliable sources that the two terrorists had been lured to a newspaper office in Beirut for an interview with an unnamed journalist. Instead of a journalist, they were attacked by SEALs who shot themselves into the building. A local journalist was also killed, and the Lebanese government and various press organizations protested the raid. In response, the Pentagon declared, "All possible precautions were taken to avoid collateral damage. However, the successful elimination of a high-value target sometimes incurs unavoidable repercussions."

The following day, an attractive but visibly upset freelance journalist, Ms. Juliette Martin, held a press conference in Paris where she strenuously protested against "malicious rumors" that she had been part of a setup.

"Anyone spreading such rumors will be held accountable," she sternly declared with a phalanx of unsmiling lawyers around her at the microphone. "You are exposing me to life-threatening danger," she concluded.

In solidarity, the mainstream media completely dropped any further mentioning of her.

A chilling realization crept up David's spine. *The Warrior might survive. What if he started connecting the dots? Who had set him up? CIA, of course, but how had they spotted his weakness and made him drop his guard?*

***

David celebrated New Year's Eve with Jens and Nina and continued to visit them from time to time in Copenhagen.

Nina had helped him to deliver and receive safe, untraceable messages to and from Diane. He had also sent messages to his mom to reassure her that he was fine but had to live under cover. Through Nina, he communicated with his lawyer to arrange for his severance payment and modest pension to be forwarded to an account in the Cayman Islands that Nina had helped him set up. Nina also helped him install anti-spyware on his computer, taught him how to use a VPN to protect his location, and installed a sophisticated alarm and surveillance system in the cottage—just in case. She offered to arrange an unregistered gun "for self-protection," but he declined.

In January, David watched the inauguration of the new President of the United States, and he could not wait to know how this would impact the work to combat domestic and international terrorism. He sent a discreet inquiry through Nina to Diane. She told him to patiently wait.

***

One evening three months into the new administration's reign, David was watching TV while enjoying a glass of red wine and reading *The Economist*. The CNN anchor announced that they were switching coverage to a suddenly announced DOJ press conference. David excitedly turned up the volume as he saw Acting Deputy Attorney General of the United States, Mr. Tom Sipowicz, step up to speak. Standing behind a podium with the seal of the DOJ and in front of the American flag and the banner of the Justice Department, Sipowicz made sure that he had everyone on stage before he started. His colleagues lined up with the demeanor of professionals who had worked tirelessly for months and now had a big announcement for the world to hear.

Sipowicz then made the announcement that would dominate the first pages of the largest newspapers in the U.S. and even some in Europe.

"Today, the Department of Justice unseals an indictment that concerns serious threats to the integrity of our democracy. Specifically, a grand jury in Washington D.C. has returned an indictment that alleges 236 federal crimes by thirty-five individuals associated with a clandestine operation named 'The Secret Brotherhood of the Christian Shield for the Protection of the White Race, or CS for short.'"

Sipowicz took a sip of water and reviewed the room. The tension was palpable. He continued.

"These individuals allegedly engaged in actions to gather information related to a number of perceived enemies of the United States and to take violent action against these targets. The CS members were recruited among military and ex-military personnel, several police departments, and branches of the intelligence community. Under the guise of operating as an arm of law enforcement, CS morphed into an autonomous operation that wrote its own laws. Enhanced interrogation techniques were at times employed to secure cooperation. It is alleged that violence was orchestrated in order to provoke counter-violence, which resulted in several fatalities. The end game appears to be a widespread armed confrontation targeting Muslims and others perceived to be unpatriotic in the USA."

Sipowicz paused. Maybe for effect, maybe for composing himself. The gravity of the indictment was not lost on anyone.

"This nation's institutional integrity is strong. We will now put an end to this threat to the core of our proud democracy. I will now call upon my colleagues to provide further details. We will take questions from the press at the end. Thank you."

David's jaw dropped as his excitement and sense of triumph blurred his senses. He could not follow the speakers'

The Benevolent World Banker

legalese any longer, but he had heard enough through Diane to think that CS was most likely the organization that had blackmailed him. He grabbed a bottle of champagne from his cellar and opened it. It was not properly chilled, but he did not care this one and only time. As he returned to the TV, the head of the FBI was speaking.

"The FBI is mandated to protect the American people and uphold the Constitution of the United States. Our nation stands as a beacon of good governance in the world. Now, we have to face an enemy from within. A vibrant democracy is a prerequisite for human and economic development."

"Amen to that!" said David aloud as he lifted his glass. Other senior DOJ officials spoke, but David was too excited to be able to digest anything further. He just emptied the bottle, relieved, and slept like a log on his couch.

The next day, he went into Skagen and bought new pants, a shirt, a pair of shoes, and got a haircut. All things that he used to dread, but that day, he was full of energy and loved every minute. He bought an ice cream, in spite of the cold, and joked with children who played in the park where he sat. At his favorite wine shop, he filled a case with top quality whites and reds. He loaded up on groceries and spent the evening grilling chicken on a tiny charcoal grill in front of the cottage. A full-bodied Australian, Penfold St. Henri's Shiraz, came loaded with dark fruit, chocolate cake, and French oak spice, and it went down effortlessly.

He sent another message to Diane, asking about the new development. Could he relax now?

Her response was ambiguous, "A battle is won, but the war isn't over. Stay put."

***

Later in the new year, he tracked down several former PhD students he had lost contact with. Most of them had followed predictable paths and reached positions of some gravitas in academia or the private sector. There was one surprise: Torben Nielsen, the PhD student who had lambasted David for selling out to the "imperialist Bank" was now a venture capitalist screening startups for profitable ideas. His dissertation on Marxist Economics had stalled. But Nielsen appeared just as passionate about his convictions these days—they were just very different.

David sent an invitation to Diane. She would be delighted to come but could not make it until June. Diane had been promoted again and could not easily get away from a string of scheduled events. Her son, Josh, was "… going through a rough patch at school …" So, she couldn't leave him now. It would have to wait until the semester was over, and he could join a summer camp.

David had gradually gotten back to better sleep through mediation, poetry reading, and long jogs on the beach that made him appropriately exhausted. He had cut down on his drinking. Alcohol made him sleepy, but it interfered with his REM sleep, he had learned. It all made him less moody and prone to crying. But he could never stop thinking about ways to see Diane again, and never get rid of the feeling that his life was missing something fundamental. Now that some doors were ajar, he got increasingly impatient for a change of scenery. But there was so much he did not know about the situation in the U.S. Would it be safe to return? Diane had advised against it for now.

***

It was June 17th, almost at the peak of the summer, and the first light came to Skagen at 3:04 in the morning. David strolled to the shore and continued north toward the tip of Jutland where the Baltic Sea meets the North Sea. It was a quiet morning with little wind, and he was alone on the beach. The sun rose at 4:17 that day, and there was not a cloud in the summer sky. He took off his sandals to get even closer to nature, to feel the cool sand under his feet.

At 8:04, he set out in his car. His father would not have approved, because it was a twenty-year-old Volvo that David had bought from a widow in Skagen. "My husband loved that car, and they do last forever," she assured him. She quizzed him on his driving habits and respect for car maintenance before she finally agreed to the sale, being satisfied that it would be in respectful hands. It was in mint condition.

David put on a CD with music by Erik Satie. His favorite was "Gnossienne No. 1." It gave him a sense of melancholy, but it fit his pensive mood. He drove slowly south through the flat landscape with his window halfway down to enjoy the breeze. The fields around him lacked drama, but exuded fertility and promise in the benevolent light. When he was still living in Denmark, midsummer had always been David's favorite time of the year when darkness capitulated, and the days seemed to go on forever.

After a five-hour ride, he arrived much too early at Kastrup airport in Copenhagen, parked the car, and listened one more time to Satie's "Première Gymnopédie." He tried to take a nap but kept waking up to check the time. Finally, it was time, and he made his way to the international arrivals' hall.

David had run the scenario a thousand times in his mind but still felt unprepared when he spotted her coming through the sliding doors. She wore a blue pants suit with a colorful matching scarf draped over her shoulders and pulled a cabin bag behind her. Walking slowly with elegant poise, she stopped right in front of David who stood frozen, unable to do anything but watch her.

"Hello, I'm Diane," she said.

"Hello, I'm David," he said.

She has cute dimples when she smiles, he thought. Just like that time eons ago when they first met.

CHAPTER 35

New Beginnings

The flame within him surged naturally and irresistibly as he gazed at Diane. David had resigned to set his ambitions into the frame of a low-key, withdrawn life in Skagen. But shut doors now swung open both professionally and personally. They spent long, delightful hours walking on the beach. No matter the weather, it seemed pleasant to slowly wander by her side. They held hands like teenagers and sat down at times in the sand to just be close.

They made love cautiously, slowly, the first time as if to reassure themselves that everything was OK. It was, and the second time around, she dressed up and seduced him with an energy that blew him away. This was the Diane who he had fallen in love with—and wanted to be with again.

There was plenty of time for deep reflection on what had transpired since they parted in haste and agony in Washington, D.C. Was the U.S. now a stable democracy? Had the solid institutions—so wisely designed by the Founding Fathers—stood the test of new, undermining forces that sought to establish an order where might is right? Diane argued the answer was "yes" on both accounts. David wanted to be convinced but was not.

"David, come back to the U.S. with me. The political situation is stable, and the Christian Shield is effectively dismantled. There are loads of other militias, but the FBI has now realized that the main threat to American democracy is not external terrorism like Al-Qaida, but homegrown, right-wing extremists."

"Sounds good, but the next election might still swing the pendulum back. Even if the ultraviolent movements are scattered and with few members, there's broad-based support for anti-democratic measures to suppress votes, gerrymander victories, and play dirty games to get the upper hand."

"David, you don't have to make a definite decision for the rest of your life. If polarization and anti-democratic measures get worse, you still have a Danish passport. But you know that there are a lot of interesting things for someone like you to do."

"What do you have in mind?"

"I know you are still committed to working on combating poverty. You saw some successes during your time at the Bank, and you used to talk about some really impressive people you met. But I also know that you were frustrated with the red tape at the Bank and the corruption and inefficiency that you encountered in the field."

"That's a long preamble!"

"OK, I have a friend who works for the International Conservation Action. It's a great organization, small, nimble, efficient. Sometimes critical of the Bank, but increasingly, they are collaborating in their field projects. They need people to work for them in the field, implementing projects. Hands-on stuff that you would love."

"Wow, ICA, that's where Julia used to work," said David and tried to battle back a queasy feeling in his stomach. The memories of her rushed through his brain, and he could not help thinking *what if.*

Diane read him like a book. "I can understand if ICA brings up tough memories for you. But there are several other NGOs like that. I can help you with contacts, so come with me and take some time to look around. You can stay up to

90 days as a tourist while you look around. A work visa can come later."

"I'm not sure I would fit in. As an ex-Banker, some people would look at me with suspicion."

"The NGOs are not all like that. You've had a short but great career at the Bank. You were much appreciated for your analytical skills and for being collegial. So these are things you can build on in that new environment."

David needed time to reflect on her proposal and changed the subject. "Do you know what happened to Bob?"

"Bob looked me up before leaving and asked me to pass on his warmest regards to you. He told me he was about to retire and go back to Lebanon. His extended family lives there, and he wanted to run an orphanage in his home village. I have his contact details for you."

"Great! What about JP?"

"He moved to Paris and is writing a book about the Bank, he wrote me. I imagine it will be a pretty irreverent satire about its Byzantine bureaucracy. His wife has opened a gallery for avant-garde abstract art. He asked a lot about you, but, of course, I couldn't tell him more than that you were OK. I have his email."

They strolled back to the cottage in silence. David pulled out a big picnic basket, and they filled it with pears, raspberries, French cheeses, and whole grain bread. He added a Harlan Estate Bordeaux Blend–an extraordinary expensive cult wine from California that he hoped would impress Diane.

They ventured out again into the pleasant breeze and strolled along the shore. It was one of those magic Nordic summer evening when the sun refused to set. David spread out a blanket on the sand, and they sat down.

"There is something else I want to discuss," Diane said as if she had just resolved something in her mind. "You once told me that you came to the U.S. with two clear goals in mind: to find a meaningful job contributing to poverty alleviation and to find a wife and start a family. Right?"

David nodded. He remembered his first mission and the talk with Bob on the flight to Kangaland. He remembered his youthful enthusiasm and his visions of how his life plan would work. He remembered falling in love with Julia and planning a life with her and kids. Then, her tragic death, his confused search for a faith to hold on to, the awkward breakup with Eva, the life-altering kidnapping, and the Kafkaesque twist with the Islamophobic organization that forced him to spy on Bob and contribute to stoking violence. So much had happened, so many obstacles had been thrown in his path—but he still carried the same fundamental ambitions.

"There's a new twist to this story," Diane said and leaned toward him. "I have a proposal that I never thought I would extend to a man." She took a big sip of the red wine and looked around as if searching for the right words. She lowered her gaze, and he thought there was a slight blush on her cheeks as she continued. "The truth is I'm in love with you, and I want you in my life."

David sat up straight in rapt attention. *She has declared her love before, but where is she going with this?*

"So, you know that I could never commit to monogamy or marriage. I will not have any more children. But I want to invite you to come and stay with me...for a while. At least give it a try. I'm not sure it will work, but I really want to give it a chance. I won't give up my other love interests for you, but I won't bring them home either. I'll play with them elsewhere, and the 'don't ask, don't tell' rule will remain."

David was too stunned to speak and collected his thoughts. *What's happening?*

An elderly couple sauntered by them closely, and they sat quietly until they had passed.

Diane resumed. "The other thing you need to know is that my son is growing up quickly and in need of a father figure—a mentor. My sweet boy is retreating in front of a screen trying to find his way in life. He's growing a shell around him and finding friends who lead him astray. He's book-smart like hell, but not a good judge of character—he's too trusting."

She shifted position on the blanket and looked at David with a troubled look on her face. "As a single mother, I've never been so challenged. I'm a good mother, but—"

"Diane, you're raising a great kid. He's—"

"Thanks, David. But a male role model would help. I work too much, and I should do more to guide him. You and Josh are both analytical thinkers, and he likes you. But you have an emotional maturity that he needs to learn from. You've changed so much since I first met you," she added with a smile.

David had met Josh only a few times. They usually played chess until Josh bluntly declared that David offered insufficient competition. Josh seemed smart and generally sweet as a kid, but things were obviously changing with age. It had never occurred to him that Diane would extend that kind of an invitation. She had spoken about the joy of getting a divorce and living in "freedom" on her own. A tornado of thoughts flooded his mind. Bewildered, he stood up and hurried off.

Diane followed. "David, talk to me! I understand this isn't the kind of family you had envisaged: a monogamous wife, vanilla sex, two sweet, over-achieving kids, a single-family home in the suburb, a garden, and all that. But at least, think about it."

They wandered on in silence. David loved the reliably rhythmic sound of the waves, the softness of the sand under his feet. He felt a sense of "home" here. David was puzzled about one thing. "You said that I've changed so much since we first met—how so?"

"You may not see it yourself, but when we first met, you were pretty nerdy, talked a lot of economic jargon, and held back emotions. But as I got to know you, you started to come out of that shell, seemed happier, joked more, even did spontaneous things...well, like calling me just to say you love me!"

The visceral reaction hit David first in the stomach. It took him a second until the mental image came into such sharp focus that it hurt: *Julia at the brunch in the Hay Adams Hotel, sitting in front of him with a slight blush on her adorable cheeks, saying "...why don't you ever call me spontaneously to share something exciting, or just to say you love me?"* It had hurt then, and it hurt now, which annoyed him greatly. He stopped and turned to meet Diane's searching look.

"Did I say something wrong?" she said and squeezed his hand.

"No, no, just old memories." He looked sideways to not show her his true feelings. He let go of her hand and hurried off to escape his emotions but soon realized that Diane was not following. *She's giving me space, but it's unfair of me to turn away. Memories of Julia must never spoil what I have with Diane*, he thought and turned back.

Diane approached him, grabbed his arm, and turned toward him still with a searching look on her face. "David, my flight leaves tomorrow, as you know. I'm not pushing for a decision now. Think about it! I have to be at the airport by 5 p.m. Can you take me there?"

"Of course. Now, let's go back to the picnic. They strolled back to the blanket, sat down, and had some more wine.

David collected his thoughts. The world had changed. It was not without risks to return to USA, but new opportunities had suddenly opened up. *Let's give this a simple structure*, he thought.

"You crazy economist, are you writing equations?" she asked.

"Yes, let me think out loud with you. My happiness (H) is a function of emotional satisfaction as well as professional satisfaction. The former is based on my vision of a wife and kids." He pointed to the variables in turn. *But Julia's tragic death and Diane's seductive appearance upended the first part of the equation. I need to revise my ambitions.* "Marriage in itself is not the point, so why not substitute with love? That's really the essence! And the joy of parenting could substitute for having my own kids." *It was not quite the same, but coaching young Josh as a young man toward maturity would be quite fascinating.* He wrote a second equation with new variables. "Not a bad alternative!"

Diane giggled at his writing but stood up to read the equations and follow his reasoning. "How can you think of your life's plan as a set of equations? It seems odd to me," she noted with her head tilted.

"Economists do this all the time. We want to capture complex real-life phenomena in simple formulas. We know very well it's not 'reality,' but it helps to organize thinking, lays the ground for rigorous quantitative analysis and…"

"I get it!" she snapped. "But tell me what I'm looking at."

David continued. "Professional satisfaction is a function of working on something ethically laudable, something intellectually challenging, and receiving decent compensation." He wrote that out with appropriate symbols.

"Isn't that what we all dream about?"

"Many of us do, but my point here is that those variables could probably be satisfied outside the Bank. I could continue to pursue the same ethical goals and would likely get more intellectual stimulus from working in the field with an NGO. Seeing results on the ground had been a highlight of my experience with the Bank, and I could get closer to that kind of feedback in a new role. Compensation would be less, of course." He replaced capital M for money with lower-case m, but the structure remained the same.

"You need to add another variable to achieve happiness," suggested Diane. She leaned down to write "+SC" in the sand. "That stands for social capital. You need friends outside of the office and in addition to your family."

David nodded and looked pleased. "I know it may seem silly, but this helps clarify my thinking."

Diane faced him and put her arms on his shoulders. "So, what's the result of this impressive formal analysis?" she teased.

"Isn't it obvious?" He inhaled deeply and blurted it out: "Tomorrow morning, I'll start packing!"

Diane let out a cry and jumped onto him with such force that he tumbled backwards into the sand. Straddling him, she gave him the kind of long, passionate kiss that he still remembered from their first date. She started to unbutton his shirt.

"Diane, people are walking along this beach, we can't…!"

"I'll be the judge of that," she declared with a confident, beaming smile.

He knew better than to try to resist.

ABOUT THE AUTHOR

The author, using pen name M.K. Nielsen, holds a PhD in Economics and had a long career as an employee of the World Bank, Washington, D.C.

REVIEWS

Dear Reader,

Now that you have read the book, please share your reflections with me and other readers in a succinct review. Just twenty words are enough for Amazon. Whether a positive or negative critique, it will help me to become a better writer, and it will inform potential readers as to what they can expect.

How to give a review:

- Go to the search bar on Amazon: http://www.amazon.com

- Enter: "ISBN 979-8-9880475-1-3"

- On the book's page, go to "Reviews," and underneath the heading, "Review this product" click the "Write a customer review" button.

  If you have not given a review before, Amazon will help you through the process.

My sincerest thanks,

M.K. Nielsen